THE
GIRLS
IN
THE
SNOW

THE GIRLS IN THE SNOW

STACY GREEN

Bookouture

Published by Bookouture in 2020

An imprint of Storyfire Ltd.
Carmelite House
50 Victoria Embankment
London EC4Y 0DZ

www.bookouture.com

ISBN: 978-1-83888-880-0
eBook ISBN: 978-1-83888-879-4

PROLOGUE

October 1995

Up and down. Side to side. Was she on the water? She didn't remember getting into her father's old fishing boat, but she must have. *God, the water's choppy. I'm getting seasick*, she thought.

"Nik, we're here." Someone pushed on her shoulder. "Wake up."

Nikki's eyes peeled open. She wiped the saliva off her mouth, her mind sluggish. "Where?"

"Your house, remember?"

A yawn made her jaw crack. Blurry images of the past few hours flashed through her head. *Stupid, stupid.* "Sorry. Fell asleep."

"More like passed out." Annmarie helped her escape her seat belt. "You sure you're okay? You still look green."

Nikki had already vomited three times in the last hour. Her stomach had to be empty. "I'm good. Where's my bag?"

"In the back. I'll grab it."

Nikki fumbled with the handle of the door and shoved it open. The house was dark; her parents would definitely be in bed. She just had to quietly sneak inside and get to her bedroom. As long as she avoided the squeaky parts of the steps, her parents would never know about what happened tonight.

She tested her balance, putting both feet on the solid ground before she carefully stood. Her legs seemed strong enough, but she still held onto the car as she tiptoed around and collected her purse.

"Thanks again for picking me up." Acid rose in Nikki's mouth. She told herself she would not puke in the driveway.

"No problem," Annmarie said. "Call me when you wake up tomorrow afternoon. We can talk more about what happened…"

Nikki preferred not to talk about tonight ever again. "Okay." She quietly shut the door and shouldered her purse.

Annmarie whipped the little Escort around the circular drive, and her headlights disappeared down the lane.

Summer wind rustled through the cornfields, and Nikki tried to walk faster. She hated the cornfields at night and wished her parents would put up some sort of security light in front of the house. She grabbed the stair rail and took the steps one at a time. The old wooden slats creaked as she crept to the door, fumbling in her bag for her keys.

She found her key and reached for the door.

And then her hand froze in midair.

The door's decorative glass pane had been shattered.

She tried the handle, and the door swung open. Fear locked her knees and made her stomach turn. Her vision cleared, her body on high alert.

Darkness greeted her, but she could see the shards of colored glass scattered on the floor.

Nikki's gut told her to run to the neighbor's. But what if her parents were hurt?

She took a shaky step inside and reached for the light switch. The sudden intrusion of light made her wince, and the hallway seemed to narrow and lengthen, like the funhouse at the state fair. Her knees knocked together as she crept down the hall toward the stairwell, listening for the sound of her father's snoring.

He was probably awake and waiting for her, she reasoned. Nikki could just imagine her parents' reaction if her paranoia about being caught after sneaking out made her overreact and waste the police's time. They didn't live in Minneapolis, she told herself. Stillwater was about as safe and boring as church on Sunday.

Thirteen steps to the second floor. Nikki once scared Annmarie into believing the thirteen steps meant the house was a spirit portal. Nine-year-old kids believed anything.

The loose railing rattled from Nikki's shaking hand. Random dark spots dotted the carpet; she rubbed her eyes, but the spots were still there. Dribbles, and then blobs that got a little larger on each step until they took a definitive shape. Shoe prints on the beige carpet leading to her parents' bedroom, a familiar swoosh logo visible in the stronger prints.

Nikki stopped outside the closed door to her parents' room.

No sound came. No snoring.

Her pulse thundered in her ears as she slowly opened the door.

Blood dripped down the side of the bed. Her mother's arm dangled off the edge, her hand limp.

More bile rose in Nikki's mouth. Her vision blurred again. Her face had gone numb, but her heart raced.

She had to be dreaming.

Then why did she smell copper and gunfire?

The hall light burned a spotlight on her mother. Nikki inched toward the bed, panic attacking her nervous system.

"Mom?"

Lifeless brown eyes stared back at her. A face frozen in anguish, blood on her nightgown pooling next to her body and dripping off the side.

Nikki grabbed her mother's hand and put two fingers on her wrist. No pulse.

Nikki's breath came in short rasps, the vodka still threatening to come back up. She remembered the bloody footsteps… the killer had walked through her mother's blood.

And then she heard it. A familiar series of creaks. Someone was slowly walking upstairs. Someone who didn't know which steps to avoid.

CHAPTER ONE

Present day

Bitter, cold wind tore through Nikki's heavy coat and snow crept into the tops of her boots as she waded through the drifts. She swore under her breath. The Arctic Circle was probably warmer than Minnesota right now.

Deer tracks covered the snow, making a path that led up to the barbed-wire fence several hundred yards to her right. Bright yellow "No trespassing" signs had been posted along the fence line. It was prime hunting ground, although only small game was currently in season. She envied the deer's ability to jump the fence and shelter in the trees; instead she was fighting the wind in the flatness of the surrounding cornfields.

A man in a thick Washington County Sheriff's coat zipped up to his nose joined her, his wool hat low on his forehead. "Agent Hunt?"

"Special Agent Nikki Hunt, FBI." She shook his gloved hand, her frosty breath filling the air between them.

"Sergeant Kent Miller with the sheriff's office. We haven't touched the bodies. Knew you'd want to see them first."

"You're certain it's the girls who disappeared two months ago?"

Bits of blowing snow freckled over Miller's dark skin. "Yes. They're well preserved, frozen solid, just like the others. But no red ribbons. That's why I was on the fence about calling you, but Sheriff Hardin insisted on notifying the FBI."

The others, meaning the five women Frost had killed over the past half-decade. Frost was the first serial killer Nikki had chased, and the only one she hadn't caught. Frost stuck to the same routine every year: he took a woman in the late fall, kept her alive for an undetermined amount of time, and then froze her body immediately after he'd killed her. A red ribbon tied the victim's hair back, and they were always wiped down with bleach, leaving little transfer evidence. Frost bounced between northern Minnesota, Wisconsin and Michigan, often taking a victim from one state and dumping her in another. He always left the frozen body in the snow at the peak of winter, in an area it would easily be noticed. A city park, an empty lot across from a high school, an unplowed parking lot—these were his places of choice. An isolated cornfield in the back of a large acreage was the last place she'd expect to find one of his victims. Nikki was certain the public's reaction was part of Frost's addiction. So why would he leave these bodies out here where it could be months before they were found?

"The Frost Killer has never left two victims," Nikki said.

"Sheriff thinks he might be bored with one victim," Miller said, a slight edge to his voice. "You're the expert, though."

"This is his favorite time of year." Nikki followed Miller's long strides into the cornfield. She'd always found them creepy. Her friends earned money in the summer from detasseling, but Nikki refused to set foot in them. Too claustrophobic. "Any idea when they were dumped?"

"Not with any certainty. We didn't have serious snow accumulation until mid-December. I double-checked, and we've had sixteen inches since then. We got about five inches of snow the day before yesterday, but the wind's causing it to blow and drift."

Thirty mph-plus winds, Nikki thought. "Who owns the field?"

"Farmer up the road," Miller said. "It's a back field, used mostly for sweetcorn."

"He probably doesn't come here much at all during the winter." Nikki wondered how many people knew this.

"Nope," Miller replied. "One of his dogs got loose and his son chased it down the lane. He's the one who found the bodies."

Poor kid. "Did the dog come into contact with the bodies?"

"No, thankfully. They're just up here."

Eight years on the job and dozens of victims should have hardened Nikki, but seeing dead children never got easier. Her throat tightened, her hands balled into fists. Child killers deserved a special place in hell.

The two girls lay on their sides, face to face. A fine layer of snow partially covered their torsos. Frayed brown rope looped beneath their bottoms and over their necks, securing them in the fetal position. Clothing covered their necks, but lividity would show if the ropes were attached before or after death. "The killer must have roped them like that because the freezer wasn't big enough."

"None of Frost's victims were like this?" Miller asked.

"So far, all of his have been laid out flat." Each victim's hands were always folded over their midsection, like a body prepared for funeral. That was a detail Nikki had intentionally kept from the press, instead describing them as laid out in the snow.

Miller shook his head, his attention on the dead teenagers. "I never stopped looking for them," he muttered.

"I'm sure you didn't." Nikki knew that every cop had cases they agonized over, and ones like this were the kind that drove a person to the bottle.

"The darker-haired girl is Kaylee Thomas," Miller said. "Madison Malone is the other."

"They're both high-school freshmen?" Frost's youngest victim had been eighteen.

"They're young for Frost, but Kaylee looks more like a senior. Maybe he targeted her, and Madison was collateral damage?" He sounded embarrassed at the theory. Frost's methods hadn't changed in five years.

"Is that the sheriff's opinion, or yours?" Nikki would bet her savings that Sheriff Hardin hadn't braved the weather to come to the scene.

"Sheriff's."

Nikki shivered from the cold. "You're the responding officer?"

Miller nodded.

"What was your gut reaction when you first saw them?"

"Initially I wondered about Hardin's theory, but there are no red ribbons. The scene feels staged to me. My gut tells me someone local did this, thinking the isolated location meant it would be spring before they were found."

"I agree, but I'm sure the sheriff doesn't like that idea," Nikki said. "Can't say I blame him. It's certainly more complicated if it's someone else."

Wind and snow stung Nikki's eyes as she knelt next to Kaylee. The girl's thick, dark hair had been streaked with blond highlights. The hem of her sweater had been torn in the back, like someone had grabbed her from behind. Neither girl wore shoes. One of Kaylee's socks had a hole in the toe, revealing her pink nail polish.

Nikki adjusted her winter gloves and carefully touched Kaylee's arm. "Are these the same clothes they disappeared in?"

Miller nodded. "Clothes are pretty much frozen to both bodies."

"Did Kaylee have the blond highlights?"

"She did them at home a couple of days before the girls disappeared."

"Is there a picture of her with the highlights?" Nikki's crime scene guru might be able to figure how much the hair had grown out—if any—before she died.

"Not that I know of," Miller said.

Kaylee's sweater was frozen tightly to her neck. Madison's fisted hands were tucked under her chin, but Nikki could see the lightweight coat was zipped to her throat.

"Why is Madison wearing a coat?"

"She had a thin shirt on," Miller said. "Her dad made her put on a coat before she and Kaylee left the house."

Nikki wondered if perhaps the girls had been ambushed, or if they'd gone into someone's home and taken their shoes off, intending to stay awhile.

A shout startled Nikki and Miller. A tall man with skinny legs and a Vikings wool hat trudged through the snow. The hat's braided tassels whipped in the wind, making the ear flaps wiggle like a floppy-eared dog.

"Are your bird legs strong enough for those boots?" Nikki asked.

Agent Liam Wilson gave her the finger. "They keep my feet warm."

Liam had joined the unit fresh from the FBI academy a year ago. His tall, lean frame and red hair earned him plenty of teasing, but he'd taken it all in his stride. His patience and attention to detail, along with his instincts, made him a valuable asset to the small criminal profiling unit.

"Where's Court?" The elements had likely destroyed any chance of finding good trace evidence, but she'd worked with Courtney Hart long enough to know she could find a needle in a haystack.

"Right here." Courtney plodded through the snow behind Liam, carrying her kit. "How frickin' deep is this stuff?"

"It's not that deep," Liam said. "You're just Oompa-Loompa sized."

"I'm average height. You're the anomaly."

"Sergeant Miller, this is Agent Liam Wilson and our lead crime scene analyst Courtney Hart. She's one of our best forensic scientists and the head of my Emergency Response Team," Nikki said. "Liam worked the last Frost case with me, and Courtney's been with me since my unit's first investigation."

Liam shook Miller's hand. "I'd say nice to meet you, but under the circumstances, it sucks."

Courtney murmured her agreement, nodding at Miller before shuffling through the snow to examine the bodies. "I followed our Frost protocol, so it's just me today. Bodies frozen like this unfortunately take a while to process, and we don't need a full team scouring the snow." She dropped to all fours and leaned over the girls' heads, her nose within an inch of their faces.

"What's she doing?" Miller asked.

Courtney looked at Nikki and slightly shook her head. Frost always used bleach to wipe his victims clean, including their clothes. They'd smelled bleach on every Frost victim so far, and Nikki firmly believed Frost wouldn't deviate from that routine. Like the body position, that crucial detail had been kept out of the media, and Nikki could count on her team not sharing the information until they were certain about trusting Miller. Nikki didn't know Miller well enough yet.

"I'm just trying to figure out how long they were covered with snow," Courtney said. "What do you think?"

"A few days, at least," Miller said. "This nasty wind helped expose them."

Liam glanced at Sergeant Miller. "No offense, but I don't think this is the Frost Killer's work."

"Neither does he," Nikki said. "Sergeant, what do you know about the farmer who owns the ground?"

"He's around our age, inherited the family farm. No record of any sort. Son's fourteen, never been in any trouble."

Nikki looked at Liam, who shivered in the brisk wind. "Is the truck almost here?"

"The rolling freezer?" Liam asked. "Yeah."

"First time I've seen it used," Sergeant Miller said. "Never dreamed it would be for two little girls instead of some poor soul who fell through the ice."

Courtney crouched beside Madison, using her high-powered magnifier on the girl's jeans. "God, this wind is a bitch. Any trace evidence is probably long gone unless it's frozen in the clothes."

"Boss, why don't you go warm up in your car and wait for the morgue truck? I'll stay with them." Liam circled the bodies, taking pictures with the digital camera.

Nikki would normally refuse, but her damned feet and hands ached from the cold.

Her mind raced ahead as she and Miller walked back in silence. Given the frozen state of the bodies, Nikki understood why Sheriff Hardin wanted to inform her. But with her family's name in the news again, Nikki wondered if Hardin hadn't jumped at the chance to bring her into town. She hadn't set foot in Stillwater in nearly twenty years, and despite the desolate location, it felt like the town was already suffocating her.

Now that she was sure it wasn't Frost, she could hand the investigation back to the local police. Nikki could go back to St. Paul and keep Stillwater in her past, where it belonged. But she knew she wouldn't be able to get the image of the two girls lying dead in the snow out of her head.

"Shit," Miller hissed. "Someone must have tipped her off."

Nikki shielded her eyes against the blowing snow. A four-door pickup had parked in front of Nikki's jeep. The woman behind the wheel watched as the refrigerated truck ambled down the drive and came to a stop behind the sergeant's cruiser. She typed something into her phone, and then checked her reflection in the rearview mirror.

"It's Caitlin Newport," Miller said. "She's—"

"I know who she is." Caitlin's last true-crime documentary had helped get a death-row inmate a new trial. In 2000, Fred Elwood was convicted of the brutal murder of his sixty-eight-year-old mother-in-law. His young niece testified she'd hidden in the closet and was certain her uncle had committed the murder, but she later recanted her story. DNA evidence had finally exonerated Elwood last year.

Caitlin hopped out of the pickup and pulled a hat over her honey-colored hair. She scanned the scene before zipping her coat to her chin and striding through the snow as though she had every right to intrude on a crime scene.

Instead of designer snow boots and a figure-flattering coat, Caitlin had opted for bulky snow pants and a well-worn parka.

Caitlin didn't usually dress so sensibly, and Nikki could tell she was trying to blend in with the locals. Sunglasses hid her shrewd eyes, but Nikki still felt the weight of the filmmaker's stare.

"My guys will take care of her." Miller motioned to the two pink-cheeked deputies tasked with standing in the frigid weather and keeping the scene clear.

The taller deputy blocked the reporter's path, shaking his head. Caitlin looked up at him with a bemused expression and then pointed toward Nikki.

"It's okay, deputy." Nikki eyed the reporter.

Caitlin smiled at the deputy as he stepped aside. She strode through the snow like a prize fighter, her attention squarely on Nikki.

Nikki raised her hand in warning. "Don't step over that crime scene tape."

"I know the rules, Agent." Caitlin's friendliness was about as real as her hair color. "I have to say I'm surprised to see you here."

"I was invited," Nikki said. "Unlike yourself."

Caitlin shrugged. "Don't be so sure of that. How's the hunt for the Frost Killer coming along?"

Nikki had encountered the reporter twice in the last two years, both times during a Frost investigation. Caitlin knew the serial killer wouldn't suddenly change his methods. "Well, it is his favorite time of year."

"Surely the police don't think he suddenly changed his M.O. and took two high-school girls?" Caitlin's surprised tone wasn't fooling Nikki.

"How do you know anything about the victims?" Nikki asked.

"Stillwater's grown since you left, but it's still a relatively small town. News travels fast."

"Fantastic," Nikki said. "I'm still not giving you information on this case."

"You're working it, then?"

"I'm here, aren't I?"

Caitlin slid her sunglasses on top of her head. Colored contacts made her eyes a chilling blue. "It's just surprising."

Nikki chewed the inside of her cheek. She'd become a household name in Stillwater. Everyone in town recognized her as the girl who found her parents murdered, and she'd been the star witness at the trial. She'd encountered Mark Todd in the house that night and was the reason he'd been convicted so quickly. Everyone in Stillwater either looked at her with pity or didn't look at her at all. And after the trial she'd just wanted to finish school and get out of town.

Caitlin was resourceful enough that she had to know bad memories weren't the only reason for Nikki to stay out of town. After all, she'd been recognized as soon as she'd left anyway—the case wasn't just famous in Stillwater—and she'd had to cut her hair, dye it blond and ask her professors at the University of Minnesota to refrain from using her last name just so she could attempt a normal life. Caitlin was trying to bait her into talking about new developments in her parents' murders. Nikki had ignored all media requests over the past month, and she wasn't about to give Caitlin Newport an exclusive.

Two death investigators approached the barricade carrying the equipment they needed to collect the bodies.

"Down the hill, cornfield's around the corner." Nikki's patience was running thin. "Newport, you need to leave. Or I'll have you escorted away from the area."

"Have the police identified the bodies?"

If Caitlin wanted information, she would have to get it from the local police. "No comment. Have a nice day."

Nikki turned her back on the woman and followed the guys from the medical examiner's office. Stillwater may have grown in the years since she'd left, but like the filmmaker said, it was still a small town, and news traveled fast. How long did Nikki have before everyone found out she was here and she had to deal with a barrage of questions she didn't want to answer?

She trudged over the hill and into the field. Courtney knelt next to one of the bodies while Liam concentrated on photographing the scene. She and her team had worked enough cases in the snow and Nikki didn't have much hope for any trace evidence. "I assume you haven't found anything?"

"Nope," Courtney said. "These poor babies are frozen just as solid as Frost's victims, which means we've got to wait at least a week for them to thaw."

"Why is that?" Miller asked.

"Thawing a body is a slow process," Courtney explained. "They need to be brought to room temperature gradually or we risk losing evidence. Appendages thaw first, so I may be able to swab fingernails. But the medical examiner won't allow the removal of clothes or shoes until the bodies are fully thawed."

"Which means at least five days," Nikki said. "What can we do today?"

Courtney nodded. "Very little. Once they're situated in the truck, I can use the UV light and look for blood or possible semen. I won't be able to take any samples until the medical examiner clears it, but we'll at least know if there's anything viable."

The death investigators struggled with the solid limbs as they carefully put each girl into a body bag.

Courtney sniffled. "I'll never understand how people can be so cruel to one another. These girls had their whole lives ahead of them."

"Some people are born evil." Nikki squeezed her friend's shoulder. "Others are made. They enjoy seeing people suffer. It's about control."

"I don't know how you do it," Courtney said. "Working with bodies is bad enough, but to have to deal with the killers, face to face? And try to understand them? No thanks."

Early in her career with the FBI, a serial killer who'd taken the lives of at least four pre-teen boys had looked Nikki dead in the eye and explained the kill as "the most satisfying thing" he'd ever done. The seasoned agent next to Nikki had blanched, but she'd remained stone-faced, unimpressed. The man went on to describe his crimes in grisly detail, clearly enjoying the reaction of Nikki's colleague and simultaneously getting more and more agitated at Nikki's lack of emotion. He'd continued to talk in an effort to impress her, to get a reaction out of her. That's when he broke and admitted to the murder she wanted to nail him for: the kidnapping and killing of a twelve-year-old boy nearly a decade before. Her peers had been in awe and more than a little unnerved by Nikki's ability to stay so remote and focused. She'd never been able to explain to anyone that her resolve came from years of blocking out the memories of her parents' murders.

"After we speak with the families, I'll issue a statement for the press," she told Miller.

"I can deal with the press," Miller said. "You're going to be bombarded with personal questions. Easier if I just make the statement."

"Don't rule out Frost," Nikki said. "Tell the press the FBI was called in because of similarities to prior Frost killings, and we're currently investigating all possibilities. If the killer intended for us to believe Frost did this, blasting all over the media that we didn't buy it will make him hypervigilant. We want him to feel safe enough to make a mistake."

"I'll make sure the statement is on the news tonight." Miller closed his eyes as Madison's body was secured in the bag. He seemed to be willing his emotions to stay in check. "And when the media asks if you're personally working the case, I'll only verify the FBI is assisting."

Nikki was grateful for Miller's discretion, but she wasn't naive enough to believe she could go unnoticed. Her reputation as an FBI agent paled in comparison to her history in Stillwater. But she wasn't here to open old wounds. She'd returned to Stillwater to find the monster who'd killed these two girls, and she would see it through either way, because finding monsters was her specialty. Everybody knew that.

CHAPTER TWO

Taking Highway 96 into town added several minutes to Nikki's drive, but the road was in far better shape. Nikki marveled at how far west Stillwater had bloated over the past eighteen years. She'd grown up as a rural farm kid, but businesses and homes populated the old fields and marshes she and her friends had once played in.

She took the long route into downtown, driving through the historic district. Nikki had spent the last two years of high school stuck with her great-aunt in one of the grand old Victorian houses. Her childhood self would have passed the days searching for hidden passageways and spirits, but Nikki had lived in a state of numbness back then. Raising her grades in order to get into a good school and get the hell out of Stillwater. Bit by bit, the memories of her life in Stillwater had faded. The call about Madison and Kaylee brought them back in blazing technicolor.

Four blocks from the sheriff's office and the shiny, new government center, a group carrying picket signs had gathered around the intersection.

Get the DNA tested.

Justice for Mark Todd.

Mark was framed. Get him out now!

Nikki slammed her foot on the brake for the yellow light and glared at the protesters. Most looked around college age and she doubted they were from Stillwater. She dug her fingertips into the steering wheel to keep from rolling down the windows and screaming.

The light turned green, and Nikki hit the gas. She couldn't think about Mark Todd right now. She had another killer to deal with.

*

Nikki was aware of the eyes on her as she walked through the sheriff's station. A gray-haired deputy peered over his cubicle, and a heavily pregnant clerk around Nikki's age slid her chair back to get a better view.

Nikki followed Miller down the hall, surprised at how anxious she was about seeing Harvey Hardin. The sheriff had been a deputy the night her life imploded. He'd been first on the scene after Nikki had escaped to call 9-1-1, and he'd guided her through various parts of the trial process. He hadn't known how to comfort her then, and Nikki had probably been a nightmare to deal with.

Miller knocked on the sheriff's open door. "Are you ready for us, sir?"

"Yes, of course." His voice was gruffer than Nikki remembered.

She stepped around Miller and barely managed to keep a neutral expression. Harvey Hardin had grown at least two pants sizes since Nikki last saw him. He had always been stout, but he had to be pushing three-hundred-and-fifty pounds. His black hair had turned a pretty shade of silver, but the excess weight in his face gave him a youthful appearance.

He hefted his bulk from the chair. "Nicole, thank you for coming to help us. Have a seat."

Nikki froze for a moment. She hadn't been called Nicole since she left Stillwater. She sat down, and Miller took the seat beside her. "I hope my team can help."

"Your record as an FBI agent is impressive," Hardin said.

"First-hand experience to the criminal mind helps." She clutched the warm coffee cup she was holding. Her fingers still hurt from the cold. She'd never had an issue with Hardin, but something about him always set her on edge. As a kid, she'd figured it was her aversion to authority figures. The people who should have protected her and failed.

"You see the protesters?"

"Freedom of speech."

"Those bleeding hearts at the Innocence Project are absolutely certain we railroaded the guy, and they're going to help get him out of prison by testing some tiny speck of DNA." Hardin's mouth curled in disgust. "You know that's not true, right?"

Nikki had only learned about the Innocence Project getting involved in Mark Todd's appeal a few days before Thanksgiving. She'd spoken with the new district attorney, who assured her that his staff was handling the defense's request. He'd told her to enjoy the holidays and not to worry about it and Nikki had done her best to put it out of her mind and focus on more important things. But she still hadn't heard when the judge planned to rule on getting the DNA tested, and she wouldn't have come to Stillwater if she'd known the appeal had become such a hot topic.

She nodded. "I'd rather focus on Madison and Kaylee, if you don't mind. That's what I'm here for."

Hardin's chair groaned as he leaned back, his meaty jowls making him look like a dangerously overfed bulldog. Nikki worried his uniform buttons might become tiny projectiles at any moment. "I just want you to understand you're going to get hit with questions, especially if Mark Todd's younger brother finds out you're in town."

"I'm not worried about it," Nikki said. "I'm only here to do my job."

Hardin's meaty hands rested on his stomach. "So, you married? Kids?"

"Divorced. Too busy for kids."

Sergeant Miller cleared his throat. "The families will be here soon."

Nikki was thankful for the interruption. "Kaylee and Madison disappeared six weeks ago?"

"Yes. Kaylee was at Madison's home. It backs up to the woods and a nature trail that's close to the lake," Miller said. "Madison texted a friend who lives on the other side of the park to let him know they were coming over and taking the trail. It's about a ten, fifteen-minute walk. They never showed."

"Just vanished," Hardin added. "Madison's cell phone was turned off, and it's never come back on again. No GPS. Her phone records don't show anything suspicious."

"What about Kaylee's phone?"

"She didn't have one."

"A teenager without a cell phone? Really?"

"Her mother confiscated it a few weeks before," Miller explained. "Kaylee was a bit of a handful. Got caught this summer sneaking out and partying with people she had no business being around."

Hardin smiled and winked at her, but his eyes were flat. He'd busted more than one underaged party Nikki had been attending.

"You didn't find anything in her phone records? No texts to suspicious people? What about her social media?"

"Kaylee only had a few contacts in her phone: her mom, Madison, her mom's work. But like the sheriff said, she didn't have it for three weeks. She only had Instagram, and it was set to private. She deleted all her other accounts last year."

"I can't fathom a teenage girl going without a phone for three weeks," Nikki said. "Did Kaylee have a part-time job?"

"Sort of. She babysat for some of the neighbors," Miller replied. "Her mom Jessica barely keeps her car running and she works long hours. Kaylee didn't have a ride to work anywhere else."

"But she did have cash?"

"Presumably."

"Then she had a cheap phone somewhere," Nikki said. "Pay as you go. No way she's cut off from friends like that."

"We searched her room," Miller said.

"She likely had it on her that day." Nikki would bet a month's salary on Kaylee having a secret phone. She just hoped Madison wasn't the only one who knew about it. "Any suspects?"

"No good ones," Miller confirmed. "Kaylee's mom had an on-again, off-again boyfriend. He was at work when the girls disappeared, alibied by several people. Miles Hanson, the boy Madison and Kaylee were going to see before they disappeared, has an alibi. His dad was at home with him all day and security footage from Hanson's front and back door confirmed the girls never showed."

"What about the parents?" How anyone could harm their own child was beyond Nikki, but the statistics didn't lie—someone close to the family was usually responsible.

"Kaylee's mom works long hours at a nursing home," Miller said. "She was at work all day. Madison's mother went to visit her parents in Northfield. Her stepdad works for a pharmaceutical company. He had a business meeting with a client in downtown Minneapolis. Restaurant receipts verified a lunch meeting around the time Madison and Kaylee left for their friend's."

The stepdad had at least an hour's drive time both ways, and probably more. "You're certain the stepdad was in Minneapolis?"

"At the time they left the house, yes. We have security-camera footage of the girls leaving shortly after Madison sent the text to her friend," Miller said. "And a witness saw them on the trail not far from Madison's house. They disappeared at some point after that."

"When did the stepdad come home?" Nikki asked.

Miller handed her a dog-eared evidence file. "He went to the office. Entered at 3:00 p.m., left shortly after 7:00 p.m. Kaylee's mother went to the Hansons' to pick up Kaylee. When she realized the girls had never arrived, she called him, and he rushed right out of the office."

Nikki sifted through the notes. Miller's neat handwriting was easy to read, and his records appeared to be thorough. "What about her real father?"

"Left when she was little and lives in California. His alibi is rock solid. He was in the hospital with kidney stones."

"What about the other kids Kaylee hangs out with?"

"She was kind of a loner. Her cousin lives in Hudson, and Kaylee started hanging out with her and her friends over the summer," Miller said. "Everyone she was known to hang out with was accounted for."

"But Kaylee didn't come around much after they got caught partying. Her cousin hadn't talked to her since before she got her phone taken away." Hardin shrugged. "I'd like to think she would have told us that Kaylee had a secret phone, but…" He spread his hands wide. "You know teenagers."

Nikki chest tightened, but she didn't look up from her notes. Everyone drove across the river to Hudson for fireworks and Wisconsin beer. "Teenagers lie to police all the time. And they're a lot smarter than we were. Most of them know you can't look at their phone without a warrant. And you'd never get one without a lot more evidence."

"Madison had a decent-sized social circle at the high school," Miller said. "None of their friends had anything bad to say about either girl."

"Which is suspect in itself." No matter how fast the world changed, the behavior of teenage girls remained predictable. There was no way some other girl didn't have a grudge against one or both of them.

"Teachers were a different story," Miller added. "Madison was the golden kid, but Kaylee was a problem child who didn't live up to her potential and had a smart mouth. She spent a couple of afternoons in detention."

"If it were just Kaylee, I'd have suspected she ran away when she was first reported as missing. But Madison isn't the type," Hardin said. "Lots of similarities to your Frost murders. That's why I invited you to check things out."

Hardin wasn't an idiot. He'd known the chances of Frost committing these murders were slim. He'd more than likely used the case as a reason to get her back to Stillwater and defer some of

Newport's attention away from him and onto Nikki. "Evidence suggests it isn't him."

Hardin nodded. "That was my thinking, but Sergeant Miller thought differently."

Miller's face heated. "I agreed with you that we shouldn't ignore the possibility."

Nikki resisted the urge to roll her eyes. "I believe we're looking for someone who knew the girls. Not a serial killer. However, as I told Sergeant Miller earlier, if we let the public believe Frost is an option, then the killer might feel safe and make a mistake."

"Good strategy." Hardin's narrow eyes studied her. "You catch serial killers, though, right? If this isn't Frost, you have no reason to stay."

Staying likely meant having to deal with Caitlin Newport as well as the scrutiny of Mark Todd's appeal. Was Nikki really ready for that? Probably not, but she couldn't walk away now. "That's not all I do. I'd like to stay and help."

Miller's phone buzzed. His face turned ashen. "Madison's family is here. God, I hate this part."

So did Nikki. She saw herself in every family member's face. "I'll go with you, if you'd like. Sometimes it's easier if you don't know the family well."

Hardin cleared his throat and looked pointedly at Miller. "She doesn't know?"

"I wasn't sure how to tell her."

"Tell me what?"

"Madison's stepfather is John Banks. He's raised her since she was little, after her real dad split."

Nikki's chest tightened. John Banks had been her first everything, until her parents died and she shut out the world. He was the one she'd been with the night her parents had been murdered. She hadn't seen him in years, and his face would be a stark reminder of the things she'd run away from.

CHAPTER THREE

"I meant to mention it earlier," Miller said as soon as they left Hardin's office. "I hope it doesn't stop you from helping us out."

Nikki walked briskly down the hall, her composure already in hand. Like every other damned thing about Stillwater, her and John's relationship was in the past. "It's okay. You don't mind my coming with you?"

"Not at all." Miller glanced at her sheepishly. "This is bad timing, but I guess you don't remember me."

She stopped and stared at him, mentally running through her admittedly sparse memories of high school. "Should I?"

"I was a couple of years behind you in school. I remember how crazy things were after that night."

"I'm so sorry," she said. "I've forgotten a lot of stuff from high school."

They walked to the family area in awkward silence. Nikki sifted through her memories, trying to place Miller. He was several inches taller than her, in good shape. She'd spotted a pair of running shoes in the back of his car.

"Wait. Kenny Miller who broke the school's single-season rushing yards record?"

Miller grinned. "That's me." He glanced at the closed door. "Thanks again for coming with me. Just to warn you, Madison's mother has gotten more aggressive since the case went cold. That's why I ended up telling them over the phone that we'd found the girls instead of waiting until they got here. She wouldn't accept anything else. She's grieving, so I try to give her the benefit of the doubt. But she can be pretty blunt. Just don't take it personal."

"It's likely easier for her to channel her grief into anger," Nikki said. "And I've got pretty thick skin, so don't worry about me."

The door flew open before Miller could reach for it, and John Banks filled the space. Nikki had forgotten how John towered over most people. His height had been one of the things that made him so successful in track.

"John, I'm so sorry," Miller said.

"You're certain it's our daughter?" Amy Banks looked like the perfect Stepford wife, right down to the manicured nails and blond hair. She hovered behind John, her arms wrapped around her petite frame. The fierceness in her eyes was every bit as intimidating as John's stature. He stared down at Nikki, his expression a mixture of pain and confusion. "That's why the FBI's been called in, isn't it?"

Sergeant Miller nodded. "You'll need to make official identifications, but yes, I'm certain it's Madison. I've seen her body myself. Kaylee's too."

Amy stepped back as though she'd been slapped. She shook her head, tears welling in her eyes. "It can't be her."

"I'm sorry, Amy." Miller's soft voice seemed to shatter the last of her resolve.

"Excuse me." Amy bolted from the room, her sobs echoing down the hall.

"Give her a minute." John sat down. He still looked lean and fit, his blond hair flecked with gray. Diamond cufflinks decorated his designer shirt. John stared at the table, lost in his grief.

"I'm sorry for your loss, John."

He looked at her with bleary eyes. "It really is you, isn't it? I thought I was going crazy."

"Yes, it's me." Nikki down sat across from him, the tragic irony of the moment nearly rendering her speechless. Twenty years ago, their roles had been reversed. Almost. The idea of burying your child was unfathomable. John clearly thought of Madison as his own.

"It's just not real. I know it's been weeks, but I still had this hope that she would come home. Who would do this?"

"The worst kind of monster," Nikki said. "I know this is extremely difficult, but can I ask you a few questions?"

He nodded. "I'm not sure what else I can tell you that the sergeant hasn't already asked."

"How long had the girls been friends?"

"Just a few months." John cleared his throat. "They played volleyball together, until Kaylee was kicked off the team for fighting."

"This is all Kaylee's fault." Amy Banks had returned, her grief weaponized into rage. "That girl barely had any adult supervision. I told Madison to stay away from her, but she wouldn't listen."

John took his wife's hand. "Kaylee wasn't a bad kid. Her mom worked all the time, so she was on her own a lot. She spent a lot of time at our house."

Amy's mouth tightened. "Not because I wanted her to."

Nikki hadn't missed the angry glances Amy gave to John every time she said Kaylee's name. She blamed Kaylee for her daughter's death, but he didn't seem to share her sentiments. Perhaps that had driven a wedge between them.

"Kaylee's mother's on her way," Sergeant Miller said.

John looked at Nikki. "I've followed your career with the FBI. Maddie, too. She was fascinated by the killer from the Ivy League schools. She wanted to go into criminal justice and when she found out I'd known you in high school, she begged me to email you so she could talk to you as part of her project for career day. I kept putting it off." John's mouth trembled and his hands fisted on the table. "Now you're investigating her murder."

Throughout grad school and her first few years with the FBI, Nikki kept her head down and worked her way up the food chain. Only a select few of her colleagues knew about her past. Six years ago, while working for the BAU at Quantico, her profile helped track down Marshal Weathers, better known as the Ivy League Stalker. Weathers had terrorized the elite schools for nearly a decade, with murders at Princeton, Brown, Yale and Harvard. Nikki hadn't been the lead agent, but luck put her right in Weathers' crosshairs. His dramatic capture at Harvard's famed Memorial Hall made national news, and so did Nikki, along with her past.

After the capture of the Ivy League Stalker, Nikki had been offered the chance to start a behavioral analysis unit in St. Paul that would serve not only Minnesota but be available to assist law enforcement in Iowa, Wisconsin and Michigan. She'd hesitated to take the job because it could eventually bring her back to Stillwater, but heading a new unit was an opportunity the bureau probably wouldn't offer her again. Her team made the news that summer after catching the resort murderer.

"To be fair, the Ivy League Stalker helped us. I don't think we would have ever caught him if his ego hadn't gotten involved," Nikki said. "They always make mistakes, eventually."

"And yet the Frost Killer is still out there." Amy's bitter tone matched the anger in her eyes. "You've failed to catch him and now he's killed our daughter."

"We can't be sure that the Frost Killer did this."

"Sergeant Miller said—"

"Sheriff Hardin was right to suggest the Frost Killer," Nikki said. "And it's important that we continue to consider him a suspect, but I'm not concentrating my investigation on just Frost."

Sergeant Miller gave her an appreciative glance. "Agent Hunt will know more after the medical examiner is ready to report her findings."

"Did she suffer?" John asked.

Nikki hated lying to grieving families but knowing the grim details of their loved one's death, especially if the victim was a child, served no purpose. "She looks like she's sleeping."

John's stoic expression crumbled. "My poor little girl. It's my fault."

Nikki could see that John's love for Madison was sincere, but she was still surprised he'd married a woman with a child. The John she'd known would have never settled down and had a family. But time changed people.

"I'm sure that's not true," Nikki said.

"It is," John replied. "I wasn't home. I was supposed to be, but a client I've been trying to land called and had time to meet with me. The guy is so busy, it's nearly impossible to get a meeting. I met him for lunch in Minneapolis. If I had been at home, then maybe she wouldn't have gone into the woods that day."

"Kaylee was already at your house with Madison when you left?"

He shook his head. "She was on her way over."

"And they would have asked to go to their friend's, and you would have said yes." Amy rubbed his shoulder. "It still would have happened."

"I need to see her," John said. "I can't answer your questions until I've seen her."

Nikki had dealt with enough parents to know the Bankses would need to see Madison before they could truly accept she was gone. "I understand. My questions can wait until morning. I assume you'll both be home?"

"Yes." John stood and looked down at her. His smile was a ghost of the one she remembered waiting for days to see. His smile always had an edge, as though he'd been starved to see her. He probably thought the same about her. "I'm so glad you're here. To work the case, I mean."

Twenty years later, John still wore the same cologne. A single whiff brought back all the memories she'd worked so hard to forget. She'd been sitting on his lap at the party, drink in hand. He'd whispered in her ear about "later," and Nikki had flushed with excitement. She'd finished her drink and then stood up to make another, but her head swam from the alcohol. John had told her to go lie down before she passed out on the floor…

"I'll see you tomorrow." Nikki turned and headed down the hall before John could say anything more. She ducked into the ladies' room and locked the door. Acid coated her tongue, and she dry-heaved over the sink until her throat burned. She splashed water on her heated face and tried to catch her breath.

She wondered if she could really work this case. The longer she stayed in town, the more emotions she'd be dredging up. But turning her back on Madison and Kaylee would haunt her, and she already had enough regrets for a lifetime.

She retrieved her bag from Miller's dark office and popped a mint into her mouth. Her smart watch vibrated with a text.

Help. In break room.

What sort of trouble could Courtney possibly get into in the break room? Nikki wondered. She hurried down the hallway, following the scent of stale coffee that followed Courtney everywhere and skidded to a stop at the open door.

"Court!" Nikki said, spotting Courtney before she even entered the room.

Courtney sat on the floor with her snow pants trapped around her ankles. She'd managed to get the drawstring at the bottom of her right pant leg tangled with her boot lace. Nikki knelt beside her and went to work on the string.

She loved Courtney dearly, but it never ceased to amaze Nikki how someone so intelligent wound up in the silliest situations. Courtney had started at St. Paul at the same time as Nikki, and during the first sixty minutes of meeting her, Courtney had managed to get herself locked in a supply closet.

"How did you get this into such a knot?" Nikki asked.

"I have no idea, but I'm about ready to cut myself loose."

"Hang on." Nikki found her nail file in her back pocket and wedged it into the knot. After the fourth try, she loosened the string enough to untie it.

Courtney stood up and shimmied out of the pants, and then wiped her face with her sleeve. Tiny white skulls polka-dotted her black leggings. "Christ, I'm sweating."

Nikki laughed and sat down, the weight on her shoulders less crushing. "I should have taken a picture of you."

"I'd kick your ass." Courtney collapsed on the chair next to her. "If it wasn't so bitter cold, I'd say we should go for a drink. God knows we deserve it."

Courtney was one of the few people Nikki called a friend. She'd spent her last two years of high school as a social pariah, pitied and gossiped about, and she'd shut everyone out of her life to survive. College had been just the opposite: being friends with Nicole Walsh earned you a badge of coolness. Figuring out who wanted to be friends because they actually liked her took more effort than Nikki had been willing to give. By the time she joined the FBI, she'd become an expert at keeping people at a distance, and that included her ex-husband. She'd intended to do the same thing with her Minnesota unit, but Courtney's big personality had cracked Nikki's defenses. They'd become close friends, and Nikki was a better person because of their friendship. And she was damn lucky to have Courtney on her team. "Did you find anything on the bodies?"

"I used the UV light in the truck. No stains, and no visible trace of anything."

Nikki had expected as much. "The sheriff's department doesn't have much physical evidence, either. They found nothing usable on the trail or surrounding areas. They disappeared in mid-October. The weather had been good, so no footprints. No sign of fibers or any sort of struggle, which makes me think the girls might not have been forced off the trail."

Liam appeared in the doorway, still wearing his floppy hat. "Why didn't I take that job in the Florida office?"

"Because you wanted to work with the best." Courtney tossed her discarded snow pants at him. "You're lucky to have us."

"Some days I wonder," he replied, looking her up and down. "Why are you sweating?"

"Long story."

When she'd learned about the DNA testing, Nikki had told her team but had made it clear she intended to let the district attorney handle things. "I'm sure you both saw the protestors. I wasn't aware Mark Todd had a following, but it sounds like they aren't going away any time soon. Anyway, I just want you both to know they aren't going to affect this case. As far as I'm concerned, that case is closed. I intend to ignore them. They aren't going to affect my ability to work this case."

"I'm not worried about that," Liam said. "I just don't want them slowing us down."

"I've been told they're keeping a respectful distance. As long as they continue to do so, they're of no concern." Nikki dreaded telling them the next part. Being around John wasn't the issue. But she didn't want Madison and Kaylee's murders sensationalized because of her past connection. "Before you hear it from someone else, Madison's stepfather is an ex-boyfriend. I was dating him when my parents were killed. It's not going to be a problem for me, but I'm sure the media is going to be all over it."

Liam nodded, wide-eyed.

Courtney shot her a quizzical look, but Nikki shook her head. As much as she wanted to tell Courtney everything, now wasn't the time or the place.

A month into their new jobs in the criminal profiling unit, Courtney encountered her first domestic violence victim. She'd spent hours collecting evidence from the woman's clothes and body, along with the crime scene, without batting a mascaraed eyelash. The second they clocked out, she'd turned to Nikki and announced they were going to the bar down the street. Half a bottle of tequila later, Courtney became one of the privileged few who knew the grim details about Nikki's past. Keeping the truth from her superiors hadn't been an option, but a decade plus since she'd become the girl whose parents were murdered, Nikki had willingly told only one person: her ex-husband. Aside from him, Courtney was still the only person at the FBI office familiar with the darkest details of that night.

Nikki looked at Liam. "I emailed you a list of all the persons of interest the sergeant compiled during the girls' disappearance. All close family and friends have alibis that other officers have already checked out. I want you to run background information on everyone."

The FBI had deeper resources than the sheriff's office, and Nikki was hoping for a lucky break.

"I think Kaylee had a secret phone, so I want you to see what you can find out about it from her cousin. Apparently they were close. Then run detailed background checks on all the sex offenders within a fifty-mile radius, especially those released around the time the girls were taken. We don't know yet if they were assaulted, but that list is a good place to start. Court, since you're in a holding pattern, can you go through the girls' social media and see if anything stands out? Maybe you'll spot something that Miller's team didn't."

A yawn nearly dislodged Nikki's jaw. "I'll go and interview the parents with Miller again in the morning. We currently have no evidence to process and it's too late to interview any witnesses. I'll go through the original investigation notes, you guys get home and let's start fresh tomorrow. It might be our last chance to get any sleep for a while."

Liam glanced at Courtney, who shook her head.

"What?" Nikki asked.

"I don't mean to be disrespectful, but now we know this isn't Frost, we don't have to work the case. You have every authority to pack it up and let the locals handle it. I've seen the protesters outside, and I wouldn't want to be around that if I were you."

Nikki forced her best fake smile. "Don't worry about me. The past will stay where it belongs. I'm here to find out what happened to those girls."

CHAPTER FOUR

Blowing snow made Nikki's drive home take twice as long. She'd blasted the radio in a futile effort not to think about the past. Long-buried memories seemed to pop out of nowhere. The sound of the floorboards creaking came into her head. That sound had saved Nikki's life, and she'd never forget it. Hiding in the closet, sweat soaking her shirt, she'd trembled with fear as the footsteps came into the room. Then he'd whispered her name, and fear turned to rage. How could he do this to her family?

She blinked back the tears. The thought of Mark Todd convincing anyone that he was innocent, much less a group of people who were willing to spend their time and energy fighting for him, burned a hole in her gut. He'd sat silently during the trial all those years ago, refusing to look at Nikki. She'd wanted to grab him and make him look at her, make him see what he'd done to her. He'd known her family for years, their family farms bordered each other's: they'd play in her family's cornfields as kids, running through the mazes, sweat pouring down their backs, laughing. The first two years of high school, she and Mark had even run in the same social circle—until Nikki met John.

Looking back, Nikki could see that she'd dropped everything for John. At sixteen, he'd been her first love. He was athletic, handsome, and a junior at Bethel University. He'd made Nikki feel special and wanted—for the first time in her life. But her parents had believed the four-year age difference was too much and when they found out—caught him picking her up one evening at the top of the field by the house—they'd forbidden her to see him. And for the first time in her life, Nikki rebelled. She snuck out to meet John a few days later, half-expecting to get caught. But she hadn't, and the rush that came with getting away with it was intoxicating.

Nikki had always been close to her parents, and growing up an only child meant she was often spoiled and doted on. Her mother was stricter than her father, who hated to tell her no. He was always the peacemaker between Nikki and her mother, and Nikki had always been able to nag him into allowing her to do whatever she wanted. But he'd sided with her mother about John, and Nikki had been furious. She barely talked to her father when he came in from the fields for dinner, and hurting his feelings felt justified.

The night of the murders, Nikki had said something rude to her father, and he'd snapped, calling her a spoiled brat. Her mother had sent Nikki upstairs with a warning not to come back down until morning. The two of them were sick of her bad attitude.

What she wouldn't give to turn back the clock and change that last conversation and wipe out the memories of their hurt faces and the tears welling in her father's eyes.

A single decision had altered the course of Nikki's life. She'd snuck out after her parents had gone to bed, longing to see John. She'd hopped into his waiting car without a shred of guilt, unaware she'd seen her parents for the last time. If she'd just stayed home, she knew they'd still be here.

Nikki wondered if Kaylee and Madison had been sneaking around with the wrong people too. Stranger abduction was rare, especially with two victims and, statistically, Nikki still had to consider the parents as suspects. Amy's anger with John might be solely grief-driven—the last couple of months would have taken their toll on their relationship, as they waited each day desperate for news, blaming one another for Madison's disappearance—but the fire in Amy's eyes when John defended Kaylee hadn't looked like grief.

Nikki turned onto her street and groaned. She lived in one of St. Paul's quiet suburbs, full of perfect family units. Highland Park was only about thirty miles from Stillwater, but it was busier, and that made it seem worlds away from the sleepy area she'd once called home. She preferred it, being closer to the city, even if the city plows always left her street until last. Thankfully her jeep breezed through the drifting snow.

Her small home sat in the cul-de-sac at the end of the street. She'd chosen lot size over square footage, and the trees surrounding the property and sea of motion lights made her feel safely cocooned.

Nikki parked in the single-car garage and made sure to reset the security code to the garage door.

A four-digit code unlocked the mudroom door; she reset it as well and then left her boots on the mat and tiptoed into the small kitchen. The dishes were dried in the sink, and the house smelled of clean laundry. Nikki hung her coat on the back of a chair and went into the living room.

Her ex-husband lay on the couch, one foot dangling off, snoring loudly. At least she didn't have to try to sleep with that noise anymore.

"Hey." She patted his shoulder.

Tyler opened one eye and yawned. "Time is it?"

"Almost midnight. Thanks for staying."

"Lacey insisted. I paid the sitter before she left." He sat up, and habit made her want to smooth the unruly lock of hair at the back of his head, but she kept her hands to herself.

She and Tyler had met at the FBI Academy when they were both new recruits. He was a good guy: stable, hardworking, faithful. He respected her as a cop and treated her as an equal—a first in her relationship history. The sex was good but predictable. Marriage seemed like the inevitable next step, but Nikki's passion for her work—Tyler would call it obsession—drove her further away.

Nikki found out she was pregnant the day she planned to ask Tyler for a divorce. But as much as they both loved their daughter, the marriage was a lost cause. Their divorce had been amicable, and while they shared custody, both tried to accommodate the other's schedule. Knowing that Lacey was safe with her father made working late nights easier for Nikki.

Nikki sank onto the couch next to Tyler. "I'll give you some cash."

He waved her off. "Is it Frost?"

"I wish, sick as it sounds. Two teenaged girls. Frozen. Bodies secured with rope to keep them in the fetal position."

"Which means the killer had limited space. Frozen solid?"

"Close enough. It will be days before the autopsy. We can't even take clothes off or look at exterior wounds without possibly damaging evidence." She rubbed her temples and wished she'd grabbed a beer from the fridge. "Fifteen years old."

"I don't know how you do it." Tyler stood and stretched. Sitting behind a desk had given him a little bit of a belly, but he still had the physique of a wrestler. Two-time state champion, as he liked to remind everyone. "Lacey had a bath tonight."

Her throat knotted. She hadn't told Hardin about her six-year-old daughter because Lacey belonged in this life, not in that one. Saying her name in Stillwater felt like some sort of curse. But it didn't protect Nikki from imagining what it would be like to find Lacey lying in the snow.

"Stop." Tyler nudged her shoulder. "You can't compartmentalize when you do that."

Nikki wiped her eyes. "Do what?"

"Think about something like this happening to Lacey."

"I thought I was the mind reader." Hollywood's ridiculous depictions of criminal profilers were a constant irritant to Nikki and her colleagues. People expected her to spend ten minutes looking over some data and come up with a dead-on profile.

"I can read you," Tyler said. "That hasn't changed."

She smiled at the hint of wistfulness in his tone. "Guess not."

Tyler still loved her. Deep down, he thought they would eventually make it work, no matter how many times Nikki told him they were better off as friends.

"Did you run into anyone involved with the appeal?"

"Well, John Banks is one of the girls' stepdads. There was a group protesting for Mark near the sheriff's office. They didn't recognize me, but I'm sure they'll have the make and model of my vehicle, along with my height and weight, by tomorrow. Oh, and Caitlin Newport showed up at the crime scene."

"No shit?"

"She didn't say anything about my parents. But she didn't press too hard about the girls' murders either. I don't know what she's up to."

"You could talk to your bureau chief. He already knows your history, and Frost is still out there. Getting someone else assigned to the case wouldn't be that difficult."

"I know. But now that I've gone to the scene and heard the details, I'm attached. I want to get those girls justice." Was that the only reason? Nikki wondered. Or did some part of her want to prove to everyone in Stillwater that she was no longer the girl who'd found her parents murdered? Nikki had clawed her way to success in the FBI despite the obstacles. She knew that people expected her to fail, for her grief and her anger to overwhelm her. But she didn't let it.

"John Banks doesn't have anything to do with you wanting to stick around?"

Nikki stared at him. "Are you serious?"

"He was your first love—"

"Twenty years ago. I haven't thought about him in forever. I want to find their killer because it's my job. Madison and Kaylee's killer has to be held accountable."

"Why does it have to be you, though?"

She smiled faintly.

Tyler held up his hands in defeat and reached for his heavy parka. "Okay, sorry I mentioned it. Just… watch yourself. If people are protesting and that reporter is around, you're going to be a target."

"I can handle it, but I'm probably going to get a room in town while we're working this case." In the lightest of traffic, the drive to Stillwater took at least forty-five minutes. As much as Nikki looked forward to quiet evenings with her daughter, she had a job to do. And she wanted to keep her as sheltered from that as possible.

"Lacey can stay at my place as long as you need her to," Tyler said.

"Thanks for being so flexible." Nikki stifled a yawn. "You sure you don't want to crash in the guest room?"

"Early meeting tomorrow. I'll pick her up from school."

Nikki walked him to the front door. "Be careful driving. Roads are still drifting over."

"I will." Tyler kissed the side of her head. It would be so easy to melt into his arms and let him distract her for a while, but she wouldn't use Tyler like that. He deserved better.

Nikki secured both dead bolts and the doorknob's lock before going to check on her sleeping daughter.

Lacey sprawled in the middle of her bed, blankets on the floor, her favorite stuffed animal on her face. Her wavy, dark hair and blue eyes resembled Nikki's, but her smile and lighthearted personality came from Tyler. They hadn't made their marriage work, but they'd definitely made a perfect kid. She considered snuggling up with Lacey, but that always ended in a sleepless night for Nikki. Lacey had been a bed hog since before she could walk.

Nikki took a long shower, letting the hot water massage her tight shoulders and nearly falling asleep. She checked the locks and security system one more time and then crawled into bed with Miller's case file, along with sticky notes and a pen. She combed through the file, adding a note about anything she needed clarified or wanted to investigate further. It was well into the early hours of the morning when she finally turned off the lamp and tried to sleep.

Her mind still felt wired, but her body quickly succumbed to exhaustion.

She could hear male laughter, followed by a strange buzzing sound and angry shouting.

She was so sick and scared.

Thirteen steps, blood on the stairs.

Nikki, you did this.

CHAPTER FIVE

Lacey's boot-clad feet bounced rhythmically against the leather seat of the car, spraying sand and grit everywhere. Lacey sang along with the radio, at least a key higher than the song playing, but at a much louder decibel. "Mommy, this is my favorite song."

Nikki smiled at her in the rearview mirror. "I thought 'Uptown Funk' was your favorite song."

Thank God for before- and after-school care, she thought, already going over everything she needed to start the investigation today. Lacey had asked why she was going in so early. "You've come this early before. A couple of your kindergarten friends will be there," Nikki had replied.

"Carly and Logan," Lacey had said. "They have to come early every day." Lacey shook her head as though that were the worst possible situation. "Mommy, are you really going to be gone all week because of a bad guy?" She knew what Nikki did, that both her parents were the good guys.

"Yes, but we can FaceTime every night," Nikki had answered.

"I don't like it."

"Me either, Lace. But I have to do my job, and it makes more sense for me to stay in town. Besides, you know Daddy will let you eat way more junk food than I do."

Lacey had grinned. "I already thought of that."

Nikki stopped in the drop-off lane and then hurried around to help Lacey out of her booster. "Backpack?"

"Check."

"Hat and gloves?"

"On my head and hands." She proudly displayed the mismatched gloves. At least they were both wool.

Nikki told Lacey her dad was picking her up from school, wrapped her arms around her daughter and wished she would stay this happy and innocent forever. She watched her run toward her friend, her hat only half on. Two little boys raced past, their mother shouted something from the car, and the older boy waved in response.

Cherish these moments, Nikki wanted to say. Some mothers will never get to drop their kids off at school again.

The Banks family lived in an upscale community on Long Lake that had been cruddy swampland when Nikki was a kid. Now perfectly maintained, sprawling homes with two- and three-car garages lined the lakefront. Between the new construction and exclusive views, the properties' taxes had to be sky-high.

Nikki wasn't surprised to see how well John had done for himself as she reached the right turn. He'd come from a wealthy family and been given every opportunity to succeed; that sort of environment made you driven, and it helped that John was charming too.

A gleaming Chevy Tahoe was parked in the driveway, along with an older model Toyota Camry. Nikki parked on the street behind Miller's cruiser. She secured the emergency brake before she joined him on the sidewalk.

"They must have company," Miller said. "The Tahoe's Amy's and John drives a Lexus. We initially processed both for evidence. Amy was screaming mad, but I told her it was protocol. Roads decent?"

"Mostly. Nice place," Nikki replied.

"John works for a large pharmaceutical company. He's pretty high up in the food chain. Amy works part-time as a bank teller so she can be here when the kids get home from school."

"Madison had one sibling?"

"A little brother. Second grade, I think."

A tall, sturdy-looking woman came out the front door, pulling it shut behind her. She started sprinkling ice melt on the wide steps.

Nikki glanced at Miller. "Housekeeper?"

He shook his head. "Family friend. Good morning, Mindy."

"Sergeant Miller, I didn't realize you were already here. I wanted to make sure these steps weren't so icy."

"Mindy Vance, this is Special Agent Nikki Hunt with the FBI."

"I'm glad to meet you, despite the horrific circumstances." Mindy's heavy winter coat added to her plump girth and she was nearly as tall as Miller. "I stopped by to check in on John and Amy."

"How long have you known the Bankses?" Nikki asked.

"Oh, for a long time," Mindy said. "Everyone's just in shock. I guess I'm a bit of a Pollyanna, but I still hoped the girls would come home safe. Amy's just a wreck. And John's, well, John."

"Stoic," Nikki said. "He was never great at showing his emotions."

"I think that's the case with most men in our generation." Mindy's smile quickly faltered. "Madison was a good kid. She had such a bright future."

Miller took the ice melt and started sprinkling it onto the sidewalk.

"Thank you," Mindy said.

"Did you know Kaylee as well?" Nikki asked.

"No," Mindy replied. "I don't visit as often as I should since my husband died, but I wanted to check in on Amy."

"I'm sorry for your loss," Nikki said. "You and Amy are close?"

"Not exactly close. Amy's very private. But she was a rock after my husband's death. I just can't imagine what she's going through."

Nikki glanced around at the snow-covered houses. "Is this a tight-knit area?"

"I think so," Mindy said. "The Burns family at the end of the cul-de-sac throws block parties in the summer. Pays for a live band and funhouses for the kids."

"People look out for one another," Nikki said.

"Absolutely."

"Would they notice a strange person or vehicle hanging around?"

Mindy thought about it for a moment. "Maybe, but there are always visitors. I can't see anyone paying much attention unless there was some kind of commotion." She zipped up her coat and pulled on gloves. "I'm sorry to be rude, but I have to get to work."

"Of course." Nikki handed her a business card. "I know you already gave a statement, when the girls disappeared, but if you think of anything else that you think could help, give me a call."

Mindy nodded. "It was nice to meet you."

The door opened once again. Dressed in sweats and an old Vikings shirt, Nikki thought John looked more like the slightly wild college kid she remembered.

"Thought I heard your voice." Circles lined his bloodshot eyes.

"Did you get any sleep?" Nikki asked.

"A little." John glanced over her shoulder and waved at Mindy. "I was going to take care of the sidewalk."

"I think she just wanted to help," Nikki said. "No one really knows what to do in these situations."

Miller joined them, finishing off the last of the ice melt, and she and Miller followed John inside. Nikki slipped her boots off, discreetly admiring the house. The entry flowed into a massive great room that offered spectacular views of the iced-over lake. Family pictures lined the mantle over the fireplace, and the entire room had a definite Dollanganger vibe. Fair-skinned and blond-haired Amy and John could have been related, and Madison and the small boy sitting on her lap were doll-like replicas of their parents. Madison easily passed for John's biological child.

"What's your son's name?" Nikki asked.

John sat on the couch, staring into the fire. "Bailey. He's with Amy's parents."

"How did he take the news?"

"We haven't told him," John replied.

"I understand it's going to be hard," Nikki said, "but you shouldn't wait much longer. The worst thing that could happen is his finding out from someone else. If you need a victim's advocate who specializes in kids—"

"We're fine." Amy Banks sat down next to her husband. The black-framed glasses she wore didn't hide her red eyes or the dark circles beneath them.

"How are you doing this morning, Mrs. Banks?"

Amy stared at her for a moment. "Fucking awful. How do you think I'm doing?"

"Jesus, be polite," John said. "She's here to help."

Nikki wasn't fazed by the woman's rudeness. She'd endured much worse from grieving family members. They needed someone to lash out at, and cops were often the easiest people to focus on. "We just met Mindy Vance. It was nice of her to stop by."

Amy's expression softened. "She's very kind. She's gone through her share of grief."

"Yes, she mentioned her husband. Your families spent a lot of time together?"

"Not in recent years," Amy said. "Madison was younger than Mindy's son, so they didn't hang out much. We just didn't have much in common."

"Were you and your daughter close, Mrs. Banks?"

"Of course we were. Aren't all mothers and daughters?"

Nikki remembered that she and her mother had argued for hours on end when she was Madison's age, and her father usually had to send them both to their respective corners.

"I've gone over your original interviews after the girls disappeared. I just have a few questions. They may seem repetitive, but it's important that I ask since this has become a homicide investigation," Nikki explained. "Did Madison ever mention anyone following her or Kaylee? Anybody new in their lives?"

"You should start with Jessica Thomas' boyfriend," Amy said. "Everyone knows he's a drug dealer."

"That doesn't make him a kidnapper," John said.

"Ricky Fillinger," Miller confirmed. "He's been convicted of some minor drug offences, but he works as a mechanic and I've told you he does have an alibi."

There was something so familiar to Nikki about that name. "Ricky Fillinger, as in all-state football?" Nikki asked.

"Yep," John said. "He blew out his knee. I heard he got addicted to the painkillers."

"His buddy alibied him, Sergeant Miller." Amy's harsh tone matched the hateful glare she gave her husband. "And guys never lie for each other, do they?"

John's jaw twitched, but he said nothing. Nikki wasn't sure if this tension was a sign of marital problems, or just the soul-crushing anger that came with losing a child.

"Our daughter was a good girl who followed the rules," Amy continued. "Whoever did this came from Kaylee's life."

"You don't know that." John's blue eyes flashed.

"Are you defending that girl?" she said, her voice rising. "She exposed Madison to things she never should have seen. And her mother's never home. How's the girl supposed to have any moral compass?"

Nikki let Miller take notes while Amy and John volleyed back and forth. Amy looked like a tiger ready to spring, and John leaned forward, his elbows on his knees, almost in a protective stance.

"She works fourteen-hour shifts at the nursing home," John said. "Not everyone has a husband who provides everything. You should remember that more often than you do."

Nikki tensed at his manipulative tone, struggling to keep her mouth shut. Amy was a grieving mother who deserved some leniency. Nikki had forgotten about John's fragile ego, but when they were dating, John had demanded gratitude for the smallest acts of kindness. Nikki realized now that he'd been just as insecure as everyone else.

After her parents' murders, she'd pushed John away. She wondered if his insecurities would have eventually caused their relationship to end if the murders hadn't happened.

Amy's fair skin turned red. "How dare you—"

"Okay." Nikki shook off the heaviness that had started to settle over her. "Let's focus on what you know about the girls' last day."

"We've told you everything already," John said.

Nikki had memorized the file the night before. "Madison texted you at 12:07 p.m. that she and Kaylee were walking the lake trail to the Hansons'. It's a ten-minute walk. She said she would text you when she arrived."

"She didn't." John put his head in his hands. "But I totally forgot to check. It didn't dawn on me until hours later that she'd never texted me."

"Maybe if you didn't spend all your time at the office, she might still be here."

John's knuckles turned white, but he said nothing.

"Listen," Nikki said. "You've both experienced a terrible loss, and you want someone to blame. But that isn't going to help you get through this. The only person who can comprehend your loss is sitting beside you."

"She was *my* daughter. My flesh and blood—"

"I loved her like she was my own," John exploded. "You know that."

Amy's jaw tightened, her lips thinned to an angry line, but she remained silent.

"Let's get back to the questions so we can get out of your hair," Miller said. "You both need rest."

Nikki continued. "Miles Hanson and his father confirmed the girls never arrived, and that Madison didn't answer the boy's text. The weather was nice that Saturday, especially for November. A jogger saw the girls on the trail between here and the halfway point."

"We know the details, for Christ's sake," Amy said. "Why aren't you out there looking for this monster?"

"We are," Nikki replied. "The neighbors were interviewed, but is there any chance they might have stopped at someone's house prior to the Hansons'?"

"Every house near the trail has either retired people or young families," Amy said. "Madison didn't know any of them. I highly doubt Kaylee did, either." Amy glared out the window, shaking her head. She clearly blamed Kaylee for her daughter's death, but something else brewed beneath the surface. Nikki needed to get to the bottom of it sooner rather than later.

Nikki glanced at Miller, who nodded and said, "We found the pepper spray in her room. Probably figured she didn't need it during the day."

"Both girls were athletic, both were capable of fighting and it's unlikely that someone was able to take them by force. My notes say that officers found no evidence of a struggle along the trail," Nikki added. "We're looking for someone the girls knew. Someone they may have left the trail with willingly."

"Sergeant Miller said the same thing when they first went missing," Amy said. "You aren't telling us anything new."

"Jesus, Amy," John said. "Let her talk."

Amy's pallid face turned red. "Excuse me?"

Nikki cleared her throat. "I've gone through all of the witness statements, including Miles Hanson's and Madison's other friends. Miles said that the girls texted to say they were headed over—and phone records show that's true. But when Sergeant Miller spoke to the rest of the friends, they seemed surprised that the girls would hang out with Miles outside of school."

"They're wrong," John said flatly. "Maddie had gone to the Hansons' more than once."

Nikki nodded. "We're headed to speak with Miles next. Maybe they did intend to go to his house and then changed their minds."

"They were seen on the trail—" Amy began.

"Before the halfway point," Nikki said. "They could have exited it at any time after that. There were other people on the trail, and no one reported seeing them or hearing any sort of a struggle. There's little chance they went into someone's house, especially since they were all canvassed, and most had security footage. I think we have to consider someone with a car was waiting for them, and the girls got into the car willingly."

"So, what now?" John asked.

"Every kid keeps secrets from their parents. We need to know what Madison and Kaylee kept to themselves."

John's sad eyes met hers. He knew exactly what she meant. "You think there's a boy involved?"

"We don't know, which is why we need access."

"What sort of access?" Amy said. "The police already went through Madison's social media accounts and her computer when they first went missing. They didn't find anything."

"Teenagers are smarter than us when it comes to technology. They know how to hide things," Miller suggested. "My people went through everything, but the FBI has better resources. I'm hoping they will find something we couldn't."

"In the meantime, we'll talk to friends, the school, any known acquaintances. My hope is that someone in their social circle has information—and chances are, they don't even realize it can help. I'd like to take a look at Madison's room."

"Sergeant Miller already did." Amy glared at her.

"Mrs. Banks, fresh eyes and a new perspective can make a big difference," Miller replied.

Amy sighed. "Fine, but I'm going with you. I don't want anything changed from the way she left it."

It wasn't the ideal situation, but Nikki could tell it was the only way the woman was going to cooperate. When her parents were murdered, Nikki hadn't let anyone else go through her mother's collection of Precious Moments figurines or set foot in their bedroom. "I'll let you lead the way, then."

The big staircase opened into a large common area with a flat-screen television and toys scattered around overstuffed chairs. Various artwork decorated the walls, ranging from finger-paint blobs to an impressive sketch of one of the big Victorian houses in the historic district. Madison's name was scribbled on the bottom right.

"She was a talented artist."

"Yes, she was. Maddie's room is over here." Amy turned left at the far end of the hall. Her fingers trembled as she reached for the doorknob. "Please don't move things around."

"I won't." Nikki opened the door, and a flicker of envy swept through her. Her own room in the big farmhouse had been painted in bright yellow, and she'd covered one wall with various posters. Her vanity and bedside table had been her parents' castoffs, and they didn't match her dresser. Nikki had delighted in making Lacey's room pretty, but Madison's room made it look drab in comparison.

A mural of a beach with white sand and a sparkling ocean covered the largest wall. Various quotes covered the adjacent wall, along with dozens of doodles. Nikki was sure Madison had decorated her own room.

"A dry-erase wall," Nikki said. "That's very cool."

A large art table sat beneath the big window that overlooked the neighborhood. All the supplies were organized and labeled, stored in containers under the desk.

"She liked things neat. She was a very good organizer." Sadness laced Amy's tone.

"It's a lovely room. May I look in the dresser drawers?"

Amy nodded, and Nikki worked her way through the dresser, searching for anything hidden. It was just as organized as the rest of the room, and she made sure to leave it that way. Madison's nightstand had several books, and a large jewelry box sat on top.

Amy hovered over Nikki's shoulder as she examined the walk-in closet. "What exactly are you looking for? If she did have any big secrets, they would have been hidden on her phone."

"Most likely," Nikki said. "Honestly, I'm not just looking for something tangible. I want to get a feel for the type of person Madison was. Now I see that she was very methodical, am I right?"

"Yes, and she was driven. She was in the top five percent of her class. She excelled at everything she tried."

And probably knotted up with tension and anxiety. Feeling the need to be the best and have things exactly as a person wished was exhausting.

"Madison didn't make snap decisions," Nikki said.

"No, at least not until she met that girl. Kaylee was always telling her to loosen up and live a little. Look where that got her." Amy rubbed her temples. "John says I have to get it together. Put on a good front for Bailey. I'll be strong for our son, but John just wants to make sure we don't embarrass ourselves with public outbursts and displays. We should grieve in private."

John had been the same way when she dated him. Their relationship was volatile at times, and he'd always been more concerned with his image than her feelings. Still, Nikki saw her opening. "Is that why you're so angry at him?"

"I never said I was angry—"

"You didn't need to," Nikki said.

"It's not meant for him. I'm just angry at the world for what's happened to my child."

Nikki tried to steer the conversation back to the couple's relationship. "That's absolutely normal, but I can see how much it bothers you when John talks about Kaylee."

Amy bristled. "He never should have allowed that girl into our home. I told him she was trouble. She just brought too much baggage into Madison's life." She folded her arms over her chest. "Are you finished?"

Nikki knew she wasn't going to get anything more out of Amy, but she sensed that Amy was still holding something back. "I don't want to cause problems between you two. But I know this about grief: it does what it wants, when it wants. Everyone grieves in their own way, and any person who thinks they can control the process is in for a big surprise. Asking for help when you need it is crucial." She walked back into the hall, trying to give Amy some space.

Amy followed her and closed the door. "Tell John that."

"I will." Nikki was certainly no marriage counselor, but she'd seen enough families torn apart by death to know what not to do, especially when kids were involved. "And I'm going to do whatever it takes to get you justice."

"Like you did with Mark Todd?" Amy said sharply.

"I'm sorry?" Nikki turned around, working to keep the frustration out of her tone.

"That didn't come out right," Amy continued, taking a moment to collect her thoughts. "I can't imagine what it's like to see the protestors when you go to the sheriff's office, and with everything being dredged up by the media, how will you stay focused on my daughter?"

Nikki hadn't seen anything on the news about Mark's appeal, but she realized now that the local paper was probably making it a front-page story.

"Mark Todd is in prison, where he belongs. And I learned to compartmentalize my life a long time ago." Nikki hoped she'd had her last conversation about Mark Todd.

CHAPTER SIX

Nikki wrapped her scarf around her face. Beyond the bare trees, a group of kids skated on the lake. The county closely monitored the lake's ice, but Nikki didn't care if six feet of ice covered the water. It only took one weak area to crack and pull someone under, especially kids.

"You skate?" Miller asked.

"Not very well. And never on the lake." She and Miller bent their heads against the wind as they made their way down the trail toward the Hansons'. "What do you think of the dynamic between John and Amy?"

"She's grieving and he's in shock," Miller said. "I think she blames him more than she wants to admit."

"Do they have a history of marital issues?"

"Not that I know of." Miller had zipped his collar up to his nose again, his voice muffled against the heavy material. "We investigated the two of them closely after the girls first disappeared. Pretty standard relationship, but losing Madison has definitely caused a big divide between them."

Nikki wondered if that was the only rift between the couple as she checked her phone for an update from Liam. He'd found a handful of registered sex offenders outside of Washington County who had been convicted of crimes involving girls around the same age as Madison and Kaylee. Local authorities had agreed to check in with the men and get back to Liam.

"Liam's working through the local sex offenders list, and he's expanded the target area." Nikki glanced at Miller. She didn't want him thinking they questioned his investigation. "It's probably a long shot, but we have to be thorough."

Miller smiled faintly. "Don't worry about pissing me off. I failed the girls. I couldn't find them, and I worked around the clock."

"I'm sure you did everything you could." Nikki tightened the scarf around her face, and her breath immediately fogged up her sunglasses.

"I was so ticked off at Hardin when he called you. But I'm glad he did."

"That's the one thing bugging me," Nikki said. "Why didn't Hardin call in the FBI earlier? Two missing kids usually warrants additional resources."

"He said we could handle it. Initially, we'd hoped they'd decided to run off. Maybe Kaylee wanted to get out of town and Madison had followed, hoping to talk some common sense into her. As the days went by, we realized that wasn't the case. But Hardin still believed we had the resources to find them."

"Calling in the FBI is always a difficult decision," Nikki acknowledged. "There's always at least one officer who resents the intrusion, and with Hardin being an elected official, he probably wanted to show the community his people could handle it. To tell you the truth, I was surprised to hear he'd become sheriff. He never struck me as the political type."

"I don't want to be disrespectful, but you can see his... weight is an issue. He's diabetic and being in the field was getting tough for him. Plus, he likes being in charge." Miller shook his head. "You remember when his niece used to come to the parties and drink and then rat us out after she left?"

"No," Nikki said. "When was that?"

"Our senior year she moved to Stillwater. Every damned time she showed up, the party was doomed."

Nikki forced a laugh. She'd been otherwise occupied senior year. The initial days after the murders were a blur, including the trial.

Once Nikki realized college was the only way to escape her past, she'd thrown herself into school and shut the rest of the world out.

"Shit." Miller stopped and glared up at the gray sky. "I'm sorry. I wasn't thinking."

"It's okay." She didn't expect people to walk on eggshells around her. Still, a familiar knot formed between her shoulder blades. "I'm going to get a room in town for a few days. Any suggestions for a decently priced place near the sheriff's station?"

Miller pursed his lips. "There are a couple of places with suites for business travelers right off the interstate. They're only ten minutes or so to downtown. You'll have more room and not be so close to the protestors."

"Good point." Nikki made a mental note to reserve a room when they were back in the car.

She tried to imagine the trail in the fall. It was paved and wide enough for three or four people to pass through. With the trees shedding leaves, the lake would have been visible. All in all, it was a peaceful place. A safe place, where two teenaged girls could easily be so caught up in conversation that someone could have snuck up on them. But witnesses who saw the girls said the trail had been relatively busy that day because of the nice weather. How did Madison and Kaylee disappear without anyone noticing something was wrong?

"Are we getting close to the Hansons'?"

Miller looked like he wanted to say more, but he only nodded. "It's the gray one on the left. I called them last night and told them we'd found the girls dead. They're expecting us."

When they got inside the house, Mrs. Hanson insisted on making everyone coffee, fluttering around her large kitchen like a nervous bird. Her son and husband sat on the sofa waiting nervously, Miles looked like his mother—both were blond, a bit on the chubby side, with the kind of fair skin that demanded sunscreen year-round. Mr. Hanson's brown hair and dark eyes made him the odd man out.

Miles eyed Nikki. "You're not wearing high heels. Female FBI agents always wear heels on television."

Nikki stuck her foot out. "These babies keep my feet warm in minus thirty-five degrees. And don't believe everything you see on TV."

Miles looked down at the cookies his mother had placed in front of him. His round shoulders sagged. "I think it's my fault they're dead," he said, reminding everyone of why they were there.

"Miles." His mother pressed a kiss to his head. "That's not true. How could you think that?"

Tears welled in his blue eyes. "They were coming to my house."

"Miles, that doesn't make it your fault," Nikki said. "Madison and Kaylee wanted to hang out with you."

He scrubbed his eyes and stared at his plate. "No, they didn't."

Nikki rested her clasped hands on the table and gave him an encouraging look. "Is there something you haven't told the police?"

Miles' chubby fingers trembled. "I didn't want to lie to the police. That's why I never said anything."

"What are you talking about, son?" Drew Hanson said. "You told me they stood you up."

"Not lying to the police is a good thing." Nikki's gut told her the girls never planned on coming to Miles' house. "Did Kaylee and Madison ask you to lie about something?"

"They wanted me to tell their parents they'd spent the afternoon here," Miles said. "Maddie wouldn't say where they were going, but she begged me to cover for them. I said okay. But then they disappeared, and the police wanted to know if they showed up here. I said no, because they hadn't."

Drew Hanson sighed. "You did the right thing by not lying to the police. But you should have told them that Maddie asked you to lie."

Miles stared at his father. "I didn't want to get in trouble."

"Miles is a good kid," his mother spoke up. "He's never in trouble."

"It's okay," Nikki said. "Did Maddie give you any details about where they were really going?"

"No, I swear. I didn't want to cover for them, but Maddie always helped me with my math homework, and we've been friends for a long time. She's responsible, too... or she was, anyway."

"How long have you known Kaylee?"

"I just met her after she started hanging out with Madison."

"What did you think of her?" Nikki asked.

"She was nice. Not like I thought she'd be."

"How'd you think she would be?" Miller asked.

Miles flushed. "She got kicked off the volleyball team for fighting. I thought she'd be mean. Plus, she's got a reputation for being kind of..." He flushed. "A thot."

"Thot?" Miller asked.

"That ho over there," Nikki said dryly. "A lovely term from social media. Why did she have that reputation?"

"Girls who didn't like her started it, I guess. I heard she'd slept with a bunch of guys and even gave one a..." He turned red and looked at his mouther. "Well, you know... in the locker room. But Madison said those were all lies. She said Kaylee was a virgin."

"You think Madison was right?"

"I didn't know at first, but after I hung around with Kaylee, I did. She's so shy and quiet. She was, I mean." He stared at his plate. "I can't believe they're gone."

"Bullying has become an everyday occurrence for these kids." Drew Hanson sighed. "The things social media exposes them to, the pressure it adds, is unreal. And it's the perfect rumor mill."

"Sergeant Miller told me you were Kaylee's English teacher?" Nikki asked.

Hanson nodded. "She had real talent. Her short stories were layered with the sort of emotion and substance usually seen in college writing."

"Do you have any copies of those?"

Hanson shook his head. "I wish I did. They were wonderful."

Nikki glanced at Miller. "You know if she had computer access at home?"

"She shared a laptop with her mother. No papers on it."

"I don't think she wrote her stories at home," Hanson said. "She spent her free period in the computer lab and often stayed after school."

"Do students have access to the cloud?"

"No," Hanson said. "But they're allowed to bring their own flash drives."

"We didn't find one in her school stuff," Miller whispered to Nikki. "We can check her room again."

"Tell me more about her papers," Nikki said. "What sort of things did she write about?"

"Why?" Miles asked. "How are they going to help you find out who killed them?"

"When I started at the Behavioral Analysis Unit, my mentor told me that profiling wasn't about the bad guy, but the victim. Profile the victim, because understanding the victim means understanding the person who hurt them. Make sense?" She'd learned Madison was wound tight and particular, and likely a stickler about obeying rules.

"Kaylee's papers might have insight into who she was." Miles looked impressed.

"Exactly," Nikki said. "She very well might have put things into her stories—even if they were fiction—that she didn't tell anyone else."

"That's fascinating," Hanson said. "I believe the overarching theme in most of her stories was being the outsider. Misunderstood and never being heard. In one story, she likened it to standing in the middle of the room, screaming at every person in her life, and no one heard her."

"Did you ever talk to her about them?"

"I tried," Hanson said. "But she didn't want to talk, and I respected her privacy. I hoped writing the stories probably helped her with whatever she was going through."

"Kaylee was aware you were Miles' father? She knew you'd be at the house?"

Hanson glanced at his son. "I assume she did."

Miles grabbed a cookie off the plate. He chewed vigorously, eyes on his father.

"I'm just asking because I assume you being home would make it difficult for Miles to cover for them."

Hanson's gaze shifted around the room and then back to his son. "That's a good question. Son, did you tell her I would be out of the house?"

Miles flushed red, his mouth set hard. He nodded.

"And you were home all day?" Nikki asked Hanson. "No chance you left and maybe saw the girls walking?"

"I wasn't going to leave my fourteen-year-old son home with two girls," Hanson said.

Miles grabbed another cookie, and his mother gave him a fresh soda. She smoothed his hair. "I don't think he can help you any more than he already has."

Nikki stood. "Neither girl ever talked about doing something they knew could get them in trouble? Meeting up with older friends or something?"

Miles chased the cookie away with a big chug of soda. "Madison told me that Kaylee had a crush on some older guy. I wasn't supposed to tell anyone."

Bingo.

"Kaylee had a secret boyfriend." Miller kicked a frozen snow clod out of his way. They'd taken the short route back to their cars, which were still parked in front of the Bankses' home. "Why didn't he tell me that when I interviewed him before?"

"Well, he said she had a crush on a guy." Nikki could feel Miller's frustration. He'd already felt like he'd failed the girls, but Nikki had reviewed his files. He'd done everything by the book and followed every possible angle.

"Was she dating him? And if so, how were they communicating? All her social media accounts and emails have been checked. We've gone over her mom's computer three times. Is he someone she's able to see every day, like with some kind of pre-arranged meeting place?"

"Maybe," Nikki said. "If he is older, he might work nearby or go to one of the local colleges. But I agree with you that she'd be desperate to communicate with him, because that's how teenaged girls are. I thought she might have a secret cell phone, and this seems like another reason she'd need one."

In the weeks when Nikki was dating John behind her parents' backs, she'd had to call him from Annmarie's house or the payphone at the laundromat. Going a day without talking with him was torture.

"I'm more concerned about the dynamic between Miles and his father," Nikki said. "Something's not right there."

Miller nodded. "I noticed that, too. What are you thinking?"

"I think Miles agreed to cover for them because Madison asked, just like he said. But I'm not sure Drew Hanson was home." A third vehicle had parked behind the Bankses' SUV while they'd been at the Hansons'. "Who does that car belong to?"

"Pastor," Miller said. "He's from the Methodist Church a few blocks over."

Nikki was more interested in the security camera mounted on the garage. She scanned the neighbors; most had at least a single camera on the garage and one at the front door. "Does Hanson have a security camera focused on the garage?"

"No, just the front and back door."

"Does either camera capture the driveway at all?"

"Not that I can remember."

Nikki found her key fob and turned the jeep on, giving the seats a few extra seconds to warm up. "Did you notice Miles' demeanor change when I asked about his dad being there?"

"He couldn't get his mouth full fast enough."

"Exactly," Nikki said. "He's covering for his dad. No chance the security footage could have been swapped for another day?"

"Not with his setup. Connected to the internet so it pulls the date and can't be altered. I went through it twice to make sure the girls never came into the house. Hanson didn't leave out the front or back door. Miles said he was home. So did his wife. I didn't pursue that angle. I guess I should have." Miller looked down at the ground and kicked a chunk of dirty, frozen snow.

"I probably would have done the same thing," Nikki said. "But after talking with Miles and his dad, I think Drew left sometime that day, in his car. No camera on the garage to capture it."

"And he makes his son lie for him," Miller said. "What kind of parent does that?"

"The kind who has a secret," Nikki said.

CHAPTER SEVEN

During the short drive to Kaylee's home, Nikki called the Comfort Inn and Suites and reserved a room.

Jessica Thomas' house was less than a fifteen-minute walk from the Bankses' home, but the area felt entirely different. Kaylee had lived in a cookie-cutter condominium that looked exactly like the other dozen on the street. The Thomas home was minimally decorated with careworn furniture, but it seemed much homier than the Bankses'.

Jessica sat at the table in her maroon work scrubs and stared vacantly at Nikki. Her long dark hair was pulled into a ponytail and streaked with grays. She had a lean look about her, with bony cheekbones and pallid skin.

"How are you holding up?" Miller asked.

Jessica's thin arms hugged her chest. "I keep telling myself to wake up. Like it's all a nightmare."

Nikki had done the same thing during the nightmares that lingered for months after her parents' murders. Her brain would desperately scream at her to wake up before she went into the house, but Nikki never managed to listen.

"This is Special Agent Nikki Hunt with the FBI," Miller said. "She wants to ask you a few more questions, if that's okay."

"Did that Frost guy do this to my girl?" Jessica asked.

"We're examining all possibilities," Nikki said.

"If it's not Frost, then why are you still here?" Jessica asked tiredly. "I know who you are, and I read the paper. I can't imagine you'd want to stick around. All the new evidence…"

Nikki's heart skidded to a stop before ramping up again. New evidence? She'd been told that Mark had asked for new evidence to be re-examined, not that there was anything new to look at. Nikki couldn't think about that right now. "Finding the person responsible for the girls' deaths is my priority."

"And what if the Frost Killer dumps some woman?" Jessica replied. "Will you just leave the case hanging?"

"Jess, you don't need to worry—" Miller began.

Jessica's voice grew louder as she white-knuckled her coffee cup. Her eyes bore into Nikki's. "I need to know that you're going to work this case until it's solved, no matter what happens."

"I'm not going anywhere," Nikki said. "I know you've answered the same questions over and over, so I'm going to try not to be very repetitive, but I do need to ask them again. That's why I'm here. And I won't be leaving until I find your daughter's killer."

"My kid's just another dead teenager to you," Jessica snapped. "If you catch Frost, you'll make national—"

Nikki reached over the table and placed her hand over Jessica's trembling ones. "I swear to you that I will see this case through."

Jessica's shoulders inched down. "I'm holding you to that, Agent."

"I fully expect you to," Nikki said. "Sergeant Miller said Kaylee was grounded and without her phone," Nikki continued. "That she didn't have permission to go to Madison's."

"She'd cut class and then was caught with a joint. I took her phone and grounded her." Jessica closed her eyes. "If she'd had her phone, maybe—"

"Don't do that to yourself," Nikki said. "You did what any parent would do in the situation."

Jessica grabbed a lighter from the small pile of odds and ends on the table. Nikki didn't see any cigarettes, but the landlord probably didn't allow smoking inside.

"Do you need a break to smoke?"

"I quit. Too expensive. I just like to have something in my hands, you know?" Jessica cleared her throat. "I worked a double shift at the nursing home that day and didn't get home until after dinner time. I was so angry she wasn't home, but I knew she'd be with Madison, so I just drove over there. No one was home. I texted Amy then, and she told me the girls were at the Hansons'. I told her I'd go get them and drop Madison at home."

Nikki looked at Miller. "Why didn't Madison go with her mother and brother to see her grandparents?" Nikki asked.

"She begged off, saying she had a big test on Monday," Miller answered.

Exactly what Nikki expected from what she knew of Madison.

"The Hansons had just gotten home from dinner. Miles said the girls never showed up. That's when I called the police."

"I know Kaylee got in trouble this summer," Nikki said. "Were things any better when she got back to school?"

"I thought so. She seemed happier," Jessica said. "But middle school was rough. Do you know how much social media can mess a teenaged girl up?"

"I can only imagine." Stillwater had two middle schools, and everyone was thrown into the mixing bowl freshman year.

"Most girls spend an hour making themselves look perfect before they even think about taking a picture. But not Kaylee. She never obsessed about how she looked until she started getting teased. I don't think she ever got her self-confidence back. Then a couple of girls on her volleyball team started picking on her."

"Teenaged girls can be awful," Nikki agreed. "Is that why she left volleyball?"

"She was kicked off the team because she stood up for herself." Pride swelled in Jessica's tone. "Madison Banks was the only girl on that team who stood up for her to the coach. All the rest fell right in line behind Jade."

"Good for Kaylee," Nikki said. "And the girls became friends after that?"

Jessica dabbed her eyes with a Kleenex. "I thought it was great. Madison was a good student, good kid, she was nice," Jessica said. "They spent all their free time together. Sometimes Madison came here, but Kaylee mostly went to her house. Madison's mother didn't want her over here. But Madison never seemed to care that Kaylee didn't come from a well-off family or have money to blow at the mall. I think that really helped Kaylee's self-confidence."

"Amy Banks didn't like your boyfriend."

Jessica snorted. "That woman doesn't like anyone below her income level. But yeah, she didn't like Ricky. Neither do I. Why in the hell I hooked up with him, I'll never know. It's over between us."

"I think we all have at least one of those guys in our past," Nikki said, and Jessica smiled back at her. "Did Kaylee like him?"

"Kaylee hated him, so he was never over here when she was by herself."

"Why did she hate him?"

Jessica hesitated. "She said he'd said some inappropriate things to her. He denied it, but I couldn't trust him."

Miller glanced at Nikki. "I'm sure you saw that in the case file. That's why Ricky was originally a suspect, but his alibi's solid."

"I did," Nikki said. "Is that why you broke if off?"

Jessica's gripped tightened on the lighter. "That was part of it."

Nikki let the silence simmer, watching Jessica become more uncomfortable as the seconds ticked by.

Miller leaned forward, his brow furrowed. "Jessica, is there something you haven't told us?"

Jessica's bouncing knee made the table shake. "I found pictures of other women on his phone."

"This was before Kaylee disappeared?"

"About a couple of weeks before."

"Why didn't you say anything to me?" Miller's voice was sharp.

"Because Ricky didn't have anything to do with it," Jessica said flatly. "You know he was visiting his brother at Oak Park Heights when the girls went missing." Oak Park Heights was the same prison where Mark Todd was housed. Was Nikki going to have one conversation today that didn't have ties to that man?

"His brother's serving eight for larceny," Miller said. "Ricky did visit that day, but he was back by the afternoon."

Jessica crossed her arms, both knees bouncing now. "He went back to work. His boss alibied him. Look, you guys didn't need to be chasing dead ends. I know Ricky didn't do it."

Something wasn't adding up. Jessica had been desperate to find her daughter, and keeping information from the police didn't make sense. "Jessica, what aren't you telling us?"

"Excuse me?"

"The only way to be absolutely certain that Ricky didn't take the girls is knowing his whereabouts at the time of the abduction," Nikki said. "Which means you were in contact with him."

"If Amy Banks hears this, I guarantee you she'll start screaming about you being involved and covering up for Ricky," Miller said.

Jessica's face turned red. "I would never—"

"Then you need to tell us everything," Nikki said. "Or I'm going to start digging into Ricky's alibi, and I will find the truth."

The woman's shoulders dropped. She rested her elbows on the table, head in her hands.

"I was with Ricky that afternoon. He came to my work when he got back into town. He was there during the time the police think they were abducted. And then he went to work. Clocked in and out."

"So why didn't you tell us before?" Miller asked.

"I need my job. And I'm just trying to help patients."

"What do you mean?" Nikki asked.

"Do you know how expensive it is to get old and die? Medicare fights coverage on everything they don't feel is necessary. God forbid the patient not be in so much pain. I just can't stand seeing them suffer. So I asked Ricky to get me something to help them."

Miller sighed. "Ricky sold you pain medication?"

"He didn't sell it to me," Jessica said. "I took them from him—used the pictures on his phone as blackmail."

"Wait a minute," Miller said. "Were those pictures of minors? Because blackmailing him with pictures of adult women makes no sense."

"If they were kids, I would have called the police, I swear. A couple of them were taken at a construction site. He'd been screwing other girls on the site. His boss would have fired him on the spot." Jessica's head dropped to her hands. "I know it's all wrong, but I swear I didn't make a dime off it. I just snuck the pills to—"

"I don't want to know the name, and I don't want to know if you received compensation for the pills," Miller said. "You realize opioids are being laced with fentanyl, right? Surely you've read about it on the news? The patient could have died from a bad batch; they're all over Stillwater."

"Ricky swore these were pure."

"Did Kaylee know you were doing this?" Nikki asked.

"I had to tell her, because she'd overheard us arguing about the pictures and wanted to know why I wasn't telling his boss."

"And she didn't negotiate to keep the secret? A phone perhaps?" A cell phone was a teenager's lifeline. Losing it was like cutting off a hand.

Jessica shook her head. "She knows what it's like for the residents. She said I should help them."

Nikki left Miller to finish interviewing Jessica while she checked out Kaylee's bedroom. She had the larger of the two bedrooms, but the twin bed and mismatched dresser took up most of the real estate, along with an old bookshelf loaded with various paperbacks from thrift stores. Nikki carefully sifted through the books in search of a phone. Mystery and science fiction dominated the collection, but a dog-eared copy of *The Outsiders* was full of sticky notes.

Two storage containers under the bed held sweaters and other winter gear. Nothing beneath the mattress or jammed inside the rickety nightstand. A portrait-sized mirror was propped on the dresser. Hairbrush, several hair ties, along with drugstore foundation, blush, eyeshadow. Nothing over the top.

A couple of Polaroid pictures had been taped to the mirror. How in the hell were those things popular again? Their picture quality had improved but was nothing like cell phone or digital camera pictures. But the instant gratification of the Polaroid probably appealed to an impatient teenager.

Both pictures featured Madison and Kaylee, smiling and happy, with Kaylee making the silly "duckface" in the second. The expensive Polaroid probably belonged to Madison.

Dresser drawers contained the usual items, but Nikki removed the slats just in case. She'd kept notes from John hidden from her nosy mother in the small crevices between drawers. No such luck with Kaylee.

There was no shelving in the small closet, and nothing hidden in the flooring. These cookie-cutter condos didn't have the same kind of hiding places as an old farmhouse.

Nikki's mother's voice rang in her head. *"I found your stash, Nicole Ann Walsh. How did you get the weed? Was it that boy?"*

Instead of answering the question, Nikki had railed on her mother for not trusting her. The pot had been hidden beneath a loose floorboard under Nikki's bed. Her mother had to search long and hard to find it.

Nikki swallowed the knot in her throat and stood, her groaning knees reminding her that forty was bearing down quickly. She hadn't expected to find the phone. Kaylee had no doubt had it on her—if she actually had one.

A memory slivered on the edges of her consciousness: a strange buzzing, a command: *Stop taking pictures.* Sweat beaded on Nikki's forehead. The phantom taste of vodka swilled in her mouth.

She went to the dresser and stared at her reflection. Her dark hair was messy from the hat and the sweat, her face pale despite feeling hot. Fear glowed in her dark eyes, but of what?

Nikki took a deep breath and pulled herself together. She'd had so many nightmares after the murders and being back in town must have triggered them again.

She looked again at the pictures taped to the mirror, willing one of the girls to give her something to work with. The pictures had been taken on the same day, in front of a brick storefront with a large bay window.

Mahoney's.

Mahoney's in downtown Stillwater.

But who took the picture?

Nikki yanked one of the pictures off.

The window reflected a tall male with a stocking cap and a dark hoodie, the camera covering most of his face. He looked to be a few inches taller than both girls, close to six feet. Wide shoulders but not overly muscular. The window wasn't big enough to reflect his shoes, but his jeans were well-worn, either from use or style.

Nikki grabbed the second picture and put the two side by side. Was that a tiny grin on the visible fraction of the boy's mouth?

Kaylee's outstretched arm was blurry and in a weird position, almost in front of her. She'd been moving when the picture was taken.

Kaylee hadn't been making the face. She was going to blow a kiss at the boy taking the picture.

Back downstairs, Kaylee's mother knew nothing of the boyfriend. She'd never asked who took the picture, she'd just been glad her daughter was hanging out with Madison. Nikki told her not to blame herself, even though she knew the woman would do exactly that.

She followed Miller outside. "Are you going to charge Jessica?"

Miller shook his head. "Not unless you push the issue."

"No, but she has to stop." Nikki's breath crystallized in the frigid air. "I don't care how pure Ricky says the stuff is."

"She will. I'll make sure of it. I did come up with one thing." He held up a small black object. "Kaylee's flash drive for school stuff. Her mother made her keep it in the kitchen junk drawer, so it didn't get lost."

"Mind if I take it?" Nikki asked.

"Once I bag it and mark it as evidence, it's yours."

"Thanks." Nikki pointed to the condo adjacent to Kaylee's house. "Is this the security camera you looked at to confirm that Kaylee left that day?

Miller nodded. "Why?"

"Did you look for visitors earlier in the day? Or the day prior?"

"We watched everything taken from that day," Miller said. "We were focused on the search and the area they'd last been seen. I didn't think to look earlier."

"You were focused on the right things," Nikki replied. "But go over the last couple of weeks. Catching him on camera is probably a long shot, but if Kaylee knew about her mother's deal with Ricky, I'm betting she tried to blackmail him, too."

"For cash or drugs?"

"I'm hoping cash, for the phone I can't find."

CHAPTER EIGHT

Nikki replaced the nozzle and closed her gas lid. Miller wanted to get a warrant for Ricky Fillinger's truck before they spoke with him, so they tabled that fun task until morning. She pulled away from the gas pumps and parked in front of the store.

Mark Todd's mugshot stared at her from the front page of the *Star Tribune*.

New evidence and disturbing details emerge about Nicole Walsh's state of mind on the night of the murders.

Her state of mind? No one on earth had a damned clue what her state of mind had been that night. This had to be the article Jessica had referred to earlier.

Nikki shoved four quarters into the change slot and snatched the paper, folding it under her arm.

Inside the busy store, her hands trembled as she made a cup of decaf coffee. She had to stay focused on the present. Getting caught up in her past wasn't going to do a damn thing to catch Madison and Kaylee's killer. She loaded her coffee with French vanilla creamer and stepped up to the counter.

"I paid at the pump for my gas." She eyed the cigarette display behind the cashier. She'd stopped smoking when she was pregnant, and it wouldn't take more than a couple of puffs to be right back in the habit. She chose a bag of candy instead and pretended sugar was less addictive than nicotine.

It seemed like she'd already been away from her daughter for days. Since Nikki's FBI unit served all of Minnesota, staying at a hotel for a few nights wasn't a new experience, but being away from Lacey seemed to sting more than usual. As soon as she was settled into the room, Nikki would check in with Tyler and Lacey. Her daughter's happy little voice was always a mood-booster.

The cashier pressed several buttons on the register and sighed. "Dang it, this thing locked up on me. Just let me reboot it."

"No problem."

A six-pack of beer hit the counter beside her with a thud, and Nikki jumped.

"Sorry." A man in a gray hoodie and paint-splattered jeans set a pack of gummy bears on top of the beer. His cheeks dimpled with his smile. "Didn't mean to scare you."

He was at least a head taller than Nikki, with a slim build but broad shoulders. A lock of dark, wavy hair had escaped his navy wool hat and curled around his ear.

"Nice combination," Nikki said. "What flavor goes best with the Corona?"

"Red, of course." His voice made candy sound ridiculously erotic. "Sugar baby."

Nikki's eyes widened. "Excuse me?"

He tapped on the bag of candy. "Sugar babies. I think you're the first person I've met who liked them."

Her entire body felt red hot. "I might have a sugar addiction."

"Hi, Rory." A second cashier opened the next register.

Rory? The name sounded vaguely familiar. Had she gone to school with him, too?

Nikki snuck a glance at him while he simultaneously counted out cash and flirted with the cashier. His wide smile and raspy voice had the girl blushing, and he clearly understood the effect he had on women.

Nikki's face still burned and not just from embarrassment. She couldn't remember the last time she'd felt something for a man, let alone felt nervous standing next to someone as good-looking as this guy. How long had it been since Nikki had a date?

"Try it now," Nikki's cashier said, his eyes on Rory. "I read the article about your brother, man. You think he'll get a new trial?"

You're going to be asked questions, especially if his brother finds out you're in town.

Nikki's stomach hollowed out, and her hands shook as she swiped the card and waited to put in her PIN number. The newspaper tucked under her arm felt like a brick.

Rory shrugged. "Who knows? He's been so fucking railroaded, I can't count on anything."

Nikki snatched her receipt and tried not to sprint to the door. "Thank you."

"You forgot your candy." Rory grinned and tossed her the sugar babies.

"Thanks." Nikki pocketed the bag and hurried outside. The cold wind almost pulled the jeep's door from her hand. "Christ." Nikki slammed it shut and caught her breath.

She knew Stillwater was still a small town, but what were the odds she'd end up at the same gas station as Mark Todd's brother? Rory had been in middle school when everything happened, and he used to follow Mark to the bonfires he'd have near the creek that ran between the Todd property and her parents'. Mark had been more tolerant of his younger brother than most, but he'd always sent him home when the alcohol came out.

Nikki remembered Mark as an average-sized, wiry guy with a plain face. Between the green eyes and the jawline, Rory had clearly been blessed with the superior genes.

What would he say if he knew who he'd been standing next to?

Rory came out of the store, and Nikki slunk down into the seat. He got into a white pickup truck with Todd Construction clearly emblazoned on the passenger's door.

Nikki had intended to read the paper at home, but the headline tormented her.

Striking new evidence has come to light, leading to a retrial of Mark Todd, currently serving a life sentence in prison for the murder of Dean and Valerie Walsh.

The daughter of the victims, one Nicole Walsh, claimed to have discovered Todd in her home when she found her parents dead. Her identification of Todd led to his arrest.

An exclusive source has revealed that then sixteen-year-old Nicole Walsh had been drinking heavily the night her parents were killed, casting doubt on her reliability as a witness.

Nikki almost ripped the paper in half. She'd taken both a field sobriety and a blood test the night of her parents' deaths and she knew that Mark's appeal was based on lies.

Both the district attorney's office and Sheriff Hardin—then Deputy Hardin, who arrived first on the scene—did not return phone calls, but Deputy Hardin's original report stated Nicole Walsh passed his initial sobriety test.

Nikki remembered the paramedic taking her blood and filling out the chain of custody paper. There must have been a toxicology report too.

If the DNA extracted from the new biological evidence is not a match for Mark Todd, it is possible his attorneys will push for a full exoneration.

Vomit rose in Nikki's throat. In the mid-nineties, DNA testing had been limited, but technological advancements meant even the tiniest samples could be tested. What had happened to the touch DNA taken from the lamp cord and the windowsill in her room?

Nikki's stomach turned. Biological evidence almost always meant blood or semen.

She threw the paper on the seat and started the jeep. The windshield wipers clicked and made a grinding sound, but only the passenger side moved.

Fantastic. She dug around for her scraper, hoping breaking up the ice would do the trick.

She'd barely rounded the open driver's door when her feet shot out from under her, her back and head hitting the icy concrete. Stunned, she lay still and tried to catch her breath.

"Don't move." Rory's worried face was suddenly inches from hers. He definitely wasn't the short kid with the even shorter hair anymore. His cap was gone, and the mess of dark, wavy hair framing his face made him seem even younger.

"I'm okay," she said, embarrassed.

"Just take a second and get your breath," he said. "Can you move your fingers and toes?"

"Yes." Sleet pelted her face and her elbow stung.

Nikki slowly sat up and touched the growing bump on the back of her head.

Rory held up three fingers. "How many?"

"Three. I don't have a concussion. I just need to get up."

He grabbed her hand and slipped his other arm behind her back. "Slowly."

Nikki closed her eyes against the vertigo, her forehead against his shoulder, her free hand on his chest. He smelled like clean laundry.

"If you're dizzy, you shouldn't be driving back to St. Paul, especially in this weather."

"I'll be okay." Nikki stepped back, heat creeping over her face. "I just need a few minutes. Stupid windshield wiper."

"Sit down and I'll look at it."

Nikki tried not to think about his last name as he helped her to the driver's seat. She mentally went through a concussion checklist while Rory cleaned off the wiper blade.

"This thing is about shot," he said. "Barely any rubber left. You need to replace it before you drive very far. There's a hardware store down the road. They can do it for you if you don't know how."

"Thanks." Nikki's father had made her learn to check her oil, replace a flat tire and put on new windshield wipers before she even got her license.

Rory leaned against the driver's door. "You're welcome, Nicole."

"How do you know my name?" She looked up at him nervously.

"I didn't until just now. At least I wasn't certain it was really you. I thought you looked familiar." He glanced at the newspaper lying on the console and then looked away.

"I should have said something," Nikki admitted. "But there were other people around, and I didn't think it was the right time or place."

"So you made a quick decision and ran. Must be a habit of yours." Rory wiped the sleet out of his hair and looked at her with disgust.

"Thanks again for your help," Nikki said. "I need to get this blade replaced and head off."

Rory still held the door. "But you'll be back, because you're investigating those two little girls' murders."

She pulled on the door again, but Rory didn't budge. She tried to focus on the anger in his eyes and not his full lips.

"You caught the resort killer, right? I've heard you have quite the reputation these days," he said. Nikki felt nervous under his gaze.

"My team and I caught him," she replied.

"Now you're after the Frost guy," he continued. "You hunt big game. Tell me, Nikki, with all your fancy degrees now, do you think you can you tell when someone's lying if you're talking to them face to face?"

Nikki felt the heat rising to her cheeks. She hadn't expected to stay under the radar but running into Rory was the one thing she'd hoped to avoid.

As much as she wanted to react to his sarcastic tone, she knew it would only egg him on. "I don't need to see your brother to tell you that he's lying," she said evenly. "I was hiding in my parents' closet when he came back upstairs. He whispered my name, and he would have killed me too if he'd found me first."

Nikki had cowered inside the closet for what felt like hours, wanting to flee. She had no idea where Mark was in the house, what he was doing, or if he was close to discovering her. She'd strained to hear his footsteps, wondering when he would enter her parents' bedroom and discover Nikki's hiding place. Her heart had pounded in her chest, and the fear had nearly paralyzed her as the minutes ticked by. And then she'd taken a chance, managed to get downstairs and out of the house, fleeing to the neighbors.

"I can't talk about your brother's case, I'm sorry." Nikki had to wrap this up before she lost her temper.

"I don't want your apologies," Rory said. "I want you to open your eyes and find out what really happened that night."

"I know what happened," Nikki replied.

Rory stared at Nikki for a moment, his eyebrows knitted together. He rubbed the back of his neck and chewed the inside of his cheek.

"What?" Nikki said. "There's obviously something else you want to say."

"There's no tox report."

"Don't believe everything you read in the paper," Nikki replied. "That reporter clearly has an agenda."

Rory shook his head. "Mark's new lawyer has a copy of the entire case file. There's no tox report."

Dread crept through her. She'd had her blood drawn, hadn't she? So much of the night had become a blur to her because she'd worked so hard to bury the horrible image of her mother's dead body. Her parents had been good people, respected by the community and neighbors. Her mother loved to volunteer at the library, working with the younger readers. She would have been a wonderful grandmother. The ache in her throat was becoming unbearable.

"Mark can fill in the blank spots," Rory said. "He's the only one who knows what happened that night."

"You're finally making sense."

"I'm talking about the party," Rory clarified. "You need to know what happened at that damn party while you were passed out cold. You told the police Mark attacked you while you were there, that he wanted you and you rejected him. That he went to your house to wait for you and you walked in once he had killed your parents. But the people protecting you back then weren't honest with you. You don't have the whole story."

Nikki jerked the door into Rory's hip. "I'm leaving now."

Rory stepped back but still held the door. "You should talk to Mark soon, before the truth all comes out."

"Goodbye." She yanked the door harder this time, and he finally moved enough for her to close it.

Screw the wiper blade. Nikki needed a hot shower and a stiff drink.

CHAPTER NINE

Nikki slipped the ice pack beneath her tailbone and tried to get comfortable in the stiff hotel bed. The aspirin she'd taken had helped her headache, but her tailbone still throbbed, and her nerves were on edge. She'd called the district attorney, but he'd already left the office for the day. She told his service to make sure he knew she would be there first thing in the morning.

She'd spent a blissful half an hour on the phone with Lacey. The sound of her happy voice and little-girl giggles had been a perfect distraction. After Nikki told her daughter good night, Tyler took the phone and started in about the newspaper article. Her ex meant well, but Nikki didn't have the energy to talk about it and telling him about seeing Rory was out of the question. Tyler could be overprotective, and Nikki would get snappy and say something she'd have to apologize for tomorrow. She ended the call with a promise to call tomorrow evening.

Nikki opened the internet browser on her phone and typed in her name. Her heart immediately sank. Today's article had been picked up by just about every news outlet in the state.

You have blank spots.

That wasn't true, Nikki thought. She remembered sneaking out of the window and meeting John at the end of the long, winding drive. They'd gone to the party. More of a gathering, really. Only a few of John's friends had been there. Nikki had felt out of place being the only girl. She'd felt dizzy later on in the night and gone to lie down, but her memory after getting home was crystal clear.

By the time police arrived, Mark had fled, but he was arrested within hours. His bloodstained clothes were found in the trash, the blood later confirmed as her mother's. His prints were all over the gun. And she was told that it was an open-and-shut case, according to Hardin and the prosecution. So, what biological evidence had the reporter been talking about? she wondered.

Nikki scrolled through the article and realized she hadn't read the last paragraph.

Nicole Walsh, who now goes by her married name Hunt, is a Special Agent with the FBI's Behavioral Analysis Unit. She's currently in Stillwater to assist the sheriff's office in the murder investigation of two local teenaged girls. She declined all requests for interviews.

Nikki had instructed her unit's office manager to weed out any media requests regarding her parents' case as soon as news broke about the DNA testing. The reporter's information wasn't wrong, but her wording suggested she'd spoken to Nikki personally. She could probably get the newspaper to make the correction, but that also opened up a line of communication she had no interest in pursuing, and besides, the comments were already pouring in. The top two appeared to be social justice warriors engaged with several posters on whether or not the sheriff's office might have railroaded Mark Todd. Some users claimed to have stories about other wrongdoings by police, a few attacked Nikki's character and one user seemed particularly fascinated with the Frost Killer, but his supposed insider knowledge was way off target.

Nikki's hand froze, and she stared at the screen.

Join our protest in Stillwater. We meet at the intersection by the sheriff's office every morning at 9:00 a.m. Agent Hunt will have to use that entrance and we're hoping to talk with her.

The user had commented with the information at least three times. She clicked on the username, but the account had been created today. Nikki had no way of tracing the identity. She fired off an email to the FBI's press liaison, directing them to ask the newspaper to monitor comments that could interfere with Nikki's investigation into Madison and Kaylee's murders.

Nikki didn't have time to ward off continuous interview requests and pushy protesters. Should she make some sort of statement asking the media to back off? The idea of giving anything more to the wolves was sickening, but maybe it would keep them at bay long enough for her to work this case.

She closed the browser and opened the group chat with Liam and Courtney. They'd already been brought up to speed about today's interviews, and Liam had come back from Hudson without anything useful. Courtney didn't have a lot to do without physical evidence, but Nikki knew she'd pressure the medical examiner to prioritize Madison and Kaylee when they could. She sent them a quick update.

Miller found us a space in the government center. Let's meet at nine tomorrow morning and figure out where to go next. Court, I'll call the medical examiner first thing in the morning for an ETA on the evidence.

Liam replied with a thumbs up. Courtney was probably asleep, but she'd see the message in the morning.

"Ouch." Nikki got out of bed and hobbled across the room. She tossed the melting ice into the trash and made sure the door was locked. The cheap wine she'd bought at Target tempted her from its spot on top of the bureau. If she opened it, Nikki would probably drink too much and end up with a hangover. Her body already felt bad enough.

She set the alarm on her phone for six, giving her plenty of time to go to the district attorney's office before heading into Stillwater. As she shifted around trying to find a position that didn't put pressure on her tailbone, ideas for her potential statement ran through her head. The objective was making it clear to the media that Nikki's priority was finding Madison and Kaylee's killer. *I understand the media's interest into my past... two grieving families... parents shouldn't have to bury their kids... prioritize...*

Despite the drowsiness settling over her, Nikki continued drafting one version of the statement after another in her head. None of them sounded exactly right.

A strange buzzing sound filled her head, followed by images too murky to understand. And then she was back in the farmhouse, her heart pounding and sweat running down her back. Blood on the stairs. The creaky step. A woman lying in a pool of blood, her face slack, her arm dangling over the bed.

Her eyes flashed open. She stared straight at Nikki. "You did this."

Roger Mathews had been elected district attorney last fall. He had an impressive run as a prosecutor, but his track record suggested he only took slam-dunk cases to trial. Nikki sat down in the chair in front of his desk and tried to keep her composure. When she'd woken up this morning, the old FBI T-shirt she'd worn to bed was drenched in sweat. She'd slept for five hours but felt like she hadn't even closed her eyes, and she still hadn't managed to loosen the muscles in her bruised back by the time she made it to Mathews' office. "I assume you've read the paper?

"I'm sorry," he said. "I was at a family event and didn't learn about it until late last night. I planned to reach out this morning."

"Good thing I'm here then." Nikki glared at him. "What biological evidence is the paper talking about? Now suddenly there's a new sample?"

Roger Mathews sighed. "I apologize for the way you found out. As I told you when we spoke before the holidays, I've only recently taken over the office. This case has moved very quickly."

"I just want answers."

"As you know, Mark's been working on an appeal for several years and asking for new DNA testing. He's been denied multiple times, and he didn't have the money for legal representation beyond a public defender."

"Until the Innocence Project became involved over the summer."

Mathews nodded. "They originally requested to test the touch DNA taken from the lamp in your room, your father's clothes and your windowsill." DNA testing had come a long way since the original investigation. Microscopic samples of skin cells could now be tested and produce what was called touch DNA. Nikki had read about touch DNA convicting people years after the crime, but she'd also heard some experts argue that certain kinds weren't reliable enough to use in court. Nikki also knew that this type of DNA testing was expensive, and with so much other evidence against Mark, she'd previously been told that no judge would approve it. "Patsy Moran convinced the judge to order the testing," Mathews said quietly.

Nikki's mouth had gone dry. "Patsy Moran took the case?"

Patsy Moran was a retired prosecutor who had tried and won some of Minnesota's grisliest murders. In 2014, a man prosecuted for the murders of four teenaged girls nearly two decades prior was fully exonerated with DNA evidence. Moran worked for the original prosecutor's office, and the conviction never sat right with her. She'd joined the Innocence Project the day after the news of the exoneration broke. She hadn't lost a case since.

"She's absolutely convinced Mark Todd was wrongfully convicted," Mathews said. "After she presented to the judge, he not only allowed the testing but signed off on a full review of the case file."

"What else are they testing?" Nikki didn't want to hear the answer, but she had to know. "Obviously it's more than some skin cells from the lamp and windowsill."

Mathews looked at her for a moment and then sighed. "Todd's attorney's discovered biological samples taken from your mother that had never been tested. The deputy who collected it wanted to test for semen but was denied by his superior."

Nikki gripped the chair arm to keep from shaking. "There was a sample that was never tested? You should have told me the minute this was found by Todd's attorneys. You told me there was nothing to worry about."

Mathews sighed. "The ADA in appeals has been handling it. She notified me last week, and I made the decision to withhold the details of testing from you until the judge made his decision."

"How could you do that?"

"Because I didn't see the need for you to hear gruesome details on what I thought to be a Hail Mary by the defense."

"So I found out through the media instead." Nikki was furious. "Hardin never said a word to me about another sample at the time."

"He didn't do the collection, and you were a kid. Given the way the case played out, he was probably trying to protect you."

The bagel Nikki had eaten an hour ago threatened to make an appearance. "But Hardin knew they were there, and he knows about DNA advancement. He should have told me."

"Hardin's certain he got his man."

"But you aren't?" Nikki couldn't believe what she was hearing.

Mathews leaned back in his chair. "I've been thinking about it. Why wouldn't they have tested those swabs? Surely it should have just been more evidence to convict Mark."

"The case is twenty years old, things happen. It may simply be an error," Nikki said, not even sure she believed what she was saying. "Mark was there that night, I saw him, and he had a motive to kill me. John testified he found Mark and me alone at the party. I'd gone to lie down, and John caught Mark trying to take advantage of me. He defended me. He saved me. So John was lying? Several other people from the party verified the story. And I was there too." Nikki remembered what Rory had told her last night. "A paramedic took my blood to test for blood alcohol level."

Mathews' eyebrows knitted together. "You mentioned that when we initially spoke in November. I assumed our staff would be able to locate the report. But we haven't. Don't you find it strange that no one could find that toxicology report? Even though John and his friends all testified that you were sober when you left the party, and Hardin stated that you passed a sobriety test," Mathews said. "As a law enforcement officer, does it make sense to you that there's no record of this?"

"I remember being in the ambulance," Nikki said. She remembered sitting there trembling on the gurney while the paramedic checked her over for injuries. Despite the warm air, Nikki had shivered with cold. "I remember the paramedic having a needle."

Mathews flipped through the dog-eared file. "You were treated for shock. Is it possible you were just given fluids?"

No, because she'd watched the blood fill the vial—hadn't she? Or was her memory that scrambled? "I—I'm not sure."

The weeks and months following the murders were mostly a blur, but Nikki remembered the prosecutor treating her like a star witness just as much as a grieving daughter. He'd painted her as a suffering, fragile child who needed to be handled with care. Nikki had been grateful for his kindness, but she knew it made the jury sympathize with her too. She'd been so naive, she believed that simply telling people what happened that night would be enough, but the trial taught her that everything in a prosecutor's case had to be calculated, down to the clothing and mannerisms. The district attorney had put her through a rigorous mock cross-examination a few days before the trial.

The nightmares started after that miserable day.

Nikki had been well into her junior year in college when she realized she'd developed a skill for reading people after her parents were killed. She kept her guard up, always hyper focused on people's body language, because everyone had an agenda.

"Nikki?" Mathews looked concerned. "Are you all right?"

"Yes," she said. "I'm just trying to get my head around all of this. I wasn't impaired when I found my parents. And I'm betting the defense played up the intoxication thing to this reporter, trying to get more people on Mark's side."

"Public opinion might appear to influence the case, and unless the defense has proof you were intoxicated, that argument won't hold water in court. The DNA certainly will, but Patsy Moran is absolutely certain none of the samples will match Mark's DNA. She's pushing for urgent testing because he's already spent enough time in prison as an innocent man."

Mark Todd must be one hell of a liar. "Please tell me the state is doing its own testing. If they've hired some independent—"

"The defense sent it to the state's crime lab," Mathews said. "No chance of bias or false results."

"Good. They're going to look like idiots when it's a match."

"Nikki, have you looked at the evidence?" Mathews asked. "I know it will be hard to be objective, but perhaps now is the time for you to do that. We can provide copies of the photos and all the reports—"

"I have a killer to catch first." Nikki stood up to leave. "Please keep me in the loop from now on?"

She held her tears in until the elevator doors closed. Patsy Moran wouldn't have taken the case if she didn't believe Mark was innocent. Why hadn't the biological evidence been tested? Why were there so many inconsistencies in the case she'd been told was rock solid? How many other lies had she been told?

Rory's face flashed through Nikki's mind. He wanted Nikki to talk to Mark and find out what really happened at the party, and Nikki understood that whatever story his brother had given him, Rory believed it. But she didn't.

Hardin and the prosecutor believed Mark Todd had crawled in the bedroom window she'd left open, knocking a bunch of things off her dresser, including the lamp. They'd painted a detailed picture

at the time. Nikki's father had gone to investigate the noise with his
.32. Nikki's room had been a mess, her vanity knocked over and
the mirror broken during a struggle, and a ligature mark on her
father's neck suggested Mark likely tried to strangle him with the
lamp cord. Police believed that's when her father lost the gun, and
Mark shot him. Nikki's mother likely tried to help her husband,
at some point running back into the bedroom to call for help. The
phone cord had been ripped from the wall.

It worried Nikki that Mathews was doubting the original
investigation. Throughout his career, Mathews had consistently
defended due process for the accused, because it was the only way
to get a true conviction. A moral conviction, he'd once said in court.
How hard would he fight for Mark's guilt if he didn't believe in it?
Mark could wind up walking the streets before the DNA results
even came in, and that was the last thing Nikki wanted.

CHAPTER TEN

Nikki listened to a playlist of supposedly calming music on the drive to Stillwater, but the repetitive, dull sounds made her sleepy. She switched to her classic rock list and blasted AC/DC as she approached the Washington County Government Center. She could do this. She wasn't some broken teenaged kid. Nikki had worked her rear end off to get where she was, and she'd faced down far scarier things than a crowd of protesters.

Their numbers appeared to have doubled since yesterday. Nikki expected them to swarm her car, but the group stayed on the sidewalk, shouting at her. She made out the word "liar," and several obscenities in the signs they were holding, but she didn't let off the gas and drove into the government complex.

Nikki exhaled a shaky sigh of relief as she circled the parking lot in search of an available space. She squeezed the jeep in between two sedans and hoped her doors didn't get scratched. She was late, and she hated walking into a room full of people waiting for her.

Sergeant Miller had found a temporary workspace for Liam and Courtney to set up shop. Unfortunately, the location was at the far end of the complex, and Nikki had parked up front.

She pulled her hat low and then zipped her parka up. Her face burned and her eyes watered from the cold wind. She ducked her head as far into her collar as possible.

"Agent Hunt." Caitlin Newport materialized out of nowhere. Nikki hadn't noticed the big truck when she'd circled the lot.

"We have no new information on the murders," Nikki said.

"The press release indicated Frost isn't responsible. That seems pretty obvious given the differences in the crimes."

"Thank you for clarifying that," Nikki said sarcastically.

"Are you staying to work the case?"

"I'm here, aren't I?" Hopefully that was enough to satisfy her for now.

"I assume you read the newspaper?" Caitlin's tone had changed; she was more businesslike, her words heavy with meaning.

"No comment."

Caitlin was undeterred. "The irony of John Banks' stepdaughter being one of the recent victims is chilling, isn't it?"

Nikki's stomach dropped. She'd suspected Caitlin had more on her agenda than Madison and Kaylee's murders. "You don't care about those poor girls at all. You're doing a piece on Mark Todd."

"It's a compelling story," Caitlin said. "Horrible small-town tragedy, the wrong man railroaded by police and finally freed by DNA, not to mention how emotional the case was when it first came to light."

"You mean me finding my parents dead?" Nikki glared at the cameraman she spotted trying to sneak out of the passenger seat of Caitlin's truck unnoticed. "You do not have permission to film me, so you might as well get back inside and stay warm."

He glanced at Caitlin, who waved him back into the truck.

"No problem." He slammed the door.

"That includes filming from inside the truck." She walked faster towards the entrance, but Caitlin easily fell into step next to her.

"I'm sorry to sound crass. No one should have to endure something like that. You were a traumatized kid who recounted the events as she remembered," Catlin said. "But the revelation that you were under the influence changes things."

"Hardin did a sobriety test. Are you the one who talked to the press?"

Caitlin shook her head. "Believe me, if I'd known, I would have come straight to you. You're saying you weren't intoxicated?"

"No comment."

"Mark had a reason to be at your house that night, but the police never wanted to listen."

"That's on them, not me."

"The new DNA evidence is going to prove Mark's innocence. The police screwed this up from the start."

"Does the Todd family know you're doing this?"

"His parents are all for it. They want their son's story heard."

"What about Rory?"

"He'll come around. I'm on their side."

Engaging with this woman was stupid. Shortly after the Innocence Project took Mark's case, Caitlin had approached Nikki for her side of the story. Nikki had been able to blow her off more than once, but with all this new evidence now coming to light, she was worried she'd have to speak out.

"Do you know how many times Mark changed his story?" Nikki asked Caitlin. Mark had originally told sheriff's deputies that he'd come to talk to Nikki, that he'd seen that the front door was busted and entered the property to check up on them. When he finally admitted to being inside the house, Mark claimed that he'd accidentally stepped in her mother's blood and the tracks were made after he discovered the bodies and went downstairs to use the phone. He said he'd been outside waiting to talk to Nikki, that he'd heard gunshots and run into the dark house, but he also said that he'd found Nikki's mother dead, checked her pulse, gone downstairs to call for help and been hit from behind. He said he'd woken up with the pistol in his hand and Nikki walking around upstairs.

"Did you know he talked to the police for hours without any representation?"

"He was a legal adult. He probably waived his rights."

"There's no evidence he did that. The security cameras in the interview room didn't record audio. Look, you're a decorated FBI agent," Caitlin said. "Have you gone over this investigation with a trained eye? When was the last time you looked at the files? Or the crime scene photos?"

The cops had told Nikki they may never have caught Mark if she hadn't come home. Her version of events remained consistent, while Mark had changed his story. His prints had been on the gun, her mother's blood on his clothes…

"No need. I got to see the real horror, up close and personal."

"You've already seen the protestors. Yard signs are popping up around town, too. People are starting to believe Mark. And they want to hear from you, especially now."

"Too bad. I have nothing to say."

"Agent Hunt." Caitlin stepped in front of her, blocking Nikki's path to the front entrance. "You need to cooperate with me. I can tell your story so that you remain a victim. You were a traumatized kid. It's the police who really screwed up here."

"Cooperate with you?"

Caitlin nodded. "That DNA is going to exonerate him. He'll be released within months and selling his story for millions. Not to mention he'll have a solid lawsuit against Washington County and maybe even you. Talking to me now is going make you a lot more likable in the long run."

Nikki closed the distance between them. "Let me make this clear, Ms. Newport. And you can consider the following a formal statement since I'm sure your phone is recording our conversation. Mark Todd's appeal will be decided in the courts. My team and I are in Stillwater to find out who kidnapped and murdered two teenaged girls. While I understand and respect the public's right to protest, I'm asking the media, which includes you, to stop asking for interviews regarding the appeal. We are already months behind this perpetrator, and I believe we have a very short window to catch him. We have to assume this could be a serial predator who could be looking for new victims. Please allow me to focus on Madison and Kaylee so we can bring this person to justice before he hurts anyone else."

"Of course the murders have to be your priority," Caitlin replied. "But don't forget that giving your side of the story is the only thing that will stop people from getting in your way."

"My side of the story has already been documented in court. If you continue to follow me around and bug me about Mark Todd's appeal, I'll charge you with harassment."

"We both know that won't stick. You're fighting the wrong person here."

"Do not follow me inside this building," Nikki snapped.

"It's a public building."

"And I'm a government agent you're harassing. Back off."

"Nicole." The filmmaker's voice lost some of its sharp edge. "Please go over the files. Or have a colleague who isn't emotionally involved do it."

Nikki heaved the glass door open and stomped into the lobby.

The front attendant looked up from her computer. "Agent Hunt?"

Nikki's chest heaved as though she'd just sprinted from the jeep. Her body flashed from cold to burning hot. She removed her hat and tried to tame her hair. The roots were damp with sweat, so the effort was futile. "Where are we set up?" she asked.

"Second floor, room 212. Take a right off the elevator."

Nikki glanced at the door to make sure Caitlin wasn't going to follow her in. "Thank you. If that woman comes inside and tries to find me, call room 212 right away."

"Sure thing."

Nikki peeled off her gloves and coat in the elevator. She found a brush in her bag and ran it through her hair before clipping it into a bun. Who the hell did Newport think she was, asking Nikki to cooperate, like she had done something wrong? At least she'd made a firm statement to the media, even though she hated giving it to her.

Room 212 was just a couple of doors down from the elevator. Nikki slowed her pace and took a deep breath to refocus, running through a mental list of what she needed to go over with her team.

Liam and Courtney had set up computers and makeshift workstations, along with a smart board. Half-empty boxes of bagels and donuts sat on a corner table, along with a coffee machine and bottles of water.

"Sorry I'm late." Nikki grabbed a donut with a mound of gooey icing. "Caitlin Newport ambushed me."

Miller looked up from his computer. "Are you serious? I ran her off this morning already."

"She's tenacious. And all excited about that newspaper article since she's doing a documentary about Mark Todd's innocence."

"I knew she was up to something." Courtney's expression made it clear she'd read the article, but she'd never bring it up in a professional setting.

Liam focused on the notes scattered in front of him.

Miller glanced at Courtney, who shook her head. Her team knew better than to push her, and Miller had good survival instincts.

Nikki tossed her half-eaten donut in the trash and sat down. "Liam, did you have any luck figuring out who was in the Polaroid from Kaylee's room?" Nikki had taken the photo for evidence, hoping to identify the person who'd taken the picture.

"I scanned it to see if we could get a better look at the man reflected in the shop window," Liam said. "The tech geeks are running it through their advanced photo software, but I don't think we're going to find much."

"I didn't expect to." Nikki shifted her focus. Courtney had already updated Nikki this morning. It would be at least seventy-two hours before they'd be able to begin examining the bodies, so her staff wouldn't even consider trying to remove the girls' clothes yet. The medical examiner expected to start the autopsies in five days, but she'd cautioned Courtney that she wasn't going to rush things and risk losing evidence, no matter how hard they pushed.

"I know we're still in a holding pattern with the evidence from the bodies, but we have leads to follow now. You'll all have read Miller's notes from the missing persons investigation. Is there someone else who knew Madison or Kaylee who hasn't been interviewed? And are there any holes in those stories? I think there are things we don't know about Kaylee's mom's boyfriend, Ricky. Courtney, Sergeant Miller has a warrant to search his truck, so I'd like you to follow us out there."

Courtney nodded. "I'm good to go. I've been going through Madison's social media accounts, trying to come up with something. But so far, she's the typical teenager."

"Look for pictures of Kaylee in Madison's social media, too. And let's interview their friends again. Liam, I think Kaylee had a phone. She didn't have a lot of pocket money, so likely a pre-paid phone. Madison's phone has been off, but is there any way the cell companies could pinpoint a connection from a pre-paid phone during the time the girls were supposed to be walking to the Hansons' house?"

"I'm not sure without the number. We don't even know what carrier she might have had. And if it's pre-paid, the text messages are long gone. Most carriers don't keep records for pre-paid calls."

"I know it's a long shot," Nikki said, "but I need you to visit the Stillwater carriers who provide pre-paid services. You'll be able to work up a list easily enough. Take Kaylee's picture around, see if someone happens to remember her. We'll need a warrant to contact the carriers about pings, and if you can find an employee who remembers her—or a manager who's willing to go through old security footage—we might be able to get records."

"I'll do my best. That's probably going to be several locations, so it might take a couple of days to get the right contact at all of them."

"That's fine. I know you'll be as efficient as possible. And let's begin searching for places with industrial freezers—what sort of places could have held Madison and Kaylee's bodies, and who had access to those places?" Nikki looked at Miller. "Did you find out where Ricky's working this morning?"

"New construction by the lake," Miller said. "I can drive, if you'd like."

"That works for me." Nikki preferred her own vehicle, but Miller's cruiser offered an extra layer of protection against Newport.

Nikki sighed with relief as Miller exited the parking lot. There was no sign of the protesters or Newport. "Thanks for the ride," she said.

"Just made sense," Miller replied.

"It does, but I appreciate the buffer if that woman shows up."

"I had no idea she was doing a documentary on your parents," Miller said. "I bet money she's brought in the protesters. They're probably paid."

"She's got Mark's family believing he has a chance at being exonerated. You think she cares about them?"

"She does as long as they're useful," Miller said. "If she shows up at this construction site, someone's leaking information. I can't believe she's doing this when we're trying to find out who murdered those kids."

Nikki bit her lip, trying to think of the right thing to say. Local police often had issue with the FBI coming in and taking over, but Miller seemed to be just the opposite, and Nikki suspected that had to do with his guilt over not finding Madison and Kaylee. "I've gone through the case file twice. You did everything you could."

"It wasn't enough." Miller sighed.

"Sometimes it isn't," Nikki said. "But that doesn't mean you're to blame. The sad truth is that we can't save them all, especially when it comes to missing kids. You know the statistics as well as I do."

An awkward silence fell between them.

Nikki started to ask about turning the radio on when she noticed the pictures. "Are those your daughters?"

Two wallet-sized school pictures of grinning, gap-toothed girls were taped to Miller's radio.

"Yep. Six and nine. It's all estrogen in my house."

"That's going to be rough in a few years."

"I don't even want to think about it. The little one's boy-crazy, too. She kissed some boy at recess last week. My wife thought it was hilarious."

"I think I kissed a boy on the playground in kindergarten." Nikki blocked out the unpleasant image of Lacey doing the same.

"Hell, I kissed three or four girls by first grade," he said. "But when it's my little girl, nah. That ain't happening."

Nikki laughed, and Miller joined her.

"I'm serious," he said. "I told her that's how a person gets really sick and ends up missing a bunch of school."

"Did that work?"

"For now," he said.

Nikki's laughter died in her throat. A large, white canvas had been mounted onto the side of a dilapidated barn. "Free Mark Todd" sprawled across the sign, the red spray paint a vibrant shock of color against the winter landscape.

"You okay?"

"I have to be," Nikki said, composing herself. She thought about Rory's insistence that his brother was innocent and wondered if he'd painted the sign. "What do you know about Mark's younger brother?"

"Rory? Not much, which means he stays out of trouble."

"I ran into him at the gas station yesterday." Nikki recounted last night's embarrassing events. "He was far nicer to me than most people would have been."

"He's grown up in the shadow of his brother's case, seeing his parents spend their lives trying to free Mark. You'd think it would have made him bitter, but he doesn't have that in him."

"How are his parents?" Nikki remembered Mrs. Todd as petite and friendly. She'd enjoyed Mark having his friends over. Mr. Todd had been reserved and usually kept to himself, but they'd always seemed like a close family.

Miller shifted in the seat. "Far as I know, they're fine. They moved to an apartment in town a few years ago. I heard Rory bought the house."

Nikki flushed, trying not to think of how good it had felt to lean on Rory's chest and breathe in his scent. She rarely allowed herself to think like this, to be so vulnerable, even with Tyler during their best times. He was good and kind, dependable. Nikki could always count on him to be there for her, but she'd never experienced the sparks other couples described. Nikki had always assumed she lacked the ability to truly connect with anyone. She'd trusted Tyler enough to tell him the details about the night her parents were murdered, but she hadn't been able to let her emotional guard down. He'd pressed her to tell him how she felt and what she was going through, but Nikki could never manage it. It wasn't his fault, but Tyler couldn't possibly understand.

But there was something different about Rory. They had both experienced the same thing, albeit from different sides. They'd both been living under a media microscope after the murders, they both understood what it was like to have their family torn apart. No matter how hard he tried, Tyler would never be able to understand what that had been like.

"There's another thing I wanted to mention," Miller said. "I would have brought it up back at the office, but you'd just dealt with Newport."

"What is it?"

"Ricky Fillinger works for Rory Todd."

CHAPTER ELEVEN

Ricky had been a football star during Nikki's first two years in high school. His speed made him one of the fastest running backs in their conference, and he'd gone on to play at a community college until the knee injury ended his football career. The school rumor mill had claimed Ricky kept a list of all his sexual encounters. Nikki had been warned to steer clear of him when she was younger, and it seemed perhaps that times hadn't changed.

A man in heavy work overalls looked up from the half-built deck of yet another cookie-cutter condo. He looked warily at them, and Nikki wondered if he was well-versed in dealing with cops. Ricky was the epitome of small-town athletic hero gone to seed: thirty pounds heavier but somehow appeared more solid than flabby. His sandy blond hair had receded a good inch from his forehead, and his ruddy skin was damaged from the sun.

"Hey, Ricky, you got a minute?" Miller asked.

Ricky stuck his hammer in his belt and puffed his chest. "Not really."

"We have some questions about Kaylee—"

"I already answered those." If Ricky was grieving Kaylee's death, he hid it well.

"Not mine," Nikki said.

"Who are you?"

"Special Agent Nikki Hunt with the FBI."

Ricky grunted and finally hopped off the deck. He still had the piercing blue eyes Nikki and every other girl in school had swooned over. "Rory Todd's my boss. He hired me even though I've got a record," Ricky said. "That don't happen very often."

"Very kind of him," Nikki said. "Your employment isn't the reason for our visit."

"He's supposed to be here this morning." Ricky grinned. "I know who you are. You sure you want to be around when he shows up?"

"I've already spoken with Rory, actually. I'm here to talk to you."

Ricky looked her up and down, his lips curled into a hateful smirk. "I read that article. How soon you think it'll be before the Todd family is suing the county and maybe even you? Like I said, I got nothing to say."

Nikki resisted the urge to unzip her coat and make sure he knew she was the one carrying a gun and badge. She'd dealt with dozens of Rickys, and almost all of them used misogyny to mask their own insecurities. They weren't used to women calling their bluff and wound up running away with their tails between their legs. "Did Kaylee ask you for money after she found out about the deal you and her mom made?"

Ricky's jaw tightened. "What are you talking about?"

"Jessica told us about blackmailing you for painkillers," Nikki said. "Did Kaylee try to do the same thing?"

"You're delusional."

"Okay," Nikki said. "So, you don't mind if I search your truck then?"

"You don't have a warrant."

"I actually do." Nikki held up the warrant. "Judge's signature is still drying. See the blue vehicle behind Sergeant Miller's? That's a senior FBI crime scene specialist. She'll be conducting the search. If she finds anything, we'll have the truck impounded and dig deeper."

"You're not going to find anything." He shoved his hands into his pockets.

"If you went to Kaylee's house, we'll see you on the neighbor's security footage," Nikki said.

"I didn't."

"You met Jessica the day the girls went missing," Miller said.

"And I was there for over an hour. Then clocked in at work. Alibied, so back off."

Nikki closed the distance between them. "Was Kaylee alone when you saw her?"

Ricky gritted his teeth.

"My instincts tell me you've been selling prescription drugs on job sites. It's hard to imagine you only sold them to Jessica. But I'm not really interested in that, I'm trying to find a murderer and I know there's something you're not telling me."

"And I'm supposed to believe this guy won't haul me in if I talk?" Ricky pointed to Miller.

"He's more concerned about finding a killer." Nikki played her trump card. "I, however, will call your parole officer if you don't answer my questions. He'll look at your phone, and they'll find out all of your dirty secrets."

"You were a cold bitch in high school and you're still one." Ricky crossed his thick arms over his chest. "She showed up at my job site a few days before she disappeared. Gave me the same spiel her mother did. But I told her I wasn't giving her money for whatever she was trying to buy."

Nikki had a hard time imagining Ricky as the type to care about Kaylee's well-being.

"You're lying," Nikki said. "She left here with something. Either you tell me what it was, or I call your parole officer."

Ricky looked more nervous than ever, and Nikki could tell she was getting somewhere. "I gave her fifty bucks, okay? Jessica barely makes ends meet and Kaylee's phone was going to get shut off. She didn't need to be going around without a cell phone—" Ricky drew an unsteady breath. He ducked his head and rubbed his eyes. "I thought her phone would protect her. Did she suffer?" Ricky asked.

"We won't know anything until after the autopsy." Nikki softened her tone. The sadness in his voice was real. He'd actually tried to look out for her. "How did Kaylee get to your job site that day?"

"Some guy in a van."

"You get a look at him?"

Ricky shook his head.

"License plate?"

"Wasn't paying attention. It was a plain grey minivan and had a Stillwater High School bumper sticker."

"You're certain?" Miller asked.

"Yep. Got no more to say."

"Don't leave town," Nikki said.

Ricky huffed and disappeared into the half-built house.

"Drew Hanson drives a grey minivan with that bumper sticker," Miller said. "His father-in-law owns Grinnell Farms. They raise cattle and pigs for farm to table."

"Industrial freezer access?" Nikki said.

"I would assume so. They slaughter their own animals and sell the meat locally to grocery stores. And farmers' markets during the summer."

"You think we could find a judge to sign a warrant to search?"

"No way," Miller said. "No judge is going to piss off a business like Grinnell Farms without strong evidence. Hanson doesn't work at the farm, and he says he was home all evening with Miles."

"Kaylee was a little taller, so from head to toe curled up and secured with the rope, she measured forty-two inches. Assuming they were put in a chest freezer, we're looking for at least eight cubic feet."

"That's some fast math."

"Can't take credit for it. Liam's the math whiz." Nikki was already headed back to the car. "We already planned to stop at the high school to talk to the girls' friends. We can pay Hanson a visit, too. Pulling him out of his class will catch him totally off guard. He'll want to answer our questions and get us out of there as soon as possible. And if he's got a chest freezer, I want it torn apart. We need—" The words died in her throat as a truck stopped next to Miller's car, blocking the drive, and Rory Todd's angry gaze locked on Nikki.

CHAPTER TWELVE

Rory shoved open the truck door and stalked towards them, his heavy boots smacking against the hardened snow. His heavy work pants were covered in dried paint, and he hadn't bothered to put a coat on over his hooded sweatshirt. His blazing green eyes locked on Nikki, and she wasn't sure if the adrenaline pumping through her veins was driven by the anxiety of dealing with him or the thrill of seeing him again. "What's going on?"

"We had questions for your employee regarding Kaylee Thomas."

"He's already been alibied," Rory snapped. "Just because he's an ex-con doesn't mean he's a suspect."

"Thank you so much for clarifying that. A decade in law enforcement has taught me nothing."

"You've been wrong before."

Nikki's patience ran out. "I have a warrant to search Ricky's vehicle. He's under suspicion of dealing prescription drugs on your property. And I'm interviewing him in relation to the murders of Kaylee Thomas and Madison Banks."

Rory flinched and looked at Ricky, who'd come back outside. "Is that true?"

Ricky still hadn't confirmed that he'd had other customers come to sites to pick up from him, but Nikki could read the truth all over his face.

Nikki pointed to the rusting pickup truck next to the house. "Ricky, is that yours?"

"Why?" Rory asked.

Nikki waved at Courtney and gave her a thumbs up. "I told you, my CSI is going to search for physical evidence tying you to Kaylee. So if she was in your truck for any reason, you'd better tell me now."

"Girl was never in my truck."

"Ricky, get back to work," Rory said. "We'll talk about this later."

Ricky disappeared again, tail between his legs. Nikki was fairly certain he was telling the truth, but she needed to be sure. Ricky's truck had to be searched.

"A judge seriously signed that?" Rory said. "With no probable cause?"

Nikki resisted the urge to tell him to lay off the true crime shows. She'd dealt with more than one jury expecting to see forensic tricks that didn't even exist. Armchair detectives turned up in every high-profile murder investigation, usually wasting precious time. "We had probable cause and we're talking about the murders of two teenaged girls."

"I'm the one who got the search warrant, and it's absolutely necessary," Miller added. "Ricky didn't tell us everything before. He's a suspect."

"In other words, you need to back off," Nikki said. "Unless you want to be charged with harassing an officer."

"Fine," Rory said. He glanced at Miller and then back to Nikki. "Can we talk privately?"

"About what?" Anxiety rippled through Nikki. She didn't want to have a private conversation with Rory. Too many of her worst memories had already been dredged up. "I'm working."

"It will just take—"

"Look," she burst out. "I can't say this enough: I'm here to find out who killed two innocent girls. I can't do that with you breathing down my neck about Mark."

"I know why you're here. I'm just asking for a few minutes."

Why did he have to do this with an audience?

Ricky peered out of the framed-out window, and Miller hovered between the house and Rory, scratching his head.

Nikki shook her head and started walking across the frozen snow to join Courtney.

"Really?" Rory said. "You're just going to ignore me and take the easy way out?"

Nikki turned so quickly her boot cracked through the thin ice coating the snow. Her heart pounded. After her parents were murdered, her life in Stillwater had been a sideshow until she was able to escape it. How long before someone other than Caitlin and Rory started following her around, wanting answers she didn't have to give?

"Easy way out?" Nikki laughed bitterly. "I became a cop because I already knew how monsters worked. Leave me alone."

She stalked over to help Courtney with her equipment.

"What's going on? Why is the owner giving you so much grief?" Courtney asked.

"It's Mark Todd's brother." Nikki put her hands in her pockets to hide their shaking. She wasn't going to be pushed around while she was trying to do her job. "If you find anything questionable, Miller has people on standby who can impound the vehicle for you."

Courtney's head moved up and down, but her gaze focused over Nikki's shoulder. "He's coming over here."

Nikki turned around, bracing for another nasty remark.

"Mark was never a monster until you made him one." Rory's voice cracked and the muscle in his jaw twitched. "I don't mean to disrespect you. I'm just asking for ten minutes of your time. Please."

She wanted to scream. Why couldn't he be mean to her instead of compassionate? Dealing with killers was easy. But instead of coming at her loaded with anger and ego, Rory seemed almost contrite. He jammed his hands in the front pocket of his sweatshirt and looked down at her with a far softer gaze than she deserved.

"I know what it's like to have people constantly coming at you. Everyone wants a piece of you. It's like they thrive off of the most miserable moments in other people's lives. We're not all that different, if you think about it." He flushed a new shade of red. "I mean, what happened to your parents is worse than anything I went through, but the attention and all…" Rory looked down at his boots. "I don't know what I'm trying to say."

"I do." Nikki had been thinking the same thing on the drive from the station. She sighed. "Listen, I do have to prioritize this case, and forensics are on the clock. I'll probably be at the government center late this afternoon. If you see my jeep, ask the front desk to speak with me. Take it or leave it."

"I'll take it." Rory's voice sounded tight. "Thank you."

Nikki nodded curtly and then turned her back to him. "Test for blood and any bodily fluids. And keep an eye out for anything that looks like it might belong to a teenaged girl."

Plenty of seasoned experts would be offended at Nikki giving them basic instructions even a new CSI would know to do.

Courtney murmured her agreement and kept working.

"Thanks, Court."

"Anytime."

CHAPTER THIRTEEN

Nikki sat with Sergeant Miller in the staff room at Stillwater High School, flanked by the principal and assistant principal. The office decor and the faces were new, but the room was familiar to Nikki. Her freshman year, Nikki had skipped her last classes to walk to the ice cream parlor with Scott Taylor, a boy she'd had a crush on since grade school. She hadn't made it off campus when one of the teacher's aides spotted her. Nikki's parents had been furious, and she'd endured in-school suspension for three days. Sophomore year, she'd been caught making out with a boy in the copy room; a couple of months later, she'd started a food fight in home economics. She wondered if schools even taught that now, but thinking about junior year would only bring more misery, and she wasn't certain she could keep a calm façade after the encounter with Rory. She refocused on the case and the students she and Miller had come to see arrived.

"Okay, girls." The principal's soft voice and laidback manner were reserved for this sort of occasion. "You've spoken with Sergeant Miller already, but this is Agent Nikki Hunt with the FBI. She has some questions about Kaylee and Madison."

The four girls sat in a row across from Nikki. Despite varying skin tones and haircuts, they all looked alike: expensive wool boots—the brown shade every girl seemed to own—skinny jeans or leggings, form-fitting shirts and too much makeup.

A tall, willowy girl with silky, black hair crossed her legs and eyed Nikki. She was confident and well-aware of it. Nikki checked her list of names. "Are you Jade?"

The girl nodded. "My mom went to high school with you."

"Oh, really? What's her name?" As much as Nikki needed to make a connection with these girls, delving into her high school years was a slippery slope. The last two had been nothing but misery and grief.

"Connie. Her maiden name was Butler. I think you graduated the same year."

Connie Butler had been the stereotypical popular girl loved by all the teachers and loathed by most of the school because of her bullying. The confidence already radiating from Jade now made perfect sense.

Jade tossed her hair over her shoulder. "Mom says it must be hard being back here."

"Don't worry about me. I know you all must be shaken by Madison and Kaylee's deaths."

"For sure," Jade said. "I'm still in shock. Not surprised, though."

The blond girl to her left elbowed her. "Jade, come on."

"Why?" Nikki checked her list; the blond's name was Taylor. The girl next to her was Sophie; the short-haired brunette on the end was Brianna.

"Kaylee was trouble." Jade's tough exterior threatened to crack. "We told Madison that, but she didn't listen."

"Kaylee punched a couple of girls on the volleyball team for spreading rumors about her," Taylor added. "And got herself kicked off the team for it."

"Not what I heard," Jade said. "I heard it was because she came on to the coach."

Brianna rolled her eyes and looked at the floor, while Taylor and Sophie scoffed.

"My sister is varsity," Sophie said. "She saw the whole thing go down."

"What happened?" Nikki asked.

"One of the varsity girls had her phone and was showing everyone the photos of Kaylee from last year. She was talking about her. Madison told them to knock it off, and the varsity girl shoved Madison and told her to mind her own business. Madison was being nice to Kaylee, telling her to ignore them, but the older girl wouldn't shut up. Kaylee had enough and socked the girl." Sophie shrugged her shoulders.

"That's when they started hanging out," Taylor said. "This fall."

"She brought her into our group without asking," Jade said.

Jade certainly had inherited her mother's holier-than-thou attitude. Connie loved to make sure the unpopular kids—usually those who lived outside of town, like Nikki—knew their place.

Brianna had yet to speak, her gazed focused on her shoes.

"But you guys were still friends," Miller said. "Madison was at your house the weekend before she disappeared."

Jade made a face. "Because I had to nag her into it. And I had to invite Kaylee. Thank God she didn't come. That's the thing—she didn't like us any more than we liked her."

Sophie and Taylor exchanged a glance that made it clear Jade's opinion didn't speak for all of the group, but the girls didn't have the guts to challenge the social pecking order.

"I liked Kaylee." Brianna's soft voice surprised Nikki. "She was nice. Quiet, but nice. And smart."

Jade glared at her, while Sophie and Taylor tried to hide their smiles.

"Did she ever talk to you about boys?" Nikki asked.

"Not really." Brianna's nervous gaze focused on the window behind Nikki.

"Are you sure?" Nikki asked. "We think she may have been dating an older boy in secret."

Jade snickered. "Wouldn't surprise me. She probably put—"

"Stop it," Brianna said. "She had a big crush on an older boy, but they weren't dating."

"How did they meet?" Nikki asked.

"Madison's known him since she was little. His name is Bobby Vance."

"Mindy's son?" Miller asked.

"I don't know his parents," Brianna said. "He's going to Mankato State."

"He's Mindy's son." Jade perched on the edge of her chair. "He is pretty cute. They used to live down the street from Madison until his dad died."

Nikki scribbled down the name and then tried to pass the picture she'd taken from Kaylee's bedroom to Brianna, but Jade got to it first.

"Cute."

"See the reflection in the window? Is that Bobby?"

Jade shrugged and then gave the photo to Brianna. "Might be. He's tall and thin. Blond hair."

"I can't tell for sure," Brianna said.

"Isn't that a restaurant in Hudson?" Jade asked.

"Why?" Nikki waited for the other two girls to look at the picture before stowing it in her bag.

"'Cause I don't think Bobby has a car," Jade said "Freshmen can't have cars on campus, and his dad died before they could buy him one. His mom can't afford it now."

"You sure know an awful lot about their family situation," Miller said dryly.

"Not really," Jade said. "Everyone knows freshmen can't have cars. And if Mrs. Vance couldn't afford their house, I bet she couldn't afford to buy him a car."

Nikki directed her question at Brianna. "Did Kaylee talk about Bobby coming home on the weekends? Or say anything that made you think she might have been spending time with him?"

Brianna shook her head. "I only know about the crush because Maddie told me."

"I think Madison was her main friend," Sophie said. "And Miles Hanson, but that was because of Maddie, too."

Because she was afraid to be herself. She wasn't high enough on the food chain to draw any sort of attention that wouldn't be negative. Four years of that had sucked. Nikki wouldn't go back to high school for any amount of money.

"What about the girl Kaylee punched?" Nikki asked. "Was there fallout?"

"Trinity's all talk. She threatened to beat Kaylee up after school, but never did anything. I need to get back to class," Jade said. "Are we done?"

"Yes." She didn't want to push the girls, to scare them. They were keeping themselves together, but Nikki could tell Madison and Kaylee's murders had upset them. "Thank you for your time." Nikki handed each girl a business card. "Please call me if you think of anything else."

The assistant vice principal told the girls to return to class, and they left single file, with Brianna lingering in the back. She glanced over her shoulder at Nikki, chewing on her lips, and then pocketed the card and hurried from the room.

Principal Phillips offered to take them to Mr. Hanson's room. She and Miller quietly discussed the student body's reaction to news of the murders, but Nikki lagged behind.

Walking through the halls felt surreal. She never dreamed she'd set foot in this place again. Not all the memories were bad, but she'd had to lose the good ones to get rid of the awful.

The more things changed, the more they stayed the same. For all the advances in technology, high school, at its core, remained a four-year survival course. The popular kids were different than the ones she'd known, but they were just as catty and cruel. Kids who didn't conform to their standards spent high school trying to fly under the radar, while the popular kids secretly feared that one day they would end up on the outside looking in. The idea that high school was supposed to be the best years of your life was hysterical. But, in the end, most people wound up an upgraded version of their high-school selves, passing on their agenda to their kids.

Jade Eby looked just like her mother, save for the darker skin tone. She seemed to have inherited the same calculating personality, the same arrogance, confident she could do and say whatever she wanted to whomever she wanted. Connie didn't even know Nikki existed until she'd started dating John Banks. They'd all wanted to be her friend after that. To her credit, Connie never pretended to be anything but mean.

Nikki spent her last two years in high school being "the girl whose parents were slaughtered." Other kids called her a freak because of what she'd seen. And some doubted her story.

Sweat broke out over her forehead as a long-forgotten memory slipped through her defenses.

"She was all sorts of messed up." Connie Butler's nasal voice bounced off the locker-room walls like an echo chamber. "I heard John was in there with her for a while before Mark. You know they were banging."

Nikki pulled her feet up and balanced on the toilet, her heart pounding. If they caught her, she'd have to stand up for herself. She wasn't afraid of Connie or her friends, but Nikki didn't want to talk to anyone about that night or anything else.

"Guess that's what happens when you date an older guy way out of your league." Shelly Peek, another cheerleader, laughed. "I can't feel sorry for her. He's always been a player."

"And a creep," Connie said. "We fooled around a couple of times last year, and he wanted to do some really kinky things. So gross."

"Nikki Walsh probably lets him do whatever she wants. Look how popular she is now that she's dating him."

"God, you guys are awful." Mary Barton was the rare breed of nice cheerleader. She sat near Nikki in English and had been nice to her long before she started dating John. "Her parents were just murdered."

"And she's putting the wrong guy in jail." Connie's hard tone echoed through the old walls. "Mark would never."

"He was, like, there," Shelly said. "With blood on his hands."

"He said he went to tell Nikki what happened at the party," Connie said.

"John kicked his ass for trying to have sex with his drunk girlfriend. He was humiliated."

Connie snorted. "I heard Mark was trying to stop John."

"How do you know that? It was a college party."

"I know a girl who was dating one of John's friends. She heard it from him."

"Sounds like a bad game of telephone," Mary said. "The cops know what they're doing. They wouldn't have arrested Mark if they weren't sure."

"Maybe," Connie said. "But Nikki Walsh was drinking enough vodka to pass out. No way she remembers everything from that night."

"Doesn't change the fact that her parents were murdered," Mary said. "You two are jerks for talking about her like this."

Small feet stomped out of the locker room, followed by a slamming door.

"Ugh, goody two-shoes."

"Yeah," Shelly said. "But I mean, she's not wrong. Just because we don't like Nikki doesn't mean we should be making jokes about her parents."

"I'm not making jokes," Connie said. "It's awful what happened. I just think she got what she deserved. Some girl from the sticks dating John Banks and acting like she's queen? It was bound to happen."

Shelly giggled. "You're just pissed off because John blew you off to date her."

Nikki wondered if she'd even asked John about Connie's accusation. She didn't really remember breaking up with him. It was as if they'd just stopped talking. But what else had Nikki erased from her memory?

"Nikki?" Miller touched her arm. "You okay?"

They'd reached the second floor. Nikki wiped the sweat off of her forehead and peeled off her jacket. "I'm fine. Just remembering."

"If you want to wait in the car—"

"I'm fine." Nikki took a deep breath to clear her head.

CHAPTER FOURTEEN

The principal directed them to Hanson's room and headed back to her office. Drew Hanson had a large classroom with a view of the south side of campus. He sat at his desk, lost in his computer, while his students worked on school-issued laptops.

"Drew? You have a moment?"

The class looked up from their work, mouths agape at the sight of Miller in his uniform and Nikki with her FBI badge prominently displayed.

"Uh, sure. Guys, I'll be right back."

Hanson followed them into the empty corridor and closed the door. "What's going on?"

"We just talked to Ricky Fillinger. Kaylee got a ride to his job site a few days before she disappeared." Revealing so much information was a calculated risk, but during their previous interview, Nikki had learned that Hanson wasn't a very good liar. If he really didn't have anything to hide and had a valid reason for giving Kaylee a ride, this was her best shot at spooking him into telling the truth. "Gray minivan with Stillwater High School bumper sticker. Miller says that's what you drive."

Hanson's face paled. "Along with dozens of other people, I'm sure. This is the only high school in town so…"

Nikki folded her arms and looked pointedly at Hanson.

Sweat broke over his brow. "Is that all?"

Nikki shrugged. "You tell me."

Nikki knew guilty people postured and had trouble making eye contact. They'd inevitably start slouching or withdrawing into themselves, crossing their arms over their chests. They just didn't trust the system. Innocent people inevitably wanted to talk. Hanson may not have done anything to the girls, but he definitely had something to hide.

She glanced into the room. Some of the students were pretending to work, but several watched with wide eyes, which is exactly what Nikki had counted on when she decided to confront Hanson. He wouldn't want her and Miller around for any longer than necessary, and his desperation to get rid of them and give the students some rational excuse would make him talk faster than any threat. Nikki had learned the technique from a veteran detective, and it had never failed her.

Sweat glistened on Hanson's broad forehead. "I-it's not what it looks like."

"Really?" Miller said. "Because it looks like you forgot to tell me you gave Kaylee a ride days before she disappeared. And you've got access to commercial refrigeration."

Hanson swayed. "Do you mean the farm? God, no. I didn't do anything to those girls."

"We've spoken to Ricky Fillinger," Nikki said. "He told us about Kaylee stopping by a job site. Why didn't you mention giving Kaylee a ride?"

Sweat glistened on Hanson's brow. "I—I guess I'd forgotten about it."

"I see." Nikki didn't buy that for a minute. "Why did you give her a ride? Her house isn't on your way home from school."

"I was headed to St. Paul, and it was cold and just about to rain. She was walking without a jacket, and I felt sorry for her. I didn't want to kick her out when she said she needed to stop and talk to her mom's boyfriend first. I figured she had to check in or something."

"Why didn't you tell us this?" Nikki asked. If what Hanson was saying was true, it didn't make sense that he'd lied.

"Because I knew how it would look," he said. "And the police would have to investigate my alibi, and I didn't want…"

"What?"

Hanson's shoulders dropped. "I didn't want my wife to find out I'd been in the city the day Madison and Kaylee disappeared. That I wasn't home. That I asked Miles to lie for me. Because I was with another woman."

It would never cease to amaze her how far a person would go to hide an affair. Hanson wasn't the first man she'd seen in the hot seat because he didn't want his infidelity exposed.

Hanson slumped against the wall like he'd been given a muscle relaxer. Confession usually brought a person relief, and Nikki knew he was telling the truth.

"Does your son know you're cheating?"

Hanson shook his head.

"Kaylee's contact with Ricky makes him a suspect," Miller said. "You should have told me you knew they met."

"But he had an alibi. I read it in the paper. So I didn't see the point in saying anything."

"Nice of you to do my job." Miller looked ready to haul the teacher away in handcuffs.

"Kaylee said she had to give Ricky a message from her mom, and she didn't have his number in her phone. We stopped there, they talked a couple of minutes, and I dropped her off at home. That's it. I didn't think there was anything out of the ordinary about it, and I felt sorry for the kid."

"Did she have a phone on her that day?"

"Uh… maybe. I think she texted someone, but I wasn't really paying attention."

"She say anything about Ricky after they spoke?"

"Just that he was a pain in the ass, and she was glad to be rid of him. I asked her why, and she said he just wasn't good enough for her mom. I left it at that." He glanced into the classroom. "I need to get back inside."

"We're going to get a warrant for your truck," Nikki said. "And your house."

"What?" His voice cracked. "No, there's no reason."

"You made your son lie about your whereabouts that day and you kept the ride from us."

"I'm telling you the truth. If you do this, my wife's going to ask questions."

"That's your problem," Nikki said. "You shouldn't have had an affair."

After securing a warrant, Miller brought in Hanson's truck for Courtney to search. She'd finished processing Ricky Fillinger's and found some suspicious stains, but the truck was old, and Ricky hadn't exactly kept it clean. If he'd had either girl in his truck—especially transporting a body—he would have recently cleaned it. His alibi was solid as well. Nikki had crossed him off her list of suspects.

Hanson produced receipts for the motel room he'd rented when he was supposedly home with Miles. Nikki had requested the motel's security footage and asked the St. Paul Police to pay a visit to the mistress to confirm his new alibi. If Hanson's wife didn't know about the affair, she wasn't paying attention. The man couldn't tell a good lie to save his life.

Nikki spent the afternoon at the government center poring over Kaylee's stories that Liam had printed from the school computers. Many of the characters in Kaylee's stories seemed to have been inspired by the likes of Jade Eby and other bullies, observed by a snarky misfit heroine who always had the strength to stand up for herself. Viewing the characters through the heroine's lens gave her a much better look into Kaylee's head. Her antagonists had reasons for their actions, even the mean girls. Most had redeemable qualities, and Kaylee's writing tended to be at its best in those scenes.

In one story, an angry young man brought a gun to school and barricaded himself in a classroom with twenty students and a teacher. The heroine believed there was good left in him and eventually succeeded in his relinquishing the gun.

Kaylee wanted to see the good in people. Despite having every reason to be bitter about her peers, Kaylee's empathy prevented her from simply turning her back.

Nikki glanced at the window for what felt like the fiftieth time. Despite wanting to focus on the case, she couldn't help but wonder if Rory was really going to come to talk to her.

"Not a damn thing." Courtney came into the room with her usual dramatic flair, dumping her bag on the table, and plopped into the chair across from Nikki. "Hanson's got some stains in his upholstery, but they aren't blood. His kid has a stash of frozen candy beneath the back seat. What is that mound of paper in front of you?"

"Kaylee's short stories."

"You printed all of those off instead of reading them on the computer?" Courtney shook her head. "You still don't own an e-reader, do you?"

"I told you that I like reading things in print instead of on a screen. Helps keep me focused."

"Okay, Gen X. Find anything useful?"

"Actually, I did. Kaylee was a fixer."

"As in—"

"Drawn to the misfits and outcasts."

Courtney made a face. "The more broken the guy, the more attracted she would have been. My sister's like that. It's why she's on her third marriage. How can you use it?"

"I'm not exactly sure yet. But she wasn't the type of person to see red flags from a guy who came from a rough life, had a bad attitude, maybe even a juvenile record. She believed in second chances, so if she had a connection to someone, I think she sticks by him."

"You said Madison was Type A, control freak?" Courtney asked.

"Very much so. Opposites attract. They probably balanced each other out."

"Maybe Kaylee was meeting someone, and Madison was with her that day because she knew the guy had issues and wanted to protect her friend," she said.

"Maybe," Nikki replied. "I've spoken to Liam and he's come up empty with the cell carriers so far. It was a long shot, anyway. But Drew Hanson confirmed that Kaylee had a phone on her two days before she disappeared, and we know she could have used Ricky's money to keep it turned on. Did Miller come back with you?"

"He's catching up on reports. Said to text him if anything important came up."

Liam's noisy entrance ended their conversation. He still wore his coat and hat, his cheeks pink from the cold. He sat down, and Nikki updated them on what she and Miller had found. "Madison and Kaylee's school friends identified Kaylee's crush. Bobby Vance. He's a freshman at Mankato State. Bobby's mother, Mindy, had been surprised when Nikki had called her, but she assured her they were just trying to talk to anyone who might have information and that she'd just learnt that Bobby and Madison had been close friends. "I met his mother at the Bankses'. Bobby was at school when the girls disappeared, but we still need to talk to him. She promised to tell him to call me if she talked to him. Hopefully he returns my call soon."

"I found something you need to see." Liam opened his laptop and quickly typed in his password. "This is from the condo next door to Jessica's house. Essentially sharing a wall means the neighbor's security camera catches anyone walking up the sidewalk."

Nikki scooted closer, expecting to see Ricky Fillinger swagger into frame.

"That's Amy Banks."

"Madison's mom?" Courtney said.

"Three weeks before the girls disappeared. She was at the Thomases' house for about seven minutes. We'll have to double-check with Jessica to make sure she didn't switch shifts or call in sick, but going by the schedule she gave us, she was at work."

"Getting time and a half on a Saturday." The same thing she'd done the day the girls went missing. Jessica would probably carry that guilt for the rest of her life.

"Madison never shows up in the footage? Maybe she came to pick her up."

"Just Amy."

"Amy never mentioned this during the initial investigation?"

Liam shook his head, the silly tassels on his hat bobbing. "She specifically said she didn't know where Kaylee lived."

"You tell Miller about this?"

"Not yet."

What was Amy Banks doing at the house and why hadn't she told them? Nikki wondered. Had Amy Banks gone behind her daughter's back and told Kaylee to stay away? Was she worried it made her look bad? Or did she have something else to hide?

"I'll call Miller on the way to my hotel. Liam, meet me at the Bankses' first thing in the morning."

CHAPTER FIFTEEN

Nikki foolishly lingered in the lobby well after Liam and Courtney headed home. The wait for the autopsies added more pressure for her team to find something to move things forward. The medical examiner wouldn't even think about letting Courtney collect evidence for at least two more days.

Why had Amy Banks gone to see Kaylee? Amy had been out of town with her son when the girls disappeared. Amy's parents confirmed the timeline, and they lived far enough away that Amy would need a good reason for being gone for hours.

"No way Amy overpowered both girls," Nikki muttered to herself. Kaylee had at least thirty pounds on the woman.

Grief had been Nikki's second skin for so long that she could easily spot fake emotion. But was Amy's grief laced with guilt? Nikki wasn't leaving the Bankses' house tomorrow without the truth.

Nikki hadn't been exaggerating to Newport about the possibility of more murders. While she was certain the girls' killer had been someone they knew and trusted, Nikki still had to consider that their killer might murder more girls.

The front desk clerk cleared his throat. "Sorry, Agent Hunt. I need to close the building and lock up."

Nikki flushed and glanced at her watch. She'd waited twenty minutes for Rory, and that was more than she'd intended to wait. She slid her coat on and shouldered her bag, irritated at her own disappointment. Not having to deal with Rory again should have felt like a good thing.

She said goodbye to the night guard and braced for the cold air, ducking her face from the wind. She hadn't gone more than ten steps when a male voice made her stop short.

"Agent Hunt?"

Nikki's hand instinctively went to the gun still secured on her hip as a young man appeared between two vehicles.

"Can I help you?"

He took a few steps toward her.

"Stop. You're close enough."

A lock of blond hair stuck out from beneath his skull cap. A few days' scruff dotted his jawline. "My name's Bobby Vance."

Nikki's shoulders relaxed, but she kept her hand on the gun. "You didn't have to come down here. Approaching a cop in a dark parking lot isn't exactly a smart decision."

Bobby's cheeks turned pink. "Ah. I didn't think of that. I was already here." He pointed toward the parking lot exit where the protestors had gathered outside of the gate. "I'm protesting for Mark Todd."

"I see."

"I took a few days off classes when I heard about Maddie and Kaylee. Wanted to be here for services and all. But we don't know when that's going to be, and I've been reading about Todd's appeal."

"You don't have to justify protesting to me. That's your right," Nikki said. "It's freezing. Would you mind going into the station for a few minutes? It's just right over there."

He grinned. "Sure. I went there first and they said you were over here."

Nikki fell into step next to him, still on high alert. He walked with his hands in his pockets, keeping his eyes on the ground. He seemed harmless, but she wasn't going to take any chances. "What are you majoring in at Mankato State?"

"I haven't declared yet. Guess I'm afraid of making the wrong choice and then wasting money on school."

She rang the sheriff's station's after-hours bell. "College is never a waste. And you'll figure it out."

A front desk officer unlocked the door. "Agent Hunt. Sergeant Miller's left for the day."

"I just need to borrow the lobby for a minute," Nikki said. "He's a friend of the Banks family, and it's too cold to chat outside."

"No problem. Just make sure the door is closed behind you. It automatically locks." The officer went back to her post behind the bulletproof glass. Nikki sat down on the bench in the lobby, and Bobby perched on the end as though he were afraid to get too close and do something to offend her.

Nikki dug into her bag for the Polaroid she'd found at Madison's house. She studied his face, hoping the element of surprise worked in her favor. "Have you ever seen this picture?'

"There was some kind of festival in Hudson last September. Maddie talked me into being their chauffeur."

Nikki had already checked, and the department of transportation only had a handful of cars registered to a Vance in Washington County. The Toyota Camry Mindy had been driving was registered to her, and Nikki had confirmed the other registrations belonged to people with the same last name and no relation to Bobby and Mindy. "It was my understanding that you didn't have a car."

Bobby looked surprised. "I don't. Mom let me borrow hers to take them."

Nikki nodded. She believed him.

"Were you and Maddie close, then?"

He shrugged. "Not like confess-your-secrets close. She went to a lot of my baseball games in the summer. She liked hanging out with older kids. I didn't have a problem with it, unless alcohol was involved. I didn't want a kid partying with us, so I usually wound up giving her a ride home before things got too crazy."

"Did she ever come to you for advice?" Nikki asked. She thought perhaps Madison might have seen Bobby as an older brother—confided in him, expected him to protect her.

"Maddie spent most of her time focusing on school." Bobby shook his head. "She was the kind of kid that had it all together, you know?"

"Right," Nikki said. "Were you at school when they disappeared?"

"I came home to help search." Bobby's voice was thick with remorse. "We must have walked up and down that trail twenty times, looking for any sign of them. I went door-to-door with my mom and we talked to a few joggers from the trail. They just seemed to vanish."

"What about Kaylee?" Nikki wanted to see if Kaylee's name would change his calm demeanor, but he still seemed the same.

"She seemed like a nice girl." Bobby jammed his hands into his pockets.

"A couple of the girls' friends said that Kaylee might have been dating an older boy. She's blowing you a kiss in that picture. And she was a very pretty girl. If you guys were dating, I need to know."

Bobby's eyes widened. "No way. I'm a freshman in college. I don't need to come back to Stillwater to find girls to date. I've only met Kaylee a few times. I know she had issues at school and her mom worked a lot. She seemed lonely, but she was happy to be with Maddie." His jaw tightened. "I can't believe this is happening."

"Did she give you her phone number?"

Bobby shook his head. "I'm sorry I can't be more helpful." He paused for a moment, fiddling with the ends of his jacket. "Can I talk to you about something?" Bobby lowered his voice, uncertainty in his eyes. "About Mark Todd?"

Nikki had expected the question. "I'm not comfortable talking to you about him. Mark's attorneys are doing what they believe is in his best interests. It will all play out in the courts."

"I know that," Bobby said. "It's just my dad talked about that night a lot. He was with you that night, at the party. I grew up hearing about it, since nothing like that ever happens around here."

Nikki's insides went cold. She didn't remember any of John's friends from that night. "Did your dad give a statement to the police?"

"I think so," Bobby said. "He backed up what John said happened. If the story ever came up—"

"Why would it come up?" Nikki said.

"John would bring it up. I probably don't have to tell you that he likes to be the center of attention. He was a hero that night, at least in his eyes." Bobby looked down at the floor and chewed the inside of his cheek.

"What is it you're really trying to tell me?" Nikki tried not to think about John using her family's tragedy as a party favor.

"It's probably nothing," Bobby said. "But a few years ago, when the case was in the media again, I think because of an appeal, we were all together at dinner. John was going on about what happened, and Amy said something about him embellishing things. Like every time he told the story, he added something that made himself look tougher or whatever. She called him out on it, and John got really mad and told her to keep her mouth shut. They started arguing, and my dad took John outside so he could cool off."

"What happened?"

"John got in Dad's face," Bobby said. "And ever since then I've wondered about it."

"I'm still not sure why you're telling me this."

"One of the protestors said that Caitlin Newport—you know who she is?"

"Unfortunately."

"Well, she told the protestors that everyone at the party lied about what happened."

"According to Mark, I assume."

"I suppose," Bobby said. "But then I remembered that argument. And I know that day stuck with Maddie."

"What do you mean?" Nikki's head felt heavy, and her chest tight.

"Maddie told me that after they went home, she heard her parents fighting about it again. She never told me details, but I suppose I wonder what was said. And if she ever pressed her parents about it. Maddie wasn't the type to let things lie."

"Thank you for the information." Sweat beaded across Nikki's brow. Her coat felt five pounds heavier. She needed to get out of this stuffy lobby. "I understand that you're protesting, but can you keep this between us? Newport will stir things up and make it harder for us to find out what really happened to the girls."

"I never thought of that. Of course, I won't say anything."

Nikki couldn't stay in the hot lobby another minute. She shoved open the door and breathed in the cool air.

"Agent Hunt?" Bobby touched her shoulder. "Are you all right?"

"It's just been a long day. Thank you for the information."

"No problem," he said. "Just please promise me you'll find out who did this to Maddie and her friend."

"I'm doing everything I can." Nikki closed her eyes as a wave of vertigo struck.

Headlights bore down on them, accompanied by the low rumble of an engine. The truck screeched to a halt.

"What's going on?"

Nikki's eyes snapped open at Rory's voice. She took a deep breath and focused on his face. Sunglasses held back his wavy hair, and he glared at Bobby.

"Bobby just came to make a statement regarding the case." Nikki's vision had cleared, but her legs were still weak, and her stomach suddenly ached with hunger. "I haven't eaten since this morning. It just caught up with me."

Bobby looked nervously at Rory. "Well, if you're okay and don't have any more questions for me—"

"I don't," Nikki said. "You're free to go."

He looked like he couldn't leave quickly enough. "Have a good night."

Bobby gave Rory a wide berth and hurried toward the lot's exit. He lit up a cigarette and glanced back at them before he turned the corner and disappeared.

"You okay?" Rory asked.

"Fine." She drew a ragged breath. "You're late."

"Sorry," he said. "I got hung up at a job."

"It happens." Nikki tried to ignore the jittery feeling racing through her since Rory had arrived.

"You okay to drive?" The kindness in his voice made her throat tighten.

"Fine. But I thought you wanted to talk."

He shook his head. "Yeah, but it's getting late, and I'm sure you have family to get home to."

Nikki zipped her coat back up. "I'm staying at the Comfort Inn and Suites for a few days. But I'm freezing, so can we take this somewhere else? Preferably some place that serves food."

"There's a bar across the river. Good pizza and wings. Total dive, but it won't be busy."

"Meaning you won't be seen with me," she said. "Makes sense."

"I don't care about being seen with you. I just don't want you to deal with any more bullshit tonight, especially since those protesters are still around."

"I appreciate that. I'll follow you there."

CHAPTER SIXTEEN

Rory hadn't been exaggerating about the bar being a dive. Nikki had spent plenty of time in them during her wilder days, and the dark interior and dated red leather booth gave her a strange sense of comfort. Nikki ordered a club soda and mozzarella sticks. Not exactly brain food, but at least she'd have something in her stomach. Her skin felt clammy beneath her warm clothes. She'd already put her hair into a ponytail but sitting across from Rory and his unreadable eyes felt like standing beneath a spotlight. She wriggled out of the sweater and fanned the collar of her thin shirt.

Rory's gaze swept over her. "Where's the scar from?"

She'd forgotten the V-neck didn't cover the pencil-thin scar below her collarbone. Three years ago, Nikki had foolishly gone alone to interview a potential witness of a second abduction, but the man was already dead by the time she arrived, and she'd been left with a scar of her time confronting the killer.

"It's nothing," she replied.

"How do you do it?" Rory sipped his beer.

"Do what?"

"This job. Your life is on the line every day. Not to mention the things you've probably seen."

"After you find your parents murdered, you start to become desensitized," Nikki said, and she realized the words came out harsher than she'd intended.

Rory looked down at the table, a lock of hair falling into his eyes. "Guess I set myself up for that."

Nikki's mozzarella sticks arrived, and she ate in silence for a few minutes. Why did she feel like the bad guy right now? Rory was lucky she'd even agreed to talk to him.

"You know that kid you were talking to was out protesting today."

"He told me."

"And you still spoke to him?"

Nikki dropped a half-eaten mozzarella stick onto her plate, irritated at the edge in his voice. "I was interviewing him. Why do I need to justify that?"

"You don't." His green eyes bore into hers, and a fresh wave of warmth spread through her body. She took another sip of club soda. Why did her brain get so muddled every time she tried to ask him a simple question? "You said you got tied up at a job. And then you show up while Bobby's hanging around."

He'd started to take another drink, but Rory slowly lowered the bottle. "What are you asking, exactly?"

"I'm just curious about your timing. Maybe you saw him show up to talk to me. And then you wait until the right moment."

Rory stared at her for a few seconds, his expression more confused than angry. "For what, exactly?

"You knew he was a protestor. There's a good chance the two of us argue. If you come in and break things up—save me, even—you might gain my trust," she said. "Putting me in a position of owing you a favor might persuade me to look at Mark's file."

He leaned forward and folded his hands on the sticky table. "But I know you can take care of yourself. You carry a gun. You don't need saving."

His husky tone and unrelenting gaze made her feel light-headed. Did he turn this kind of charm on for everyone? "No, I don't. But your timing—"

"I fired Ricky," he said quietly. "I didn't want to, but he admitted to me that he had been dealing at one of my job sites. He says he's done, but I can't allow that. I've worked too hard to risk my business and reputation."

"You did the right thing."

He peeled the label off the beer bottle, his gaze boring straight into her. "Nicole, I didn't wait around to see what the protestor would do. I'm grateful you're talking to me."

"Fine." Nikki believed him for now. "It's the cop in me. I'm naturally suspicious."

"So, what's it like to be a mind reader?" Rory asked, still looking at her intently.

"We hate that term." She felt bad being so blunt with Rory, unsure what he wanted to gain from making conversation with her. "We study behavioral patterns, in an attempt to understand how one piece of behavior predicts another and then another. It's not mind reading."

"And it works?" Rory asked, intrigued.

"It's a tool. If it were a magic solution, Frost would be in prison."

"You learned all of that from the FBI?"

"I have a master's in psychology. I wouldn't have made it into the academy without it, much less gone into profiling."

"But you get why people do the things they do." He said it flatly, and she realized where this conversation was going. That's what they had come to do. Rory probably had little interest in her life outside of that.

"To an extent," she said. "But that comes over the course of an investigation."

Rory pushed his beer aside and folded his arms on the table. "But you've never looked at my brother's case with a trained behavior analyst's eye, have you?"

"No," she said. "Do you really think I could be objective?"

"If you knew the things I do, yes. It would be hard, but you're too good at your job not to be."

"You overestimate my—"

"I've read all about you," he said. "You've been featured on a couple of police shows, and your peers were kind of in awe with how well you read people."

She flushed at his compliment, not knowing why she felt embarrassed by Rory saying this. She was used to being analyzed in the press for years, but it felt different coming from him. "I guess seeing violence like I did is both a curse and blessing. It made me hyper aware. Obsessed, almost. If I'd only understood him better, I would have realized what your brother was capable of."

"You didn't realize because he isn't capable of it."

Nikki admired Rory's loyalty. "What did you want to talk to me about, specifically?"

He ran a hand through his hair and Nikki couldn't help but watch, her eyes trained on the way it settled on his brow. "I'm absolutely positive that you would see things differently if you sat down with the case file. There are so many things that don't add up."

"D.A. Mathews told me that was the defense's position." Her stomach knotted. "Did you leak any of the new details about the case to Caitlin?"

"I would never do that," he said. "It was probably someone from the Innocence Project."

Should she really trust him? What if he was recording the conversation?

"Can I see your phone?" she asked.

"Why?" he replied, moving back slightly as if shocked by the question.

"I want to make sure you're not recording me. I'm here to talk to you, not the attorneys."

Rory looked irritated but slid the phone across the table. "It's unlocked."

He didn't have a lot of apps, and voice memo wasn't turned on.

"Thank you." She slid the phone back to him. "Look, I know you want to believe your brother, and I've been told about the new

DNA testing and evidence. But it doesn't change what I remember. You know what happened earlier in the night from my testimony. John found Mark on top of me at that party. I woke up and Mark was hovering over me and I screamed." Nikki hugged her arms to her chest to hide her balled fists.

"Is that how you remember it?" he asked softly.

She hesitated. "Yes."

"There's no way you don't have blank spots. Mark says you were completely blasted and passed out. You didn't go into that room to sleep it off."

"I'm sure that's his version. I never denied drinking, but I was told my sobriety was confirmed when I gave my statement. There's nothing unreliable about what I saw." She waited for him to mention the missing report, but he didn't seem to know.

"You're remembering what you've been told happened."

"That's not true," Nikki said, anger growing inside of her.

"Nicole, how do you know Mark was going to rape you?"

"His hands were on my shoulders. He was straddling me."

"And then John's your hero," he said dryly. "Do you remember fighting with him earlier that night?"

"Yes." John always had to be the center of attention, especially hers. He didn't like her mingling with other people at parties. Nikki usually complied, but that night she'd drunk enough that she didn't care. John had pulled her into the hallway, and they'd argued. He'd gone on about her embarrassing him, how she'd been flirting with every guy. He usually succeeded in manipulating her into an apology when they argued, but her liquid courage had prevailed. She'd told him to shove it and gone for another drink. And then another. "We argued all the time." Nikki shouldn't be talking about John to anyone given her involvement in Madison's case. "But I'm not sure what that has to do with Mark. He's the one who killed my parents and waited around for me so he could finish what he'd started at the party."

Rory's eyes shined with sympathy. "I'm sorry for what you went through, but Mark didn't do it. He'd come over to wait for you, yes. But then he heard the shot and went inside. That's why the front door was broken into. He found your mom, but he was hit on the back of the head before he was able to get help—"

"Why didn't the killer shoot him?" Nikki asked. "He'd already killed one person and a second one was dying. Shooting Mark would have been the only option."

"The killer used your dad's gun. The chamber was empty. He had to subdue Mark," Rory said. "Mark was hit on the back of the head—that's a documented injury."

"From John kicking his ass earlier in the night."

"His skull was cracked. The X-rays were taken two days after the murder, so the prosecutor got them ruled inadmissible. You'll see them when you look at the case file." Rory was leaning against the table again, his hands close enough to touch.

Nikki set back against the booth. "Then he smacked his head hard during the fight. It's easier to crack a skull than you might think."

"Was he bleeding from the back of the head when he left the party?"

Nikki didn't reply; she couldn't remember if she'd been inside the house or standing in the front yard when Mark ran off.

"He refused to go to the hospital and get stitches because he knew the cops were already looking for him," Rory said. "He has the scar to prove it."

"Then it must have been bleeding when he left."

"There was no blood on the side of your house where he supposedly climbed into the window. None on the windowsill. They did find his blood in your parents' room, several feet from the bed. He was knocked out, his skull cracked and bled on the floor. He came to and went downstairs looking for a phone. You came home. He panicked and almost ran. But he didn't know if the killer was still inside, so he went upstairs to get you."

So now Mark was actually her knight in shining armor. "His memory's awfully good for someone hit hard enough for the skull to crack."

"He didn't remember all the details right away, but it didn't matter because Hardin made up his mind the minute you told your story. Getting even with Mark fell right into his lap."

"What are you talking about?"

"Mark was having a relationship with Hardin's wife."

Bitter stomach acid rose in Nikki's throat; she couldn't believe what she was hearing. "What?"

"She was only a few years older than him. He worked for them during the summer, cutting their grass and doing odds and ends. She was lonely, I guess. Mark said she invited him in to cool off, and one day, things went too far. It went on for months, but Hardin caught them after a while."

"That is—" She couldn't get the words out.

"Relevant," Rory said. "Hardin busted Mark for possession of weed two days later—weed that Mark had never seen. Mark spent two weeks in jail. Few months later, he's in the wrong place at the wrong time and Hardin's the officer in charge. You honestly think he's going to be impartial?"

"Hardin wasn't the only cop…" Nikki's voice faltered. Someone else had collected the evidence, which meant Hardin hadn't worked the case alone. "Of course Mark's going to say all of this, but it doesn't mean you should believe him," Nikki said.

"Hardin and Marie got divorced six years ago. She confirmed everything. If you read the case file, you'll see why Patsy Moran believes Mark."

Nikki's head spun. She was able to tell herself the new evidence was a mistake, that she was drug tested, that her own testimony was reliable. But she'd never considered any of these motivations before. Had Hardin really railroaded Mark Todd for revenge? "Mark was there. No one else had motive."

"Hardin never looked for anyone. And that's not all—"

"I've heard enough." Nikki needed space to think and she needed to focus on Kaylee and Madison. This wasn't why she'd come back to Stillwater, and she wasn't going to let anyone else be killed because she couldn't handle her emotions. She put a ten-dollar bill on the table and stood. "I need to get some rest. I have the double homicide of two teenaged girls to focus on. I can't be distracted, I'm sorry." She hurried out of the bar, fighting tears.

"Nicole, wait."

She didn't stop walking, but Rory's long legs easily surpassed her stride and blocked her path.

"Why are you telling me all of this, Rory? If you believe Mark's innocent, then you should hate me, and it doesn't matter if I'm aware of all of this or not. I can handle you hating me." Much better than she could handle his kindness.

"Maybe I'm weak. That's what Newport said when I refused her interview about your being back in town." Rory stepped into her space, close enough that she could smell the sweet scent of his laundry powder. "You were a traumatized kid. When it comes out that the DNA doesn't match Mark, you'll be the scapegoat. You aren't the bad guy. You lost your parents. Hardin and anyone who helped him screw my brother are the ones who need to be held accountable. And they will be. And you forgot your coat."

"Thank you." Nikki looked up into his green eyes. He was taller than she'd realized. She pulled her coat on and walked to her jeep.

"Drive safe," Rory said.

She waved her hand without looking back. The jeep's cold engine sputtered to life. Nikki didn't wait for it to warm up, driving too fast out of the parking lot, finally letting the tears fall.

CHAPTER SEVENTEEN

Nikki gave up on sleeping around 3:00 a.m. Between her dreams and everything Rory had said, her exhausted brain wasn't sure what it actually remembered.

She made a pot of coffee and sat down at the little table next to the hotel window. Miller planned on searching Hanson's house this morning, but she didn't think he'd find anything. He'd also said Hanson's mistress had backed his alibi, and St. Paul police confirmed the two of them had been at the hotel the afternoon the girls disappeared.

Madison and Kaylee had gone with their killer willingly, Nikki was certain. Two capable teenaged girls weren't abducted off a trail right behind several houses. Ricky had an alibi, and if he had somehow been involved, his ego was too big for him to stay quiet. He was the type to skulk around the investigation, getting off on outsmarting the cops. Bobby Vance didn't have a car, and Miller had already confirmed Mindy was visiting friends in the city that day. Bobby had taken the picture, but that had been several weeks before Madison and Kaylee disappeared. Had Kaylee started dating someone else?

Liam still hadn't found any suspects with access to industrial freezers other than Drew Hanson, and they didn't have enough evidence for a warrant. All of the sex offenders he'd found recently released nearby had iron-clad alibis. And Nikki was going to have to tell him that she still didn't have Kaylee's phone number—tracking it seemed less and less likely.

Nikki felt like they'd focused a lot on Kaylee, but she couldn't stop thinking about Madison. Everyone seemed to agree that Kaylee was at the center of everything, but Nikki wondered if Madison was more than just a perfect student.

If her mother had visited Kaylee's house, she was going to find out why. And Bobby's comments about John rattled her. Why was he arguing with so many people about her parents' case?

Her phone vibrated. Dread seeped through her as Miller's number flashed on the screen. Early-morning calls were never a good sign. "What's up?"

"We have another body," he said.

Nikki leapt out of the chair, slopping coffee on her nightshirt. "Do you know who it is?"

"Female in her early twenties. She was left to the elements like the girls, but she's not as frozen. Medical examiner's on her way."

Nikki shoved her coffee aside. Had she been too slow to find Madison and Kaylee's killer and cost another woman her life? "Text me the address. I'll leave in ten minutes."

Rush hour and lane closures made the drive to the scene three times longer than it should have been. Heritage Square Park was a small, quiet park tucked away in one of the newer residential areas on the west side of town.

Nikki scowled as she recognized the two people standing near the swings.

She parked in an illegal zone and jogged across the street to join Miller.

"Why is Newport here?"

Hardin's bulk eclipsed the reporter's trim form, and she had to look up when she spoke to him. She was speaking very quickly, hands on her hips as Hardin nodded obediently.

"Hardin called her as soon as the call came in this morning," Miller said. "He's trying to play nice with her all of a sudden."

And Nikki knew why. If Rory was right, Caitlin's documentary on Mark Todd would expose Hardin's mistakes—or worse—that night. She hadn't been able to get Rory's words out of her mind ever since she left the bar. Was Hardin really capable of putting an innocent man in jail?

"Agent Hunt," Caitlin called. "What do you think of Frost leaving a victim here in Stillwater at the same time you're here on a separate case? Seems like a message for you."

"I haven't even seen the body," Nikki snapped. "May I have a moment with the chief?"

"Of course."

Nikki felt the reporter's gaze as she led Hardin to the other side of the swings. "Chief, between you and me, I don't need to see the body to know Frost isn't involved."

"Now how do you know that? Besides, she's got a red ribbon in her hair just like Frost's girls."

"I can't share that information, but I'm asking you to trust me. The red ribbon is common knowledge."

Hardin hitched up his pants. "That's some ego, Hunt."

"It's not ego," she said. "It's simple fact."

"She's been left in the snow, in a public place, and she looks to be the same age as the other women he killed."

"He never leaves two bodies in the same year, let alone three," Nikki said. "Will you please just tell the media that we're looking at all angles and leave it at that?"

Hardin glared down at her. "You said that after Madison and Kaylee were found. Now we have another body."

"Exactly," Nikki said. "If this is the same killer, he's made his first real mistake. Excuse me."

She stalked past him, and Newport closed in.

"No comment."

"I haven't even asked you anything yet."

"Saving you the energy."

"She's not one of Frost's." Newport lowered her voice. "She's frostbitten. That means she died out here. Frost's girls are already dead when they're put on ice, right?"

"How do you know she's frostbitten?"

"I overheard your people talking," Caitlin said.

"Of course you did." Nikki turned to Miller, who'd trudged through the heavy snow to join them. "Would you have one of your deputies escort Ms. Newport to her vehicle?"

"No need. I'm sure I'll see you later." She sauntered toward the street.

Nikki followed Miller past the snow-covered gazebo. "Newport claims she overheard the medical examiner say the victim was frostbitten."

Miller scowled. "I don't trust her as far as I can throw her."

"But the woman did have frostbite?"

"Quite a bit," Miller said. "Poor woman died out here. I just hope she wasn't conscious."

Nikki and Miller quickly reached Liam and Courtney, who were standing in the middle of the small park, examining the area between a swing set and a large tree. "Where's the body?"

"Hardin had the jurisdiction to have the medical guys bag her and take her in. She's been out here for a while, and this is a family park. Liam and Courtney were already here, and you were stuck in traffic."

"It was Hardin's call, anyway. I can't fault him for wanting to get her out of here. What do you guys have so far?"

"Hispanic female, approximately five foot seven, about one-hundred thirty, one-hundred forty pounds. Frostbite means blood still flowing, so she was left out here alive." Liam handed her his phone, and she scrolled through the pictures he'd taken of the body.

At first glance, it was easy to see why someone without intimate knowledge of Frost's methods would think the victim belonged to him. She lay flat on her back, arms and legs spread like a snow angel. The true position of Frost's girls—flat on their backs, arms folded over their midsection—had never been made public. Her dark hair had been pulled to the side and tied with a red silk ribbon. But Frost's ribbons were red velvet—another detail they'd kept out of the media.

"We might be able to get a fingerprint from the ribbon," Courtney said. "I think we all know it won't match Frost's."

The victim had been wearing makeup, including false eyelashes. Her skimpy dress and heels suggested she hadn't intended to be in the cold for more than a few minutes. The fishnets she wore certainly weren't going to keep her legs warm.

"Every finger is significantly frostbitten," Nikki said. "What did the medical examiner say about getting prints?"

"It doesn't look like her fingers got to the point of splitting open, so she's hoping they can warm her up and peel the skin off with tweezers to get prints."

Close-up photos of the back of the woman's head showed possible blunt force trauma. Blood caked her dark hair. The fishnets had been torn in the front, exposing both thighs, which also had black patches of frostbite. A small bird tattoo on her left ankle might be their quickest way to identify her.

"Something hit her hard in the head," Nikki said. "Had her bleeding been stopped before she came out here?"

"The medical examiner thinks so," Liam said. "Which means she was hit and then left to die hours later. We won't know without the autopsy."

"The medical examiner was able to move her limbs," Courtney said. "She doesn't think she was out here for more than a few hours. But Frost's victim's being frozen solid isn't public knowledge."

Bits of red dotted the area where the body had been. "Frost's girls never bleed. Did the wind blow very hard this morning?"

"Nope," Courtney said. "I checked as soon as we got here. The wind was light, and the snow looks like it's been rolled around in."

"That means whoever dumped her waited and came back to stage her body."

"Exactly." Courtney pointed to the impressions in the snow. "She was dragged out here. And whoever left her tried to cover their tracks. No good impressions of the footwear. Looks like they basically shuffled. It's impossible to tell if they made more than one trip, but I can't rule it out, either."

"From a parked car, or was she attacked walking down the street?"

"I found a fairly fresh oil spot along the street, but I can't say for sure when it was left."

"I canvassed that side of the park," Miller said. "No one saw anything, and no one has security cameras with the right angle. I've got a deputy going to door-to-door to make sure we cover every side of the park."

"At least we can rule out her passing out drunk and freezing to death." Nikki went back to the first picture of the woman. "We've let the public believe that Frost is still a suspect in Madison and Kaylee's murders. And this is a pretty clear attempt at copying his methods."

"But Madison and Kaylee were too frozen to be manipulated into a specific position," Liam said. "And why weren't there red ribbons on their bodies?"

"Because I don't think the killer initially meant for them to be considered Frost victims," Nikki said. "Remember, that field is remote. He meant for them to be found in the spring. But fate intervenes and our public statement is that we aren't ruling Frost out yet. So, when he dumps this woman, he makes an attempt at Frost's methods, but he doesn't get the body position right."

Courtney's eyes widened. "Meaning he thinks that adding another body to the mix will push you further toward Frost and farther away from him? But a basic internet search should have told him enough about Frost to realize you'd never buy it."

"He's not a planner," Liam said. "This poor woman was killed out of desperation."

"Exactly," Nikki said. "We need to find out who she is. Liam, get her description on the news, along with a picture of her tattoo. Make sure the information goes to both Wisconsin and Minnesota media." She turned to Miller. "Did your deputies turn up anything at Hanson's house this morning?"

"Uneventful. He doesn't have a freezer, and there's no sign of one recently being moved," Miller said. "His wife wasn't surprised when we showed up with the warrant."

"He probably gave her a sterilized version of events," Nikki said. "Did you get my message about Amy on the security video of Kaylee's?"

Miller's mouth tightened. "I can't believe she didn't tell me that. Do you think she could be involved?"

"Anything is possible, although I have a hard time believing she killed her own child. I need to brief Hardin. Walk with me?"

"Absolutely. I stopped by Brianna's place last night," Miller said. "Her dad and I played football together, so I'd hoped that would be my in to talking with her. But her father's out of town on business, and Brianna told her mother she's got nothing else to say and that we needed to leave her alone. Apparently, she's got anxiety issues as it is."

"She definitely knows something more," Nikki said. "But pressing her mother doesn't sound like a good idea. She works at the library, right?"

Miller nodded. "I think her next shift is in a couple of days."

"I gave her my card. If she does know anything relevant, maybe a third victim will convince her to call." Nikki was determined that no one else was going to be killed on her watch. This case had to be solved as soon as possible.

Hardin had retreated to his vehicle, his big belly pressed against the steering wheel. Nikki rolled her eyes. If he got in an accident, that steering wheel would be coming out of his ass, she thought to herself.

Hardin rolled down his window. "Well?"

"Zero chance Frost did this," Nikki said. "Good chance it's somehow related to Madison and Kaylee's murders."

"How in the world do you get that?" Hardin asked.

Nikki explained her theory to Hardin. "From the disturbance to the snow, it's likely she rolled around in the snow, probably fighting to get up, before she died. He came back and arranged her and probably put the ribbon on her."

"Then why couldn't this be Frost?"

"Frost immediately freezes his victims after they're dead," Nikki said. "Their bodies are pristine. He wouldn't deviate from his routine and allow a victim to get frostbite. That mars the beauty of it to him."

Hardin sighed. "You've already said Madison and Kaylee aren't Frost victims, either."

"To you," Nikki said. "But not to the public. He's still in play. The girls' killer didn't expect us to find their bodies, and when we did, he started to panic. Frost gives him a lifeline. I think this woman's death may have been an attempt to push us towards Frost again."

Hardin chewed his lower lip. Nikki didn't remind Hardin of his earlier certainty that Frost had struck in Stillwater.

"You know as well as I do that most killers aren't as smart as they're portrayed on television. If this is someone who killed the girls and didn't expect them to be found, he's in a panic right now. He most likely believes killing this woman leads us away from him, and we need to let him believe that."

"I can keep the press information brief," Hardin said.

"You have to walk a fine line," Nikki said. "Don't commit one way or the other."

Hardin's chin jutted out. "I know how to deal with the media, Agent."

"And I know Frost," she replied. "He's methodical, and he's ruled by his ego. If you push the narrative too far, he will do something that very clearly proves he's not responsible. That blows our strategy, not to mention possibly getting someone else killed."

"Fine," he said. "You think our victim knew something about the murders or was she just a decoy?"

"That's the million-dollar question. We'll know more after she's identified and autopsied." Nikki smiled sweetly. "Why did you call Newport?"

Hardin scowled. "I'm just trying to get her attention off us."

Miller had walked over to speak with a deputy. Hardin already seemed off his game. If she asked about the blood test now, she might get an honest reaction.

"Where's the blood test I took that night? To check my blood alcohol level."

Hardin's expression didn't change, but he stiffened, his hands gripping the steering wheel. "What are you talking about?"

"A paramedic took my blood the night my parents died. You knew I'd been drinking."

"I gave you a sobriety test," Hardin said. "You passed easily."

"I remember the paramedic and the needle."

"You were in shock and dehydrated," he said. "They put an IV in. They wanted to take you to the hospital, but you refused."

Nikki vaguely remembered the argument about the hospital. She'd arrived on the neighbor's doorstep, screaming and pounding on the door. The neighbor called the police. At some point, the police had left the crime scene to speak with Nikki, and the paramedics had shown up.

"They took my blood," she said, wanting to feel certain, as doubt crept through her.

Hardin rolled his eyes as though she were an irritating toddler. "That never happened. You told me you only had a few drinks and hadn't had anything for at least three hours. You passed the sobriety test. But evidently you weren't honest about how drunk you were."

"That's not true," she said. "I had sobered up."

"The facts don't matter. It's perception." Beads of sweat dotted Hardin's forehead.

Nikki tried to keep her voice calm. "At least now I know exactly what I'm dealing with."

"What's that supposed to mean?" Hardin's face had gone red.

"What do you think it means?"

"That you're a cocky FBI star who is worried about her reputation," he said. "If your testimony is ultimately thrown out, you're going to look like a pariah who lied."

"Or a traumatized teenager who was a victim of a poorly run investigation," she snapped.

His dark eyes narrowed. "You'd better watch out who you cross, Hunt."

"Then don't try to manipulate me. You're not nearly as good at it as you think."

"You should be focused on these murders instead of wasting time in the past."

Nikki's hands balled into fists. "I'm completely focused."

"Tell Miller to keep me up to date." Hardin gunned the engine and peeled away from the curb.

Nikki's body trembled with anger. How could he accuse her of lying about the tox report, much less her sobriety? He knew she'd been drinking that night because she'd admitted to it, and he performed the field sobriety test himself. She'd been a traumatized sixteen-year-old kid, and she'd trusted Hardin when he said she had passed the test. What else had Hardin lied about? What if Rory was right?

Miller headed towards Nikki. "What the hell's going on?" he said, reaching her.

Nikki had to focus on the murders, and Hardin was Miller's boss. He didn't need her emotional baggage. "We need to get this woman identified as soon as possible."

"We will," Miller said. "Your theory makes sense. But what if this woman has no connection to the girls?"

"Obviously we need to hear what the medical examiner finds during autopsy," Nikki said. "But at this point, I'm certain this is our killer trying to distract us. And Liam's right, it stinks of desperation. Someone waited for her to die and then staged her body so she looked like Frost had killed her. That action alone suggests we're dealing with the same person who killed Madison and Kaylee."

"I'm on it," Miller said. "While Liam's getting her picture to the media, one of my deputies and I are going to show her picture to everyone already interviewed about Madison and Kaylee."

"Good thinking. Catch them off guard." Nikki unlocked her jeep and started the engine. "Keep me in the loop. I'm going to get Liam. We're going to pay a visit to Amy Banks."

CHAPTER EIGHTEEN

Nikki and Liam stood outside the Banks home, shivering. Liam rang the doorbell a second time, while Nikki stared blankly at the expensive glass panes.

Liam turned around, concern on his face. "Everything okay?"

"We have a third victim on our watch," Nikki said. "Everything is not okay."

"That's not what I meant. You seem distracted."

Hardin's insistence that her blood hadn't been drawn tied Nikki in knots. She kept thinking about Mark Todd's affair with Hardin's wife. Would he have gone to such lengths to get revenge? He'd been certain of Mark's guilt, hadn't he? The alternative made her tremble with anxiety.

She felt Liam's eyes on her. He was every bit as perceptive as Nikki. She didn't want her team to think she wasn't fully committed to the current case, and she felt terrible that her confusion might have cost a woman her life.

"I'm just trying to work out this guy's motivation. If we're right, he's desperate now. That puts any number of people in danger."

"As cold as it sounds, I hope it's someone else," Liam said. "If it's some kind of domestic, perhaps this woman didn't suffer as badly as Madison and Kaylee. The positioning of their bodies felt so much more brutal. But maybe I just don't want to believe this woman's dead because we haven't caught our guy. Why in the hell isn't she answering?" Liam hit the doorbell a third time.

Seconds later, the door cracked open, and a pair of frightened blue eyes stared up at them. The boy looked to be around Lacey's age; his tousled blond hair and serious expression made him look like a mini-John.

"Hi there. It's Bailey, right?" Nikki showed him her badge. "My name is Agent Hunt, and this is Agent Wilson. We know your mom and dad. Are they home?"

The door widened an inch, revealing the Kool-Aid stain around his mouth. "You're trying to solve my sister's murder."

His soft voice made the words sound obscene.

"We are. Are your parents home?"

"My dad's working. Mommy's asleep."

"Could you wake her up? It's really very important we speak with her."

"I already tried. She's sleeping real hard."

Nikki and Liam glanced at one another.

"Does she usually sleep that hard?" Liam asked.

"No." Bailey's voice trembled. "She said she was hurting all over and was going to take some medicine for it and go back to bed."

Nikki glanced at Liam, and he spun on his heel and headed back to his car. Before he'd joined the team, Liam had worked in narcotics, and overdoses were a common occurrence. He still carried naloxone out of habit. Naloxone was capable of reversing the effects of an opioid if administered in time.

Liam jogged back to the door, the small black kit in his hand. "You know how to do it?"

Nikki nodded. She'd taken a class on the overdose drug a couple of years ago. She smiled down at Bailey, trying to hide her nerves from the little boy. If Amy had overdosed, time was of the essence. The drug only worked if the person's heart hadn't completely stopped. "Will you let me come in and check on your mom? Sometimes pain pills make people extra tired."

Bailey unlocked the storm door and then held it open. He hugged his chest and looked between them. "She'll be okay, right?"

"Why don't you stay with Agent Wilson while I check on your mom." She pointed to his sweatshirt and he looked down at the logo. "Vikings fan, huh? Agent Wilson had tickets on the fifty-yard line last fall."

Bailey's eyes widened, and Liam knelt down. "Dude, it was so cool."

Nikki hurried up the stairs, already searching for her phone, content that Bailey was distracted. A superhero movie played on the television in the upstairs common area. A half-eaten Pop-Tart and a glass of juice had been left on the small table. Bailey must have been responsible for his breakfast.

The master bedroom was three times the size of Nikki's. Amy Banks lay in the king-sized bed, blankets tangled around her and her eyes covered with a silk mask.

Nikki hit the emergency button on her phone and felt for a pulse on Amy's cool wrist. Her heartbeat was weak and possibly irregular.

She took the mask off Amy's eyes. "Amy, wake up."

There was no response and Nikki could feel that Amy's breathing had slowed.

"What did you take?" she said, aware that Amy couldn't hear her.

She found an empty bottle tangled in the sheets: 40mg of oxycodone, prescribed to John Banks three months ago. Take one tablet in the morning for lower back pain.

"Christ." Nikki shook Amy again, hoping to see movement behind her closed eyes. She thought the Bankses were having problems when she'd visited their house, worried their relationship wasn't solid enough to deal with the strain of Madison's death, but not for one moment did she imagine Amy was suicidal. How many pills had she taken? "Amy, come on. You have a little boy and husband who need you. Wake up," she whispered.

Nikki opened the kit and grabbed one of the Narcan nasal sprays. She carefully inserted the nozzle and pressed the plunger.

Amy immediately coughed and gagged.

"Mrs. Banks, just relax," Nikki said. "You're going to be okay."

Amy finally opened her eyes. She glared at Nikki. "The hell you doing in my house?"

"You overdosed on oxycodone. My partner is with your son. I'm going to let him know you're okay." Nikki hurried into the hallway. "Liam?"

Bailey appeared at the foot of the stairs. "Is my mom okay?"

"She's awake. Give her a few minutes, and I'm sure you can come up."

"We already called Mr. Banks," Liam said. "He's on his way. Paramedics, too."

"Good."

"I don't need paramedics." Her shrill voice carried into the hallway and down the stairs. "I'm not an addict. My child was murdered."

"What happened to Mommy?" Bailey asked.

"She took too much medicine." Nikki met him halfway up the stairs. He didn't need to see his mother until she looked more like herself and had her head somewhat straight.

"Why?"

"She's just really tired and made a mistake."

Bailey seemed pacified, but his eyes were still worried. "When can I go see her?"

"I need to talk to her for just a few minutes. Then she's all yours."

The little boy grabbed her hand. "Don't take very long."

Nikki's throat knotted. "I won't."

When she returned to the bedroom, Amy was sitting up on the bed, a silk robe wrapped tightly around her thin body. "I guess I'm supposed to say thank you." She sighed. "I just needed to sleep."

"They make pills for that."

"My prescription ran out, and I have to go back to the doctor to get it filled. That's the last thing I want to do right now." Amy slowly made her way to the bed and sat down. "I just needed a couple of hours. John said one would help me relax, so I took a few extra." Her eyes widened in horror. "Is Bailey okay? Does he know what happened?"

"He's downstairs with Agent Wilson talking about the Vikings. I told him you took too much medicine by mistake. John's on his way."

Amy closed her eyes.

"You don't want him here?" Nikki asked, sensing that John's presence was the last thing Amy wanted.

"I don't need a lecture from him," she replied.

"I'm sure he's going to be happy you're all right."

Amy's cold gaze met hers. "You don't know him at all."

"He's not going to be happy you're all right?" Marital problems and stress aside, Nikki couldn't see John being that callous, especially now.

"I'm not discussing my marriage with you." Amy walked shakily to her vanity unit.

"You're grieving an unimaginable loss," Nikki said. "It's understandable that you're having a tough time, and you and John should be able to console one another. No one else will feel the loss like you do. You're lucky to have one another."

Amy stared at her reflection, tears welling in her eyes. Her small body shook as she sobbed. "What am I supposed to do now?"

"Carry on." The words came out harsher than Nikki intended. The woman's grief was contagious, and Nikki's heart ached for the two girls and their families.

Amy stared at her. "Carry on? That's it?"

"Yes, uncaring as it sounds. We have no other choice when bad things happen. And you have a little boy who loves and needs you."

"What if I can't get it together for him? I don't want to get lost in grief and fail him."

"Then don't," Nikki said. "Go to grief counseling. Take Bailey with you. Use every resource available to help you both heal."

Amy reached for a box of tissue and dried her tears. "Why did you come over in the first place? Is there news?"

Nikki didn't want to set her off again, but she had to know the truth. "I came here to ask you why you visited Kaylee's house a few weeks before the girls disappeared." Amy turned back to the mirror and started brushing her wild hair. "You told me you didn't know where she lived."

Amy stiffened and turned around to face Nikki for a moment. "I asked her to stay away from Madison. She was a bad influence."

"How so?"

"She got kicked off the volleyball team for fighting. She skipped school. I didn't want Maddie around that." She turned back around to continue with her hair.

"And what did Kaylee say when you asked her to leave Madison alone?"

"She said no," Amy replied. "She had the gall to tell me I couldn't buy everything in life. Like she was some sort of expert on relationships."

"Did Madison know you did this?"

Amy yanked the brush through her hair, her hand trembling. "Kaylee said she wouldn't tell her, as though she were giving me some sort of leniency. I was just trying to protect Madison. All it takes is one bad friend." The hairbrush hit the vanity hard enough to rattle the perfume bottles. Amy put her head in her hands. "I still can't believe this is happening."

"I know," Nikki said.

Amy's bloodshot gaze met hers. "How did you do it?"

Nikki tried to mask the wave of pain that swept through her. "I did everything wrong. I tried to block everything out and get through school so I could leave. I shut out my friends. I learned to compartmentalize—to a fault. Don't do things my way. Find a grief counselor and a group. There are several in the city. I can give you some referrals."

"I'll think about it."

"Mrs. Banks," Nikki said. "I want to find out who did this, but I can't if you don't tell me everything."

"I have." Amy took a deep breath. "Thank you for everything. Will you please send Bailey upstairs?"

"Sure." Nikki hesitated. "There's one other thing, and I hate to do it now, but I'm here and I'd hate to bother you again."

"What is it?"

Nikki told her about the woman found in Heritage Park. "I think there's a connection to Madison and Kaylee, but we don't even know this woman's name. Would you be able to look at a photo?"

"Of her body?" Amy turned green.

"Just her face," Nikki said. "There's some frostbite, but it's not too graphic."

Amy still looked uncertain, but she nodded.

Nikki opened the photo Liam had texted her earlier and zoomed in so that just the woman's face showed. She turned her phone to face Amy.

"No." Relief colored Amy's voice. "I don't recognize her."

"Thank you. I'll be in touch." Nikki headed downstairs. Bailey jumped up from the bottom step and hugged her. "Thanks for helping my mom."

If something happened to Nikki, she felt sure that Tyler would take care of their daughter. She would be loved and given all the help she needed. Nikki had a gut feeling that Bailey wouldn't be so lucky if something happened to Amy. She hugged him back, and then handed him one of her cards. "Put this somewhere safe, and if you need anything or want to talk, call me. Any time, okay?"

Bailey looked at the card as though she'd handed him a great treasure.

"Go on and see your mom. Agent Wilson and I will hang around outside for your dad."

Bailey shot off upstairs.

Liam closed the front door and Nikki shouldered into her coat. Bright sun glinted off the snow and made her eyes hurt.

A burly paramedic was trudging up the sidewalk.

"She overdosed on oxycodone," Nikki said. "I administered a single dose of naloxone. She seems stable."

"Nice job," the medic said. "We'll check her over and make sure she doesn't need to go to the hospital."

"Go easy on her. She's just lost her daughter, and she didn't want the paramedics coming in." Nikki waited until the medic went inside and then turned to Liam. "It was John's oxycodone. Prescribed a few months ago."

"I heard her yelling at you," Liam said. "She sounds like a lovely person."

"Grief makes a person lash out," Nikki said. "Thanks for distracting Bailey."

Liam grinned. "I did more than that. He said his dad had a neon Vikings sign in the garage, and of course I just had to see it. The Bankses have a standard standing freezer that's stocked full. No way the girls would have fit into it."

"Thank God. Getting a warrant for their freezer would have put Amy over the edge." Nikki could see a silver Lexus come to an abrupt stop in front of the house. "That's John." Nikki headed down the steps. "Amy apparently told Kaylee to stay away from Madison during her little visit. That's it."

"You believe her?"

"For now."

John jogged down the sidewalk and slipped on a patch of ice. Liam caught his arm before he fell.

"Thanks." John's face was ashen, with dark circles around his eyes. "What happened?"

"She's okay." Nikki glanced at Liam. John was likely to be more candid if Nikki spoke to him alone. "You mind if I speak with John privately?"

Liam gave her a knowing look. "Sure. I want to talk to the paramedics before we leave anyway." He headed back into the house.

"Bailey's with Amy right now, along with the paramedics," she said. "She overdosed on your oxycodone."

His eyes widened. "I told her to start with half a pill. She's never taken painkillers."

"She wanted to sleep, so she took more than one. Luckily, Liam carries naloxone. I don't know if the ambulance would have got to her in time."

"Christ, she's never done anything like that."

"She seems vulnerable, John, I can't imagine what she's going through," Nikki said. "Just be there for her. I think she might need to talk to someone."

"I know," John said. "It's just hard to think about breaking down in front of a stranger."

"Because you were taught to be strong and in control." Nikki smiled sadly. "But nothing prepares us for a loss like this."

John's eyes misted over and he cleared his throat. "Why did you come over this morning? Is there news on Maddie's case?"

Telling him about Amy's conversation with Kaylee might drive a further wedge between the two, but John deserved to know. And hearing it from Nikki might soften the blow, as well as any potential fallout with Amy.

"Kaylee's neighbor has a camera that captures part of her front walk. We found out Amy went to Kaylee's house a few weeks before the girls were taken. She wasn't there long," Nikki explained. "But she said she warned Kaylee to stay away from Madison and Kaylee refused."

"You think Amy had something to do with this?" John shook his head. "No way. She would never hurt anyone."

Would she pay someone else to hurt Kaylee? Nikki might be able to use the security footage to get a warrant for Amy's financial records to see if had made any large withdrawals since the girls' disappearance, but she still couldn't see her being involved with Madison's murder. Her grief was too raw. "I don't think she would, but I still had to ask. She didn't even tell us she went there."

"Why would she keep that a secret?" John shook his head. "I just don't understand."

"Pride," Nikki said. "Listen, don't let this come between you two. Not telling us was wrong, but it ultimately didn't affect the outcome."

"I don't have the energy to fight with her," John said. "Especially after today. If she did something foolish and—" He looked down at the ground and rubbed his eyes. "I don't know what I'll do."

Nikki awkwardly patted his arm. "Try to be there for her. Make sure she knows how much you love her. And let her be there for you."

John squeezed her hand. "I'm sorry you had to come back to Stillwater, but I'm glad you're here."

The wind gusted, and Nikki caught the sweet scent of his cologne. She pulled her hand away and took a step back. "I do have a couple of questions."

Disappointment flickered through John's eyes. "Sure."

Nikki told him about her conversation with Bobby Vance—minus the part about John's ego. His bragging and embellishing his role that night hadn't surprised her. "Bobby remembers there being tension between you and his dad."

"I don't remember that day, but I'm sure there was. Bob suffered from severe depression. He couldn't find a medication that helped." John's eyes misted. "Maddie was always curious about crime stories. When the Innocence Project announced they were reviewing the case, Maddie got really into following it. She was thinking about law school." John's teeth dug into his lower lip. "So much ahead of her."

"I'm sorry." The Innocence Project hadn't filed any formal motions until after Madison and Kaylee disappeared, but the news media had run at least two articles in the fall about the possibility. "Did the two of you talk about the case after that?"

"Probably," John said. "But I was mired in a project for work. I wasn't as present as I should have been."

The regret in his voice reminded Nikki of her own. She didn't have the heart to tell him the feeling never completely went away.

"Why did you talk to Bobby?" John asked.

"He was friends with Madison and we have reason to believe that Kaylee might have had a crush on him." Nikki told him about the picture. "But he was pretty insistent that he didn't return her feelings."

"He's a good kid. Maddie always looked up to him." John glanced at the house. "If there's nothing else—"

"Unfortunately, there is. A woman was found dead in Heritage Park this morning. We think she may be related to Madison and Kaylee's murders. I'd rather be the one to tell you—I'm sure it will be on the news in a matter of hours."

John stared blankly at her. "Why do you think it's the same killer?"

"I can't go into specifics," Nikki said. "But we haven't identified the victim yet. Would you mind looking at a picture of just her face?"

John paled but nodded.

Nikki handed him her phone with the image already cued up.

"Sorry, but I don't recognize her," he said, immediately.

Nikki slipped her phone into her pocket. She really wanted to ask him about that night; so much of what Rory said had made her feel uncomfortable. But standing here in front of John, she still felt like she could trust him. Their relationship had been tumultuous at times, but he'd always been honest, even if he knew it would cause a fight.

"What's wrong?" John asked.

She flushed, surprised he was still able to read her so well. But she knew she needed to focus on the case.

"I heard about the documentary," he said. "That woman is determined. If there's anything you want to ask me to put your mind at rest, you know you can, Nikki."

"I think they're going to question the reliability of my testimony," Nikki said, unable to stop herself. "Even though I passed Hardin's sobriety test."

The crease between John's eyes deepened. "You'd had some vodka that night, but you also hadn't eaten. I remember you had a bit of a headache and went to lie down."

"Was that when I woke with Mark hovering over me?"

"I never heard anyone scream like that." John's jaw tightened. "You know I broke the hinges on that door? I wanted to kill him."

"You and a couple of your friends took him outside, and you beat him up."

"Kicked his ass." John's gaze drifted past her, a flatness in his eyes. "His nose was bleeding—pretty sure I broke it. We got blood everywhere, all over his jeans."

"When you saw me the next day, after it happened, did I talk about taking a blood test?"

John's eyebrows knitted together. "That sounds right. Look, Nik, that filmmaker is just using this story for her own gain," John said. "Mark Todd was caught red-handed."

"Almost red-handed. If the DNA they've found doesn't match Mark Todd, then I helped put an innocent man in prison."

John stepped toward her and gently took her shoulders. "Nikki, you were there. I'm sure the DNA evidence will shut him up once and for all. Where's this DNA even from?" John asked.

Nikki couldn't bring herself to share the details. "I don't know."

He squeezed her shoulders, and for a moment she thought he might pull her in for a hug. "Exactly. This is all a waste of taxpayers' money."

John's voice was so soothing, she almost believed he was right.

CHAPTER NINETEEN

Nikki rubbed her eyes and reached for her phone. It was nearly midnight, and the evening news was replaying on the muted television. When had she fallen asleep? She'd spent the rest of the day scouring missing persons cases from the tri-state area. The medical examiner hadn't been able to get decent fingerprints from the woman in the park, and Nikki didn't have access to a facial recognition program. By the time she'd checked all the files, her vision seemed like a blur of faces.

Thirty minutes video chatting with Lacey had helped clear Nikki's head. Her daughter had a vivid imagination and an even more expressive face, and Nikki loved listening to her stories. Lacey missed her mom, but she was having fun with Tyler especially since Daddy tended to be lax about things like healthy snacks and bedtime. Nikki had desperately needed the time with her daughter, especially after seeing yet another young woman's life cut short.

Tyler had asked if she had any problems with the Todd family or the protestors. Nikki had thought about discussing Rory's information with him, but something held her back. She wanted to keep Rory to herself for now, and she couldn't spend time on his brother's case right now. She'd gone back to work and eventually fallen asleep with her notes scattered over the bed.

Nikki sat up and gathered her notes. Maybe she'd see something she'd missed earlier. A picture of the victim's tattoo and a composite of her face had been sent to every media outlet in the tri-state area. She hoped the tattoo would catch someone's attention. Kaylee's mother and the Bankses didn't recognize the woman, and both

Hanson and Ricky Fillinger had told Miller they'd never seen her before. Yet Nikki couldn't shake the feeling that this murder had something to do with the two girls.

The victim hadn't gone into the park on her own two feet, but the blow to her head had stopped bleeding before she was dragged through the snow. They needed to find the crime scene.

At least the autopsy results would be available soon since the woman hadn't been frozen solid. Madison and Kaylee's were still a few days away. The medical examiner estimated she'd been outside no more than five to six hours before she'd been found. Given the residential neighborhood, it was unlikely anyone would notice her being dragged out to the park in the middle of the night, unless they worked an odd shift. Miller's deputies were still canvassing the area around the park, hoping for a break.

A familiar face appeared on the television. The conference had been previously recorded—the sun was setting in the window behind Hardin. Nikki turned the volume up with a sinking feeling.

"Sheriff Hardin spoke to the media late this afternoon regarding the murders of Kaylee Thomas and Madison Banks, as well as the unidentified woman found in Heritage Park this morning."

Hardin stood behind a podium that barely hid his belly. "We are working around the clock to find the person responsible for the deaths of poor Madison and Kaylee, as well as the unidentified woman in the park. The FBI hasn't ruled out any suspects, including the serial killer known as Frost."

Hardin asked for questions and then scanned the audience. He pointed to a mousy-looking woman in the front. She asked about Mark's retrial and the validity of Nikki's testimony given her intoxicated state.

"She passed a sobriety test," Hardin said.

"What about a toxicology test?"

"Nicole Walsh claimed she'd only had a couple of drinks, and she passed the sobriety test. We took her at her word."

Nikki couldn't believe it. Was her memory that messed up?

"Do you think Todd's appeal is distracting Nikki from the case at hand?"

"Yes, because you keep asking about it," Nikki said to the empty room. Every time she tried to focus on Madison and Kaylee, something about her parents' case came up. Why didn't the media have their priorities straight?

Hardin paused and glanced at the camera as though he were thoughtfully considering his answer. She knew Hardin had a working relationship with at least one local reporter. Perhaps the reporter had been instructed to ask that specific question. "I have some concerns, yes." Nikki's jaw throbbed from clenching it. "It's not a reflection on her abilities at all, but she's not superwoman. I think it's asking quite a lot for her to work in Stillwater right now."

"Are you asking her to leave the case to the locals?" another reporter asked. "Given the lack of movement on the girls' disappearance, it seems your department needs the FBI's resources."

Hardin bristled. "I plan on working closely with Agent Hunt from here on to ensure she stays on task."

Nikki rewound the television and paused on the reporter in the front row. She took a picture with her phone and then zoomed in as far as she could without distorting the image. The reporter's badge indicated she worked for the *Star Tribune*, and her first name was Molly or something close. Her last name only had four letters.

Nikki dug into her bag for the article about Mark's retrial that she'd read in the paper.

Written by Molly Dahl.

Nikki's phone buzzed, and Miller's number flashed on the screen. She didn't bother with a greeting. "Your boss planted that reporter and the questions she asked."

"I had no idea until the piece ran on the news," Miller said. "But that's not why I'm calling. We have an ID."

CHAPTER TWENTY

The Doll House was a "gentlemen's club" that supposedly catered to a higher-end clientele, touting its view of the St. Croix Vineyards as an exclusive perk, along with high-quality dancers. The building's location on a dead-end road provided discretion. The exterior was decidedly understated, but inside looked like every other strip club Nikki had seen: dark, with lots of shiny chrome and several different stages.

"Sorry to drag you out of bed," Miller said.

"It's fine." Anger still coursed through her. "I wasn't going to sleep anyway. Who called in the ID?"

"Strip club owner, Bart Gibson. He's waiting for us in his office."

It was a slow night, with only a handful of patrons watching the two women who were dancing.

Nikki and Miller showed their badges and were led into a backroom by a bored-looking waitress.

"Cops are here for you," she said.

A petite man wearing a black polo shirt waved them into a tidy but small office. Miller introduced himself and Nikki.

"Her name is Janelle Gomez. She's only been working here for a few days. She didn't show up for her shift yesterday morning, so I thought she'd flaked. Couldn't believe it when I saw her tat on the news."

"You have a morning shift?" Nikki asked.

"Business meetings," Gibson said. "Married men skipping work, that sort of thing. Money obviously isn't as good, but she was new."

"Do you have any contact information for her next of kin?"

Gibson shook his head. "Story she gave me was that she left Eau Claire to get away from an abusive ex. Never mentioned any other family."

"Was she friendly with any of the other girls?"

Gibson shrugged. "Not that I know of. She kept to herself, but she wasn't here long."

If Janelle had really escaped an abusive ex, he could have caught up with her and left her in the park to die. Nikki had seen the lengths men would go in order to keep control. But those were almost always spur-of-the-moment crimes of passion, and she couldn't see an abusive ex sticking around to wait for Janelle to die so that he could go back and stage her body.

"We need you to go to the Washington County Medical Examiner's office and make a formal ID," Miller said.

Gibson paled. "Can't I just do that from a picture? I know it's her from the tattoo, anyway."

"You'll be in a separate room from the body. They have a video feed set up for occasions like this," Miller explained. "What's the address you have on file for her?" Most strip clubs paid in cash only, but usually had some kind of residential address for their workers for tax purposes.

"She was staying at the Starlight Motel across town," he said.

Miller left his card, telling Gibson to have the dayshift girls call as soon as they came in.

"I'll swing by here before lunch if I haven't heard from them," Miller told Nikki on the way outside.

"I assume the Starlight is the kind of place where you pay by the week?" Nikki asked.

He nodded. "We had a big drug bust there a couple of months ago. There's supposed to be a night manager, but whether or not someone's actually in the office is usually hit or miss. You want to wait until morning?"

"We're already behind," Nikki said. "But it's late. I can handle it myself if you want to head home."

Miller shook his head. "There's been a couple of stabbings at that place recently. Liam is still an hour away, and you shouldn't go without backup. And the employees are all familiar with me. They're more likely to trust a local."

"I'll follow you, then."

The Starlight Motel only had twelve rooms—six on each floor. Nikki shaded her hands and peered through the dingy front entrance. "It's closed, but there's a light on in the back office."

Miller banged on the door.

A skinny white guy with saggy pants and dirty shirt emerged from the back office, a cigarette dangling out of his mouth. He walked to the locked door and pointed to the "closed" sign.

Miller slammed his badge against the door.

The night manager rolled his eyes and opened up.

"What?"

"We need to see Janelle Gomez's room."

"She staying here?"

"Yes, and we believe she's been murdered," Nikki said.

He took a long drag from the cigarette and blew it in their faces. "Terrible. But I can't just let you into her room without a warrant."

"Sure you can," Miller said. "It's a possible crime scene."

"Possible ain't enough."

"I know this place is still running drugs," Miller said. "What am I going to find if I go into your office?"

"Nothing, 'cause you got no reason to search." He folded his arms and smirked.

Miller looked at Nikki. "You smell weed?"

"Yep. Sounds like probable cause to me."

"I let you in there, and I get in trouble," the man said.

Nikki showed him a picture of Janelle the club had used in its flyers. "We believe this woman was hit in the back of the head and left to die in the park. She might have been staying here since she came to town a couple of weeks ago. Either let us into the room or I'll come back with a warrant to search this entire shithole."

"Right, lady." His pockmarked chin jutted out. "I'm not stupid. You can't get no warrant for the entire place."

"She's with the FBI," Miller said. "That means she can do a lot of things. You willing to take that risk?"

The man threw his cigarette onto the concrete and stomped it out. "Stupid cops. I have to get the key."

Nikki surveyed the motel while Miller made sure the manager didn't run. Its single dumpster was full. If someone had tossed anything from the room, it should still be inside.

Nikki and Miller followed the manager past the other first-floor rooms. For a woman running from an abusive ex, a room on the end wasn't the best choice. "Did she ask for this room?"

"No idea." He lit another cigarette and knocked on room six. "Anyone home?"

"Unlock it," Miller said.

"Wait." Nikki grabbed the man's arm. "Don't touch it."

"The hell you talking about?"

She shined her flashlight app on the dark smudge near the doorknob. "That looks like blood and fairly recent." Nikki slipped her gloves on and snatched the key without asking. "Get back."

She checked the knob for other blood spots. She unlocked it and slowly turned the knob enough to open the door a crack and then motioned for Miller to push the door open from the right. Nikki stepped back and took out her gun, ready to back Miller up from the left.

He shoved the door open, keeping his body on the other side of the doorframe.

Nikki swept her light across the room. "Empty. Bathroom door closed."

Miller reached in and found the light switch, and the room was bathed in yellow light.

The bed appeared to have been hastily made. Nikki crept forward and pulled back the jungle-themed cover.

The right side of the bed had a bloodstain the size of a large cooking pot. It had spilled over onto the side, with dried streaks down to the box spring.

Suddenly Nikki was sixteen years old, staring at her mother's body, her outstretched arm dangling off the side of the bed.

Nikki pivoted past Miller. Anger she'd spent twenty years burying now simmered on the surface. She had to keep it together. If Nikki fell apart now, she wouldn't be able to put herself back together again. She breathed in the frigid air and tried to focus.

"You all right?"

"Yeah, sorry," Nikki said. "Guess we found our crime scene."

CHAPTER TWENTY-ONE

Janelle Gomez was paid up to the end of the week. She had been living out of two small duffel bags, but so far, they hadn't found a cell phone or computer. Liam had spoken to Janelle's mother on his drive into town. She told him that Janelle had canceled her phone and purchased a pay as you go in an effort to hide from her ex.

"Eau Claire police are looking for him." Dawn had broken by the time Liam and Courtney arrived, and Nikki had spent the past few hours collecting evidence.

"Housekeeping isn't exactly good in places like these." Nikki didn't want to think about what had gone on in this room over the years. "These sheets could have DNA from previous guests."

"Looks like the pillowcases are missing," Liam said. "The killer probably wrapped them around her head while transporting her."

Miller picked up the small lamp lying in the corner. "The base is covered with dried blood. Hopefully we'll get fingerprints."

Liam nodded. "Our killer hits her with the lamp hard enough to incapacitate her and then takes her to the park to leave her to suffer."

The room had only one small chest of drawers, and Janelle's few clothes were folded inside. Her wallet had been left on top of the clothes, her driver's license and fifty dollars cash still inside.

"Clearly this wasn't about money," Nikki said. "It's almost as though he wanted us to identify her."

"Condoms, a couple of packs of cigarettes, matches from the strip club." Courtney had moved on to the bedside table. "Her killer must not be a smoker. No way these are left behind."

Nikki's head spun from lack of sleep. "We need to find out if Janelle told anyone about having someone new in her life."

"I'll go back to the strip club and talk to the girls who take the morning shifts," Miller said. "Maybe I'll get something useful. The Eau Claire police are sending a detective to notify the family in person."

Courtney finished labeling an evidence bag. "I've got plenty of fingerprints from this room to analyze, and I'm hoping to get some off the ribbons in Janelle's hair. If I could get my hands on the physical evidence from Madison and Kaylee's remains, I could compare to the trace evidence we've found here."

A familiar weak sensation came over Nikki. "I'll call the medical examiner and get an ETA on the way back into town. And then we need to get some food."

CHAPTER TWENTY-TWO

Nikki sat in a back table at the Main Cafe, a mom-and-pop staple in the commercial historic district. Many of the two- and three-story buildings had endured since the nineteenth century. Nikki's mother had been on the committee responsible for the commercial historic district being placed on the National Registrar of Historic Places in 1992. The boom since then had been incredible.

"I can't get over how much Stillwater has changed," Nikki said. "Downtown looks totally different with all the boutiques and kitschy stores."

"Tourist trap equals money." Liam looked around the busy diner. "I'm freaking starving."

"You're always starving." Courtney rolled her eyes. "I'm positive you have a hollow leg."

"Here comes the server, thank God."

Main Cafe served breakfast until they closed in the afternoon, so Nikki and Courtney ordered eggs and bacon, while Liam asked for the lunch special that sounded big enough to feed three people.

Nikki tried not to inhale the coffee. She already felt lightheaded from no food and too much caffeine.

"You've been up all night?" Courtney asked.

Nikki didn't mention she hadn't slept much the night before, either. "I dozed in the jeep while I was waiting for you guys."

"You look exhausted."

Nikki shrugged. "I'll get a nap in."

"Did you and your friends spend a lot of time downtown back in the day?" Liam asked.

"Sometimes. I was a rural kid, so we usually wound up at someone's house."

Liam stared into his coffee, his hands tight around the cup.

"Liam, what are you thinking?" Nikki asked.

He bit his lower lip, his face pink beneath his freckles. "I've worked with you long enough to know you can handle whatever's thrown at you. But the public perception may be different, especially after the newspaper article and Hardin's press conference."

"To hell with public perception." Courtney stirred her coffee.

"Liam's right. Public perception matters," Nikki said. "And I'm sure Hardin's going to try to get me off the case. It's not really hard since we're here on invitation."

"You're not going to let him tag along, are you?" Liam asked.

Nikki rolled her eyes. "As if he could keep up. I plan to avoid him as much as possible and I really doubt he's going to push me too far. He just said he was keeping a close eye on me to help his image." She glanced at her phone. "Miller texted that he's at the club. He's getting a list of anyone who came into contact with her since she's been in town."

"Eau Claire police called me on the drive here," Liam said. "Janelle filed a restraining order against the ex, Kendall Jones, a few months ago," Liam said. "They've got a BOLO out on him, and his prints are in the system. He's got a domestic violence arrest from two years ago, along with a misdemeanor drug charge."

Courtney pulled out her phone and started typing. "I'm telling the lab to compare any fingerprints lifted to Jones. Maybe we can rule him out that way—if he didn't kill her." She frowned. "But I still don't get it. Making her look like a Frost victim brings you to the scene. If this is the same killer, you'd think he'd want you doing the opposite."

"Not if I thought Frost killed her; I'd drop the girls and focus on catching him," Nikki said. "Which brings us back to the possibility that Janelle didn't know the girls or their killer at all and was just a sacrificial lamb."

Courtney leaned out of the booth and made a face. "Newport's coming into the restaurant with some of the protesters. I recognize the girl in the red coat and the chubby dude with the Vikings jacket."

Nikki rubbed her temples. "Is Caitlin following us or is this the only decent breakfast place left in town?"

"The special is cheap and supposed to be delicious." Liam's double cheeseburger with a massive side of waffle fries looked like a heart attack in progress.

"Surely you'll need a box?" Nikki asked.

"What for?"

Nikki rolled her eyes and dug into her eggs.

"Newport's sauntering over here like she owns the place," Courtney said. "Her buddies are all watching."

"Agent Hunt, nice to see you." Caitlin still wore sensible clothes, but her face was suspiciously made-up. "I was shooting some background shots when I noticed your jeep."

"Spare me," Nikki said. "We're working here, Caitlin."

"Have you identified the victim in the park?"

"No comment," Nikki said.

"I heard about Amy Banks. The poor woman is going through hell. Did you learn anything new when you visited the school?"

Nikki knew it must have been Jade Eby who'd reported their visit to her mother, who'd gone straight to Newport.

"How's Connie doing, then?" Nikki asked. "I assume she's the one who told you we visited the school."

Caitlin shrugged. "It's important that I speak to the people in town who lived here when you did, preferably ones who knew both you and Mark Todd."

"Connie didn't know me."

"What about Annmarie?"

Nikki's blood ran cold. "You called her?"

Annmarie had been Nikki's best friend since they were little, and she'd picked Nikki up at the party the night her parents were killed. After the murders, Nikki felt like the only way to survive was shutting everyone out and focusing on school so she could get out of Stillwater and forget everything. Annmarie had been the only person Nikki made a valiant attempt to stay in contact with, but Annmarie was a painful memory of Stillwater, so Nikki eventually pushed her away, too. She did at least know that she was a nurse and lived somewhere in Wisconsin.

Caitlin nodded. "She told me to fuck off and to never call her again."

Nikki drained her coffee, trying to hide the swell of pride she felt. She shouldn't have been surprised that her oldest friend wanted nothing to do with the documentary, but Annmarie certainly didn't owe Nikki her loyalty.

"Have you looked at the evidence, yet?"

Liam shoved his plate away. "We're discussing official police business. Please leave."

Caitlin looked around. "It's a diner. I can't eat?"

"As long as you don't sit with us," Nikki said.

"That's right." Courtney swung around to face her. "Take your ass to your table before I help you get there."

"Are you threatening me?"

Courtney stared her down.

"Unprofessional," Caitlin said as she walked briskly back to the group of protestors sitting around a large table, Bobby Vance among them. Nikki looked over her shoulder long enough to see that he sat quietly with his arms over his chest; he seemed partially separated from the others.

"Sergeant Miller's just arrived." Courtney waved him over.

Miller sat down next to Nikki and looked at Liam's half-eaten cheeseburger. "You going to finish that?"

Nikki laughed at the look on Liam's face and passed Miller her toast. "You find anything out from the day shift?"

Miller ate the toast in a few bites and then drank the water Courtney offered him. "You won't believe it."

"Excuse me." A man wearing an old peacoat and corduroy pants had slunk over. "Are you Nicole Walsh?"

Nikki took out her badge. "Nikki Hunt, Special Agent, FBI."

He smirked. "Is that supposed to scare me?"

"Do you want me to scare you?" Her temper threatened to boil over.

"You put an innocent man in prison. For twenty years," he began to say.

"Enough," Miller interrupted.

"Leave it alone, Doug." Bobby Vance appeared at his side and tugged on the other man's arm. He was a couple of inches shorter than Doug but far more lean and muscular. "She's working. And this isn't helpful to Mark's case."

"Listen," Nikki snapped. She appreciated Bobby stepping in, but she could stand up for herself. "I don't have to answer to you or anyone else. You have a problem with the conviction, talk to Sheriff Hardin."

Caitlin's eyes lit up like a predator's as she walked over. "Are you saying Hardin deliberately mishandled the case?"

"I'm saying that I was a sixteen-year-old kid. My statement alone didn't convict Mark Todd. Go bark up the right tree."

Doug pointed his finger at Nikki. "You need to admit you were wrong before shit gets out of control. People are angry."

Bobby moved toward him, but Miller blocked his path. "Are you threatening a law enforcement officer, Doug?" Miller's tone sounded even more threatening than his physical stature.

Doug held up his hands. "Everyone just wants to hear from her."

"I already gave Ms. Newport my statement," Nikki said. "My team and I are one hundred percent focused on these active murder investigations."

"We have a right to protest," Doug said. "First Amendment."

Nikki struggled to keep her tone steady. "I respect that right. You do not, however, have the right to impede my investigations."

Bobby rolled his eyes. "He just wants to be included in her stupid documentary."

"Doug, you aren't helping Mark's case at all." Newport turned to leave and then glanced at Nikki. "Agent Hunt, if you ever want to discuss your feelings about Sheriff Hardin, give me a call."

Why couldn't Nikki control her big mouth?

Newport dropped a couple of bills onto the protesters' table on her way out of the restaurant.

Doug glared at Nikki, obviously torn between pride and common sense as Bobby lingered behind him.

"Go on back to your table, or I will take you down to the station," Miller said.

"I almost forgot. The FBI does whatever it wants and gets a free pass." Doug puffed out his chest, emboldened once again. "Is that why you joined, Agent Hunt? To hide behind the badge?"

Liam stood, red-faced. "Do you know anything about respect?"

"Big guy finally stands up for his girlfriend." Doug smirked at her. "How are we supposed to count on you to catch those poor girls' killer? You can't even see what's right in front of you."

"Oh, I see what's in front of me." Nikki stepped around Miller and glanced at the rest of the protestors. She lowered her voice. "Which girl over there are you trying to impress?"

Doug shoved Nikki out of his face. "Fuck you."

Bobby grabbed Doug's coat collar and threw him into a nearby table. Doug got to his feet and lunged, but Miller caught him by the arm.

"You were warned." He snapped cuffs around Doug's wrists. "How stupid are you?"

"No fighting in my restaurant." Main Street's owner had come out of the kitchen.

"It's under control," Miller said. "Doug's going to the station with me."

Nikki mouthed a "thank you" to Bobby and then glanced at the frazzled owner. "Sir, do you mind if I use the back door to exit? I won't be setting the alarm off?"

"No, you come through the kitchen," he replied, holding the door open for her.

Nikki followed him, head down, hands clenched. She hated walking away and leaving the mess for Miller and Liam, but she wasn't sure how much longer she could control her temper. Why did these people think that berating her would help Mark Todd? Didn't they care about justice for Maddie and Kaylee, too? At least Bobby had the guts to stand up for the girls. Newport should have stepped in from the beginning instead of waiting for Nikki to say something worth pouncing on.

Why had she engaged? Nothing had changed except Caitlin had fodder for her documentary.

She thanked the owner and stepped out into the alley. Cold wind sliced through her sweater. Nikki inhaled the freezing air, trying to clear her head and focus on the present. There were still so many threads that didn't make sense to Nikki and she was getting impatient. She should have the results from Janelle's autopsy within the next few hours, but it wasn't quick enough for her. She needed to ask Brianna more questions and find out if Madison and Kaylee had other friends with vehicles, as well as locate Kaylee's phone. The killer's efforts at distracting her hadn't completely failed. Her workload had doubled, and so had her frustration.

She hadn't had an opportunity yet to ask Miller if he'd found anything out from his interviews at the strip club. She was getting more and more irritated that Mark's retrial was getting in her way and every moment considering that he wasn't her parents' killer was a moment not spent investigating her case. Her ability to compartmentalize was a skill she'd long prided herself on.

Her devotion to her job was one of the many things that had come between Nikki and Tyler. She had a tendency to become hyper focused and forget everything—and everyone else—in her life until Lacey came along. Finding out she was pregnant had sent her life into a brief tailspin. Nikki had been terrified that if she couldn't balance her job and a husband, she'd fare even worse with a child. She'd never been so grateful to be wrong. Lacey had brought a sense of clarity to her life and a purpose beyond chasing bad guys. Nikki had become even more compartmentalized, determined not to let the darkness of her job interfere with being a mother.

This case had changed everything. What if she couldn't keep her focus together enough to find the killer?

Nikki wrapped her arms around her chest, shivering with cold. "Damn it." She'd left her coat inside. Nikki tried the door, but it must have automatically locked from inside. She found her phone and texted Courtney. The last thing Nikki wanted to do was walk around front. Caitlin and the protesters were no doubt lingering, waiting to pounce again. Nikki would freeze first.

Tires crunched through the snow. Nikki's stomach lurched into her throat as a familiar pickup half-slid around the corner.

Rory Todd rolled down his window. "Need a ride to the sheriff's office?"

"Are you following me?"

"I eat here every day."

She tightened her sweater against the icy wind. "I'm just waiting for Courtney to bring me my coat."

"You have a knack for leaving it behind. At least get into the truck and wait so you don't freeze," he said. "Your lips are already turning blue. I won't bring up my brother's case. Scout's honor."

Nikki's fingers ached with cold. It could be several more minutes before someone came with her coat. She sent Courtney a second text, telling her she had a ride and asked her to bring her coat to the station.

Her heart fluttering with nerves. Nikki grabbed the door and climbed into the big truck. "I need to get to work, so we can head to the station now, if you don't mind."

Rory smiled at her. "I don't mind at all."

CHAPTER TWENTY-THREE

Rory's truck was surprisingly clean for a contractor, save for the floor mats. Trying to keep them clean during a Minnesota winter was futile.

Rory drove in silence, staring straight ahead. His wool hat lay on the seat between them, his dark curls held back by sunglasses.

"What?" His green eyes caught hers as he stopped for a yellow light.

Nikki flushed. "Nothing. I was just thinking…"

"About what?"

She wasn't about to tell him she'd been admiring his hair. "Just about how awkward this is."

He laughed and then cleared his throat. "I saw your jeep and then noticed Newport's truck. I planned on laying into her, but when I saw Miller exit the diner with someone in handcuffs, I knew something was going down."

"How'd you know I was out back?"

"Didn't see you inside or in the car. Figured you made a quick escape."

"Thanks for the ride," Nikki said. "One of the protestors had a few things to say to me and it got out of hand."

Rory glanced at her. "That kid from the other night?"

"No," Nikki said. "He actually tried to defuse the situation. It was someone else who thinks they know better than the police."

Rory didn't say anything, and Nikki hurried to clarify.

"It's not that I don't support what the Innocence Project lawyers are doing. There are wrongful convictions that need to be overturned. And if this guy was serious and not trying to impress someone, then I respect his passion. But he doesn't get to talk to me the way he did. What happened to respecting the badge?"

"Bad cops make people disrespectful. But you're not a bad cop," Rory said quickly. "And some people just have a problem with authority."

"He pushed me," Nikki said.

Rory's jaw tensed. "He did what?"

"I kind of baited him into it," Nikki admitted. "Miller had warned him once, so he arrested the guy. I'm not going to press charges, but he can sweat it out at the station for a while."

"Good." Rory circled around the government center complex. "Newport's done nothing but rile people up. My parents think the documentary's the only reason the Innocence Project is involved."

"Newport uses that to her advantage," Nikki said.

"But my mom did all the legwork. She's the one who found out about the DNA—sorry. I said I wouldn't talk about it."

Saying anything more about Mark's case was foolish, but Nikki couldn't stop the words. "Your mother found the samples that weren't tested? How? I mean, why didn't the defense already know about them?"

"I was going to tell you about that the other night before you left the bar. Mom ran into the deputy who'd done the evidence collection back then. He works in a different county now. He told her about the biological sample from your mother, and he mentioned some were taken from Mark that have somehow disappeared. He didn't like the way the investigation was run from the beginning. Hardin was adamant the sample wasn't bodily fluids. The other deputy had the latest equipment and training. He believed it was a big enough sample to test, even if the results wound up being inconclusive. He understood the science, Hardin and the sheriff didn't. Hardin's influence won."

Why had Hardin been so against testing the sample? DNA had been used successfully in court by the early nineties and had been responsible for both convictions and exonerations by 1993. She understood the budgetary issue, but cops had been as afraid of DNA as they were excited by it. She'd heard countless stories in her first years on the job about detectives wanting everything tested because they didn't want to have their convictions thrown out later because of DNA. A wrongful conviction was a huge black mark on a law enforcement career.

"That's why Patsy Moran took the case." It all made sense now. "She's spoken with the deputy. He's convinced her as much as Mark has."

"There's something else," Rory said. "I probably shouldn't be telling you this, but it's not your fault, and if some reporter like Newport finds out—"

"Finds out what?" Nikki was sick of being the last to know.

"That same deputy remembers the paramedic telling Hardin that you should have a tox screen, because you weren't acting like a normal shock victim. It took her a while, but Patsy tracked down the paramedic. He's working in Minneapolis now, but he remembers the case. He's willing to testify that he completed the tox screen and sent it to the hospital to be tested. But the hospital has no record of receiving it."

Nikki almost shouted in relief. She'd been right about the blood test, which meant her memories of the night were accurate. Her brief vindication quickly ebbed. "The local hospital? Not the state lab?"

"Stillwater used the hospital lab back then," Rory explained. "That was before the state lab started doing all the testing for every county. Anyway, there's no record of the test, but the paramedic says you had more than just alcohol in your system."

"But I didn't." Nikki's mouth had gone dry.

Rory glanced at her. "He said you kept talking about not being able to wake up. He thought it was nonsense at first, but you started talking about the party and that you couldn't wake up no matter how hard you tried."

Nikki couldn't speak, her mind cartwheeling with the information. She'd only had a few drinks that night, but they had been more vodka than cranberry juice. She remembered talking with John and his friends and then …

Did she actually remember making the decision to lie down? John had said something about her needing to lie down, but suddenly Nikki realized she didn't remember going down the hall and into the room.

"I swear I didn't do anything other than drink. I think a couple of people at the party had pot, but there weren't any hard drugs lying around."

"Is it possible someone slipped something into your drink?" he asked softly.

"No one really knew about the date-rape drug then," Nikki said.

"Liquid ecstasy was also legal at the time," Rory said. "I know it wasn't deemed an illegal substance until 2000. In the eighties and nineties, athletes used it as a performance enhancer."

"I'm aware of that." The high dose of GHB in liquid ecstasy made a person helpless when combined with alcohol. While a smaller dose produced a euphoric effect that some athletes claimed gave them an edge, research proved that to be false. She knew what Rory was getting at. John and his friends all ran track in college. Maybe one or more of them used the drug because they believed it made them run faster. "John was by my side most of the night. If one of his buddies tried to put something in my drink, he would have noticed."

"I'd imagine he would."

The words hung between them, their implication clear. "John had no reason to drug me. I mean, we'd already…" Nikki flushed, annoyed at how easily Rory could get to her. "And frankly, the only person with motive would have been Mark. He's the one who tried to attack me."

Rory's jaw clenched, and for the first time looked like he was ready to lose his cool. "Then why did Hardin bury the tox test?"

"I'm sure he didn't. It was probably misplaced at the hospital." Did she really believe that anymore?

Rory stopped in front of the county government building. "I hope you're right, but if you aren't and news about the tox report comes out, everything changes. I called Patsy this morning and asked her not to leak it. She said that she had no intention of talking to the media unless the report was actually found. But if word gets out, the protestors are really going to be after you."

Nikki stared at him, the flush on her cheeks morphing into a rush of emotion. "You called her to protect me?"

Rory shrugged. "I told you that I saw you as a victim. Besides, you're here on a case. It takes precedence. Get this bastard off the streets, and then sit down with the evidence. That's all I ask."

"I will, I promise." Nikki hopped down from the truck. She didn't want to believe Hardin could have been so bitter he would let a killer go free in order to punish Mark for sleeping with his wife. But if her tox screen had come back with drugs in her system, her entire testimony would have been thrown out.

Had Rory used his conversation with the defense attorney as a way to make Nikki feel obligated to look at the evidence file? Nikki realized she didn't care if he had. It was still an act of kindness she desperately appreciated. "Thanks for the ride."

Rory stared at her a beat too long. "You're welcome."

CHAPTER TWENTY-FOUR

Nikki sat down in one of the conference room chairs and stared blankly out of the window. Could she really have been drugged that night? It seemed impossible, but even if the paramedic had been wrong in his assessment, he had no reason to lie about the blood test. Was Hardin so blinded by his anger at Mark Todd that he'd risked his job and buried the test?

Nikki shook her head. Lost evidence was an unfortunate part of the job. New procedures and better training made a huge difference, and a mistake like that would have been much more likely back then.

Rory was getting to her. His faith in Mark made Rory's argument seem solid, but once Nikki looked at the evidence, she would be certain the right man was in prison. Still, she hated the idea of crushing Rory's hopes. He was the only person in her life who had any clue what it had been like to live under the microscope of the murders. What would happen to him when the DNA proved once and for all that Rory had wasted years of energy on his brother?

Nikki had to get her head straight. Rory wasn't a part of her life. He was an acquaintance, and they were connected by tragedy, but that was it.

The door swung open, and Courtney sauntered in. "Here's your coat. Guess who I just saw leaving the complex?"

"No clue."

"None other than Rory Todd." Courtney plopped into the chair next to Nikki. "I assume he was here to talk to you? Seems like he's done a lot of that in a short time. Not that I mind seeing him. He's easy on the eyes."

"He gave me a ride from the diner."

Courtney's eyes widened. "I wondered how you got here. Why's he being so nice when he should hate you?"

"He wants me to look at my parents' files. He's certain Mark's innocent."

"So he's buttering you up?"

"He's not like that." Nikki spoke more vehemently than she'd intended, and Courtney grinned.

"Oh really. Do tell."

"We're supposed to be working a case." Nikki frowned.

"We are," Courtney said. "But we're also friends. I just want to make sure this guy isn't taking advantage of you. Besides, I know that look. You're wound tight inside and desperate to talk to someone."

Maybe Courtney was right. Talking things out in an investigation often helped things make more sense, so why shouldn't it work for her Rory situation?

Nikki sighed and started with falling on her rear at the gas station. She told Courtney about her conversations with Roger Mathews and Rory about the untested evidence.

"You went to a bar with Rory and didn't tell me?" Courtney swiveled in one of the chairs.

"I really haven't had the chance," Nikki said. "Janelle was found the next morning, and we've been busy."

"I'll let it slide for now. You just promised him that you would look at the evidence, which means he must have said something pretty convincing."

Nikki rested her head on the back of her chair. "I'm beginning to wonder if my testimony was reliable back then. I was always told that I'd sobered up and the toxicology report proved I was a reliable witness. But there's no record of the tox report, and I know my blood was taken." She didn't want to divulge the information about the paramedic until she knew more.

"It was a long time ago, and with everything being transferred from paper to digital, things could have been lost," Courtney said. "Did you do any drugs that night?

"That's one road I didn't go down." There was no evidence anyone had liquid ecstasy at the party. She was making too many wild assumptions, and if Rory hadn't hinted at it, Nikki never would have considered the idea.

"Then I don't think you have anything to worry about," Courtney said. "It's on record that you passed the field test. The rest is on the police."

"I still want to know what happened to the tox test." Maybe she hadn't actually been drugged, but the tox report instead showed her blood alcohol level was still high enough to be an issue on the stand. That would have made Hardin look foolish, and it would have put the case against Mark in jeopardy.

"I've got a friend in records. I can ask her to look for the test. In a perfect system, all results from the hospital labs should be entered into the state database."

"Can you trust her not to go to the media?"

Courtney nodded. "I wouldn't ask her if I didn't."

"Then do it. Just keep everything between us."

"Are you starting to think Mark could be innocent?"

"I don't know, but I'm starting to wonder if I put my trust in the right people back then. I was scared, I was shocked, I'd just lost my parents." The implications made Nikki's stomach turn. If Mark Todd was truly innocent, he was just as much of a victim as Nikki. She'd known Mark since they were kids. Why hadn't she ever stopped to consider his side of the story?

Because she'd never considered a police officer could lie. And she'd never allowed herself to think about that night or the days following. She'd put what happened in a box and never thought about it again.

"Is he telling the truth?" Confusion fogged up her brain. *She'd been drinking, laughing, dancing. And then everything blurred into darkness. Her head felt like it was full of cotton.*

"Come on, Nik. What do you think? It's your own fault. You were all over him earlier, anyway."

"No, I wasn't."

John rolled his eyes. "Everyone here saw it."

She slapped him, maybe. People laughed; everyone was watching. And then what?

"Nikki." Courtney's voice brought her back from her memory. "We'll figure this out. Once we've caught our killer, you'll have all the time in the world to revisit your parents' case."

Nikki appreciated Courtney's support, but she wasn't sure she could stay focused. "Thanks for listening."

"Liam just texted me. He said he was trying to get a hold of you," Courtney said. "Remember Miller saying he got something good at the club before everything went down?"

Nikki's head felt like a fifty-pound weight as she nodded.

"You're not going to like it."

Nikki sat up straight, adrenaline trickling through her system. "What is it?"

"Two of the morning shift dancers recognized John Banks. He's a regular."

CHAPTER TWENTY-FIVE

Roan Pharmaceuticals was on the north end of the Minneapolis metro area. Tucked between two large interstates, the location provided relative privacy in the middle of a high traffic area. Nikki circled the campus in search of Liam's silver Prius. He'd offered to drive, but he had some things to catch up on in the office, and his driving her to Stillwater and then back into the city didn't make much sense. He'd taken her back to the café to pick up her jeep, and the quiet had given Nikki time to think.

At the very least, John had lied to her about knowing Janelle. Nikki had been careful about the information she'd shared with the Bankses, but if John had killed Madison and Kaylee, he was close enough to the investigation to realize that another murder would be a good distraction.

Was he capable of such horrible things? An hour ago, Nikki would have insisted he wouldn't have hurt anyone. But her conversation with Rory changed everything.

After the trial, she had worked hard to bury her memories of that night, training her mind to immediately discard any snippet that might break through. They were just blurry blips of memory, and most of them never made any sense. Nikki had always blamed it on the trauma she'd experienced, but what if Rory was right? What if she'd been drugged?

John had gone to college on a track scholarship. In high school, he'd been the state champion in the 800 meters and anchored a winning relay team his senior year. Nikki remembered John saying his first two years running college track had been average.

But he was determined to be a top-five runner his last two years. Hearing that he used performance enhancers wouldn't surprise Nikki. But she rarely refused him for sex, so why drug her? And would he have known what the GHB could do if she were already intoxicated?

Nikki had been a junior in college when the date rape drug became national news and a big issue for college campuses. As a resident advisor, she'd worried one of her girls would end up a victim. She and another RA worked together to account for every girl on their respective floors, and as far as Nikki knew, nothing happened to any of her residents.

But just because its effects weren't nationally known in 1993 didn't mean that some users weren't aware of it. The lack of rape reporting—especially date rape—also meant it could have been an issue before the media found out.

Courtney was heading back into St. Paul to process evidence, but she'd promised Nikki to do some research on the known effects of drinking and liquid ecstasy in the nineties.

Nikki debated asking John flat out, but they'd come to investigate his connection with Janelle. And she wanted more information before she confronted him about the past. Right now she only had a missing blood test and theories.

She finally located Liam's car and parked nearby. Liam joined her and they walked toward the main building together.

"Where are we on the industrial freezers?" Nikki's face stung from the cold wind.

"Just about every restaurant and grocery store has at least one," Liam said. "So far, I haven't connected any of those to Madison or Kaylee."

"What about hunters?"

"You know how many people have a hunting license?" Liam asked. "And then there are the poachers. But the only connection to an industrial freezer is Hanson, and his alibi is good. We aren't getting a warrant for his father-in-law's place. You didn't bring Sergeant Miller, I see."

Nikki shook her head. "He's busy with Doug and paperwork, but I spoke with him before I left. Both morning-shift waitresses remembered John Banks. He allegedly has a couple of favorite dancers, but neither one of them is working today. They'll be on tomorrow, so plan on talking with them."

Roan Pharmaceuticals' network of buildings and skywalks rivaled a small hospital, with the sales and marketing department spanning an entire floor.

"I showed him Janelle's picture, and he lied to my face." Nikki wasn't leaving the building until John told the truth.

His administrative assistant said John wasn't taking any meetings today, but she changed her tune when Nikki and Liam showed their badges. She led them to a corner office with a bank of windows.

Nikki beat the assistant to the closed door. "We can take it from here, thank you."

The woman looked irritated but nodded.

Nikki knocked on the door and opened it without waiting for a response. "Hi, John."

John jerked his head off the desk. He'd obviously been asleep. His hair was disheveled and his eyes bloodshot. "Nikki. I wasn't expecting you," he said, and then looked at Liam. "Who are you?"

Nikki stepped forward. "He's Agent Wilson. He was at your house when Amy overdosed. How is she?"

"Okay," John said. "She's trying to focus on Bailey. Have you found something? Or are you here about the autopsy results so we can finally bury Madison?"

Nikki sat down in the big leather chair in front of John's desk and Liam took the other one. The corner office had an impressive view of the snow-covered park surrounding the campus. "Director of Sales and Marketing for big pharma. That's pretty high up in the food chain."

"I guess." John rested his chin on his hand. "Why are you here?"

"The autopsies aren't complete yet," Nikki said. "I'm here about the murder of Janelle Gomez."

"Who?"

"The woman found in the park," Nikki said. "You told me you didn't recognize her."

"Oh, right. Sorry, I'm exhausted. Haven't been sleeping much." John rubbed his eyes. "What about this woman?"

"Her boss at The Doll House is the one who identified her," Liam said.

John nodded. "I know that place."

"We know," Nikki said. "Two of the dancers said you're a morning regular."

He sighed and reclined in his chair. "Look, I'm not proud of it. Things haven't been great between Amy and me since Madison disappeared. I go a few times a week to blow off steam. But I don't pay for sex."

"I really don't care about your personal affairs," Nikki replied. "I do care that you're the common denominator between Madison, Kaylee and Janelle."

John paled. "You're not suggesting I hurt Maddie, are you? I would never."

"We cross-referenced Janelle's shifts with the girls' accounts. We know you've been at the club during her shift. And we're getting a warrant for the security videos from inside the club. The owner says they cover every angle. So, you might as well tell the truth now." Nikki placed Janelle's promo picture onto his desk. "You don't recognize her? That's the story you're going with?"

"I don't remember seeing her there. I only interact with a couple of girls," John said. "The rest are just in the background."

"When was the last time you went to the club?"

"The day Madison and Kaylee were found. In the morning, before we got any news."

"And you haven't been there since?"

"No." He slumped back in the chair. "I'm too damned numb to do anything but come to work and try to be present at home."

"We'll see you on the security videos. You might as well be honest now and stop wasting our time."

"Christ." John slammed his hands on the desk. "I'm telling the truth, Nikki. Why are you on my ass about this?"

"I'm doing my job."

"Then you're doing a pretty bad job of it. You're here, wasting time on me instead of looking for the bastard who killed my daughter." His hard eyes focused on Nikki and a feeling of anxiety seeped through her. "You're supposed to be one of the best. Or is the media right? Are you too focused on Mark Todd to do your job?"

"The media has no idea what they're talking about."

"Then why are you going around asking about your blood test? And hanging out with his brother?"

"Excuse me?"

"You didn't think I'd find out about that? Stillwater's still a small town, and I've got connections everywhere. People think you're trying to butter up Rory because you're afraid your reputation's going to be ruined."

Nikki had been stupid to think John had changed. He was still the same guy who wanted to keep control. But she wasn't the same insecure girl who dutifully gave in to him.

"I have zero worries about my reputation. I just want to make sure the right man is in prison."

"You know he is, for Christ's sake. Rory's manipulating you to feel sorry for his brother."

"That's not what he's doing."

"Then what is it? Why are you hanging out with him instead of looking for Maddie's killer? Are you that hard up for a man's attention? Just like old times, then."

Nikki bristled. John's demeanor had changed so quickly, but something about his reaction felt normal to her. "We have reason to believe Janelle might have been drugged. Would you know anything about that?"

Liam stiffened but didn't call her bluff.

"Why?" John snapped. "Because I work at a pharmaceutical company?"

Nikki stared at him, letting the implication linger.

John's face reddened, a flicker of nerves in his eyes. "Get out of my office."

Nikki stood, turned on her heel and walked out with Liam beside her. Her hands trembled with anger. How had she forgotten John's manipulative side? Nikki knew exactly how to deal with people like him, but she'd allowed him to back her into a corner.

Liam walked in silence next to her until they reached the elevator. "What's this about drugs?"

She didn't want to tell him about her conversation with Rory, especially after John's accusation. "Just a hunch. I wanted to see his reaction."

"You definitely ticked him off," Liam said. "Why didn't you put him in his place for talking to you like that?"

Nikki pushed the button and then shoved her hands in her pockets. She couldn't meet Liam's gaze. "I did."

"Did you not hear him imply something was going on between you and Rory? Or that you weren't doing your job?"

"John thrives on the power he gets from drawing people into arguments and then twisting things around to be their fault. I'm not going to give him the satisfaction." Nikki wished she believed her own reasoning.

"Is that what he was like when you two dated?"

"Yes, and it appears he hasn't changed all that much."

"You do realize he's scared of you, right?" Liam asked as the doors opened. "Maybe he used to manipulate you out of insecurity or whatever, but he's scared of you. He knows you have the power to make his life miserable."

"Only if he's done something." Nikki changed the subject before her emotions overwhelmed her. "You sent the security videos to the geeks at the office, right?"

"They'll be finished by tomorrow afternoon."

John's proclivity for strip clubs and possible adultery still didn't give him a motive to hurt Madison and Kaylee. Kaylee had tried to blackmail Ricky; would she do the same thing to her friend's father? What if John had gone after Kaylee and Madison had been collateral damage?

And where did Janelle Gomez fit into the picture, if she even fit at all? Maybe she really had been killed by someone else who'd been smart enough to use the current interest in Frost to cover his tracks.

John claimed he'd started hitting the strip club after the disappearance, but Nikki had her doubts. The Stillwater-Hudson area had at least ten so-called gentlemen's clubs. Janelle working at John's strip club of choice couldn't be a coincidence.

"Dig into John's extracurricular activity. Find out if he's a frequent flyer anywhere else and if he's really as hands-off as he says. Check public record and see if he and Amy have ever been legally separated or a motion filed. I want to know how good his marriage actually is, and neither one of them is going to be honest."

"Any suggestions on where to start?"

"The strippers," Nikki said. "He came to them for comfort and to get his ego fed. If he talked shit about Amy, he said it to them."

CHAPTER TWENTY-SIX

Nikki reset the house alarm and headed to her bedroom. She'd decided to swing by the house after the visit to Roan Pharmaceuticals to get some clean clothes and then stop at Tyler's to surprise Lacey.

Nikki wished she didn't have to drive back to Stillwater. She'd kill for a night in her own bed. She sifted through her closet and chose two pairs of jeans, but all of her tops seemed frumpy. Not that her usual attire made her look sloppy, but the jeans hugged her curves. She might as well find tops that did the same thing.

"Who am I trying to impress?" she muttered. Before she allowed herself to think of the answer, the house plunged into darkness.

Nikki shuffled across the room until her knees hit the bed. She felt around for her phone and then turned on the flashlight feature. The house seemed eerily quiet as she hurried down the hall to the front window. The neighbor's lights were on.

"So are my driveway lights." She spoke to the empty space as she peered out of the front window. The lights were motion-sensored, but Tyler's truck wasn't in the driveway. Her garage only had one stall.

Alarm bells were screeching in her head. The neighbors still had power, but she couldn't see all of the houses on her side of the street. Maybe it was a partial outage and she just couldn't see who else was affected.

The circuit breaker was outside, protected by a padlocked cover. The padlock was key coded, so picking it was impossible. Nikki didn't even know the code by heart.

Her security system had a backup battery that would supposedly last at least twelve hours in an outage. The panel by the front door indicated the alarm was still on. Nikki had no idea if the security cameras were still recording.

She peeked around the window, searching for signs of an intruder. No fresh footprints in the snow, but the breaker was on the side of the house, just a few inches to the left of the dining room window.

Nikki slipped around the table, dread settling into the pit of her stomach. Something wasn't right.

The window suddenly exploded, glass flying like shrapnel. Nikki raised her arms in front of her face, but pain burst across the side of her head. Her knees hit the floor hard.

CHAPTER TWENTY-SEVEN

"So much for unbreakable glass." Nikki pressed the ice pack against her head. The bleeding had stopped, but the wound still burned. Someone had broken into the protective cover on her house's circuit breaker to cut the electricity. Her security cameras covered the front and back doors, along with the garage, but the shooter had avoided all of them. "It looks like whoever did this parked down the road and climbed over the fence and headed straight for the circuit breaker."

"Thank God it was only an air gun." Tyler had been furious when he found out she had a head wound and still drove to his house to surprise Lacey. "How did they know you were even home?"

"They didn't," Nikki said. "I didn't even know I would be home until I was halfway to Roan Pharmaceuticals. And I didn't tell anyone but Liam." Knowing that someone had cut the power and then waited to see her moving through the house was bad enough, but what if Lacey had been home?

Nikki had accepted the dangers of her job years ago, but the idea that her daughter could be in danger sent a wave of fear through her. The sight of her mother's bandaged head had scared her, but Nikki distracted her with pizza. By the time they'd finished eating, Lacey seemed to have forgotten about the injury. She'd spent the rest of the evening snuggled in Nikki's lap until her bath.

"I suppose people use air guns for target practice." Tyler leaned against the kitchen counter, arms across his chest.

The .177 pellet had busted through the glass with precision, and the responding officer had told Nikki the air gun used was likely a higher-end model because of the likely distance between the snow tracks on the side of the house and the window.

"My guess is the person came to send a message." "Liar" had been spray painted in red across the siding, right above the circuit breaker. "It's got to be one of those protesters. One of them caused a scene at the diner and shoved me. Miller kept him at the station for hours, but one of his buddies must have followed me home. The tracks in the snow look like generic snow boots, likely a man's size ten or eleven."

"You didn't say anything about having issues with the protestors."

"It isn't any of your concern." The words came out more harshly than she'd intended.

"It is my concern when it puts our daughter at risk."

Nikki glared at him. "That's why I'm staying in Stillwater, and I called you tonight. What else do you want me to do?"

"I don't know," he snapped. "I don't understand anything you do anymore."

"I can't do this with you right now. No one in Stillwater even knows I have a daughter. I've kept her completely out of this. And my address is unlisted. Someone either went to a lot of work to find me, or they followed me."

Unless Newport had done the dirty work, but as much as Nikki disliked the woman, she couldn't see her sending her minions to commit violence.

"Has anyone else been hanging around?"

Nikki immediately thought of Rory and flushed. He wouldn't do such a thing. "Not really."

"What about Frost?"

"What about him?"

"You're letting the media imply he might be responsible for the Stillwater murders. If his ego is as big as you say it is, maybe he's pissed and sending you a message."

Nikki had already thought about Frost and ruled him out. "This isn't the sort of message he would send. It's too crass. And he knows I don't really think he's the killer."

"How could you possibly know that?"

"Because it's my job, Tyler."

"Yeah, well your job's going to get you killed one day."

Nikki gritted her teeth. Tyler had never been comfortable with her working in the violent crime unit, and he wasn't capable of fathoming her need to understand why people committed such terrible crimes. Nikki often wondered if his real issue was jealousy over the recognition she received for her work, but she didn't dare bring the idea up. The argument always ended in a stalemate. "I can handle it."

"What about Lacey?" Tyler demanded. "If something happens to you, what am I supposed to tell her? That Mommy chose—"

"Stop." Nikki stood up, shaking with anger. "Don't say another word."

Tyler's cheeks reddened. "I'm not trying to make you feel bad."

"That's exactly what you're trying to do. It's what you always try to do when it comes to my job. This is what I do, and it's not going to change," Nikki said. "How many times do we need to have this argument?"

The muscles in his jaw twitched. "No need to have it. You aren't going to change."

"Neither are you." Nikki gathered her coat and bag. "I'll call Lacey tomorrow."

"You're seriously driving back to Stillwater tonight? With a head injury?"

"I'm fine."

Tyler closed his eyes for a moment. "Look, I know we're mad at each other, but please stay in the spare bedroom tonight. It's late, and you've got to be tired. I won't bother you anymore tonight. And you can take her to school before you go to work in the morning. Lacey will be so happy."

Nikki wanted to tell him no, but her exhausted body overruled her emotions. "Okay, Tyler. But this doesn't change anything."

"Don't worry," he said. "I gave up on you changing a long time ago."

CHAPTER TWENTY-EIGHT

The air bullet had hit her hard enough to draw blood, but the wound was superficial. The bruise, however, was not. By the time Nikki arrived at the medical examiner's office in St. Paul the next morning, the welt above her ear looked like the mark from a branding iron, and the two-inch-long purple bruise along her scalp was impossible to hide. But she had received the call from Liam just after she'd dropped Lacey off at school, and she knew now more than ever she needed to solve the case and get out of Stillwater. Time away from Lacey was tearing Nikki apart and she wasn't any safer for it.

The medical examiner's office in St. Paul handled the death investigations of multiple smaller counties, including Washington County. Its location in the big medical complex in downtown St. Paul meant parking was usually hit and miss. Nikki finally found an open space in the east parking ramp. She walked as fast as possible in her heavy snow boots, and by the time she checked in with the front desk and joined Liam at the medical examiner's office, her head had started to ache again. They walked in silence to the autopsy suite, Nikki's nerves on edge. The fact that the chief medical examiner wanted to go over things with the bodies present was not a good sign, but at least she was finally getting answers now that Madison and Kaylee's bodies had defrosted.

Dr. Blanchard was already waiting for them, impatiently tapping her foot. "You're late." Melissa was the state's first African-American chief medical examiner. Nikki had worked with her on several cases, and while her no-nonsense approach intimidated some, Nikki appreciated it.

"My fault," Nikki said. "I'm sorry."

Blanchard raised an eyebrow. "You run into a door?"

"Something like that."

"Right," Blanchard said. "First, Janelle Gomez. Her family wants to give her a proper Catholic funeral, so I've released the body. She was hit with a blunt round object. The lamp you found at the motel is the likely culprit."

"Did she die instantly?"

"No, given the level of frostbite on her body, I think she was alive for at least a couple of hours after she was dumped," Blanchard said. "X-rays show a lot of healed breaks, so she's definitely been battered. But no sign of sexual assault and nothing to suggest she had sex prior to her death."

Nikki felt a surge of relief that Janelle hadn't been sexually assaulted. The way she'd died, alone and in the freezing cold, was bad enough. "If her ex did this, I would expect signs of a beating. What did the Eau Claire police say?" Nikki asked Liam.

"Still looking for him as of late last night," Liam said. "I planned to call for an update after we finished here. Dr. Blanchard, when do you expect the toxicology report?" Liam asked.

"I've asked the lab to rush it, but you know how that goes. As for Madison and Kaylee, you need to see the bodies."

Blanchard unlocked the suite and Nikki tried not to recoil at the potent aroma of formaldehyde. Madison and Kaylee's bodies lay on the steel gurneys, covered by a sheet. Their clothes had been carefully removed, the pictures taken, the autopsy performed.

Blanchard pulled Kaylee's sheet down to her chest. Her blue, pasty skin had lost much of its elasticity. Large purple bruises covered her neck. "Kaylee died first."

"Strangled?"

Blanchard nodded. "After what appears to be consensual sex. A condom was used, and there's no tearing or damage; we sometimes see that with assault. She was alive when it happened. It also appears she remained on her back for a while, because lividity set in, as you can see. However, being frozen can mess that up, so it's not an absolute. What is definite, however, is that Kaylee was coming out of rigor mortis when she was frozen."

Nikki must have heard wrong. "Excuse me?"

"Both her knee and hips joints have clear postmortem tears," Blanchard said. "The lower extremities stay in rigor the longest. Kaylee wasn't completely out of rigor when she was forced into the fetal position."

"Which means she'd been dead, what, eight to twelve hours?" Liam asked.

"On average, yes."

"This sounds ignorant," Nikki asked, "but there's no way these tears could come from being partially frozen first and then secured into the fetal position?"

"It's unlikely. A partially frozen limb would be harder to move than one coming out of rigor."

The killer hadn't known what to do with the bodies initially. They'd been hidden somewhere. "What about Madison?"

"The girls had pizza before departing the Bankses' home, and that's what I found in Kaylee's stomach. Madison's was empty. Her bowel, however, is full," Blanchard said.

"So, six to eight hours to digest," Liam said. "Usually a bowel movement within a day or two?"

"Usually, but it could be a bit longer." Blanchard removed Madison's sheet.

Nikki and Liam both gasped. Her frozen clothes had hidden the litany of bruises on her body. Her arms and feet had clear ligature marks.

"No sign of sexual assault, but her fingernails are broken, along with a couple of fingers."

"She fought like hell." Nikki jammed her hands at her waist. She'd learned a long time ago to never put herself in the victim's shoes, but as a mother, seeing the horror Madison had endured made her want to leave the room.

"She has a couple of bruises here"—Blanchard pointed to Madison's right arm—"that are lighter and have just enough yellow to make me think the healing process had started."

"How did she die?" Nikki asked.

"That brings me to the worst part."

"There's something worse?" Liam asked.

"Lividity showed she died in the fetal position, tied up. She experienced both liver failure and kidney failure. Her heart was compromised as well." Blanchard moved the sheet so they could see Madison's hands.

"Frostbite," Liam said.

"Jesus Christ. She froze to death?"

"She had internal bleeding. The back of her skull is broken from blunt force trauma. Her brain bled and swelled, which means she didn't die immediately. She may not have been fully conscious, but the frostbite proves that she was alive when she was tied up and put into the freezer."

"And Kaylee had been dead for several hours, if not longer." Liam looked at Nikki.

"Blunt force trauma is evident in both Madison and Janelle, and both died in severe conditions," Nikki said. "Was Madison left to freeze to death intentionally, like Janelle?"

"It's very possible, but the killer may have assumed she would die much faster than she did. I swabbed underneath all three victims' fingernails," Blanchard said. "But we're days away from any results. Courtney picked up both girls' clothing yesterday. Madison wore a belt and a watch. We're looking for fingerprints."

Nikki was already texting Courtney for an update.

Blanchard carefully turned Madison's arm so that her palm lay face up. "See the lower part of her forearm?"

Nikki's breath caught in her throat. The marks had likely been relatively fresh before Madison became incapacitated in the freezer. "Are those... letters?"

"I think the first one looks like an 'P.'" Dr. Blanchard squinted at the scratches. "Or possibly an unfinished 'R.' I can't tell if the second is supposed to be a letter or a number."

"It looks like a vertical line," Nikki said. "Maybe an 'I.' Probably not 'S' or 'G'. Or 'C'."

"'J,' 'O,' 'Q,' are out. 'X,' 'Y,' and 'Z' too. But that still leaves plenty of possible letters." Liam shook his head. "That's a lot of variables."

"She had fake nails," Nikki commented. "Those are too dull to make scratches like this."

"Shellac," Blanchard said. "Once the base loosens, they're relatively easy to pull off. Her right index fingernail is missing the shellac and the nail is jagged and clogged with Madison's own blood. These scratches happened shortly before she died. They're not particularly deep, but they had no chance to heal. The cold actually preserved them."

Madison had carved into her own flesh so her killer could be found.

CHAPTER TWENTY-NINE

Adrenaline pumped through Nikki. "Kaylee was probably killed within a couple of hours after their disappearance, but he took his time with Madison. He wanted her to suffer while Kaylee's death looks relatively painless."

"Kaylee had sex with him and then he kills her," Liam said. "Madison could have been collateral damage."

"Maybe," Nikki said. "But Miles Hanson said Kaylee was a virgin. Assuming he's right, Madison and Kaylee might have just gone to hang out and then Kaylee decides to have sex with the killer."

"Did the killer plan to murder Kaylee all along? Why not just strangle Madison too? Why make her death so much more brutal?"

"Strangulation is extremely intimate and almost always driven by a volatile temper that snaps," Nikki said.

"Bobby was Kaylee's crush," Liam said. "Is there any chance he's lying?"

"They disappeared on Saturday. Bobby doesn't have a car, so he would have needed Mindy to pick him up. Miller questioned everyone close to the family and checked all their alibis. Mindy was at work all day Saturday, and both she and Bobby told me that Mindy picked him up early Sunday morning so he could come home and search. That also matches what they originally told Miller in October."

"I've re-interviewed all their friends now," Liam said. "There are no other male friends with cars, and I still haven't been able to find the cell phone data to narrow down a pick-up location."

"Are you still going to talk to John's favorite girls at the strip club? We need to find out anything he might have told them that he didn't tell us. Can we see if they recognize anyone else from our list of suspects?"

Liam nodded. "They're both working this morning, so I'm headed to The Doll House from here. What about that other friend of Madison's? Have you talked to her again?"

"She only works two afternoons a week. Fortunately, today is one of those days. I think she's hiding something," Nikki said. "After you're done at the club, go back through all the interviews and look for any combination of first and last names starting with 'P' and 'I.' Local businesses and residents, too, although there may be too many. Talk to the geeks in the computer department. They might have a program to help narrow down results."

"What about the fake nail?" Liam asked.

"Madison's shellac was French tip. If she peeled it off in the freezer, her killer may not have noticed it when he moved the bodies. No one outside of the investigation needs to know about it right now, or about the initials on her arm. On the off chance the nail is still in the freezer, we don't want to give the killer a chance to get rid of it."

CHAPTER THIRTY

Nikki was surprised to see the library so busy. With most young people engrossed in their phones and social media lives, she'd expected a quiet afternoon. The computer lab was nearly full, a handful of people were in the process of checking out books, and a group of teens hung out in the activity area playing cards.

She found Brianna organizing shelves in the mystery section, wireless headphones cutting her off from the world.

Brianna removed her headphones, looking warily at Nikki. "What are you doing here?"

"Would you believe I was just browsing for a book?"

Brianna shook her head.

"I didn't think so." Nikki smiled, trying to set the girl at ease. But she stood at attention, ready to bolt.

"Are you allowed to question me without my parents or an adult?"

"Not as a suspect, no," Nikki said. "But I just wanted to ask you a couple of questions about Madison."

"I already talked to you. My mom told the police to leave me alone."

"But you didn't tell me everything."

"Yes, I did." Brianna turned back to the bookshelves.

"Do you know what kinesics are?"

"No." Brianna crammed a book into the already tight row.

"It's a broad term for nonverbal communication. Body language. Like you just shook your head when you said 'yes, I did,' instead of nodding. And young people—especially those who aren't normally deceitful—get really jittery. Kind of like the way you're rocking back and forth on your heels."

Brianna stilled. "I don't know anything else that will help you."

"Maybe you don't," Nikki said. "But you'd be surprised at how many times supposedly inconsequential details blow a case wide open. Don't you want to find out who killed your friends?"

Brianna's lips trembled. "Of course."

"Listen, I know how tough high school can be. Saying the wrong thing can get you kicked out of your social circle, and then suddenly you're a pariah. But that's only temporary, Brianna. Not doing the right thing leaves you with a lifetime of regret. Don't abandon Maddie now."

Brianna's eyes filled with tears. "Her parents were fighting a lot."

"Did Madison say why?"

"Her mom hated Kaylee. Mrs. Banks said something about Kaylee doing sneaky things no one knew about. She needed to be put in her place."

Nikki already knew this from speaking to Amy. "Did you talk to Kaylee about this?"

Brianna nodded, chewing the inside of her cheek.

Nikki stepped forward and touched her shoulder, gently turning Brianna to face her. "Why did Amy feel that way?"

"When Kaylee first started hanging out with Madison, she told her about some night last summer when she'd gone to Hudson with some older friends and used a fake ID to get into a bar. Some drunk older guy kept hitting on her, grinding up on her. He asked if she would let him take some pictures of her, in private. She told him to fuck off."

Nikki's stomach soured. She didn't like where this was headed.

"Then one night, a few days before they disappeared, Madison overheard her parents fighting. Her mother, mostly. Her little brother came into Madison's room crying and saying it was his fault," Brianna said. "He'd been snooping through Mr. Banks' office and found a box of pictures. Mr. Banks was in most of them, and there were different women, and they were naked. Some weren't even awake. Mrs. Banks got really upset, so Bailey felt like it was his fault. Madison told him it wasn't, and that whatever happened was between their mom and dad. Madison intended to confront her parents about it. She was certain Mr. Banks was the one who approached Kaylee. She was going to ask her about it."

"Did she talk to any of them?"

"I don't know. They disappeared the next weekend. I think her mom made her promise she'd let her handle things." Brianna crossed her arms over her chest, her fingers leaving pressure marks on her skin.

"Did Madison see the pictures?"

"I don't think so," Brianna said. "But Maddie knew they must have been as bad as Bailey said because her mom was a wreck."

"Why didn't you say anything before?"

"Parents fight, don't they? Madison loved her stepdad, and they were close. Just because he cheated on Maddie's mom doesn't mean he'd hurt Maddie, right?" Brianna hugged her chest, her gaze pleading with Nikki to agree.

"I can't answer that right now, but I promise to keep digging until we know what happened to them." Nikki thanked Brianna for her honesty and walked outside in a daze.

Nikki could see that at least six more protestors had joined the group outside the government center when she arrived. Doug folded his arms over his chest and stared at Nikki. She ignored him and scanned the group.

Bobby stood on the other side of the entrance with a couple of protestors Nikki recognized from the first day she'd arrived. Nikki pointed to the parking lot, signaling him to follow her, and then pulled into the nearest parking spot.

She heard the shouts as soon as she stepped out of the jeep. The entrance didn't have any sort of barricade, and the rest of the protestors seemed to be warning Bobby that he was crossing a line. At least the group respected the law enough to protest outside of the parking lot.

Bobby stopped a few feet away from her. "Just so you know, they're all recording this on their phones. It's like I'm crossing a picket line or something. They're going to pounce when I come back."

"I can take care of that."

Most of the protestors quieted down as she approached, and Doug's crude voice was quickly hushed by a young woman half his size. She stepped forward, her cell phone pointed at Nikki.

"Agent Hunt. Are you going to talk to us about Mark Todd?"

"I legally can't talk to you about him," Nikki replied. "Mark Todd is appealing his conviction, and I'm not only a witness, I'm an FBI agent. Believe it or not, my speaking to you could have a negative effect on his case. I'm sure Ms. Newport would tell you the same thing."

"Then what are you doing?" Doug replied, coming forward.

"I'm working an active murder investigation. One of the victims was a family friend of Bobby's, and I have a couple of things to verify with him. That's the only reason he's speaking with me, so please don't ambush him when he returns."

She walked back to Bobby.

"I need you to be completely honest with me. I don't think you would hurt Madison, but I need to know if you're aware of anyone else Kaylee or Madison was spending time with before they died."

Bobby looked stunned. "I already told you I don't know anything else. They spent so much time together: gossiping, chatting, running about just the two of them. It's why Madison and I weren't as close anymore. They were best friends. And I hadn't seen either of them since I took them to Hudson."

"All right," Nikki said.

"Did she suffer?" Bobby's voice cracked. "Could the medical examiner tell if it was quick?"

"You don't want to hear the answer to that," Nikki replied. "Are you staying in Stillwater until the funeral's over?"

"Um, I think so. My professors have been good about me doing online work."

"I'm glad," Nikki said. "And I have a favor to ask."

His eyes lit up. "Of me? Sure."

"You'll go back to school after the funeral and not get hung up here with the protestors. If you're passionate about Mark's innocence, there are things you can do from campus. Don't let all of this interrupt your life."

Bobby looked down at his scruffy shoes. "My life's already been interrupted plenty, Agent Hunt."

"I know it has. Losing a parent is awful, especially when you're young." She almost laughed at the irony of her saying those words to someone who believed her own parents' killer might be innocent. She didn't know how Bobby's father had died, but she knew what it was like to lose someone. "If I'd stayed in Stillwater after I graduated, I don't know what would have happened to me. It's great to come back and see friends and family, but it's okay to live your own life and heal. I'm sure that's what your father would have wanted." She turned and started walking toward the main building's front entrance before her emotions spilled into unprofessional territory. "Good luck, Bobby."

Nikki ducked her head against the wind and wished she'd parked closer to the front entrance. She'd just made it into the warm lobby when her cell vibrated in her pocket.

Adrenaline rushed through Nikki at seeing Courtney's name on the screen.

"Please tell me you have the results of the DNA and fingerprint testing."

"Well, hello to you, too."

"Sorry." Nikki shouldered her phone and rubbed her hands together. She kept forgetting her gloves, and her hands were constantly freezing.

"We found prints on Madison's belt and they match those found on Janelle," Courtney said. "The weird thing is that they don't match any of the prints lifted from Janelle's motel room."

"What about her ex? His prints are in the system."

"Negative for both. If you can get a warrant for John's prints, I can analyze them."

Nikki worried it was too soon to take John's fingerprints. She wanted to have a solid case first so that he didn't have the opportunity to run. "Thanks, Court. I'll let Liam and Miller know. They're headed home for the day, but I'll be available if you find anything else."

Nikki went straight to the administration desk. She showed the attendant her badge. There was something else she needed to do.

CHAPTER THIRTY-ONE

Nikki set the case file aside and dug into the Chinese food she'd picked up on the way to her hotel. She moaned in appreciation as she bit into the sesame chicken. Tao's had always been her favorite Chinese restaurant in Stillwater, and the food was just as amazing as she'd remembered.

She ran through her notes from the day while she ate, hoping something would jump out at her.

Liam had spoken with the two dancers John always requested at The Doll House. Both said that nothing specific about him stood out other than being a good tipper. He'd complained about his wife, but no more than any other guy. He never mentioned children. None of the girls felt he acted inappropriately with them, and none of them remembered any specific interactions between John and Janelle.

The information should have eased her mind, but Liam had saved the best for last. John had told Nikki that he started going to The Doll House after Madison went missing, but both dancers said John started coming to the strip club a full two months before the girls disappeared. The club's owner had emailed Liam six months of archived security footage. Liam and Miller had stayed late at the sheriff's office and were currently going through the recordings. John seemed to visit the same time every day, between 10:00 a.m. and 2:00 p.m.

If Brianna's information was accurate, the Bankses' marital problems had started well before the girls disappeared and he'd lied to Nikki. And if what Briana said about the pictures Bailey had found was true, were the women simply sleeping or had they been drugged? And if he'd drugged those other women, what had he done to Nikki that night? Is that why her tox screen had been buried all those years ago? Nikki wondered just how far John would go to bury this.

Minnesota was a no-fault state, and Amy would get half in a divorce regardless of the reason for it. Did he have a motivation for keeping his affairs a secret?

Madison's injuries were key. Whoever had killed the girls had treated them very differently. John could have killed someone in a fit of passion, but would he beat up his own daughter and leave her to freeze to death?

John certainly knew the press strategy regarding Frost. He also knew how stubborn Nikki could be when she made up her mind about something. Staging Janelle's killing to look like a Frost victim could have been his way to lead her off course.

But if John had been getting away with drugging and raping women for years, he knew how to choose the right victim, how to lure her and how to cover his tracks. Leaving fingerprints was a rookie move. Unless the stress of covering up his crimes caused him to make a costly mistake.

Everything pointed to John, and yet nothing added up. Maybe stepping away from the case for a little while would help her figure out what she'd missed. She grabbed the remote and turned on the television, searching for anything to take her mind off the case and clear her head. Infomercials and reality television didn't exactly help.

She glanced at the table, half-wishing she hadn't asked the district attorney to send her copies of her parents' case file. Did she really want to do this?

She had to. If there was any chance Mark was telling the truth, Nikki owed it to her parents to find their real killer. And to help get Mark out of prison. Nikki had put her trust in John, and for the first time in her life she was questioning him. What if everything he'd told her was a lie? What if he'd slipped the liquid ecstasy into her drink? What had he intended to do to her?

Nikki lifted the lid and tossed it aside. A copy of the evidence log sat on top. Her father's bloodstained pajamas and slippers, her mother's nightgown and the bottom bedsheet, and various items from Nikki's room and the nightstand were listed, with the chain of custody stating they were currently in the prosecutor's office pending testing, in addition to the swabs taken from her mother's face.

She started with the photos. Her hands shook, and the contents of her stomach threatened to make an appearance. The images had already been scorched into her brain, but the photos contained details she'd forgotten. She had to look at them with a trained eye. The first few shots consisted of the exterior of the house. Then photos of the bloody footprints on the stairs and upstairs hallway. The photographer had followed crime scene protocol and worked from the outside of the scene in, so the first picture was a full shot of the bedroom. Her mother lay on the bed, arm dangling off the side, blankets on the floor, including her grandma's quilt. Nikki couldn't stand to have it around afterwards, so she'd put it in storage, along with other items she couldn't look at but would never get rid of.

There were defensive wounds on her mother's hands. Her face was slack, sightless eyes wide.

Nikki spread the pictures out on the table and then dug through until she found the coroner's report. A bullet had grazed her mother's shoulder and then embedded into the wall as she likely fled the killer after she'd gone to check on her husband. Marks on her feet showed she'd probably been dragged and then thrown back into the bed. Had she fought him off and then tried to get up, only to have him shoot her in the stomach?

The coroner estimated she took several minutes to die.

Your mother died instantly. She didn't suffer. Hardin had made it a point to comfort her with the information. He'd said it several times in the days after the murder.

The coroner didn't indicate how long it took to accumulate that much blood loss, but given the body temperature and blood coagulation state, he estimated she'd been dead for an hour or more, which put time of death between 1:00 a.m. and 2:00 a.m.

Nikki had found her at 2:17, and the blood had already clotted on the sheet.

Postmortem bruising on her mother's wrists indicated both hands had been grasped by the killer. There was also postmortem bruising on her cheeks, chin and neck. Nikki thought it looked like the killer had held her hands over her head, and that indicated a sexual assault. Any cop with an ounce of sense would have come to the same conclusion. No wonder the deputy collecting trace evidence had issues.

Had Hardin lied to Nikki about her mother's sexual assault to save Nikki some grief or to save his investigation?

She took a break and opened the cheap bottle of red she'd picked up earlier. Anger coursed through her. Her parents' lives had been brutally cut short and Nikki's only solace had been knowing their killer was in prison. But what if she'd been wrong this whole time?

She sifted through the paperwork, re-reading the detailed accounts from John and his friends. There was no mention of Nikki passing out or acting incoherently, nor were there any notes about drugs being at the party. Was Nikki putting too much stock in the paramedic's story? Trauma made people say strange things.

Why would Hardin lie about the tox test? The paramedic had nothing to gain from his involvement, but Hardin had everything to lose.

Nikki sifted through the exterior photos again. The farmhouse they lived in sat at the end of a long, circular drive. Surrounded by mature trees, it had been nearly invisible from the gravel road. At the time, the rural area had several well-used dirt and gravel roads, but in general the only traffic belonged to the people who lived in the area. The handful of families watched out for each other. If someone saw a strange person or vehicle, they would have reported it.

Mark Todd's parents had a small farm about a half a mile away. He could have taken a few different routes to her parents' house, but the fastest was straight through the cornfield.

Hardin hadn't looked for other suspects because there weren't any.

Gunshot residue tests hadn't been taken due to the close quarters and proximity of the victim to Mark. At least one thing had gone in favor of due process. If Mark really was innocent, he would still have residue from checking her mother's pulse.

Nikki looked at the diagram used to show her father's wounds. The bullet had embedded in the base of his skull, indicating her father was either kneeling or in the process of getting up when he'd been shot. Nikki realized that if Mark was standing up and her dad had been kneeling, at that close range, his pants would have been hit with blood spatter at the very least.

Nikki studied the photographs of Mark's clothes. There appeared to be a couple of small blood spots on his hip, but they could have been from contact with Nikki's mother.

Budget and inexperience meant that no blood spatter analysis had been done, but a damning report in 2009 completely changed the science of blood spatter, so any analysis likely would have been rejected if Mark received a new trial.

Nikki looked at the pictures of Mark Todd for a long time. Blood smeared the Led Zeppelin logo on his T-shirt, his jeans appeared mostly clean, as did the top of his shoes. Nikki wasn't a blood spatter specialist, but the white Nikes that Mark wore when he stepped in her mother's blood and made tracks should have some sort of spray on the top, even if just a droplet, from shooting her father. If the deputy had been right about the angle, Nikki had a hard time believing those Nikes would be clean.

Photocopies of Hardin's original notes, mostly witness interviews and tips, were clipped together. Nikki flipped through the pages, recognizing familiar names, including Bobby's father, Robert. He and two other friends verified John's account of the night, but where were the others? There had been at least a dozen people at the party before Nikki had gone into the bedroom. Even if they'd left by the time Mark tried to attack her, Hardin should have made sure every person had been interviewed.

Hardin's interview with Nadine Johnson, the neighbor who'd allowed Nikki inside and called the police, was more detailed than the partygoers'. Relief washed over Nikki when she realized that Nadine's statement matched her own memories, but it quickly evaporated when she read the final sentences.

Nadine had heard a loud engine roaring down the gravel road around 2:00 a.m. She'd still been awake when Nikki came pounding on the door thirty minutes later. Nadine told Hardin the engine reminded her of the muscle cars that used to race on the dirt tracks.

A vehicle racing down the gravel road that time of night wasn't uncommon, especially on the weekends. But a muscle car speeding past in the same timeframe as her parents' murder was something entirely different.

Mark Todd drove a beat-up station wagon.

John's restored 1968 Shelby Mustang's engine had been so loud that whenever Nikki snuck out, she had to walk all the way down her parents' long driveway to meet John. He'd park on the side of the gravel road, and Nikki always heard the car's idle before she was halfway down the drive.

Everything seemed to lead back to John Banks.

Had Hardin brushed the information off because it didn't bolster his case against Mark?

Nikki gathered every piece of evidence, carefully putting it in order. She corked the wine and rinsed her glass. The hotel suite was chilly, so she turned up the thermostat.

Her parents had argued over the heat every winter.

Tears welled in her eyes. She unzipped her suitcase and pulled out the manila envelope she'd taken from her nightstand drawer the previous night. The envelope contained their last family photo, taken the summer before the murders.

Her throat constricted. She couldn't remember the last time she'd looked at their pictures. Her father had been tall and lean, his hands perpetually calloused from working on the farm. He'd worn his farmer's tan with pride, and his hair never quite behaved. He'd slicked it back for the picture. Her mother hated it.

Nikki looked more like her mother than she'd realized. Same dark, wavy hair, porcelain skin and strong cheekbones. Her mother never showed her teeth when she smiled because she'd been embarrassed by their crookedness. She'd taken a second job waiting tables to help pay for Nikki's braces. Had Nikki ever thanked her for that?

Fat tears rolled down her cheeks and splashed onto the picture. She carefully wiped off the moisture and put it back into the envelope.

Nikki didn't know if Mark had killed her parents anymore. But she couldn't stop running from the idea. If Mark was really innocent, then everything that Nikki knew was a lie. Even worse, his innocence meant the real killer was still out there.

Nikki scrolled through her contacts. Civilians had to make their appointments during normal hours, but she hoped the number she'd found had a human being monitoring it.

A tired male voice answered the phone. "Minnesota Correctional Facility."

"This is Special Agent Nicole Hunt with the FBI. I need to set up a visit with an inmate as soon as possible."

CHAPTER THIRTY-TWO

Nikki pulled into the snowy driveway, her nerves on edge. Nadine Johnson's two-story house looked as she remembered, but the willow trees were much taller, their bare branches growing well past the roof. Nikki had played house beneath those long branches during Nadine's summer barbeques, enjoying the strawberry lemonade Nadine had made especially for her.

Nadine had to be nearing seventy now, still living in the little cottage a couple of football fields from Nikki's old house. Nikki used to walk through the big strawberry patch in the summer to visit her. She'd taken the same route escaping from Mark when she'd fled the house that night: ran as fast as she could through the gardens, not knowing if she was being followed, if she'd even make it there.

After the murders, Mrs. Johnson wanted Nikki to stay with her, but the courts had given Nikki's great-aunt custody of her. And Nikki shut Mrs. Johnson out as she'd done the others.

"So you're telling me that Amy Banks knows John was, at minimum, cheating, and that he might have drugged women?" Liam's voice filtered through the jeep's Bluetooth system.

"According to Brianna, yes, Amy saw the pictures. But without more evidence, John's drugging them is just speculation. They may have been sleeping."

"I doubt it, but I guess people have weird fetishes."

"Janelle had GHB in her system." Nikki read the email from Dr. Blanchard out loud. "Given the high quantity, probably taken within a few hours of her death. She was also intoxicated."

"I've talked to Janelle's mom and sister. They both said she didn't do drugs. And she's got no arrests on file."

"Blanchard said she would have definitely been incapacitated."

"Forcing her to take it would make her easier to control," Liam said. "What about Madison and Kaylee?"

"Both negative," Nikki replied.

"You know what bugs me?" Liam didn't pause long enough for her to reply. "John's probably six feet tall and still in good shape. He wouldn't need drugs to control her."

"Not physically, but the drugs would keep her quiet. My issue is this sudden major mistake. If John's been doing this for a long time, he knows how to cover his tracks. Assuming he didn't kill any of the women in the pictures, why kill Janelle? Did she wake up and threaten him?"

"He's coming apart because of Madison," Liam suggested. "Even if he didn't kill the girls, he's under a lot of stress. He drugs Janelle and does his thing, and then something happens, and she ends up dead. He panics and tries to leave her as a Frost victim to cover his tracks."

The theory made sense, but it didn't sit right with Nikki. They didn't have enough for a clear picture, and bringing John in for questioning—much less arresting him—was out of the question without concrete evidence. Brianna's story needed to be corroborated.

"We need Amy Banks to confirm she saw the pictures." If Nikki's suspicions were correct and John had done the same thing to Nikki all those years ago, Amy was less likely to confide in her. "I asked Miller to talk to her this morning, but without proof that John killed her daughter, she's unlikely to turn on him. Are you going to Eau Claire?"

"On my way now. Janelle only brought the necessities when she moved. A lot of her things are at her mother's. It's probably a waste of time, but I want to go through everything."

"It's not a waste of time. Tiny details usually make or break a case. And we know they were killed by the same person."

"You sure you don't want to go with me?" Liam asked.

"I wish I could, but I'm following a possible lead." She waited for him to press her for details, but they'd worked together long enough that he trusted her.

"Let me know what you find."

"Will do."

She ended the call and immediately started second-guessing herself. But she wasn't just here on personal business. John was a murder suspect. Questioning Nadine about what she heard the night her parents were murdered was prudent. If he'd lied then, what else had he lied about? And what else had he done?

Nikki locked the jeep and walked toward the house, taking a familiar path.

Nikki took a deep breath and knocked on the door. Would the woman even recognize her?

Mrs. Johnson looked exactly the same, with whiter hair and a slightly stooped posture.

"Nicole Walsh? Is that you?"

"Hi, Mrs. Johnson. Can I come in?"

"Of course." She smiled. "And it's Nadine, please. You're not a kid anymore."

Nikki followed her into the familiar house, her throat knotting. The furniture had changed, but the general arrangement remained the same. Two chairs flanked the big bay window that overlooked the old Zephyr line. Her parents had loved the now-defunct dinner train, and every time they had a romantic night out on the Zephyr, Nikki would sit at the window watching the train rumble past. The route was now Brown's Creek Trail. "You still have a lovely view."

"Thank heavens," Nadine said. "I was afraid when the train stopped running the bulldozers would come next. But the nature preserve is just lovely."

"You look well."

"I can't complain." Nadine studied her for a moment. "Your hair is shorter. I told you cutting it to your shoulders would make it curl."

Nadine had owned a successful hair salon for years in downtown Stillwater. Beauty salons like Nadine's had been the center of town. Nadine always knew everything about everyone; people came to her with gossip, especially their neighbors.

"You were right. I spent so many years dealing with that long mess."

"Would you like some coffee? I just made some."

"No, thank you."

Nadine sat down in front of the window. "Please, sit down. You're with the FBI. A profiler, right? Like the ones on television?"

"Something like that. I'm working on the murders in town."

"Just awful." Nadine's voice trembled. "Awful there are people in this world who do such things."

"It is. Which make my job even more important."

"You wanted to be a teacher," Nadine said. "Or a social worker."

"That was before," Nikki replied and she didn't need to say any more. "Did you see the article in the paper about me?"

Nadine waved her bony hand. "It's disgusting what these journalists can say nowadays."

"That's kind of why I'm here," Nikki said. "I haven't thought about that night for so long, and people are asking me to remember it all over again. Everyone's telling me different things, and I'm second-guessing my own memories."

"Why on earth would you do that?"

"Because Hardin knew I'd been drinking. He says he just did a field sobriety test, but I swear a paramedic took blood for a tox test. Hardin says I was just getting fluids."

"You were definitely dehydrated," Nadine said. "You reeked of alcohol. But I watched you pass the sobriety test. And then they took you to the ambulance for fluids."

"So I am just imagining things?"

"Not at all," Nadine said. "You were in such shock, and I didn't want to let you out of my sight. I watched your blood being drawn."

"Where was Hardin?" Relief washed over Nikki, but a new sense of dread settled over her. The tox report had definitely gone missing.

"That I don't remember. You were my sole focus. And as for your own memories, you had a traumatic experience most people can't even fathom. Of course your memories are jumbled. Why are you being so hard on yourself?"

It had taken years for Nikki to process her mother's death. To stop wishing her mother was there for a crisis. But being back in Nadine's house reminded her that Nadine had been her mother's friend. They should be growing old together, harassing Nikki about seeing Lacey and having more grandchildren, while her father puttered around the farm looking for a hobby.

Nikki put her head in her hands. "I've worked so hard to make the past stay in the past. Now it's like I can't get away from it."

"You can't escape the past," Nadine said. "Especially your childhood. Good or bad, those experiences shape who you grow up to be. Your past is tragic, so you gravitated towards justice. I'm not surprised you're a profiler. You were always so observant. You picked out little details about things no one else noticed."

Nikki wiped her eyes. "The last time I cried was when I had my daughter."

"You have a little girl?" Her face lit up.

"Lacey. She's five. I haven't told anyone here about her." She found her favorite picture of Lacey on her phone. It had been taken last fall, when Nikki had been raking leaves and Lacey made the giant pile her sandbox.

"She's beautiful." Nadine smiled. "She has your hair and eyes."

"Her father is blond and fair-skinned. We're divorced. But friends. Totally amicable."

"Good," Nadine said. "That's all that matters for your daughter."

"He's an agent." Nikki hesitated, trying to think of the right way to explain the reason for her visit. She didn't want to give Nadine the impression that Hardin mishandled the case, but she had to ask about her statement. "I finally looked at their case file last night. I tried to look at it from a cop's point of view."

"How did that go?"

"Not well, but I did see some things that didn't make sense," Nikki said. "The reason I asked about the blood test is because there's no record of it in the file. And some forensic details don't add up. Then there's your statement."

Nadine tapped her fingers on the chair arm. "I have a feeling I know what you're going to say."

"You do?"

"I told Hardin that a loud engine woke me up," Nadine said. "The weather was so nice, and my bedroom window faces the road. I was certain it was a muscle car, because my dad and brothers were all muscle car fanatics. I tagged along to car shows more times than I can remember. I know what they sound like. But Hardin chided me. He said there was no way I could tell if it was a muscle car or just a truck missing a muffler. I wanted to smack some sense into him, and he knew it. Then he starts blabbing about the road being far enough away that no one would be able to tell the difference."

"That's not true." She paused, then, "I knew someone who drove a '68 Shelby Mustang."

"I know you did," Nadine said evenly. "And so did Hardin. But he dismissed the idea."

The implication made Nikki dizzy. "But Mark was in my parents' house."

"And John Banks wasn't the only person with a loud car," Nadine said. "But considering the two of you were dating, why wouldn't

Hardin take me seriously? Not to mention the other deputy suddenly transferring."

"Who?"

"Deputy Anderson took the samples. I believe he had special training. He transferred to another county several months after the trial. One of my gals at the salon worked at the sheriff's office, and she said Anderson didn't like how things were being run and wanted out. He and Hardin clashed over your parents' case."

"Hardin never looked at anyone other than Mark," Nikki replied. "Did you know about Mark and Hardin's wife?"

Nadine sat her coffee on the side table. "I'd heard rumors that summer. Mark's mother came in regularly, and she was upset at times. I heard she tried to confront him and he denied it, but everyone I spoke to was certain he was lying. Hardin had a temper, according to some people in his inner circle," Nadine said. "They said he was vindictive. Do you think this was some kind of revenge against Mark?"

Nikki chose her words carefully. "I think Hardin lacked the capacity to be objective about Mark. Deputy Anderson never should have been overruled. Have you spoken to anyone on Mark's defense team at the Innocence Project?"

"They came to see me a few weeks ago," Nadine said. "I told them everything I just told you. I should have tried to reach you, but it didn't seem like it was my place. I'm sorry."

"No, no, that's fine. I just wanted to make sure they were aware." Nikki should have let the district attorney give her the details before she stormed out of his office the other day. No wonder Roger Mathews had doubts about retrying the case. "I should get going."

"How long are you in town?" Nadine asked.

"Until I solve the murders," Nikki replied.

Nadine paled and hugged her. "Oh, good Lord. The horrors you see, Nicole. Please stay in touch. It's lonely out here. Maybe you could bring your girl around, when this is all over?"

"I will," Nikki said, and she hoped she meant it. "Nadine, if Mark is innocent, do you think… do you think John could have done this?"

"Sweetheart, that question has haunted me for years." Tears built in Nadine's eyes. "I hope you can figure out the answer so your parents can finally rest in peace."

CHAPTER THIRTY-THREE

Nikki followed the winding drive to the farmhouse where she grew up, her heartbeat accelerating. She remembered how her father was forever complaining about Nikki's friends driving in the grass when they made the loop in front of the house. The driveway was gravel now, instead of dirt, and a couple of new trees provided shade in the front yard, but the willow tree Nikki played under still dominated the landscape. The farmhouse had new siding, windows, and shutters. The old barn was gone, replaced by a hibernating vegetable garden.

She left the jeep running and slowly crossed the yard, following the same path she'd taken that night. She remembered how badly her legs had wanted to give out, how she'd taken the porch steps one at a time. How the door had stood open, with glass everywhere.

"Can I help you?" A young woman with a baby on her hip stood in the doorway.

"I used to live here," Nikki said. "A long time ago. Sorry to bother you."

Her eyebrows knitted together. "Are you the girl whose parents were killed?"

That's exactly who she was, no matter how hard she tried to pretend. "My name is Nicole."

The woman bounced the fussing baby. "Did you want to come in or something?"

The cop in Nikki surfaced. "You should never invite a stranger in the house, even a woman."

"Aren't you with the FBI?"

Right. Everyone knew she was in town. "You don't mind?"

"I have to put him down for his nap, but if it's something you need to do…" She held the door open. "I'll leave you alone."

Nikki's feet suddenly felt filled with lead. Could she really do this? The young mother headed down the hall into the kitchen. The strawberry wallpaper her mother had so painstakingly hung had been replaced by cheery yellow paint. The vinyl flooring in the hall was gone, too. Engineered hardwood had taken its place. Her father had laid the vinyl himself, cutting his hand during the process. He told everyone he'd bled for the house and then proudly showed his scar. The irony almost made Nikki bolt for her jeep, but she forced her legs to move.

Nikki walked by the living room; the fireplace looked the same. Even the wooden mantle remained.

A few more feet, and then the stairs on her left. The hallway led into the kitchen, where the phone had hung on the right wall, next to the dining room doorway.

Mark's version of events had him going downstairs, probably still woozy, in search of a phone, in a dark, unfamiliar place. He'd tried to save her mother and ended up with her blood on his shirt. What about his hands? Nikki didn't remember seeing a photograph of blood streaks on the wall, but if Mark had really had his bell rung, she'd expect him to need help staying steady.

If his head had been bleeding, did anyone look for a blood trail other than the footprints he'd left after stepping in her mother's blood? If Mark had bled onto the wood floor, it was possible the blood stain had set into the wood. If it had, the stain might still be visible.

The kitchen flooring had been the house's original hardwood. Her father applied fresh stain every few years, declaring this was the last time and they were covering it with vinyl. It never happened, but someone had finally upgraded the flooring to tile.

There was different carpet on the stairs. Plush, not the tightly woven Berber she remembered. Thirteen steps; the fifth, sixth and seventh still squeaked.

Nikki scrubbed the tears off her cheeks and kept walking. Her parents' old bedroom had been completely redone, and the bed was on the other side of the room. Nikki waited for the memories to bombard her, but she remained numb.

Her room at the end of the hall was now a nursery. A changing table sat in the spot where her father's body had lain.

Nikki's throat tightened. Everything had changed, the time her family spent in the house wiped out, as though the Walsh family never existed.

She went back downstairs and found the homeowner in the kitchen. "Thank you for letting me come inside."

"No problem."

The phone no longer hung on the wall, and a portable island countertop sat against the back wall. Like the hallway, the kitchen floors had been replaced by engineered hardwood. "This is nice work."

"Thanks. My husband has done most of the upgrades. The old oak trim doesn't match. He was supposed to replace that in the summer. You know how men are."

Could it actually be the same trim from twenty years ago? Her own house was fifteen years old, and the trim had only been treated, never replaced. Nikki knelt in the corner where the phone had been. The trim was definitely old, but clean.

"I like the yellow paint," Nikki said. "Very cheery. My mother had strawberry wallpaper. It was expensive at the time."

"It was still here when we moved in a few years ago," the woman said. "The house had been pretty neglected. I liked the wallpaper, but it was in bad shape. Some of it had peeled off in places, and that wall in particular was a mess." She pointed to the wall where the phone had been. "It had brown, splotchy stains in several places. The wall behind it was fine, so it wasn't a water leak."

"Good thing." Nikki's throat had gone dry. "Water destroys everything."

*

Nikki drove too fast out of the driveway, the jeep sliding into the road. The spot may not have been blood, and even if it were, Mark had come from downstairs. He might have gone into the kitchen to try to clean off. None of this meant he wasn't the killer.

The crime scene photos had focused on the stairs and bedroom, along with the front door. Nothing of the kitchen or the back hallway. No mention of any type of blood marks downstairs.

"He didn't get knocked out," Nikki said to herself. "That's why there were no prints."

Or were there simply no pictures of the prints he'd left because Hardin feared they would threaten his slam-dunk case?

Anger swelled in her gut. Tears blurred her vision. "Bastards." She pounded the steering wheel. "Why can't this all just go away for good?" She never should have stayed in Stillwater. Her boss would have assigned someone else if she'd asked. But she had to stay and prove to all the people who remembered her as "that girl whose parents were murdered" that she'd turned out fine. Better than fine. She put the worst of humankind away for life.

Nikki let go of the wheel to dry her face, and the tires hit a patch of ice. The jeep skidded to the right, dangerously close to the deep ditch. Nikki overcorrected and careened across the road in front of a fast-approaching white truck. She barely registered Rory's angry face before he jerked the truck out of her path.

Nikki pumped the brakes, and the vehicle regained traction on a clear patch of pavement. Heart pounding, she pulled onto the shoulder.

Rory's truck had partially skidded onto the side of the road, and snow flew as the big tires worked their way back onto the pavement.

Please keep going.

He made a U-turn and parked behind her.

She snapped open her seatbelt and stepped out of the car. Rory was already bearing down on her, red-faced.

"Nicole?"

The wind burned her damp face. "I'm sorry. Is your truck damaged?"

"No, but you could have killed us."

"Why are you out here? Did you follow me?" The tremor in her voice made her want to scream.

He glared at her for a moment, his jaw set hard enough his teeth had to be grinding. "Why would I follow you?"

"How should I know?" she snapped back. "But it sure seems like you show up at the right moment. You're telling me that's just coincidence?"

"Nicole, I live in my parents' old house. I'm on my way home."

She wanted to sink to the ground from embarrassment. "Well, if there's damage, I'll pay for it."

"What happened to your face?"

She touched the still-sore welt. The swelling had gone down, but the bruising was still prominent around her hairline. "Ran into something."

"That's not what it looks like." He brushed her hair out of the way. "Looks more like something hit you."

Her throat ached. She knew she needed to get back in her car and try to think.

"Why are you crying?" Rory's voice had shifted to the same intimate tone he'd used at the bar. It would be so easy to tell him everything.

"It's nothing. I—"

The anger in his green eyes had been replaced by concern. He gently touched her shoulders. "And shaking?"

She needed to get away from this man before she did something foolish, like throwing herself into his arms. "Well, like you said, I almost killed us."

"No, this was before that. It made you drive like a lunatic. What's going on, Nicole?"

Her name rolled off his tongue in a way that made her entire body burn. "I need to go."

"Not until you've calmed down." Rory's hands still rested on her shoulders. "The road is too slick to be driving like that. What are you doing out here, anyway?"

"I came to check on Nadine Johnson." Nikki pressed her lips together, but the words still came out. "And then I stopped by the old house."

His expression softened. "You shouldn't have done that. At least not alone."

"Stop it," she said, the wind making her voice even more shrill. "Stop being so nice to me. By all rights, you should hate me."

"I told you, it wasn't your fault."

"But how can you say that? How can you look at my face and not be reminded of your brother and what happened? Just seeing me should upset you."

Rory was silent for a moment. "By that logic, you should feel the same way about me."

"You don't understand."

"You think Mark killed your family. I'm his little brother trying to prove he didn't. Why doesn't the sight of me upset you?"

"How do you know it doesn't?"

He moved closer, his hands sliding from her shoulders to her neck. A couple of curls peeked out from his cap. His pink lips parted, and then his gaze flashed down to meet hers. He grabbed the zipper of her parka and slowly closed it all the way to her chin. He put his hands in his pockets. "Did you look at the case files yet?"

"Yes."

"What did you think?" he asked softly.

"I think that I want to see those DNA results."

CHAPTER THIRTY-FOUR

Nikki glanced at her tired colleagues sitting around the conference room table. After her run-in with Rory, she'd rejoined her team at the government center. Two hours later, they were still going back and forth over various scenarios. "Madison's injuries indicate she may have been the main target and killing her was personal."

"If she knows anything, Amy's protecting him," Miller said. "When I spoke to her earlier, she insisted John was home the night Janelle was murdered. She also said she had no idea what Brianna was talking about. She never saw pictures of any sort."

"What about Bailey?"

"They wouldn't let me talk to him."

Nikki glanced up from her notes. "John was home?"

"Took the rest of the week off," Miller said. "I asked if he'd be willing to get fingerprints done so we could rule him out for Janelle's murder. Slammed the door in my face. And we don't have enough evidence to obtain his fingerprints if he doesn't want to give them up."

"Whoever tortured Madison hated her," Liam said. "And so far we don't know anyone who did."

"John Banks is the common denominator between the three victims," Nikki said. "And I don't trust Amy's story. She's already lost her child. I think she'd do anything to keep the rest of her family together, and that includes convincing herself John is innocent."

"But what's John's motive for killing Madison and Kaylee?" Liam asked. "It's got to be more than just the threat of exposing his affairs. One of them must have had something so strong on him he felt trapped. And he takes it out on Madison, because he feels betrayed."

"Why let her freeze to death and suffer?" Nikki said. "Even if he's angry enough to kill her, it's hard to imagine him wanting her to suffer that badly."

"She may have been unconscious when he put her into the freezer," Miller said. "Maybe he thought she'd just slip away peacefully."

"Or he's a selfish, sadistic asshole." Liam rested his elbows on the table and looked at Nikki. "We know he approached Kaylee at the bar during the summer. What if he was having a relationship with her? He might not be the same person you knew twenty years ago."

Nikki glared at him. "I know exactly who he is, Liam. Head back into the city and pay a visit to Roan Pharmaceuticals. Take your time and talk to the people who work closely with John and try to figure out how they really feel about him. The company CEO is a major Vikings supporter. Attends training camp, has his own box, has dinner with the owner. Football's your in. Show them pictures of all three girls—see if anyone recognizes them."

"You're the boss." Liam grabbed his things and hurried out of the room.

Miller cleared his throat. "He didn't say it very well, but I understand his point."

"So do I." Nikki glanced at her watch. She had thirty minutes to make her appointment. "I'll see you tomorrow."

"You sure you're all right, Agent Hunt? If you need to talk about anything—"

"I'm just tired, like everyone else."

And it was time to stop running from her past.

CHAPTER THIRTY-FIVE

Nikki checked her coat and bag at the front gate of Oak Park Heights. She'd locked her gun and wallet in the car. After the metal detector showed she wasn't hiding any other weapons on her person, the guard put her things in a locker.

In her early days with the Behavioral Analysis Unit, Nikki had the distinct honor of being the only junior agent chosen to attend prison interviews with serial predators. Every visit reaffirmed Nikki's lifelong belief that schools really were like prison. Oak Park Heights had only the essential architecture, with white walls and the speckled beige floors she remembered from middle school. Stairwells provided a pop of green, but the next floor featured the exact same design. The only thing that changed was the security level. Despite Mark Todd's incarceration for double homicide, good behavior over the past two decades had earned him a cell in the lower-security area on the first floor.

She followed the guard past the cell block and down a wide hall that led to a common area.

"I heard the resort killer writes to you from prison," the guard said; his gruff voice made the question sound more like an accusation, but Nikki gave him a pass on manners. Prison guards had one of the hardest jobs in law enforcement.

"Every once in a while," Nikki confirmed.

"Think you'll ever catch Frost? I heard he's very smart."

"He'll make a mistake one day. They always do."

The guard stopped at an open door. "We've never had a problem with this guy, but I'll be out here. The door is unlocked. I've been told that thirty minutes is the most I can give you."

"Thanks." Her hands were clammy and sweat dampened the back of her neck, but there was no turning back now. She held her head high and walked into the room.

Mark Todd stood as she approached, a nervous smile on his face. He looked the same as Nikki remembered, but he'd gained twenty pounds of muscle and a head of gray hair. Nikki could see a prison tattoo covered part of his thick forearm. "I couldn't believe it when they told me you were here," he said. Nikki's heartbeat accelerated at his friendliness. He made eye contact easily, showing her that while he was nervous, he wasn't intimidated.

She pulled a chair a little bit away from the table and sat down. "What does the blue uniform signify?" Nikki asked, trying to start the conversation off lightly. She was used to seeing prisoners in orange uniforms, but she was often visiting the most violent of them.

"My job. I work in welding. Got my associate's for it in here." Minnesota's prison education program was among the best in the nation, and the state had experienced a small but consistent drop in repeat offenders among those who earned a certificate or degree, but Nikki was surprised Mark had done this. "I'm going to work for Rory when I get out." He spoke softly, as though trying to explain himself carefully.

"He's very loyal to you," Nikki replied.

Mark nodded, running a hand through his short, gray hair. "You're the big-time, huh?" he said, motioning at her badge.

"I'm just an FBI agent."

"Not what I've heard," Mark replied. "You know gossip travels faster in prison than it does in high schools. Couple guys you've arrested said you're relentless. One said you mind-fucked him—his words. He called you an ice-cold bitch."

"I'll take that as a compliment."

"Use some vitamin E on that or it might scar." The concern in his eyes was unsettling.

Nikki pulled her hair over her ear to cover the still aching welt. "You should have your attorney here. The security camera doesn't record audio."

Mark shrugged. "I trust you."

What was it with the Todd men and trust? Nikki thought.

Nikki set her phone on the table and turned on the voice notes app. "I want this on the record. I'm protecting myself. Rory said I needed to ask you about the party," she began. "He said he wouldn't tell me himself, that it's your story to tell."

"Sounds like Rory." Mark nodded. "Do you remember drinking and then going to sleep it off? And then waking up to what you thought was me attacking you."

Nikki's nightmares had returned in full force over the last few days, but they were longer this time, with hazy images she never made out. Nikki was afraid the murky images from her decades-old nightmares had been trying to tell her something she didn't want to know. "Yes, but I've only recently been made aware that I can't trust what I saw. I was told I was sober enough…"

Mark ran his hands over his face. "I can't believe no one's told the truth in twenty years."

"Mark, what is it you think I need to know?"

Mark sighed. "You were out cold. Like a limp doll and John was laughing and trying to wake you up. He tossed you over his shoulder and carried you down the hall. Before he shut the door, he sticks out his tongue and gives everyone in the room this look. He comes out ten minutes later and asks if anyone wants to have a turn with you."

Nikki's damp hands slipped on the metal chair.

"He said you wouldn't wake up for a while. He'd taken your clothes off and you didn't even flinch. We didn't believe him at first, but he had a Polaroid camera, and there were… pictures."

The sound of the Polaroid camera ejecting a picture had been the odd buzzing noise that haunted her dreams for so long. Such a distinct sound, and yet Nikki had never allowed herself to recognize it. Did John still have the pictures he'd taken of her?

"Did he… do anything to me?" Nikki gripped the side of the chair.

"He said he didn't, but he wanted to see what happened if someone else tried. I convinced them that I'd known you the longest so I should get to go first."

"You did what?"

"It was me or John's buddies, who all seemed to think it was a great idea. I had to play along, so I locked the door and said I was going to take my time. Then I started trying to wake you up. Every now and then, you would mumble something, but I couldn't get you coherent. I went to pick you up so I could sneak us out of the window. John started knocking and yelling. Then you started screaming, and I went over to tell you it was all right, and your eyes opened and you thought…"

Nikki hadn't had vodka in years, but she tasted it now, her senses overloading. "Why would you do that?"

"Because it was the right thing to do. I should have had the guts to stand up to him in front of his friends and call the cops instead of trying to hide from him. Anyway, you know what happened after that. John kicked my ass and I ran."

"His friends never—"

Vodka vomit on the grass. Shouts and laughter. John's angry voice rising above the others.

Nikki had been so angry, screaming at John. Had she smacked him? Or someone else?

"His friends had his back and covered their own asses, but they never touched you," Mark said. "I was at your house that night because I wanted to tell you what happened, even if you didn't believe me. I wanted you to know what John was really like." Mark shook his head. "I made a mistake waiting until you came home. I didn't care what you thought about me, but I wanted to make sure you were safe. I waited in your old barn, but I'd been hurt pretty badly by John and I passed out. The gunshots woke me up. I had to bust the glass in your front door to get inside. I heard her crying." He paused. "I'm sorry."

Nikki's heart was in her mouth thinking of her mother, but she had to keep going; this was just another interview, just another suspect. "I'm fine," she said, and Mark nodded.

"I ran up the stairs and found your mom. She was bleeding from her side, but she was still alive. I tried to stop the bleeding and stepped in the blood. It must have got her lung because she was spitting up blood and trying to talk."

Nikki tamped the image of her mother down and focused on Mark. "What was she saying?"

"I couldn't understand her, but I think she was trying to warn me he was still in the room. He came up from behind me and hit me in the head. I woke up with the gun in my hand. Back of my head was busted open. I went downstairs to find the phone. Then you came inside."

"Did you touch anything?"

"Downstairs? Probably. My head was ringing, and I couldn't walk straight."

Just as she'd feared. His blood trail had never been mentioned, much less photographed for evidence.

"What motive would I have for killing your parents?" Mark said.

"You wanted to punish me for what happened at the party." Nikki felt like she was coming apart from the inside. It's the motive she'd held onto for years. "You climbed in the window I'd left open."

"There wasn't a stitch of trace evidence linking me to your room because I wasn't in it. My DNA isn't going to be on the clothes that are being tested."

"If that happened with John at the party, why didn't you say something to the cops?"

"I did," Mark said. "But Hardin didn't believe me, said I tried to take advantage of a girl blitzed out of her mind. I knew he wouldn't listen, since I'd been with his wife. Dumbest mistake of my life. After John's friends backed him up, I knew I had nothing. I was just a kid, Nikki."

"What were their names?"

"Who?"

"His friends?"

"I don't remember their names, but I told Hardin who they were. They should be in the file."

Nikki was almost certain they weren't. Her head was swimming with all this new information, but for the first time she trusted what she was being told. And she was sitting across from an innocent man she'd helped to convict. Her family hadn't been the only one destroyed that night.

"Do you think it's possible John put something in my drink?"

"I've never seen anyone that out of it after a few drinks. So unless you were drinking straight vodka…"

"I wasn't." Drinking that much would have likely caused alcohol poisoning and she certainly wouldn't have woken up quickly, but if her drink had been spiked with liquid ecstasy, the effects wouldn't last nearly as long. Depending on the dosage, the drug could have started wearing off after a couple of hours. But it still would have shown up in her tox screen. "You told Hardin that, didn't you?"

Mark nodded. "He told me I was a pathetic liar."

Anger coursed through her. Ever since Rory told her about the paramedic's statement, she'd wondered why John would bother to drug her since they were already having sex.

Now she had the answer. He'd offered her to his buddies and planned to take pictures. Liam was right. He was a sadistic son-of-a-bitch. And Mark Todd was sitting in prison for a crime he didn't commit.

And if Mark didn't kill her parents, she could think of only one other person with reason to come to her house—the same person Nadine heard racing down the gravel road.

Nikki couldn't help but wonder if the photos of her were the ones that Bailey found. If Amy had seen them. That's why she'd automatically hated Nikki.

Nikki stopped the recording and stood on weak legs. The guilt threatened to overwhelm her but wallowing in pity wasn't going to help Mark. "Thanks for talking with me, Mark."

"You know I didn't do this, don't you?"

Nikki could only nod. Mark was telling the goddamned truth.

CHAPTER THIRTY-SIX

Nikki didn't remember driving back to Stillwater or even making the decision not to go home. She wasn't sure she could have hidden her rage from anybody. Her stomach growled and she couldn't remember when she had last eaten, but she wasn't staying long, and then she'd treat herself to some greasy fast food before going back to St. Paul.

Rock salt littered the sidewalk and porch as she walked up to Rory's house, but a fine sheen of ice still made the short walk treacherous. The curtain in the front window fluttered and the front door opened before she even had a chance to knock.

"What are you doing here?" Rory's hair was slightly wild, like he'd been running his hands through it. His thin white T-shirt revealed several tattoos on his upper arms.

"I honestly don't know," she said and he opened the door to let her step inside.

An acoustic guitar was propped against the far wall. An eighties movie played on the muted television. Beige carpet, chocolate-colored furniture, a few pictures on the wall.

Common sense told her she shouldn't be in the house, that she should have made her way back to work to find out what was going on, but it was too late for Nikki to speak to her team and Rory made her feel safe—even if Nikki had no clue why she was so terrified. Maybe it was because for the first time in her life she was facing up to what had happened to her.

This was the house Mark and Rory had grown up in. Nikki had been inside more than once, usually when Mark's parents were already asleep and he brought three or four friends back after a party. They raided the refrigerator, and Mark's dad always woke up and said that no one was driving if they'd been drinking. Nikki lived close enough to walk home, but plenty of kids had crashed in the Todds' living room over the years.

"You want a drink?" Rory asked.

"Just water." She followed him into the small kitchen. It looked just as she remembered, right down to the old flowered wallpaper and butcher-block counters.

Nikki took the bottled water he offered and sat down at the table. What was she doing at this man's house, invading his life? It was selfish of her. If she wanted company, she had Tyler.

"What are you thinking?"

"That things have become a colossal shitshow."

Rory sipped his beer. "Your investigation?"

"Everything. I went to see Mark." He looked at her, surprised. "You're right. He didn't do it."

Rory stared at her for several long seconds before draining his beer. The intensity in his eyes was so intimidating she looked away. "What exactly convinced you?"

How could she explain it without sounding like a stubborn fool? she wondered. "I've always thought of a murder investigation as a kind of patchwork quilt," she started. "You don't know the pattern at the beginning, but as the pieces come together, the pattern finds itself. It's the clear way to make the quilt. That why cases built on strong circumstantial evidence get people convicted."

"And the pattern in Mark's case?"

"It's a fucking mess. It doesn't make sense that they were able to get him convicted. And Mark… I earn my living by understanding human behavior. I know a manipulative liar when I see one, and I didn't see that in him." Nikki swallowed the stupid sob working its way up her throat. "I'm so sorry."

"Don't," Rory said. "I wanted to hate you. Hell, I have hated you, even though Mark never blamed you, I did—"

"I can never make it up to your family."

"We don't want you to," Rory said. "Not long ago, I would have said the opposite. But going through all of this with Mark and his attorneys helped me to understand that Mark was right about you being a victim."

"Hardin told me this week, when the paper came out, that he had no idea I was under the influence. Shamed me for possibly putting the conviction in jeopardy. But he knew, because he knew what happened at the party. Mark told him what John tried to do to me. And I think he drugged me, just like Mark told Hardin that night."

Her voice threatened to break as she explained about the noise in her dreams, the fuzzy bits and pieces that flared up after she came back to Stillwater, and the building panic that she'd forgotten something crucial.

"John's friends did nothing. They never told the truth." Nikki's hands balled into fists. "I'm going to contact Mark's attorney and let him know she can back up his version of events."

"Thank you," Rory said.

"I can't stop thinking about those pictures. If John didn't destroy them, they're still out there."

"He wouldn't have kept them," Rory said. "They're too incriminating."

Nikki didn't mention the box of pictures John's son had found. Those pictures were more than trophies. They helped him relive the moments he craved. Nikki understood why people did terrible things and it meant she couldn't tell herself the lies that Rory did, the ones that might help her sleep at night.

And Mark's story fell in perfectly with Brianna's information. Was there more to John and Amy's argument? Was Kaylee in the pictures? Or Madison? She felt sick at the thought, but at this point, she had to believe that John was capable of anything. Had Madison somehow found out and that's why he'd killed the girls?

"I've spent almost twenty years pushing people away so that I didn't get too close. Even my ex-husband. Mark and I had been friends, and after what happened, I felt like I couldn't trust anyone." Nikki couldn't believe how badly she'd misjudged her ex-boyfriend. "How could John have done that? How could I not have known what he was capable of?" She shook her head in disgust. "I was wrong the whole time."

Rory sighed. "When I started high school, I was so grateful to be just another face in the crowd. But people always asked about Mark, and most either wanted to know more about the murders, or they wanted nothing to do with me at all."

"That's my fault," Nikki said.

"It's not," he replied. "Anyone in your position would have thought the same thing. The police failed Mark. You're a cop—can you imagine being so single-minded that you didn't look under every rock for evidence?"

Nikki thought about Liam's accusation that she'd been trying to come up with a reason for John's possible actions instead of just admitting he was a cold-blooded criminal. "That's one of the reasons we work cases in teams. Personal agendas cause mistakes." She couldn't stop thinking about one of Mark's initial comments. "Mark talked about how prison gossip travels, and one of the guys I'd locked up called me an ice-cold bitch."

She'd obsessed over the words the entire drive from the correctional facility. They were nothing special, yet they cut her deeply. They kept running through her mind, only in John's voice.

You stupid ice-cold bitch. You'll pay for this.

"I think John Banks killed my parents. And I think he might be the person who killed these girls."

CHAPTER THIRTY-SEVEN

Running on little sleep, Nikki consumed two energy drinks quickly the next morning. Her entire system felt jittery. She'd spoken with the district attorney and the new information she'd gathered hadn't shocked Mathews as much as her change of heart. His hands were mostly tied until the DNA results were back, but Nikki now felt like she was doing the right thing for Mark. And for Rory too.

Nikki could barely concentrate on the road. She whipped through traffic at a reckless pace, white-knuckling the steering wheel. How could Hardin live with what he'd done? He'd put an innocent man in jail, and he'd left a killer in Stillwater and now three girls were dead. Marching into his office and accusing him wasn't the most professional way to handle things, but Nikki wasn't sure she could remain professional much longer.

She barely acknowledged the front desk officer when he buzzed her in, heading straight for Hardin's office. "You're a liar."

"Excuse me?"

"I've been to see Mark and I know everything."

"Mark Todd's a liar." Hardin didn't look away from his computer.

"No, you lied, and don't you dare say it's because you were protecting me."

"I really don't like your tone."

"I really don't like that my parents' killer is still out there, and an innocent man is in prison thanks to you." Nikki made sure her voice carried into the hall. "Tell me, did you consciously decide to fuck Mark Todd over because he'd been with your wife, or did all that happen naturally?"

"You are out of line."

Nikki slammed a file onto his desk. "You ran a shitty investigation and buried evidence. The district attorney called Patsy Moran this morning, and she happily connected him with Deputy Anderson. Where are the pictures taken of the blood prints in the hall? Or the kitchen chair that Mark held onto when he went in search of a phone? Their disappearance was the last straw for Anderson."

Hardin's face turned red, his double chin wobbling. His meaty hands clenched into fists, and the anger simmered in his dark eyes. "I have no idea."

"You had no real scientific training, and yet you convinced the sheriff that some evidence wasn't worth testing. You ignored Nadine Johnson's report of a muscle car racing down the road in the middle of the night."

"Big deal," he said. "It was the weekend."

"John Banks drove a '68 Shelby Mustang, and you knew it," Nikki replied. "I know Mark told you about the pictures of me and that he thought I might have been drugged, and that's why you buried my blood test, isn't it?"

Hardin pointed a fat finger at her. "I suggest you stop right there. I'm not going to have my career destroyed—"

"If John Banks has kept that up all these years, how's that going to look for you?"

"You actually think John killed your parents? That's ridiculous. Maybe I made mistakes, but we got our man. I stand by that conviction."

"You should know I intend to speak on Mark's behalf when the DNA exonerates him," Nikki said, and stormed out.

CHAPTER THIRTY-EIGHT

Telling Hardin off left Nikki exhilarated. He talked a big game, but he'd make a terrible poker player: he refused to make eye contact and constantly shifted his posture.

Now that Nikki had faced up to John's lies, she wondered if he was the person Kaylee had gone to see. Was John the person Kaylee had had sex with before she died?

"Agent Hunt." Miller jogged down the hall to catch up with her. "Agent Wilson's in my office. He's found something you really need to see."

"What's going on?" Nikki closed the door to Miller's office.

Liam paced back and forth. "The loading dock at Roan Pharmaceuticals is on the same side of the building as John's corner office. I noticed the emergency exit door when you and I first went to Roan. The security videos we were provided to confirm John's alibi were of the main entrance and the employee entrance on the opposite side of the building. John used the main entrance when he came into the office that day, and he left from it that evening. I walked around the campus yesterday and finally realized the emergency exit near John's office is actually a stairwell that leads right down to the loading dock. Look."

Nikki took his phone and looked at the pictures he'd already cued up. The emergency stairwell was clearly visible through the building's enormous glass windows. The stairwell opened onto the side of the big dock. Anyone who used the exit just had to walk down a short set of concrete stairs to reach the grounds. "Did you request the security videos?"

Liam nodded. "The security firm Roan employs said I needed a warrant. I'm waiting for it, but I talked to a couple of the warehouse guys who'd come out for a smoke. John's been known to use the stairwell in the middle of the day when the weather isn't terrible. He's friendly to the workers and always returns in about thirty to forty-five minutes. A couple of other people confirmed he walks around the campus."

"Madison and Kaylee disappeared on Saturday," Nikki said. "She texted Miles Hanson at 12:45 p.m. that they were heading to his house. A jogger spotted them roughly five minutes later, not far from the Bankses' home. The receipt for John's lunch meeting is marked as 1:15 p.m. There's no way he's the person who picked the girls up."

"No, there isn't," Liam said. "But it doesn't mean he didn't kill them."

"Kill them?" Miller said, astonished. "We have reports that he had affairs, but we don't have anything that suggests he's capable of murder."

Nikki sank into a chair. "No, but I think he might have murdered my parents."

"What?" Miller asked. "Why would you think—"

"I've spoken with Mark Todd." Nikki looked at Liam.

"What?" Liam asked.

"I've been through the evidence that they're using to retry Mark, and his story suggests that John is lying, that he came to my house that night. It also suggests that not all of the women in his photos were there willingly."

"Jesus," Liam said, looking at Nikki. Nikki knew she didn't need to say that she was one of those girls. "If Madison and Kaylee were going to confront him about those pictures, he would have panicked—"

"And if anybody else got a closer look at them, John may have been connected to my parents' case. Especially with the retrial happening," Nikki replied.

"The news talked about it as early as October," Miller said. "Mark's parents told a local reporter they were speaking with the Innocence Project. They believed they'd found evidence to reopen the case. I remember because Hardin was livid."

"So, John's already nervous and then the girls confront him about the pictures," Liam said. "Kaylee's murder is quick, but he takes his anger out on Madison."

"And the initials Madison tried to scratch into her arm?" Liam asked.

"I have no idea," Nikki said.

"Where does Janelle fit into this?"

"She worked at the club he frequented. He could have easily found out she was new and down on her luck. He uses her to mislead us, but he has some fun along the way." Disgust rolled through her.

"We need to get his fingerprints," Liam said.

"And his DNA," Miller said. "But without a court order—"

"That will take too long," Nikki said. "But I have an idea."

CHAPTER THIRTY-NINE

Nikki sent a text to Courtney and told her to expect to have John's fingerprints by the end of the day. She fidgeted in the passenger seat and wished she'd taken the jeep. Miller drove too slowly. She needed to get control of her emotions. John would sense her weakness and exploit it. Nikki had to approach him just as she would any other suspect. They had enough circumstantial evidence to scare John into talking, and she intended to push him into letting his guard down and making a mistake.

"How do you want to play this?" Miller asked as they approached the Bankses' front door.

"You lead with Liam's information. I'll follow up about the pictures." Nikki jammed her hands in her coat pockets. She couldn't allow John to see her anger.

He finally opened the door after Miller rang the bell three times. The reek of vodka threatened Nikki's gag reflex.

John looked at them in confusion. "You have news."

"Developments," Miller said.

"Is Bailey in bed?" Nikki asked.

"He's upstairs watching TV."

"Where's Amy?"

"She's resting in the living room."

"Good. She should hear this too." Nikki held her breath as she walked past him into the living room.

Amy looked up from the couch, her eyes glazed. "Agent Hunt?"

"Did you take more painkillers?"

"No, just my sleeping pills." Amy slowly sat up. Her hair was matted, and she hadn't showered in a couple of days.

Miller caught Nikki's eye and then looked at the kitchen. Empty takeout boxes covered the counter, empty liquor bottles in the sink. Nikki clenched her fists to keep herself from saying something she'd regret. "Sergeant Miller has some questions for you."

"Yeah? Does he have information about who killed our daughter?" John took a long drink from the porcelain Disney World souvenir cup on the table next to him.

"Some of Roan's dock workers said you like to use the emergency stairwell and take long walks," Miller said. "We've got a warrant for the security footage from the Saturday Kaylee and Madison disappeared."

John stilled. "You won't find me on it."

"Maybe not, but you've lied to us so many times I don't know what to believe," Nikki said. "I heard you like to take pictures."

John stared at her a beat too long. "Doesn't everyone?"

Tension simmered in the air between them. "Did you take Polaroids of me at the party when I was knocked out?" Nikki made sure to emphasize the last two words. She was counting on John losing his temper.

"What are you talking about?" John shifted in his chair, not meeting her gaze.

"You took pictures and showed them to your buddies. Asked them if they wanted a turn. Mark got to me before anyone else could."

Contempt shined in his eyes. "Who told you that ridiculous story?"

"Mark Todd."

"Come on, Nik. Why would I do that?" John's bitter laugh sent a fresh wave of anger through Nikki. She thought of Mark Todd in his prison uniform, somehow able to seek justice without lashing out at her like she deserved. The man had spent half his life in prison for a crime he didn't commit, and it had all started because Nikki had trusted the man sitting in front of her.

"Maybe I was a trial run to see if the liquid ecstasy mixed with alcohol was as bad as people were beginning to say it was."

"I never did liquid x."

"Doesn't mean you didn't have it," Nikki said. "It was legal then."

"This is too much." Amy's shrill voice shook. "You're supposed to find my daughter's killer, not get all caught up in Mark Todd's appeal. I knew this would happen."

Nikki glared at her. "John tried to pick up Kaylee at a bar this summer. He wanted to take her picture."

"I already know about that," Amy said flatly. "We worked through it."

"Your husband tried to pick up a teenage girl, and you worked through that?" Nikki had hoped to rattle Amy's faith in John with the information about Kaylee. How could she have known and said nothing to the police?

"He didn't realize she was underage," Amy snapped. "He didn't even know her name until Madison brought her to the house after volleyball practice."

"That's why you went to Kaylee's," Nikki said. "To buy her silence."

Amy's small frame vibrated with anger. "Yes, I did try to pay the girl to keep quiet. When Maddie brought her over, John freaked out. I finally got it out of him that he'd been drinking with some work people in Hudson and made a pass at her. He was terrified she was going to say something."

"She didn't take the money?"

Amy shook her head. "She said she'd stay quiet for Maddie's sake. She didn't want the money. I told John if he ever did something like that again I'd leave him and take everything."

"And what about Janelle Gomez?" Miller asked.

"John admitted to me that he'd been going to the strip club," Amy said. "He also says he didn't have any interaction with that woman. He was here the night she was murdered."

"Forgive me if I don't trust your word right now," Nikki said.

"I don't care what you trust," Amy snapped. "I'm telling you the truth."

"When did Bailey find the pictures?"

"What pictures?" Amy glanced at John. He looked pointedly away from her.

"The ones of naked girls," Nikki replied. "Madison told one of her friends about the big fight after Bailey found them."

"The girl's either lying or misunderstood Maddie. Bailey didn't find any pictures." Amy had regained control, her tone cool and far too calm. Was she going to hold this over John's head and punish him her own way, or was she afraid of being charged for not reporting the pictures?

"I'm tired of being questioned." John took another drink. "I have an alibi, for Christ's sake. You're so screwed up about your parents that you aren't capable of thinking about anything else."

John's expression was carefully neutral, but Nikki recognized the desperation in his voice. She was getting to him.

"Here's where we stand," Nikki said. "By morning we'll have warrants for your financial records, plus this house, your office and any other property you own. We'll be up your ass until it bleeds."

John hurled the heavy stein towards her. It hit the floor with a thud and cracked into several pieces. "Kaylee's got the secret boyfriend. That's what you told me the other day. Did you ask Bobby Vance about her? I know she had a crush on him."

"He's been cleared," Nikki said. "And you're pathetic for trying to pass blame onto him."

"Then it's some other older guy. Kaylee screwed up and got our daughter killed."

"Kaylee died first, likely days before Madison. Your daughter was beaten and left to die in the freezer. She suffered tremendously." Nikki hated to be so callous in front of Amy, but the woman needed to get her head out of her ass. Protecting John was very likely protecting her killer.

Amy's cries almost pierced Nikki's resolve.

Rage flashed through John's eyes as he stood up and towered over her. "I hope you're happy, Nicole. You could never be subtle about anything. Fucking theatrics. Now Amy's a wreck again." He stomped into the kitchen.

"Mommy?" Quick footsteps sounded on the stairs, and then Bailey rounded the corner. He hurried to his mother. "Mommy, what's wrong?"

Amy's body shook with sobs.

"Mommy?" The little boy's voice trembled with fear. "Mommy!"

Amy slowly sat up, tears running down her face and dripping off her chin. She took a deep breath and drew Bailey into her arms. "Mommy's really sad about Madison, honey."

"Me too."

She pressed her forehead to Bailey's. "Why don't you come upstairs and have a camp out with me tonight?"

"Okay." Bailey glanced into the kitchen. "What about Daddy?"

"Don't worry about him. It's just you and me tonight." Amy took his hand.

As soon as they left the room, Nikki nodded at Miller and then went into the kitchen where John sat, drinking whiskey straight from the bottle.

"The fuck do you want?"

"Justice," Nikki said.

"Then find out who killed Maddie, because I sure as hell didn't do it."

"Oh, I will," Nikki said. "And I won't stop until I have the truth about everyone you've hurt."

"What the fuck are you talking about?"

She could shatter his perfect nose in a single, well-placed punch. A knee to the groin would put him on the floor. Nikki would stand over John with all the power, just as he'd probably done with her father. "I'm talking about my parents. Mark's innocent. Their killer has had twenty years of freedom, but his days are numbered. I will bring him to justice."

He sneered at her. "You're delusional."

"You're a sexual predator who's assaulted his last woman."

"Get out of my house."

"No problem. See you soon."

She glanced at the table next to John's chair as she made her way through to the living room and back to the front door.

Miller had bagged up the broken pieces of the stein.

CHAPTER FORTY

Nikki's yawn nearly split her head open. Across the big conference room table, Liam didn't look much better. He stared at his tablet, his eyes drooping. He'd delivered the bagged stein to Courtney at the lab last night and hung around while she processed it, hoping to at least have fingerprint confirmation. But since the stein was in so many pieces, Courtney had to piece it back together in order to get a full print. She'd promised to have something for them this morning.

Liam stirred his coffee. "Did you sleep last night?"

"Not really." Nikki had replayed the confrontation with John a dozen times, trying to remember every little nonverbal cue and wondering if she was being objective or seeing what she wanted to see. She still wasn't certain.

"Taking the cup from his house—how much is that going to hurt us in court?" Liam asked.

"He threw it at me," Nikki said. "Technically it's evidence in the assault of an FBI agent."

"I have to admit, I wasn't sure how you were going to make it work. But you were right about the drinking. And damned if you don't know how to push a person's buttons."

Nikki cracked a smile. "Years of practice, my friend."

Liam shoved the tablet away from him. "Even with the algorithm, I can't narrow down enough names to figure out the initials. There are just too many factors."

"Too damned many," Nikki said.

"Precisely."

"You ran them in various combinations? Like maybe Madison was so out of it she messed up the order."

Liam gave her a dirty look. "That's the first thing I did."

"Sorry, grumpy." Nikki's phone vibrated with Courtney's number. She turned the speaker phone on. "Please tell me you matched John's prints."

"I wish I could."

Nikki's adrenaline evaporated. "What?"

"I'm still waiting on DNA, but John's prints didn't match any taken from the motel room," Courtney said. "He wasn't with Janelle in that motel room."

"What about Madison's effects?"

"A partial match on the watch, which will never hold up in court since they lived in the same house."

Liam looked as defeated as Nikki felt. "Do you have anything good to tell us?"

"Maybe," Courtney said. "I got the results back on some of the hair I lifted from the girls' clothes. It's cat hair. It's on both of them, but Kaylee had much more, like she'd practically lain in it."

"Can you tell what kind of cat?"

"Not without more testing."

Liam drummed his fingers on the table. "I didn't see a cat at the Bankses' place."

"Kaylee didn't have one either. Or the Hansons, at least not that I saw." Nikki felt numb. Could she have been that wrong about John? Had she been so caught up in her past that she hadn't been objective about his involvement in the girls' murders?

"Too bad we can't go door-to-door asking for cat hair donations."

Nikki's phone vibrated with another call from an unknown number. Normally she'd let it go to voicemail, but she had made calls to a few places that might have blocked numbers. "Court, hang on." Nikki put her on hold and then accepted the new call. "This is Nikki Hunt."

"Nikki?"

She sat up straight. "Bailey? What's wrong?"

"Daddy's scaring me." Bailey's frightened whisper was barely audible. "He says he's going to hurt Mommy. And she's crying."

"Are you somewhere safe?" Nikki was already shrugging her coat on.

"I'm in Madison's room."

"Lock the door. We're on our way."

Liam grabbed his coat. "What's going on?"

"John Banks is losing it."

Nikki hit the brake and slid back down the Bankses' street. She'd alerted emergency services as soon as she got off the phone with Bailey, and two Washington County Sheriff's cruisers blocked the driveway, lights flashing.

Sirens squalled a block away, and the ambulance came around the corner.

Nikki bolted from the jeep and raced up the slick sidewalk. "Agent Hunt with the FBI. Where's Bailey?"

"We haven't located him." She recognized the deputy from the crime scene when they'd first found Madison and Kaylee's bodies. "We have a single white female, beaten pretty badly. No sign of the husband or the boy."

"Liam, look outside and in the garage." Nikki took off upstairs and ran to Madison's room. The door wasn't locked. "Bailey?" Nikki yanked open the double closet doors and shoved her way through a sea of clothes. Bailey wasn't in the room. He wasn't anywhere in the house.

She nearly fell down the stairs. The paramedics were trying to stabilize Amy. Her face was a purple mess, with a deep gash in her temple, a black eye and a bloody mouth.

"Amy, it's Nikki, can you hear me?"

Amy moaned, her swollen lips purple.

Nikki grabbed her hand. "You're going to be okay. Did John take Bailey?"

Another moan, this one far more distraught.

"Do you know where he'd go?" John's parents were in Florida. Would he try to flee? "Amy, please, if there's any place, we need to know."

"Her jaw's broken," the medic said. "She can't talk."

Nikki opened the notebook app on her phone and handed it to Amy.

The phone quickly slipped from Amy's hands. Her eyes fluttered closed.

"We have to take her." The paramedic tossed Nikki her phone, and she moved out of the way.

"Liam, we need to put out an APB for John Banks. He's driving a Tahoe and he's a danger to the boy and anyone he encounters."

CHAPTER FORTY-ONE

"The entire area has the information." Miller had arrived a few minutes after the ambulance left with Amy. "Checkpoints are set up on every feasible way out of town. Airports are being monitored. His face is being broadcast everywhere. He's not getting far."

Nikki wanted to believe Miller. The deputies had entered the Bankses' house seven minutes after Bailey's call. John's car was already gone, but they couldn't have gotten very far.

This was her fault. Nikki had pushed John too far, and they were no closer to finding out who killed the girls. Bailey and his mother had paid the price for her impulsiveness. "Property records?"

"Nothing in Washington County," Miller said. "My people are looking statewide. We haven't found anything in John's or Amy's name."

Nikki studied the family photos, trying to will information from them. One had been taken outdoors, in a field that could have been anywhere. She wrangled the picture from the frame and checked the back. No date or location. She didn't remember his parents owning any other property, but a lot of things changed in twenty years. "Check under Ronald and Madge Banks, too. His parents live in Florida, but they might have a residence somewhere around here as well."

Liam tried to get into the Bankses' laptop, but the password protection locked him out. "Fucking Mac. I'll need a warrant to get their tech people to unlock this."

Nikki searched the cabinets and drawers looking for anything that might point her in the right direction. John's desk and office were suspiciously clean. No sign of his pictures, but her gut said he had them stashed somewhere.

"Agent Hunt? Sergeant Miller?" The big deputy gestured to the front door. "A friend of the family is here."

Mindy Vance, wearing only sweatpants and a baggy sweater, stood in the doorway, shivering. Worry lined her round face. "Are Amy and Bailey all right?"

"Amy's seriously injured, and John has taken Bailey. He's in serious danger."

Mindy sagged against the doorway. "I told her he was a ticking bomb. Amy's gone through so much already."

"Did Amy or John know you were coming over?" Nikki asked.

"Amy did," Mindy said. "She wanted me to get Bailey and take her to her parents. She wouldn't tell me why, but I could tell she was scared. She sounded much worse than she did yesterday."

Nikki motioned for her to come inside and led her into the kitchen, away from the sea of cops. "You talked to her yesterday?"

Mindy sat down on one of the tall barstools. "She called to tell me that they had confirmed more details for a memorial for Madison. She wanted to make sure I'd heard about it."

"How did she sound?" Miller had joined them.

"Exhausted. Almost robotic. But that's what you do when something awful happens, isn't it? You put your head down and go through the necessary motions." She glanced at Nikki and then quickly looked down at her hands.

"You've known the family for a long time." Nikki waved Liam over from the computer. "You remember Agent Wilson." Mindy nodded. "Did Amy ever give you the impression she was afraid of John?"

Mindy tugged at her graying hair. "Afraid, no. But John's a powerful man. He likes to put on a certain façade for everyone, and he would certainly get frustrated if she didn't go along with everything he set out."

"Bobby told me about the argument over John's heroics the night Mark attacked me." Nikki worked to keep the venom from her tone. "It sounded like Amy embarrassed him."

"That's right," Mindy said. "I'd forgotten. She said something about his embellishing every time he told the story. My husband took John outside to calm down. Things were never the same between them after that, and they just got worse."

"What happened between your husband and John?" Miller asked.

"John convinced Bobby to come work for him at Roan. He promised him a guaranteed number of clients, which meant the opportunity for large bonuses. That's not how it worked out, and Bobby felt he'd been misled."

"John didn't agree?" Had he ever liked to admit when he'd been wrong? Nikki wondered.

"He said Bobby wasn't the salesman he'd once been. Bobby suffered from severe depression, and that just made it worse. He couldn't afford to just quit his job since he hadn't worked at Roan long enough to have much severance. And then he was gone. He couldn't take it anymore." Mindy wiped the tears off her cheeks. "John and Amy came to the funeral, and I was cordial. But I'd only spoken to her a handful of times since, until Madison went missing."

"Did she ever talk about John hurting their daughter?" Nikki had suspected Mr. Vance had died by suicide, but how much of his decision could be attributed to the secrets he might have kept for John?

"My God, no. John Banks is a lot of things, but he loved Maddie like his own. She called him Daddy and thought the sun rose and set on the man." Mindy's lips pressed into a tight line. "But you said he hurt Amy, and I never would have imagined him doing such a thing. Why do bad things always happen to good people?"

"I wish I had an answer," Nikki said. "Can you think of any place John might have taken Bailey?"

Mindy twisted a stray sweater thread around her finger. "Well, the boys always liked to camp. Fishing, not hunting. My husband didn't like guns, and John wasn't going to get that dirty."

Nikki glanced at Liam and Miller and knew they were both thinking the same thing. A freezer for the fish. "What kind of fishing? Lake fish? Bluegills, that sort of thing?"

"Sometimes, but they used to get a charter and go out on Mille Lacs. They wanted to catch the big trophy fish."

"That's up in Aiken County, off Highway 169," Miller said. "People fish for muskies and walleyes. Big ones in there, too."

"Did they stay at any of the resorts?" Little fishing resorts were scattered along 169 all the way into the Boundary Waters.

Mindy made a face. "They never liked staying in those places. John said they weren't clean enough. The three of them went in on a cabin just north of Lake Mille Lacs. I don't know if John still uses it."

Nikki looked sharply at Miller, who looked like he'd just won the lottery. "Do you remember where the cabin's located?"

"Maybe, if I look at a map. I haven't been up there in a long time, but all three families took the kids a couple of summers when they were much younger. Bailey wasn't even born yet." She glanced from Nikki to Miller. "He'll be okay, won't he? Parents are supposed to protect their kids at all costs. John wouldn't hurt his own child."

"Let's hope not," Nikki said. "Would you help me locate the cabin? Whatever you can remember will be a huge help."

Liam quickly pulled up a detailed map of the area on his tablet. Mindy put on a pair of reading glasses and studied the screen.

Nikki pulled Miller aside. "He took the girls to the cabin. Is there any chance the security footage from this house and the surrounding ones were altered?"

"Not according to my tech people."

"Liam said the county judge is hedging on the warrant because Roan's such a powerful company. Can you update him? Maybe he'll sign the warrant for the emergency exit footage when he learns a child is missing."

"I'll do my best."

"Agent Hunt." Liam's voice was sharp with excitement. "I've got the cabin's location. We can make it in two hours if we haul ass."

CHAPTER FORTY-TWO

It felt like they'd been on Highway 169 for days, and they still had at least fifteen minutes to go. "I can't believe the main route to all the fishing resorts up north hasn't been widened. Traffic is even worse than it was when I was a kid." Nikki cut into the left lane and gunned past a slow-moving vehicle.

"It's January," Liam said. "Are all these people ice-fishing?"

They'd been stuck behind a trailer carrying two small ice-fishing shanties for the past five miles, and passing zones were few and far between thanks to the many curves and villages the road ran through.

"Probably," Nikki said. "People love it for some reason. We always came up in the summer."

"You and Tyler?"

The image of Tyler trying to endure the relentless mosquitoes and cleaning fish would have made Nikki laugh if they weren't racing to save a kid's life. "God, no. My parents and me. We always came up the last two weeks in August."

"What about school?"

"Minnesota schools start later because of the lake season," Nikki explained. "Why do you think the state fair is in September?"

"Makes sense. Where did you go?"

"A little family-owned place called Satkos on Fawn Lake. My dad went there as a kid, and he knew the owners." Every year, as soon as August started, Nikki's mother began to stress about packing and planning for the trip. What should they take from home, and what should they buy from the stores up north? Having enough fish for multiple dinners was never a guarantee, so meals had to be planned ahead. By the time they actually left for the trip, Nikki was so irritated with her mother's fussing she wanted to scream. They were going on vacation. Why did so many things have to be planned?

But she understood now. Taking Lacey anywhere for two days meant planning, let alone spending two weeks in the boonies. Nikki wasn't sure she could manage it.

"I waited all summer for that trip," she said. "The same families usually went at the same time every year and stayed in the same cabins. I have a lot of good memories from that place."

They'd stopped going the summer before high school. Money was too tight, and the crops weren't doing well. Nikki had told herself she was too old to go fishing, but she'd secretly been heartbroken. Starting high school had been scary enough, but losing one of the last rites of her childhood made it even worse.

"Yeah, well the signal through here sucks. I can't even access public records."

"Call the office—"

"I texted Courtney."

"Does she have access?"

"I gave her my user information." Liam paused. "Don't you want his head on a platter? I mean, this guy, he's done terrible things to you, if he really did kill your parents… How are you so calm?"

For some reason, Rory's face flashed through her mind. "I just want justice," she said. "For my parents. And for Mark."

Lake Mille Lacs stretched over 132,000 acres, and most of the private property was only accessible by dirt roads. The lake had only a handful of public access points, and most were shuttered for the winter. The majority of the resorts were owned by people who didn't live in the area during the winter, but a few, like the one Nikki's family went to, lived on the property year-round. Just the thought of being shut up and at the mercy of the ice and terrain made Nikki anxious.

"The county isn't plowing the roads that lead to private access. Which means John had to barrel through big snow to get to the cabin. That's why he took the Tahoe instead of his car." Nikki pointed to the tire tracks cutting through the deep snow covering the private road.

Nikki parked as far onto the shoulder as she could. "We're walking from here. Otherwise we're likely to spook him."

She and Liam checked their weapons, expecting to have to confront John, and gathered extra ammunition. Bitter cold made her bones ache, but Nikki left her heavy coat in the car, opting for a lightweight jacket she could easily move in. She pulled her wool hat low on her forehead and tightened the scarf around her face.

Liam pocketed his phone. "Courtney said John's the sole owner now. She left the Cities about an hour ago. And she double-checked property records—the cabin's the only address on this road. It's a dead end."

At least they wouldn't have to worry about not having a signal to contact her. She and Liam trudged through the heavy snow along the edge of the road.

"There's only one set of tire tracks," Nikki said. "Whoever made them is still at the cabin."

The cabin's peaked roof emerged through the bare trees. No smoke came from the chimney. Most of the places up here had gas furnaces, but Nikki had no way of knowing if John had lit the pilot light.

Her maternal instincts flared at the thought of poor little Bailey being stuck in a freezing cabin, terrified of the person who was supposed to protect him.

The Tahoe was parked in front of the cabin, blocking their view of the door. They crouched behind the vehicle, and Nikki motioned for Liam to stay put. She inched around the right side, ready to shoot if John ambushed her.

Her teeth chattered with cold, yet her scalp prickled from sweat beneath the wool cap. Her breath unfurled in wispy clouds. She clapped her hand over her mouth. Had the blinds in the single front window moved?

She held her breath. The blind shifted again, a space appearing between two of the plastic slats.

"He knows we're here." Nikki shifted into a better position, ready to take a shot if she needed to. She took a deep breath. "John, it's over." Her voice sounded fragile in the freezing emptiness. "I'm not up here alone. I've got backup, with more cops on the way. Amy told us everything."

If John realized he'd broken his wife's jaw, Nikki's bluff might piss him off enough to open the door.

"We just want Bailey safe." Nikki moved closer to the front of the vehicle. "Let him go, and we'll deal with this mess later."

Would she really allow him to run? He had the money and resources to disappear, especially if he didn't have a small child in tow. Trading a chance to escape over Bailey meant her parents' killer may never be held accountable. Her parents hadn't seen justice in twenty years. Bailey was just an innocent little boy with his whole life ahead of him. And Amy Banks didn't deserve to lose both her children.

"John, I swear to you, let Bailey walk out of there, unharmed, we'll take him somewhere safe. You can run. I'll keep hunting you, but letting Bailey go will give you a fighting chance."

The cabin's door trembled. Nikki held up her left hand, signaling for Liam to get ready. The old door continued to rattle until the swollen wood finally broke loose and opened.

Nikki's heart jammed in her throat and nearly swallowed her.

Bailey stood in the doorway, dressed in a snowsuit and boots. His blond hair stuck up in the back, as though he'd taken off his hat.

"Bailey, can you walk out to me?" Nikki asked. "Your daddy's going to let you come home and see Mommy."

Bailey shook his head. "Daddy's not here."

Was John playing some kind of trick?

"I'm going to take a look around," Liam said quietly.

Nikki waited until he'd slipped around to the other side of the Tahoe. "Where's your daddy?"

Bailey shuffled outside, his heavy snow pants slowing him down. "He said he had to leave. He messed up and was in trouble. That I should wait for you because you'd figure everything out and come to get me."

"How long has he been gone?"

"He didn't stay after we got here. He just said you'd come."

Liam appeared on the other side of the small cabin, pink-cheeked. "Footprints leading away from the back door, men's boots, single track. There's a small storage shed, too, but the footprints go past it, and it's locked tight."

Bailey looked up at Nikki, increasingly nervous as they towered over him. "Agent Hunt, can I see Mommy now?"

CHAPTER FORTY-THREE

Bailey refused to leave Nikki's side, so they walked back to the jeep to get her coat while Liam searched the cabin. She wanted to scoop him up in her arms and hold him tight, but she wasn't sure she could contain her emotions if she did. Bailey gripped her hand as they picked their way down the icy road. His nose was pink from cold.

Nikki knelt in front of him and zipped his coat so the big collar covered the lower part of his face. "Try to keep your face tucked into this. The wind's going to chap your face."

His watchful blue eyes studied her. "Why did you have a gun?"

Lacey had asked her the same question after she'd discovered Nikki's gun case in the back of the jeep. "I'm an FBI agent. Sometimes I have to deal with people who want to hurt me or others. I carry the gun in case I have to protect myself."

Bailey looked up at her with serious eyes. "You were going to shoot my dad."

"No," she said. "But cops have scary jobs, so we have to be extra cautious and assume the person we're looking for might try to hurt us."

"Is Mommy okay?"

"She'll be all right."

"Daddy was so mad at her." Bailey's voice shook. "I never seen him that mad."

Nikki tried not to shiver. "What happened?"

"Mommy kept yelling at him about Maddie and her friend. She said that he did it, and he was going to admit the truth." Tears ran down his chubby cheeks. "Did he really hurt Maddie and Kaylee?"

Nikki wiped his tears with her gloves, unable to shake off the guilt. She shouldn't have made Amy think that John had hurt the girls until the fingerprints came back. If she hadn't let her need for personal justice get the better of her, this likely would have all been avoided. "No, I don't think he hurt her. And he's a good daddy, right?"

Bailey nodded vehemently. "The best."

"Do you remember the night you found those pictures?"

His eyes popped wide. "I'm not supposed to talk about that."

"I understand, but I'm trying to help you and your mommy, remember? I can't do that if you don't tell me everything."

"They were in a big box." He looked up at her solemnly. "Like the kind printer paper comes in."

"Why did you open the box?"

"I didn't mean to," he said. "But I knocked the lid off when I was playing. I shouldn't have told Mommy about them. That's when everything went bad." His lip quivered.

She held his shoulders. "You didn't cause any of this, I promise. After you found the pictures, did you tell your mom?"

He nodded. "She looked at them and then got really mad."

"Do you know if she looked through all of them?"

Bailey chewed his lower lip. "She told me to go play in my room."

"Did you?"

"For a little bit, but then I snuck back to Mommy and Daddy's bedroom. The door was mostly closed, but I peeked."

"What did you see?" Nikki struggled to keep the nerves out of her voice. Bailey had been through enough without thinking he'd said something to upset her.

"Bunches of pictures all over the bed. Mommy was looking at them and crying."

"Were the pictures printed out like the ones that go in frames? Like does Mommy ever take a picture with her phone and then have it printed out and framed?"

Bailey nodded. "I think there were lots of those. But there were square ones. Like thick and kind of old-looking."

How did she describe a Polaroid picture to a kid his age? The technology would seem ancient to him. "Did they look like the picture had been printed on a thick, plastic-like white material? Like the actual picture was framed in white?"

He nodded. "Those were weird. Mommy was really upset about those."

"Did she tell you that?"

"No," he said. "But she kept picking them up and staring, like she was trying to figure something out. Mommy saw me in the door and made me go back to my room. Then I heard Maddie come home. Mommy told her to come here."

Nikki worked to keep her face and tone neutral. Amy had shown Madison the pictures. "Did you hear what they talked about?"

"I heard Mommy crying and Maddie yell. Not at Mommy, though. Just like really surprised. And Mommy kept asking about her."

"Who's her?" Nikki kept waiting for him to tell her he might have seen a picture of her in John's box. Maybe she was giving herself too much credit, since twenty years had gone by. She definitely didn't look anywhere near sixteen now.

"I don't know," Bailey said. "She just kept asking Maddie if she was sure that was her. She kept saying yes," he said, playing with the end of his mittens, concentrating hard in an attempt to remember. He reminded her of Lacey when she'd had a bad day at school and was making sure not to miss a single detail. "And then Maddie came back and told me everything was going to be okay. But it wasn't. She was angry every time she saw Daddy. And then she and Kaylee were gone." His eyes welled up.

Nikki's heart broke for the little boy. "I know it's hard to understand, but sometimes really bad things happen, and it's no one's fault." She took his hand and led him to the jeep.

CHAPTER FORTY-FOUR

Bailey finally agreed to watching a movie on the DVD player in the jeep as long as Nikki drove it up to the cabin. She needed to examine the cabin and Bailey wanted to be able to see her. He was still scared, and with the visits that Nikki had made to Bailey's house in the last few days, she was the person he felt the most comfortable around. After updating the APB on John, she enlisted one of the Mille Lacs County deputies to keep an eye on him and joined Liam and Courtney inside the cabin.

"I can't imagine multiple families staying here." Courtney's equipment took up half the floor space. "Even if there are three bedrooms. Where do the kids sleep?"

"Didn't you ever go camping as a kid?" Liam asked. "Who cared about sleep?"

"I prefer indoor activities, thank you very much."

"Kids are usually stuck sleeping wherever there's room," Nikki said. "Probably on air mattresses."

In addition to the three bedrooms and single bathroom, the cabin had a decent-sized kitchen space that opened into a carpeted living area.

"Smells like mothballs and dust." Courtney ran her gloved finger along the dirty windowsill. "I think it's been a while since anyone stayed here."

Nikki looked through the bag of groceries John had left on the counter. Fruit, cereal, bread, plus ham and cheese. He'd also left two gallons of water and a couple of blankets Bailey said his dad always kept in the truck.

"He never intended to hurt Bailey," Nikki said. "He likely took him on the spur of the moment and then panicked. So, he gives him enough to keep him warm and fed for a couple of days and then leaves."

"Counting on you to find Bailey quickly," Liam said. "That's a risk."

"He must have known we'd find the cabin in his financials. He's the sole owner, right, Court?"

"Bought the other guy out after Robert Vance's death. The third friend, Larry, moved to Illinois to stay with family a couple of years ago. He's got pretty bad Parkinson's and didn't use the cabin anymore. Says he hasn't spoken to John since then."

"He locked the Tahoe," Nikki said. "But it does have OnStar. It would have taken a warrant, but we could have located him using their GPS. John surely knew that."

"Agent Hunt?" One of the county deputies ducked his head into the doorway. "We got into the storage shed. Something you guys need to see."

Dread weighed her down as they followed the deputy out back through the knee-high snow. They reached the open door, and Nikki's stomach hollowed out.

A chest freezer sat against the back wall with its lid propped open. Another deputy snapped pictures of the inside.

"Did you find blood?"

"Some," the deputy said. "And a fake fingernail."

Nikki glanced at Courtney, and they both pushed past the deputy.

"It's big enough he could have put one on the bottom and stacked the other on top, like we thought." Liam stood behind them, able to look over both their heads.

The medical examiner believed most of Maddie's bleeding would have been internal, save for her superficial wounds. But she'd torn her skin to leave the initials on her arm.

"Pink shellac nail." Courtney used tweezers to extract the nail that had been partially stuck in the dried blood. "It's definitely the same kind Madison wore when she died."

"But this makes no sense," Nikki said.

Liam looked at her. "It's pretty clear to me. He brought her to the cabin, killed her, then stashed her until he thought it was safe—"

"That's just it," she said. "John's the sole owner of this cabin. The storage shed has electricity and the shed is locked. Those girls could have stayed hidden in that freezer for years. Why dump them? And why aren't his fingerprints on Maddie's belt?"

"Perhaps he unraveled. Panicked. We agree the killer has been getting more and more desperate. It makes sense that he was struggling with what he'd done before we even got here. Perhaps someone else does use the cabin. Maybe John had an accomplice," Liam said. "What if the second mark on Maddie's arm was an unfished 'T'? As in Todd."

Nikki stopped what she was doing and stared up at him. "What?"

"The first initial on Madison's arm could have been an unfinished 'R' instead of a 'P.' If the second was an unfished 'T'—"

"Rory hasn't even been on the suspect list."

"What's to say he wasn't involved?"

"You're not thinking clearly at all," Nikki said. "There's nothing that ties him to either girl."

"But he helped you get to that conclusion," Liam said. "He's hung around you, showing up at the right times. Is his being involved really that far out there?"

Nikki knew people. She would have seen something in Rory. But she'd been wrong about John.

"He's a local. How hard would it be to get information on John? How well do you really know the guy? Honestly, if he wasn't good-looking and being so nice to you, wouldn't you be asking the same question?" Liam held up his hands before she could respond.

"That came out wrong, but you know what I mean. Hell, I don't even know what I mean."

Nikki paused. Nothing Liam had said made sense, but Nikki was beginning to question her own instincts. Was it worth her asking the question?

CHAPTER FORTY-FIVE

Lacey was fast asleep by the time Nikki called later that night, and she told Tyler to let her sleep. Nikki just needed to see her little face and hear that she was safe. Tyler had heard about Bailey's abduction on the news and wanted to hear all about his rescue, but Nikki had been too tired to tell him anything but the bare minimum.

They'd dropped Bailey off at the hospital after leaving the cabin. Amy was recovering, and Amy's mother had gathered her sleeping grandson in her arms and breathed him in. Nikki had watched as her wrinkled hand cradled the back of his head as she promised him that Mommy would be okay, and that Grandma and Grandpa would take good care of him until Mommy was ready to come home.

She found herself driving to Rory's house and she sat in the jeep for a while with the lights off, wondering what the hell she was doing.

Nikki was sure that Rory couldn't be involved, but she wouldn't be able to rest until she'd talked to him. Liam had questioned her too many times, and she needed to prove to him that he was wrong about Rory.

Sleet pelted Nikki's face as she knocked hard on the door. Rory had probably been in bed for hours. She knew construction workers got up early, though tomorrow was Saturday. Wasn't it? Nikki realized she had no idea what day it was.

Go home, for God's sake, a voice told her.

The door opened, and a shirtless Rory stared down at her. His hair was even more wild than usual, standing on end. His thin flannel pajama pants left little to the imagination.

"Nicole, it's two a.m.," he said, his eyes half closed.

"I know," she replied. Sleet dripped off her face. "I have to ask you something."

"It couldn't wait? Or did you just really want to see me?"

Her face burned. "It couldn't wait."

He smiled and opened the door.

Nikki's heart pounded as he shut the door, his back muscles flexing. And even then, she couldn't help but wonder about his cologne. God, she was tired.

"What did you want to ask me?"

She'd come to ask if he was capable of killing two teenaged girls and an innocent young woman because she hadn't been able to stop thinking about Liam's theory. But now she was at his house in the middle of the night, and facing him, she couldn't even bring herself to say it.

"Nicole?" Concern laced Rory's husky voice, and Nikki wasn't sure what she should do.

"Rory, I need to ask you about Madison Banks," she said.

"That's pretty much the last thing I expected you to ask." He gently touched her shoulders. "What about her?"

She was sure he could hear her heart pounding. "Did you ever meet her?"

His big hands slipped around her back and pulled her to his bare chest, his chin resting on the top of her head. "No, I don't think so. Why are you asking?"

Nikki exhaled, her head dropping to his shoulder. Nikki flushed as she told him about John taking Bailey and Liam's theory. Now that she was here in Rory's arms, the entire thing sounded ridiculous. "I don't think you did anything, but I had to admit to myself that if the situation were any different, I would have at least questioned you."

"What situation?"

Her entire body burned with embarrassment. "This situation."

Rory brushed the hair out of her face.

"Everything's just unraveling. So many things happened right under my nose and I still didn't see it. Not just in the past but with this case, too. I can't trust my own judgment anymore."

"Even now?"

She wrapped her arms around Rory's slim waist and buried her face into the warm nook of his collarbone. His arms tightened around her, evidence of the effect she had on him flush against her stomach. "I honestly have no idea."

Rory's lips brushed the top of her head and then moved to the shell of her ear. "Well, I trust your judgment."

Butterflies tore through Nikki. She raised her head and skimmed her lips along his sharp jawline. She couldn't see his eyes, but she felt the heat of his stare before his lips touched her forehead, and then her nose.

"Rory."

His lips found hers, and she sighed into his mouth, melting against his strong chest. He traced the lines of her back before lifting her into his arms. She wrapped her legs around his waist, and the emotional defenses she'd spent a lifetime creating shattered.

Rory's mouth moved to her neck and found the spot beneath her ear. Nikki gasped and threaded her hands through his silky hair. He moaned softly, and she tilted his head back for another kiss. She clutched his face, desperate for him to make her forget all of the bad things she'd endured and the mistakes she'd made.

He was gentler than she deserved, slowly stripping off her clothes and touching every part of her with his lips and his mouth until she was completely at his mercy.

Nikki's hands tangled in his hair, her back arched as he carried her upstairs and into his bed and her mouth opened in a silent cry.

She gave herself to him completely, her fingernails digging into his shoulders, his name louder and louder on her lips. Had she ever felt this content? She couldn't even remember the last time she and Tyler had been together, and after the divorce, she convinced herself she was too busy with work and Lacey to care about anything else.

CHAPTER FORTY-SIX

Nikki's hair was still damp when she finally made it to the hospital the next day. Thankfully she kept a change of clothes and necessary toiletries in the jeep for the all-nighters that usually cropped up during a major investigation. She could still feel Rory's body entwined with hers, and she'd hated to leave so early in the morning, but she needed to get back to work. A BOLO had gone out for John as soon as he took Bailey, and every law enforcement agency in the tri-state area was looking for him. Miller had set up various checkpoints around Stillwater, and the state police had been called in to handle searching the vast north woods area. Lake Mille Lacs was part of the Mille Lacs Band of Chippewa Indians, and the tribal police had been called in to search the twenty-thousand-acre reservation.

She checked her texts again. Thankfully, Liam hadn't blown up her phone while she'd been with Rory. He'd only called once to make sure she was all right. His text an hour ago said he had a warrant for John's financials and would check in later.

The deputy posted outside Amy's room said her parents had taken Bailey to get some rest, but they planned to return today. Amy had been in and out of consciousness, refusing any pain medication for her jaw.

Her eyes flashed open as soon as Nikki touched her arm. "You look better than yesterday."

Amy grabbed her hand and squeezed, tears building in her eyes.

"You're welcome." Nikki took the empty seat next to the bed. "He's a good little boy. And John never intended to hurt him."

Amy groaned and pointed to her mouth.

"Don't try to talk." Nikki opened the notes app on her phone and handed it to her. "I'll ask questions, you type the answers, unless you can just nod or shake your head for no." Amy nodded. "Mindy Vance said John used to co-own the cabin with his friends Robert and Larry. Is that true?"

Amy nodded.

"Madison and Kaylee were put in the freezer in the storage shed behind the cabin. We found the nail Madison used to scratch those letters into her arm."

Tears streamed down Amy's face.

"I know it's awful, but she was telling us something important, and it doesn't make sense for it to refer to the cabin, even if she didn't know John had bought the other two out. If she was coherent enough to scratch them into her arm, then she knew where she was when she was put into the freezer. Can you think of anyone Madison knew with the initial 'P'?" Nikki still had no idea what the second initial was meant to be, but she was fairly confident the first one had to be a 'P.'

Amy shook her head.

"I need to know where the pictures are, Amy. They're evidence now."

Amy's mouth twitched. *Told him I burned. But they're in my safety deposit box. Key code is 2-79-54.*

"Madison obviously got her toughness from you."

That other girl? From the park? John said she wasn't his type. That he never touched her.

"Do you believe him?"

All girls in pictures were fair skin. White. Change type?

Just like me, Nikki thought. "That's a good question. When it comes to serial predators, the answer is usually no."

CHAPTER FORTY-SEVEN

The houses around Liberty Newman Island were just as expensive as the Bankses', and the land value probably even higher given the popularity of the island. In high school, Liberty Newman Island had been more than make-out central. Nikki had attended more than one party on the island, and she and Annmarie had nearly started a massive fire when they'd snuck out here to smoke pot the summer after sophomore year.

A large foreclosure sign stood in Mindy Vance's front yard. Boxes were piled high in the minivan parked in the middle of the driveway. The house had a slightly unkempt look compared to its neighbors: the snow needed shoveling and one of the down spouts looked loose. Taking care of such a big place alone had to be difficult, especially when your spouse had died.

"Damn. Poor woman."

Nikki rang the doorbell. Footsteps tromped near the entryway, as though someone were running down the stairs.

Mindy opened the door, a fine sheen of sweat on her forehead. "Agent Hunt. Is everything okay?"

"I just came to let you know Bailey's fine, but John is on the run. I don't expect him to come around here, but you should be aware if you haven't seen it on the news."

"Oh dear." Mindy brushed the dust off her pants. "Forgive the way I look. I'm packing. Please, come in."

The house looked older than the Bankses', and the fake wood floors and run-of-the-mill trim made Nikki think it probably wasn't as well made. Most of the living area looked as though it had been packed away. Even the walls were bare, save for the dust lines that surrounded whatever had hung in that spot.

"I'm sorry about your foreclosure."

"Thank you," Mindy said. "My husband's life insurance carrier is contesting the policy. I don't make nearly enough money to cover the mortgage, so here we are."

"Why are they contesting?"

"Because they're greedy assholes," Mindy said. "Do you have any idea where John might have gone?"

"Actually, I was hoping you might have some ideas. Your husband and John had been friends since college?"

"High school, actually. They did everything together."

"I used to date John back then. I met Bobby at a party once. I'm sure you know the story. Your son told me John talked about that night fairly often."

Mindy's eyebrows knitted together. "Yes, he did. But Bobby Sr. and I started dating right out of college, so that was before my time."

"I wasn't much fun to be around back then," Nikki said, smiling warmly.

"I've been reading about the new evidence and testing and obviously your son has been going to the protests. It must be awful for you."

"It's not great," Nikki said. "But right now, my priority is finding out who killed Madison and Kaylee. And Janelle Gomez."

"Who?"

"The woman found in the park the other day."

"And her death is connected to the other murders?" Mindy wiped her pink face with a napkin.

"It's looking like it." Nikki leaned against the kitchen doorway as Mindy fluttered about. Yesterday she'd seemed resigned and quiet, but Mindy was a trembling ball of energy. She didn't seem to know what to do with her hands.

"I thought John killed the girls. Isn't that why he ran in the first place?" Mindy picked at her ragged thumbnail. The tip of her index finger looked raw from biting the nail.

"Most likely," Nikki replied. "But we can't be one hundred percent sure yet. That's why we need to find John."

"Well, I hope you can figure it out. Those poor girls deserve justice."

A big, furry cat trotted into the room and jumped onto the counter.

"Get down, Mace. You know better."

The cat looked at Mindy and then started cleaning its paw. She swatted it off the counter.

A loud buzzing rose in Nikki's head. "He's beautiful. What breed?"

"Maine Coon," Mindy said. "He's Bobby's. That cat drives me nuts, but his dad gave him Mace for his birthday just a few months before he died."

"Bobby must be very attached, then?" Nikki asked.

"He missed her more than me when he was in Mankato." Mindy quickly looked away, both hands white-knuckling the counter.

Nikki hoped her smile appeared genuine. "I'll let you get back to packing. Good luck with the move."

"Thank you," Mindy said. "If I think of anywhere John might have gone, I'll contact you."

"Please do." Nikki walked down the hall at a neutral pace, mind racing ahead. Something about Mindy's demeanor wasn't right.

The front door opened before she reached it, and Bobby stood on the other side looking just as nervous as his mother.

"Agent Hunt, I saw your jeep. What's going on?" He glanced behind her. "Mom?"

Nikki turned around, her arm raising instinctively, but Mindy was closer than she'd realized. Something hard and cold hit her temple, and Nikki fell to her knees. Her head rang, her eyes crossed. A second slam to the back of her head sent her careening into the darkness.

CHAPTER FORTY-EIGHT

Nikki blinked a few times before realizing she was stuck in total darkness. She touched the knot on the back of her skull but felt no sign of bleeding. Her head was pounding. She picked through the fuzzy images in her mind, trying to remember what happened.

Mindy Vance. She'd gone to Mindy's house and suddenly realized something wasn't right. She'd been going to leave and then Bobby had appeared… She'd been knocked out and she had no idea for how long. Where the hell had they taken her? she wondered. She knew it wasn't the cabin—it had a distinct smell that she couldn't detect. She reached into her coat pocket for her phone, but they had been smart enough to take it. Nikki extended her arms above her head and then in front of her. Wide, angled wooden slats with a few centimeters of space… she must be in a closet.

Her smartwatch. She sighed with relief as she reached for it before remembering she'd left it at Rory's this morning. Nikki had no way of contacting anyone, and nobody knew she'd gone to Mindy's house.

Shifting to her knees, she tried to look out between the slats, but the room was dark. How long had she been in here?

The closet seemed empty, but there had to be some sort of a bar to hang clothes on. She stood slowly, bracing against the wall as dizziness swept through her. She raised her hand and found a wooden bar. Plastic brackets on each end held the bar in place. Nikki braced against the right end of the bar and pushed hard, hoping the plastic was as shoddy as the rest of the house.

A loud crack sent a wave of fear through her. She stood motionless, listening. A full sixty seconds passed and no one came into the room, so she pushed the bar again. It snapped away, and Nikki yanked it out of the other bracket.

She ran her hands along the door and came to a vertical space large enough to put her fingernail in. Maybe she could bust through the cheap wood.

"You can't get out." Bobby's tired voice came from the other side of the door. Nikki hadn't heard him come into the room. Had he been waiting? she wondered. Someone as slight as him could easily sneak in without her hearing if the floor was carpeted. "Mom used a bungee cord."

As soon as the big Maine Coon had jumped onto the counter, warning bells had gone off in Nikki's head. The cat was Bobby's, and that was the source of the hair they'd found on both girls' clothes. They'd probably been in this house shortly before their murders—and most likely killed here. Courtney had found cat hair inside the freezer, probably transferred from the bodies. Assuming it was a match, the girls had been taken from this house to the cabin.

Madison hadn't carved a 'P.' She had tried to write 'B V' for Bobby Vance. The 'B' hadn't been finished.

"Bobby, please let me out. I can help you."

"I'm not stupid, Agent Hunt."

She tried to imagine the soft-spoken boy who'd come to her defense at the diner as a killer. He wasn't a seasoned criminal, nor was he driven by an urge to kill. Everything he'd done had been impulsive, but why would he kill Madison and Kaylee? What was Mindy's role in all of it?

"I know you aren't. You're also not a cold-blooded killer."

He didn't answer.

Nikki peered out between the door slats. "Can I talk to your mom?"

"She's not here. She went to the store to stock up on stuff before we leave."

What did they plan to do with her?

She had to stay levelheaded. She could talk her way out of this.

"Where are you going?"

"I can't tell you."

"Why did you kill Madison and Kaylee, Bobby? I know you cared about Maddie," Nikki said. "It was obvious every time we talked about her."

"That was before I knew her dad killed mine." His voice dripped with anger.

"I thought your father died by suicide."

"How'd you know that?"

She hadn't been sure, but she'd started to wonder after Mindy said the life insurance refused to pay out. A company like Roan Pharmaceuticals had good insurance, but if an employee hadn't been on the policy long enough, a lot of companies fought paying out if the cause of death had been ruled a suicide. "That's my job. Why did he do it?"

Nikki heard a click, and then light filtered through the door. "Because John Banks made him keep his secret about what happened at the party the night your parents were murdered."

"Listen to me," Nikki said. "I know now that John killed my parents. I also know he's harmed other women. That's what he did to me that night."

"And Mark Todd went to prison. My dad drank because of his guilt and then finally killed himself. John Banks is still a free man."

"I promise you he's not going to be a free man much longer," Nikki said. "I can find him, but you've got to let me out of here."

"Can't do it." His voiced cracked.

"What about Kaylee? Why did you kill her?"

"I really liked her." Some of the venom drained from his voice. "That was an accident."

"I believe you," Nikki said. "I could tell you were a good kid as soon as I met you. Sometimes things get out of our control, and we get caught up in other people's problems. Is that what happened?" She had to wonder if Bobby was Mindy's puppet in her desperate need for revenge against John.

"It was still my fault."

"What happened?" Nikki could tell that he was desperate to tell someone. It was why Bobby had spent so much time opening up to her—each time they'd spoken about the case, he seemed relieved. As if his conscience was eating him from the inside out. "Bobby, I think deep down, you know you can trust me." Nikki wished she could make eye contact with him. Eyes were the easiest to read.

"I know you know what it's like," he said. "For one moment to change everything. I didn't kill your parents. I wasn't even born. But what John did that night ruined my life. Kaylee understood," Bobby said. Nikki could tell the girl meant a lot to him. She knew herself how hard it was to make friends. "Kaylee wanted to see me because I was home for the weekend. They decided to ditch their friend if I picked them up. She was a good person."

"You picked them up and brought them over here?"

He grunted.

"I didn't rape her, before you accuse me of it. I would never. She wanted me to be her first. She'd asked me once before, but I told her no. When she asked again, I figured, what do I have to lose? And then she told me that John had flirted with her and I lost it. I couldn't control my anger. She told me to calm down, it was no big deal. Almost defending him. The next thing I knew, I was strangling her. I just wanted her to shut up. I didn't realize I was squeezing that hard."

Nikki knew she didn't need to say anything else. Bobby was so full of guilt, and he'd reached his breaking point. Now he'd started talking, he wouldn't be able to stop.

"I was panicked, and Madison came in from the living room and started knocking on the door and she started freaking out, threatening to call John if I didn't open up." Bobby laughed bitterly.

"I told her it was an accident, but she started calling me a murderer. Her dad ruined my family, and she's calling me a murderer." He drew in a shuddering breath. "I hit her, hard. And after that, I couldn't stop. I was so angry."

John Banks had started a domino effect. His cowardice had taken his friend's life, along with Madison and Kaylee.

"Was Madison still alive when your mom came home?" Nikki asked.

"Don't talk about my mom." She'd hit a nerve.

"I understand that she's trying to protect you," Nikki went on. "But your mother could have saved Madison's life. That means she can be charged with her murder, not just as an accessory."

"She was too late," Bobby said. "She came home, and I told her, and then she went into my room. I'd tied Madison up in the hall. Kaylee was in my bed. Mom freaked out. She tried to save Maddie, but she was dead."

Nikki's heart raced. "That's not true, Bobby. Madison was alive when she went into the freezer."

"You're lying."

"The medical examiner's certain. She had frostbite and likely died of hypothermia before her head injury killed her. She had a chance, and your mom knew it, right? Did you check Madison's pulse or try to see if she was breathing after your mom came home?"

He kicked the doors. "Shut up."

Nikki flattened herself against the back of the closet, holding the bar tightly. She could get out of the closet if she pushed Bobby far enough. "A good prosecutor's going to paint your mother as the mastermind behind this. I just can't figure out where Janelle comes in."

"I said shut the fuck up." Bobby used both feet this time, and the door buckled, its cheaply made hinges snapping off the wall.

Nikki jammed the wood rod between the hinge and door, forcing it away from the frame.

Bobby's frightened blue eyes appeared in the gap she'd created.

Nikki shoved the rod into his face as hard as she could, and then reared back and nailed him a second time.

He screamed and stumbled back. Nikki used the rod like a crowbar, snapping the top hinge. She kicked the door far enough away from the frame for her to squeeze out.

Blood poured from Bobby's nose.

Nikki dug her knee into his chest and pressed the bar across his throat. "Give me your phone."

"It's in my back pocket."

"Get it out and dial 9-1-1."

"You'll have to kill me first."

Nikki pressed down on the bar with all her strength. "You terrified my daughter."

"Not me." He gagged.

"Another charge for your mom, then."

Bobby wriggled the phone from his back pocket.

"9-1-1, now."

Tears welled in his eyes. "I'm not going to jail."

"Cooperate, and the prosecution will work with you. But kidnapping an FBI agent won't help your case. Make the call, and I'll talk to the DA on your behalf."

Bobby closed his eyes. "My mom's gonna kill me."

"No, honey. I'm going to kill her." Mindy stood in the open doorway with a pistol pointed straight at Nikki. "Leave my little boy alone."

Nikki stood, holding the wooden bar like a baseball bat. Bobby rolled onto his knees, sobbing. "Your little boy's a murderer. So are you."

Mindy stomped into the room until the gun was just a few inches from Nikki's face. "This isn't an air gun. And I'm pretty sure I won't miss at this range."

How quick were Mindy's reflexes? Would she be able to react and pull the trigger before Nikki slammed the bar against her head?

"Think about your little girl," Mindy said. "Do you want her to grow up without a mother? You know how that feels, don't you?"

Nikki dropped the bar, shaking with anger.

"Good," Mindy said. "Bobby, stop crying and use the bungee cord to tie her hands."

Bobby obeyed, blood congealing at the end of his nose. He looped the nylon cord around Nikki's wrists until her circulation was nearly cut off and then tied it.

"I've got zip ties in the kitchen." Mindy looked at her. "Start walking."

CHAPTER FORTY-NINE

Nikki's legs ached as she stumbled down the stairs sandwiched between Mindy and Bobby. Mindy seemed to vibrate with rage. Bobby was still her best shot at getting out of this alive. A part of him knew what he'd done was wrong. Mindy had already passed that point. She only cared about her family's survival. Her son was all she had left, and Nikki knew she would do anything for him. Just like she would do anything to protect Lacey.

Lacey wasn't going to grow up without a mother. Nikki would find a way to get out of this, no matter the cost.

Bobby zip-tied her wrists behind her back and then used the bungee cord to pin her to one of the kitchen chairs. "What are we going to do with her?"

"Take her with us. Get rid of her somewhere she won't be found."

Bobby held an ice pack to his nose and stared at his mother. "You're going to kill an FBI agent?" he whispered.

"I'm going to do whatever it takes to keep you safe," Mindy snapped. "That's what I've been doing the entire time. I won't let our lives be destroyed like the Todd family. Do you know what it's been like for those poor people? They were pariahs for years, and John Banks had everything."

"Mark Todd is innocent," Bobby said. "I'm not."

"That girl seduced you," Mindy replied, more to herself than her son. "Madison pushed you too far. She apparently didn't care that her father ruined so many lives."

"But won't I be just like him?" Bobby said. "If I run off and let someone take the fall—even if it's John Banks—aren't I doing the exact same thing?"

"Yes," Nikki interrupted. "No one has more reason to hate John Banks than me. But I can bring him to justice. Bobby, I can get you a reduced sentence if you help me. The truth comes out and everyone is free. But not like this."

Mindy rolled her eyes. "Surely you aren't that naive? Without my husband's side of the story, how are we to prove how John's actions affected our family?"

"All of the evidence is there. If the defense lays it out just right, it will be obvious to everyone in the room that Bobby never had a chance."

"Bobby killed two teenaged girls," Mindy snapped. "No one's going to give him a pass for having a shitty life."

"One," Nikki corrected. "You knew Madison was still breathing when you put her into the freezer, didn't you?"

Mindy looked at her son. "She wasn't."

"She had frostbite," Nikki said. "She died in that freezer, which makes you an accessory at the least. But the prosecutor will charge you with second-degree murder. I've seen Kaylee's body and her autopsy. There's no sign she was raped or beaten. She was strangled, but a good defense attorney can make the case for your son—"

"We can't afford a defense attorney," Mindy spat. "Just be quiet and let me think."

"Mom, if we kill her, we'll never be safe. We'll be on the most wanted list by tomorrow."

Nikki glanced at the microwave clock. Almost eight p.m. Time to tell Lacey good night. She swallowed the rising knot in her throat. Liam had to know something was wrong. And Rory expected her at his house tonight. Her jeep had specialized plates and she'd parked right in front of the Vances' house.

Bobby seemed to read her mind. "I put her car in the garage. We leave her tied up and run, right now. By the time she's found, we'll be long gone."

"And still be wanted by the FBI. That's a done deal no matter what we do with her."

"At least we won't be wanted for killing her. Canada's only a few hours away."

Mindy was at least four inches shorter than him, but she seemed to tower over her son. She smacked him across the face, the ice pack flying out of his hand. In the few days since Nikki had first met her, the stress had pushed Mindy to her breaking point. She seemed like she was capable of anything. "She knows what you did. I'm trying to cover up for your idiocy."

Unshed tears shined in Bobby's eyes. "No one would have thought of us if you'd just stayed away from the Bankses."

"Don't you dare blame this on me," Mindy shouted. "You brought this on us."

"I'll speak for you at trial," Nikki said. "I can make a case for both of your mental states. God knows I understand a mother trying to protect her child."

Reality seemed to be sinking in on Mindy. She leaned against the counter, her hands shaking. "That's all I was trying to do. He made his mistakes, but he's learned from them. Haven't you, honey?"

Trying not to squirm and draw attention to herself, Nikki found the metal hooks of the bungee cord and carefully separated them.

Bobby seemed unfazed by her words. "You killed that dancer. How was that protecting me, Mom?"

"Amy told me the police didn't think Frost killed the girls," Mindy said. "I had to do something to lead them away from you, especially since you'd started getting friendly with this woman."

"You didn't even know Janelle?" Nikki asked.

"I knew she'd lead you to John," Mindy said. "He goes to that filthy club. His favorite girls have little ones at home, and I'm not a monster. But I found out Janelle had no one."

"She had a family in Wisconsin," Nikki snapped. "She was someone's child, too."

Bobby's nose had started to bleed again. "Maybe I should just turn myself in. I'll take the fall for Janelle. I deserve to be in prison."

"Are you fucking kidding me?" Mindy screamed. "After everything I've done to protect you? I lost my husband and my home. Now you want me to give you up, too?"

"I want you to be free, Mom."

She laughed and pointed the gun at him. "I will never be free. And you're not leaving me."

The ear-splitting sound of the gun discharging drowned out Mindy's scream. She stared at her son, her hand trembling. "I swear I didn't mean to. My finger just twitched."

Bobby seemed frozen in shock for a moment, and then turned around to look at the bullet embedded in the wall. She'd missed his head by an inch.

Mindy started to cry, the gun falling to her side. Nikki lunged, dropping her shoulder into the woman's chest. Mindy fell backwards, her head connecting with the granite countertop. She sank to the floor, streaking blood down the white cabinets.

Nikki twisted, trying to grab the gun, but her hands were too tightly tied behind her back.

Bobby snatched the weapon up. "She's dead."

"She's still breathing," Nikki said. "You need to think long and hard about the next few seconds."

He glared at her, the rage in his eyes terrifying. "I tried to stand up for you, and you killed her. Get on your knees."

Nikki backed against the wall. "You can still run and leave me here, tied up."

"You killed my mom. Now I'm going to kill you. Get down on your knees. You can die like your father did."

Nikki's entire body chilled. "How do you know he was kneeling?"

"John told my dad everything that night. He made my dad help him cover it up." Nikki sank to her knees. Robert Vance hadn't just suspected and lied about John not leaving the party. He'd known the entire time and let an innocent man spend his life in prison.

Bobby stepped over his mother, his face white with rage. "My dad was a victim. He didn't have a choice."

"Everyone has a choice," Nikki said. "You don't think I'm angry as hell? My parents are the ones he killed. I testified against an innocent man because of John's friends backing up his story. I understand grief, and I understand you."

"You don't know me."

"I know you well enough to realize that you would have come forward if your mom hadn't tried to protect you. I know you're drowning in guilt."

The gun shook in Bobby's trembling hands as Nikki spoke. His wild eyes made it clear he wasn't going to listen to her. "General rule of holding someone at gunpoint," Nikki said. "Check the window before you step in front of it." She ducked her head as the window above the sink shattered. Bobby's arm buckled from the impact of the bullet, and the gun fell to the floor.

CHAPTER FIFTY

"The paramedics said you should go to the doctor." Liam stretched his long legs in front of him and glared at Nikki. They'd spent the last hour at the sheriff's station getting each other up to speed. After realizing Nikki had gone MIA, Liam and Miller had launched a frantic search for her, eventually retracing her steps to Amy Banks. She'd been in a fog of painkillers, but eventually remembered Nikki had mentioned going to the Vance home. By the time Miller arrived, the jeep had already been hidden in the Vances' garage. Mindy told him Nikki had stopped by earlier but hadn't stayed long. Liam had used his connections at the DOT to get access to the traffic cameras and discovered Nikki's jeep had never left the Vances' neighborhood.

Bobby had been taken to the hospital for stitches and would be in a cell by morning. Mindy had regained consciousness in the ambulance and tried to convince the paramedics that Nikki attacked them and was trying to frame her son.

Nikki understood the woman's desperation to protect her child, but Nikki couldn't fathom covering up such a horrendous thing for Lacey. Then again, thinking about Lacey spending the rest of her life in prison made it easier to understand Mindy's desperation. News stories covered the details about the victims and the perpetrator, but rarely touched on the lifelong destruction it caused in both families.

Nikki wasn't sure it would make a difference, but she intended to speak to the district attorney about everything the Vances had endured from the ripple effect of John Banks' crimes. She was relieved at least that someone alive knew what happened the night her parents died. Perhaps she could get Bobby to admit what his father told him when they finally found John.

"I will, tomorrow." Nikki finished her third cup of water. She hadn't realized how thirsty she'd been until she'd walked out of the Vances' house. "Is Courtney still at the Vances'?"

Liam nodded. "They're processing his bedroom first, because it's probably where he killed Kaylee."

"Any sign of her phone?" Nikki's lip stung every time she spoke.

"Not yet," Liam said. "He probably tossed it in some lake."

Nikki had refused to leave the house until Courtney arrived and could see for herself that Nikki was going to be fine. "What about the furniture? The house is half-empty."

"Some of it has been sold," Liam said. "Probably the pieces we need. But Mindy rented an apartment in town, so we've got a team going through stuff. I think we've got more than enough to charge both of them."

"I don't think Bobby had anything to do with Janelle's murder other than moving the body—and I'm not sure he helped with that. Mindy's tall and stout. She could have handled Janelle on her own. Hopefully we only match Mindy's prints to the motel room." Nikki and Miller had gone through the garage, looking for anything that could have caused the blunt force trauma to Janelle's head, but Mindy had likely tossed it after she dumped her at the park. Nikki's statement would go a long way to convicting Mindy, but she wanted her case to be rock solid. "Where's my jeep?"

"One of Miller's guys drove it here." Liam raised an eyebrow. "You're not driving it tonight. I can take you home."

She flushed and looked down at her phone. Rory had sent her multiple messages that evening before finally calling Miller and telling him that something was wrong. By then, Miller and Liam were on the way to the Vance house. They'd promised to keep him updated.

Nikki had texted him that she was okay and would explain later, and he immediately asked her to come stay with him tonight. She still hadn't replied.

"Lacey excited to come home?"

"Yes. She's already making plans." Fortunately, Tyler had managed to keep Lacey occupied, and she didn't even know Nikki had been missing, but he'd woken her up so that Nikki could tell her she could come home tomorrow. Tyler offered to come to Stillwater and get her, but Nikki assured him she'd be fine and to get Lacey back to bed.

The judge signed off on the warrant for Roan's additional security footage, and Liam had scoured the hours of tape while Miller searched. John hadn't left the office the Saturday the girls disappeared, but the day before, Mindy Vance had walked around the side of the building and waited on the sidewalk. She had her phone to her ear and looked angry. After a couple minutes, John exited the back door in clear fury. The two argued for several minutes, and the argument ended with Mindy pointing her finger at John's face. Whatever she'd said rendered him speechless.

"Mindy knew what he'd done to my parents because her husband told her. She probably demanded money for silence. I don't know if Maddie confronted him about the pictures, but he must have known Amy went through them. Between Mindy's information and the pictures of me, he was nervous. Did you get his financials?"

"He withdrew five thousand dollars from his personal savings account that day," Liam said. "Then two thousand the following month, same day."

"Mindy's house was still foreclosed on. Her husband must have left her with a lot of debt."

"Several coworkers at Roan said Bob Vance liked expensive things and tried to keep up with John's tastes. He probably has credit card debt, and the collectors came after Mindy."

"Where's Hardin?"

"On leave," Liam said. "And probably well on his way to retirement."

Nikki was still pissed that Hardin hadn't been at the station. He'd have to face her eventually, especially when the DNA results finally came back.

"Unless he's got a secret account, John hasn't made any withdrawals since he took off," Liam said. "No activity on his bank or credit cards."

"John's used to living in comfort," Nikki said. "I can't see him on the run for very long."

A deputy poked her head into the breakroom. "Someone's here to see you, Agent Hunt."

Nikki slowly got off the couch and followed the deputy into the lobby. Ice and aspirin had helped her head, but her entire body ached. Tomorrow would be even worse.

Her heartbeat stuttered when she saw Rory pacing.

"Jesus, Nicole." He crossed the lobby in three long strides and wrapped his arms around her. "Are you okay?"

Too overwhelmed to speak, she leaned her head against his chest and nodded. The effect he had on her was stronger than any medicine. The tension drained from her shoulders, and she was suddenly exhausted.

"What are you doing here?"

"You really thought I'd get that text and just wait for answers? I knew you were missing. God, I was so worried." He brushed her hair back and inspected her face. "Why is your lip swollen?"

"The knot on the back of my head is worse," she said. "Mild concussion. But I'll be fine."

Sleepiness began to crash over her like a tidal wave.

CHAPTER FIFTY-ONE

Nikki slept until nearly noon. She vaguely remembered asking Rory to stay at the hotel and the feel of his warm body next to hers before succumbing to her exhaustion. She was disappointed when she woke up and saw the note he'd left on her pillow, but he had to be on a job site early. Nikki texted him for the address so she could stop and say goodbye before heading home. The idea of not spending tonight with him bothered her more than it should, but getting to lounge around at home with her daughter would more than make up for it.

She stopped at the station to check in with Miller, but he'd stayed late working on paperwork last night and hadn't come in yet. Hardin's office door was locked. Nikki texted Miller to let him know she'd like to sit down with him and the district attorney before charges were officially filed. She intended to make sure Mindy was charged with the murders of Madison and Janelle.

"Glad to see you're all right, Agent Hunt." The deputy who'd been with Miller when she'd first arrived in Stillwater stood next to the administration desk, chatting with the desk sergeant. "Nice work."

"Thank you, deputy. You guys stay warm."

Outside, Nikki ducked her head from the frigid air, but her face still ached from the cold as she made her way to the jeep. Wind gusted between the cars, bringing with it the cloying scent of cologne.

"John."

He was sitting on the curb in front of her jeep, hiding in plain sight. A wool hat hid his blond hair, and several days' worth of beard made him look haggard. He looked up at her with bleary eyes.

"I saw the news. It's my fault. All of it."

"You're right. My parents weren't the only ones who suffered because of you." Nikki couldn't hold the question in any longer. "Did you put liquid ecstasy in my drink? Is that why I passed out?"

"I just wanted to see what would happen," John said. "I took the pictures, thinking you'd wake up."

"Then you decided to invite your buddies for some fun."

"Just to see if you'd wake up. I swear I wouldn't have let—"

"Oh my God, shut up, you pathetic excuse for a man. Why didn't you just stay at the party after I left?"

He looked away, a tear streaming down his cheek. "I snorted a line after you left, and I was so fucking mad at you. The guys were making fun of me."

Poor John and his fragile ego. "You planned to wait for me. Were you going to rape me like you were going to let your buddies do?"

"I just wanted to talk to you."

"Bull," Nikki said. "You were big John Banks. You had a reputation to protect. No girl was going to get away with embarrassing you in front of your friends. So you crawled through the window and planned to jump me when I came home."

John angrily swatted the tear off his cheek. "Your dad heard me. He was going to call the police."

"And you couldn't have that," Nikki said. "Because then people would have found out what you'd done to me, and that I wasn't the first. Mr. Perfect couldn't deal with jail."

"I'm not perfect. And I told you, I was high. And mad as hell. I just lost it."

She wanted to hit him. "You could have let my mother live."

"She knew it was me," he said.

"Why did you assault her?"

"Because she was a cold bitch who never gave me a chance," John snapped. "She went off about how I wasn't good enough for you, and now I'd just proven it. Next thing I know, I was…"

"Assaulting her. The DNA we lifted from your house is going to match the biological evidence taken from Mom. And then we're going to find all the women who starred in your photo shoots."

"Amy destroyed them." His jaw tightened. "So good luck."

"She lied. And I know where they are."

John hung his head, shoulders slumped in defeat. "Bailey's okay, though. I knew you'd find him."

"You traumatized him," Nikki said. "He saw what you did to his mother. But he's going to be fine."

"Nikki, I swear to God, if I'd known how unstable Bobby was, I wouldn't have let Maddie near him."

"That's not why this happened. You know that. His father kept your secret, and it destroyed his family. Just like you destroyed mine and the Todds'. Madison and Kaylee's deaths are on your hands as much as anyone."

"You're right." John stood, and Nikki drew her gun.

"Turning yourself in?"

"We both know I deserve worse than jail," he said.

"That's up for the courts to decide."

"You can do it for them." John took a step closer. "Say it was self-defense. No one will know the difference."

"I will."

John smacked his chest. "It's what I deserve, Nik. And it's what you really want, isn't it? I killed your parents. Your mom pleaded with me and I laughed at her. I told her I'd turned you into a slut—"

Nikki raised the gun, aiming it at his face.

"Yes," John said. "Do it. Then it will be over, for both of us."

Her hand trembled. No one would question self-defense. Her parents would finally receive justice, and by Nikki's hand. Wouldn't that be poetic?

But Mark Todd wouldn't get to see John in prison. All the woman he'd raped wouldn't get to file charges and look him in the eye at trial.

Bailey's worried face, the fear in his voice.

You were going to shoot my dad.

"Do it," John said. "Please."

"No," Nikki said. "I made a promise to your son. And I intend to keep it."

"Goddamn you, Nikki." John's hands balled into fists. "I'm not going to jail."

"I'm not shooting you." He was a still a coward who didn't want to face the consequences for his actions.

"You will." He stalked toward her, eyes as wild as an angry cat's, and pulled a fillet knife out of his coat. "Or I'll fucking cut you. And then I'll go after your daughter."

Nikki pulled the trigger.

The bullet tore through the fleshy part of John's thigh, but she'd missed the femoral artery. Miller wasn't the only good shot.

He collapsed, writhing and screaming in pain.

"Stop crying," she said. "It missed everything vital. You're going to live to become some burly dude's prison bitch."

"You fucking bitch."

Nikki ignored him and waved to the deputy who'd burst out of the station, gun drawn. She held up her badge. "John Banks just tried to attack me with a knife. You have cuffs?"

The deputy tossed her the handcuffs and then took the knife from John. He put pressure on the gunshot wound and called for medics.

John said nothing. He stared straight ahead, refusing to look at Nikki.

She knelt in front him and locked the cuffs onto his wrists. "John Banks, you're under arrest for the murder of Dean and Valerie Walsh."

EPILOGUE

Ten days later

Nikki reached for her coffee cup only to realize it was empty. She checked her phone to make sure she hadn't missed Rory's message, even though she would have heard the warning ding. The courthouse was part of the large Washington County government complex, and she'd found a parking spot far enough away to hide from the media but still provide a view of the front entrance.

She glanced in the rearview mirror. Most of her bruises had yellowed and were covered with makeup, but they were still noticeable. Over the past few days, she and Lacey had made a game out of learning makeup tricks to cover them.

"Mom, what are we still doing here?" Lacey bounced in her booster seat. "I thought you already talked to the judge."

Nikki had given a statement in court this morning, while Tyler had been with Lacey. She'd looked Mark and his parents in the eyes while admitting what she now knew of that night and apologizing for the pain they'd endured while she'd been trusting the wrong people. Asking for their forgiveness was unfair. "I did, but I'm waiting to hear the outcome."

"Of what?"

"The case I spoke to the judge about."

"In the prison?" Lacey rubbed her fingers across the window.

Nikki smiled. "That's not a prison, it's a courthouse. It's where we decide if someone is guilty or innocent."

"How?" Lacey asked.

"I have to find proof that someone did what they're accused of so that they can be held accountable."

"And your friend's in there, right?"

Nikki hadn't introduced her daughter to Rory yet. She didn't even know where their relationship was going, and she certainly wasn't bringing Lacey into it yet. "Yes, he's there supporting his older brother who spent a long time in prison for a crime he didn't commit. We're hoping that's fixed today."

None of the new DNA that was tested matched Mark's. But it did match John Banks, who refused to speak with anyone, including an attorney, in an effort to be treated as a psych patient. It wasn't going to work. He would stand trial for the murders, and the district attorney had already identified half a dozen of the women in his photos from the house, including Nikki. They'd all agreed to testify that John had drugged them, just as he'd likely done to Nikki. But first he would be tried for the murders of Nikki's parents.

Someday, Nikki would tell Lacey about her grandparents. She'd buried a lot of good memories along with the bad, and she wanted Lacey to know how amazing her grandparents had been.

"Why was he in prison if he didn't do it?"

"Because the police didn't do their job right," Nikki said. "That's why it's so important to make sure we have the truth."

Nikki's phone chimed. Her chest tightened as she opened the text.

Full exoneration. He's a free man. Thank you.

Nikki hadn't expected the complex emotions that surged through her. She was happy for the Todd family but angry for her parents and all those affected by John Banks. What would Rory's parents say when he told them about seeing Nikki? If that's even what they were doing. She didn't want to label things just yet. Easier to let go if she believed they were just casual.

"Look at all the people," Lacey squealed.

A throng of media rushed the courthouse steps as Mark Todd walked out a free man, his parents on one side and Rory on the other. Mr. Todd walked with a cane, and his wife slightly stooped, but they were both beaming.

Rory looked incredible in a suit.

"Does that mean your friend won?"

"Yes, he won. He and his family are talking to the reporters now."

Actually, Mark's lawyer was talking to the media. Mark looked down at the ground, clearly overwhelmed by the chaos. Caitlin Newport stood with the attorneys from the Innocence Project, probably dreaming about her next Emmy. Nikki was still deciding if she would do anything more than give Newport a statement for her documentary. In the end, Newport had been right about Mark's innocence. And she hadn't treated the facts like tabloid journalism. Nikki could always use another ally in the media.

Sheriff Hardin was noticeably absent. He'd refused all media requests, letting Washington County's legal department issue a statement on his behalf. While it did acknowledge the DNA evidence could have been tested earlier, the statement didn't include an apology or admittance of failure.

Rumor was Hardin was stepping down. Miller had promised to keep Nikki updated.

A message from Rory lit up her phone.

Going to my aunt's to celebrate. You can stop by if you want.

Nikki wasn't sure she was ready for that. Mark's parents hadn't been openly hostile, but she doubted they'd welcome her to a celebration.

Need to spend day with Lacey. Happy for you all, she replied.

"Mommy, I'm hungry."
"I know, honey. Give me just one more minute."

Okay. Call me tonight?

Nikki quickly sent a thumbs up and hoped she wasn't coming across as too cold. They were all navigating uncharted waters.

"It's been a minute, Mom. I'm dying of starvation here."

Nikki laughed and merged into traffic. She listened to Lacey chatting as she drove through town and thought about how life tended to come full circle. A few weeks ago, Nikki wouldn't have considered setting foot in Stillwater, and when she did arrive, everything felt foreign to her. Stillwater had grown and changed, and yet so much of it stayed the same, just like Nikki. She was no longer the wild teenager, but she remembered those days much more clearly now. She wasn't as scared to look back at the past.

Nikki wasn't sure exactly where her life was headed, but she was no longer "the girl whose parents were murdered."

And that was good enough for now.

A LETTER FROM STACY

I want to say a huge thank you for choosing to read *The Girls in the Snow*. I'm very excited about the upcoming books in the Nikki Hunt series! If you enjoyed *The Girls in the Snow* and want to keep up to date with all my latest releases, just sign up at the following link. Your email address will never be shared, and you can unsubscribe at any time.

www.bookouture.com/stacy-green

In 2012, two cousins named Lyric, aged ten, and Elizabeth, aged eight, disappeared from Evansdale, Iowa. The two girls had been riding their bikes and had been spotted earlier in the day but then disappeared with very few leads. At the time, my own daughter was six years old, and I followed the case, like so many parents, praying the girls would somehow be found alive. Their remains were discovered several months later, but the case is still unsolved at the time of writing. The case took its toll on the FBI agents who were called in to help the Iowa Bureau of Investigation, and it still continues to haunt Iowans.

While *The Girls in the Snow* is vastly different from the Lyric and Elizabeth case, the idea of two young people disappearing with no leads is something that's always stuck with me. The toll that cases like this take on the law enforcement officers working them is enormous and something I wanted to explore with this new series.

I hope you loved *The Girls in the Snow*, and if you did, I would be very grateful if you could write a review. I'd love to hear what you think, and it makes such a difference helping new readers to discover one of my books for the first time.

I love hearing from my readers—you can get in touch on my Facebook page, through Twitter, Goodreads or my website.

Thanks,
Stacy

StacyGreenAuthor

@authorstacygreen

@StacyGreen26

stacygreenauthor.com

ACKNOWLEDGMENTS

There are so many people who helped this book come together. Thank you to my husband for never losing faith in me, and to my daughter for always being honest and willing to listen to my ideas. And a special thanks to her for letting me measure her to see how big of a freezer I needed.

Thank you to Kristine Kelly for being there through all of my writing and life's ups and downs. Thanks to John Kelly for his fabulous tour of Stillwater all those years ago, and special thanks to Jan Barton for her love and friendship.

Stillwater, MN is a very real town and is considered the birthplace of Minnesota. It's a charming, historic place on the St. Croix River, and an idyllic spot for a small-town mystery. Many thanks to the Washington County Sheriff, as well as the Hennepin County Medical Examiner, for their help with my research questions.

Thank you to John Douglas for his guidance on profiling a case and reminding me to always start with the victim. Thanks to Lee Lofland, Sirchie, and Writers Police Academy for helping me create believable cops.

Thank you to the Minnesota Innocence Project for taking the time to answer my questions.

I want to give a very special thank you to my Bookouture editor, Jennifer Hunt. Working with her has been an amazing experience, and I'm so grateful she had enough faith in me to stay in touch until the time was right for us to work together.

Finally, thank you to my readers for sticking with me. I hope you love Nikki Hunt, and I'm excited for the series' future!

Printed in Great Britain
by Amazon

45826626R00176